**Karin Baine** lives in Northern Ireland with her husband, two sons and her out-of-control notebook collection. Her mother and her grandmother's vast collection of books inspired her love of reading and her dream of becoming a Mills & Boon author. Now she can tell people she has a *proper* job! You can follow Karin on Twitter, @karinbaine1, or visit her website for the latest news—karinbaine.com.

**Sue MacKay** lives with her husband in New Zealand's beautiful Marlborough Sounds, with the water on her doorstep and the birds and the trees at her back door. It is the perfect setting to indulge her passions of entertaining friends by cooking them sumptuous meals, drinking fabulous wine, going for hill walks or kayaking around the bay—and, of course, writing stories.

Discover more at millsandboon.co.uk.

# REUNION WITH HIS SURGEON PRINCESS

## KARIN BAINE

# RECLAIMING HER ARMY DOC HUSBAND

## SUE MacKAY

**MILLS & BOON**

First Published in Great Britain 2020
by Mills & Boon, an imprint of HarperCollins*Publishers*
1 London Bridge Street, London, SE1 9GF

Reunion with His Surgeon Princess © 2020 by Karin Baine

Reclaiming Her Army Doc Husband © 2020 by Sue MacKay

ISBN: 978-0-263-27973-3

**MIX**
Paper from
responsible sources
FSC™ C007454

Printed and bound in Spain
by CPI, Barcelona

# REUNION WITH HIS SURGEON PRINCESS

## KARIN BAINE

MILLS & BOON

For Tammy and Kieran xx

# CHAPTER ONE

'I NEED YOU.' Apparently, that was all Kaja had to say after five years apart to get Seth Davenport back in her life.

Now here he was striding through the airport in his short-sleeved, blue cotton shirt and linen trousers, wrinkled from the flight. Time and distance melted away as she watched him walk towards her, her heart beating that little bit faster the way it always had when he was around. He hadn't seen her yet, distracted by his travel companion. It gave her time to study this older version of the man she'd loved when they were both very different people. A world away from where she truly belonged.

His hair was longer than she remembered but remained as unruly as ever. His sun-kissed brown locks refused to be tamed, curling behind his ears and framing his tanned face. The dark scruff of his beard roughened the smooth jaw line hiding in the bristles and when those unfathomable brown eyes met hers she had to swallow down the sudden thirst she'd worked up. The physical changes were minimal but there was one huge difference in his life that would take some getting used to.

'Seth, Amy, welcome to Belle Crepuscolo.' She advanced towards them the way she would when meeting any foreign dignitaries or people of importance arriving in her country. With her arms raised in welcome, she kissed him on both cheeks, telling herself this was nothing out of the ordinary. She knew she was lying to herself when his beard rasped against her skin and the mere touch of him caused a total blood rush to her head.

'Thank you for the VIP treatment, Kaja. It is Kaja, isn't it? Or should I address you as Your Majesty?' There was a twinkle in his eye as he said it but also an underlying tang of bitterness in his tone. Understandable in the circumstances.

'Kaja's fine.' She kept the smile painted on her face as the small hint at her betrayal hit its mark on her conscience. There was so much she had to apologise for, to explain, but nothing would take away the hurt she'd undeniably caused him five years ago. The best she could do was make this stay as comfortable as possible for her visitors.

'Well, Kaja, we've had a lovely trip so far. Haven't we, Amy?' Seth turned his attention to the munchkin clinging onto his hand.

'I'm glad they took good care of you. Now, if you're ready, you'll be escorted to the palace. Would you like that, Amy?' Kaja hunched down to talk to the little girl, trying to make a friend but understanding that this must be overwhelming for her. She'd been dragged away from the only place she'd ever known and flown halfway across the world. It was natural the child should be wary.

Amy looked to her father for guidance on the matter and when he nodded his head, she copied him, her brown curls bobbing in agreement.

When Kaja extended her hand, the child accepted it, her little fingers curling around the stranger she was being urged to trust. Amy smiled up at her with eyes so much like Seth's, Kaja's heart felt as though it were being torn into tiny pieces. The four-year-old was a walking reminder that Seth had moved on from their relationship all too quickly.

Within a couple of months of her leaving he'd married and started a family. A life he'd offered to Kaja first, so it was her own fault he'd found someone else. When he'd proposed, he'd been offering her a commitment she'd realised too late she couldn't give in return. It had been the wake-up call she'd needed to snap out of the dream she'd been living in England with him. She wasn't anything like the woman she'd pretended to be to Seth or their work colleagues. Princess in her own country, she had responsibilities and duties she'd been avoiding in her quest for a normal life. As much as she'd wanted it, it was beyond her grasp. None of it real when she hadn't even confided her true identity to Seth. A betrayal so great she couldn't bring herself to tell him she'd lied to him from the moment they'd met.

She had no right to be jealous now when she'd fled England without giving him an explanation. She was lucky he'd been willing to even speak to her again. Never mind come all this way to do her a favour.

'I'm sorry to hear about your father…and your mother, of course.' It was Seth who addressed the reason for this reunion first. Although, it wasn't a conversation she particularly wanted to have in front of her security team, who were shadowing their journey to the exit.

Her mother's death from a heart attack soon after Kaja's return to her homeland was one more layer of guilt heaped upon her shoulders. She'd been so intent on living a 'normal' life she'd distanced herself from her family and lost precious time she could have spent with her mother. A regret she'd thought she could make up for by falling into line with the rest of the family and throwing herself into what was expected of her as a princess. Including marrying someone out of duty rather than love.

Kaja was sure it hadn't taken Seth too long to work out her true heritage from the ensuing press coverage of her mother's death, though she'd kept it from him and everyone else while living in Cambridge.

The unspoken *Why?* and the hurt she'd caused were blazing so brightly in his gaze she was forced to turn away.

'Thank you. I wasn't able to help my mother but I'm hoping you can do something to save my father.' After years of being on dialysis, her father's kidneys had failed. They were lucky that he hadn't had to go on a waiting list for a new organ when her brother had turned out to be a match and was willing to donate one of his kidneys. With Seth one of the UK's most esteemed transplant surgeons, he was the first person she'd thought of when the nephrologist had told them dialysis was no longer working.

She reminded herself that was why she had brought Seth here. Not to resolve old personal issues or pick up where they'd left off—if that were even a possibility. Which it wasn't.

'We can discuss the details later.' The tensing in Seth's jaw gave her chills. It would seem he hadn't forgiven or forgotten after all and why should he? In the intervening years she'd yet to come to terms with her actions at that time and the consequential events.

She nodded, knowing it was a conversation she couldn't avoid. Seth had come all this way to help her family and an explanation for running out on him was the least she could give him in return.

'Are you really a princess?' A tiny voice broke through the adult tension.

'I really am.' She was second in line to the throne of

this principality after her father and brother but a four-year-old wouldn't be interested in the politics or boring small print of her position. In a little girl's eyes, at least, she had all the trappings of a fairy-tale princess. Of course, the reality was much different and less enchanting than the bedtime stories.

'Do you have a glass coach and a fairy godmother?' Clearly, Seth had no problem in letting his daughter believe in the fantasy, regardless of his own experience and knowledge that happy-ever-afters didn't exist.

'I'm afraid not. I wish I did but this is it.' They stepped out onto the pavement, the sun warming Kaja's skin again after the chill of the air-conditioned airport.

The white limousine with her chauffeur at the helm was a privilege she didn't take for granted after her years using public transport in England. Although it likely wouldn't impress this Cinderella-loving youngster as much as an enchanted pumpkin and mouse coachman.

'I suppose this will have to do.' Seth let out a long whistle.

Kaja was aware this wasn't the norm for most people and only served to highlight the differences in their worlds.

Isak, her cheery chauffeur, got out, tipped his cap, and opened the door for them to get into the car.

'If you can bear it… Alderisi Palace is a short distance from here.' She stood back to let her guests climb onto the back seat first, seeing Amy's eyes light up when she heard their destination. If she had been disappointed by meeting Kaja, hopefully her home for the next few weeks would better live up to expectation. At least trying to keep a small child entertained should distract her from the prospect of her brother and father's operations. Along with the man who'd be performing them.

Her personal security guard, Gunnar, was riding up front and Amy had chosen to sit on one of the long side seats in the rear, leaving her and Seth on the back seat. Despite the vast car interior she found the amount of secrets and ghosts wedged in around them suffocating.

Amy was humming to herself and dancing one of the dolls she'd pulled out from her backpack along the leather upholstery, completely oblivious to the rest of the world around her.

'I hope having Amy with me isn't causing you any inconvenience.' Seth leaned across to speak to her privately, his warm breath brushing her cheek the way his fingers used to right before he kissed her...

'No. Not at all,' she said much too loudly, and sprang back from further thoughts of his touch upon her.

'I don't have anyone else to take care of her. Gran passed away last month. Although she hadn't been able to watch her for some time. Alzheimer's,' he confided, letting that one word fill in all the details he failed to give her.

Finding out he had a daughter when she'd contacted him had come as a shock. She hadn't expected him to be frozen in time in their semi-detached house, waiting for her call, but having it confirmed he'd led another life after her still hurt. Especially when he had the one thing she could never have. A child.

Kaja hadn't had time to mope around after her lost love due to her mother's passing. Then she'd been determined to atone for the neglect of her family by throwing herself into the royal duties she'd avoided until then. She'd met Benedikt at a fundraiser for the public hospital where she worked in the emergency department once a week; a position she'd had to fight to keep hold of as some measure of independence. Although her brief working week meant she'd never really fitted into the hospital team as well as the one she'd worked with in England.

Benedikt had been older than her and from one of Belle Crepuscolo's wealthiest families. She'd believed marriage to him, becoming a power couple on the world's stage, would please her father, to whom family and tradition meant everything. That somehow a prestigious match would fill the void left by her mother and make up for the years she'd abandoned her post in her home country. Having a baby was part of that duty, to secure the family line and make her husband and father happy. Her failure to get pregnant and her spouse's philandering shattered that dream. Benedikt's affair and subsequent filing for divorce to marry his pregnant mistress had played out for the world to see and gossip about. Whereas Seth's life was a closed book to her. One she suddenly wanted to binge-read.

'I'm sorry to hear about your grandmother. I know you were close.'

'Yeah. Her and Gramps raised me as their own. Now they've both gone I'm a bit lost, to be honest. I think the trip out here will do Amy some good to get away from my moping around.' His sad smile was one she could relate to, having lost her own mother and still having to function for other people's sake.

At a time when a person simply wanted to wallow and wail over the loss of someone important in their life, one had to plaster on a happy face for appearances' sake and pray it would stop everyone else falling apart too.

'I assume your wife couldn't get away to join you here?' She didn't imagine the child's mother would let her come out here unless she had other serious commitments preventing her from being with her daughter.

'Paula and I...er...aren't together any more. Haven't been for some time.'

'Sorry. I didn't know.' Once she'd heard he'd married so quickly after their separation she hadn't wanted to know any more. She'd simply accepted he'd moved on without her and taken steps to do the same. Something she'd later come to regret.

'Yes, well, Amy was the best thing to come out of that relationship.' His steely set jaw and change in his tone conveyed there were bad feelings lingering about the situation.

'You share custody?'

'No. Her mother left and never looked back. It's just the two of us now. That's the way we like it, isn't it, Ames?' The little girl nodded, though she couldn't have heard the nature of their conversation.

Kaja got the impression this was a mantra he repeated often so they'd both believe it.

'You certainly seem as though fatherhood is agreeing with you and she's gorgeous. A real credit to you.' She could see Seth as a single dad, braiding his daughter's hair and organising playdates. He'd always wanted children even though they'd both been busy with their careers. It was a topic she'd tried to avoid. She could see now that it was because she knew they would never have been able to settle down as a family. Not when she hadn't been honest with him about her background.

Ironic, when she probably couldn't have given him a baby anyway. Irregular periods and her failure to get pregnant with Benedikt had led to a diagnosis of polycystic ovaries and the end of her marriage. Not even the invasive laser treatment she'd undertaken to try and fix the problem could prevent her husband from straying.

Now Seth was a father she was certain Amy was top

priority in his life. Despite his dedication to his profession and his patients, Seth always put his loved ones first. Unlike her. In looking out for her own interests Kaja had managed to hurt the man she'd loved and her family.

He'd looked after his grandparents in their old age and he'd been committed to her during their relationship. To the point of proposing marriage.

Now she'd invited Seth back into her life she was reminded of everything she'd lost when she came home.

'Thanks. It's not exactly how I saw my life panning out but I wouldn't be without her for the world.' The proud father confirmed what Kaja had already seen for herself in the short time since their arrival.

'You're lucky to have each other.' Seth was currently having a dolls' tea party in Amy's honour on the back seat of the limousine. Anyone could see they had a special bond. One she was quite envious of when she'd never get to have that close relationship with her own child. Even if continued treatment meant she could conceive some day, it was a lot to go through without a guarantee of success. To her, love, marriage and children were all inextricably linked and Benedikt had proved that without one of those links everything else fell apart.

'You never thought of having kids yourself?' It was the sort of question adults asked each other all the time, catching up on each other's news after losing touch. Yet it touched a still exposed and very raw nerve.

'I thought about it. It just didn't work out for me.' Even saying that, reducing what she'd gone through to a vague disappointment brought forth a swell of sadness from the pit of her stomach threatening to swamp her. It was the ensuing anger that had accompanied that period that had prevented her from drowning in her sorrow altogether.

'I know you've had a rough time too.'

There. Her humiliation was complete to find Seth hadn't missed the spotlight shone on her own disastrous marriage, even if he wasn't party to the devastating details of her infertility problems.

'I never was very good at making those big life decisions.' She'd wondered how differently her life would've turned out if she'd accepted his proposal and settled in England for good. Although, it wouldn't have solved the problem that had caused the end of her marriage. She'd loved him too much to ever force him into a future without the family he was born to have.

'We all make mistakes. What's important is that we learn to forgive ourselves, as well as each other.' He fixed her under his gaze, warm like melted chocolate. She hoped it was his way of telling her he'd forgiven her for her past mistakes. If they'd been somewhere more private, perhaps in better circumstances, she would've asked him for clarification and taken that as a cue to apologise. There'd be plenty of opportunity to do so over the course of the next few days when they'd be living under the same roof.

'That can be hard to do when you know you're the facilitator of your own downfall.' No one had forced her to leave Seth, marry someone she hardly knew or to stay in a country where she no longer garnered any respect. She'd managed that all by herself. It was no wonder she'd been given the dubious nickname of 'The Unlovable Princess' when it was such an accurate description.

'I don't think you have it as bad as you make out, Princess. You might take all this for granted but look around you. This is priceless.' Seth wasn't telling her anything she didn't know or showing her things she hadn't seen before. Although, as he leaned across her to direct her gaze out of the window, she wasn't inclined to tell him so. It was an age since she'd been this close to a man, *this* man, and she revelled in the warmth of his body and the masculine scent of sweat and cologne clinging to his skin.

Belle Crepuscolo, as the name suggested, was a beautiful country. Landlocked by Switzerland, Italy and Austria, it had an enviable climate and a culture influenced by all the surrounding countries.

While Seth watched the blur of blue skies and sprawling whitewashed villas flash by the window, Kaja was more interested in the view she had. Seth was more a sense of home to her than the vista outside and she realised everything she'd truly left behind in England that fateful day.

'There's more to life than money and sunshine. That old adage holds true. None of it can buy you happiness.' To her, privilege had become a prison. It kept her trapped in a life she was desperate to break free from.

Her happiest time had been during those rain-drenched, barely-time-to-sit-down working days in Cambridge. At least then she'd had Seth to come home to. They'd cooked dinner, curled up together in front of the telly and made love in their own bed. Nothing out of the ordinary and yet it had been everything. Being so close to him now reminded her of those cosy nights in when she'd been pretending she could lead a normal life. Before reality crashed in and reminded her it wasn't possible.

'That's easy to say when you have this on your doorstep. What else could you possibly want?' He turned his brilliant smile on her and she was powerless to hold her tongue or tell him anything but the truth.

'Love.'

She saw that spike of pain on his face before he composed himself and returned to his own side of the car. They both knew she'd had that once in her life and thrown it away. The Unlovable Princess deserved everything that had come to her since then.

Seth hadn't been as prepared to face Kaja as he'd thought. For some reason he'd thought he'd fly out here, do the job he was required to do and, once he'd seen her, all that past hurt and betrayal would melt away. He'd got it into his head that facing her would make him realise everything had turned out for the best. After all, if Kaja hadn't run out on him he wouldn't have slept with someone else on the rebound or had Amy as a consequence. While he regretted the hasty marriage, he'd never be sorry for his daughter's existence. She was his everything.

He'd known the minute he'd set eyes on Kaja again closure wasn't going to be achieved so easily. It didn't matter that five years had passed, that they'd both married, and divorced, since, or that he'd become a father. In that moment, seeing her again had transported him back to the day he'd proposed. When she'd rejected him, packed her bags in the middle of the night and disappeared without a trace. All the confusion and fear of that time was tied up in the memory. Along with the anger and sense of betrayal he'd felt when he'd seen her on the news as word of her mother's death had spread. A princess. He'd had no inkling of her heritage, couldn't imagine Kaja as anything other than his busy surgeon girlfriend. Until now.

She'd swapped her green scrubs and sneakers for pink silk and diamonds but she was as beautiful as ever. As though her fairy godmother had waved a magic wand and enhanced her natural beauty for the oblivious prince who'd needed it spelled out to him what an amazing woman she was. It was unfortunate her real Prince Charming had turned out to be anything but, according to the papers. Seth took no pleasure in reading about her heartache but perhaps there was something to be said for the commoner she'd snubbed after all. Seth had loved her for who she was, or, at least, who he'd believed she was, with no need for a substitute.

He knew what it was to be hurt and to think you were inadequate. After all, he'd been abandoned by a teenage mother who'd thought having a baby would ruin her life and a wife who'd pretty much thought the same about him and their daughter. Kaja hadn't even bothered to give him a reason why his love wasn't enough for her.

Despite their personal history, Kaja had deserved better than being cheated on. Just as he'd deserved better than being ghosted.

'I mean, when it comes down to health matters we're no better off than the average person. We can fly the best renal surgeon out here to perform the transplant but there's no guarantees my father and brother will survive. If anything happens to them I'll have no one left in my life.' Her voice broke. It was at odds with the cool composure she'd shown at the airport. He'd known in that instant she hadn't regretted her actions when she'd seemed so personally unmoved by seeing him again. Meanwhile his insides had been churning as though he'd hit turbulence even after he'd stepped off the plane.

For a split second he'd wondered if she'd missed him or what they'd had together. She'd quickly shut down that idea, letting him know it was her family she was getting emotional over. He should've known better. Kaja's family was all she'd cared about in the end. It was a pity he hadn't known about their existence until it had been too late to do anything.

'Hey, have a little faith in your transplant surgeon. Nothing's going to take them away from you. Besides, don't you have a whole country to keep you company?' Since his gran had passed he'd been more aware than ever of his limited social circle. With his time no longer eaten up talking to carers or visiting the home, outside work Amy was his whole world. While he was content with that, he knew it wasn't healthy for a four-year-old. Before that cruel disease had robbed her of cognitive thought, Gran herself had made him swear to get a life of his own after she'd gone. To take Amy to see the world and have adventures.

Kaja's call for help had been a well-timed gift, an easier way out than forging new friendships in a place where he'd happily existed on the periphery of society. His busy life as a renal transplant and general surgeon made it challenging to balance work and home life. As a result any thoughts of another romantic relationship had gone on the back burner in favour of spending time with his daughter and grandmother when he could. Now he'd packed up and fled the country with his daughter so he didn't have to face life without the woman who'd been the only constant in his life. This trip had been the cowardly way out of his grief and he knew that sense of loss would be waiting for him on his return.

Kaja might be feeling sorry for herself now but she had no idea what it truly meant to be abandoned by the ones you loved. He'd been abandoned by his own mother and wife. Whereas she was the one who did the abandoning.

Kaja disputed his take on her life with a, 'Hah!'

'Daddy, look!' Amy was straining to see out of the window. He leaned over to see what had caught her attention.

His mouth dropped open as they drove up a winding avenue lined with blush-pink cherry blossoms and crystal-clear dancing water fountains.

'Home, sweet home,' Kaja mocked as the imposing mansion at the end of the drive came into view.

Gleaming white stone pillars, marble steps and balconies on every level of the ornate building gave it the appearance of a grand, layered wedding cake. A congregation of immaculately dressed people spilled out to meet the car. Seth immediately unbuckled Amy's seat belt and took her hand so she didn't get lost in the throng.

'Baby, we're not in Cambridge any more.'

# CHAPTER TWO

'I'LL GET THAT for you, sir.'

'Let me take your bag for you, sir.'

The car had barely come to a halt before there was a flurry of helping hands refusing to let Seth so much as open the door on his own. He clutched Amy closer in case she was spirited away by Kaja's staff with his luggage.

'Hold my hand so you don't get lost, sweetheart.'

'I suppose it is all rather much.' Kaja winced.

It hadn't been his intention to make her self-conscious about her life here. She must have preferred it to the one they'd had together as she'd left it behind so readily.

If they were going to spend the next few weeks under the same roof they were going to have to get along. All issues—personal or socio-economic—would have to be set aside in order for him to treat her father. His patients' backgrounds were none of his business unless it impacted on their health. From everything he'd seen so far, Kaja's father had the best of everything money could buy. Including health care. However, his status wasn't going to affect Seth's ability to do his job. He always did his best regardless of wealth or the status of his patients.

'I'm sure we'll get used to it.' He flashed her a grin. Reassurance that they could make this work. It was his duty to put the minds of his patients' family members at ease where he could. Even if these were unusual circumstances.

'Daddy? Can we have a sleepover in the princess castle?' Amy tugged on his shirt, her eyes wide as she took in the majesty, the likes of which he'd only seen in picture books.

'See?' he said to Kaja with a laugh. 'I think we'll fit in just fine.'

'Good. Why don't we go in and I'll show you to your rooms.' The worry lines marring her forehead evened out into a smile matching his daughter's.

Now that the palace staff had disappeared inside with his belongings it was slightly less intimidating. At least, until they walked through the doors.

The 'wow' escaped his lips before he could temper his reaction. It was difficult to say anything else when faced with the sheer opulence of the décor within the palace.

The rich purple and silver colour scheme combined with the draped silks and brightly coloured tapestries lining the walls was how he imagined the genie's pad inside the magic lamp looked.

When the imposing oak door swung shut, echoing through the halls, it made the situation very real. The heavyset dude who shadowed Kaja's every move without saying a word remained on the outside acting as a sentry.

'Your apartments are this way.'

Not room, he noted as Kaja led them up a flight of steps to the 'apartments'.

'There is an elevator should you wish to use it but I prefer to take the stairs otherwise I'd never get any exercise.'

The Kaja he'd known would've been bored rigid at being chauffeured everywhere, barely allowed to lift a finger. Like him, she'd been someone who'd thrived on being busy, being needed, and had enjoyed her privacy. The alone time they'd spent together had been more precious than he'd realised.

'I don't think you have anything to worry about on that score.' He could see she'd lost weight and some of her curves but none of her beauty. She had an elegant grace about her now befitting a princess. That look-don't-touch vibe was so different from the warm, tactile Kaja he'd planned to marry.

She paused on the steps with her hand resting on the mahogany bannister and slowly turned to look back at him. It was then he realised her backside had been in his eyeline when he'd made that last comment, and he attempted to backtrack.

'I mean, I'm sure you get a workout simply moving from one room to another in here. A few circuits sprinting up and down these steps every morning will help keep me in shape too.' It wasn't a total lie to cover his tracks. He'd let his gym membership lapse when he'd been busy running between Amy's childcare and Gran's nursing home. He'd have to begin a fitness regime when the hospitality thus far had been so effectively displayed. Getting fed around here didn't seem as though it was going to be a problem. Especially when there were silver dishes piled high with juicy citrus fruit and pastel-coloured almonds dotted around the palace at regular intervals.

'Uh-huh.' Kaja gave him a disbelieving look then carried on up the staircase.

Amy broke away from him, sprinting on up to reach the landing first. Not waiting for the adults to catch up, she bolted down the corridor, giddy at having so much space to go wild in after being cooped up in a plane for so long.

'Amy, keep the noise down and don't touch anything.'

He had visions of her bursting in on an unsuspecting dignitary and causing an international incident as she treated the place like her own. A child her age had no comprehension of the complex relationships going on around her. Only the scope of the place for potential fun and mischief. Seth didn't know if Kaja understood what she was in for hosting his daughter.

'Oh, don't worry. You're the only ones on this floor apart from me and the staff. She won't disturb anyone. Bruno and father are already at the private hospital where you'll be working. I'll take you to see them later. I'm sure you and Amy would appreciate some time to settle in first.'

'Thanks. That's very kind of you. I think a nap might be in order.'

'No problem. I know at your age you need all the sleep you can get.'

The jibe caught him off guard, as did the mischievous grin she was sporting. It was a glimpse back at the girl who'd teased him constantly about being a whole three years older and of the close relationship they'd once had.

'Ha, ha. I was thinking more of Amy.' He would never admit the day had taken its toll on him as well, albeit on a more emotional level than he'd anticipated. If Kaja remained unaffected by his presence after all these years as she seemed, there was no point in letting her know he still had unresolved feelings surrounding their past.

He'd only jumped into the relationship with Paula because he'd been so desolate without Kaja and he'd needed someone to provide the company, the intimacy he'd lost with her gone. In hindsight he could see that by rushing headlong into that relationship he'd opened himself up to further rejection from Paula. They hadn't known each other long enough to survive a pregnancy and a marriage so soon after meeting. Perhaps he'd been so keen for the family he'd pictured with Kaja he'd transferred those dreams unfairly onto his spouse. In some way perhaps he'd also wanted to prove his absent mother wrong, prove that it was possible to have a successful career and children. And that someone could love him and want him in their life. Though as of now, the only person who did was his daughter.

'Of course you were…' She patted him on the shoulder with the tease but he noticed the flare of panic in her eyes when she realised what she was doing and snatched her hand away again. It was too late for him to forget her touch now he had physical proof this wasn't a dream and she was real after all.

'Now, this is where you will be staying.' She snapped back into courteous hostess mode and opened the ornately carved oak door etched with leaves and flowers, leading to a suite so big Seth feared he'd lost Amy already. The gold and cream colour scheme wasn't easy on the eyes as it screamed money. Along with not being childproof.

'Just us? I'm sure we could fit in a few more single-parent families if you wanted to open this up as a holiday retreat.' He wasn't trying to be facetious but this one room would swallow up his entire house and still leave enough space to build another.

Kaja ignored the comment, picked up a porcelain bell from the glass table just inside the door and gave it a tinkle. Immediately, one of the staff he'd seen outside appeared in the doorway.

'This is Nils. If you need anything ring the bell. He's here to assist you in any way he can.'

'I really don't think that'll be necessary.' He wasn't aware how long it had taken Kaja to get used to having people running around after her but he was sure it was longer than a few weeks.

His home with Kaja in Cambridge had once been their oasis away from the outside world. A private place to be themselves away from the stresses of hospital life and people who wanted something from them. That hadn't changed for him. He was still in the same house and it remained his safe haven. No matter how luxurious Kaja's residence was, he wasn't going to trade his and Amy's privacy to take advantage of the perks offered.

He couldn't imagine Kaja slobbing around in her PJs here on a day off, eating cereal out of the box and binge-watching her favourite TV shows. Mind you, he couldn't see this perfectly polished princess knowing how to chill out at all any more.

'It's no trouble at all, sir. I'm at your disposal.' The deferential bow didn't go any way to assuaging Seth's discomfort at having someone at his personal beck and call.

'I think that will be all for now, Nils.' Kaja dismissed her employee on his behalf. It was disconcerting to find she could summon this impressive male specimen at the mere ring of a bell. Although Kaja's personal life was nothing to do with him any more. He was here in a professional capacity. To perform a life-saving operation, then get the hell out of fantasy land and back to the real world.

'Seth, I know you value your privacy but you're going to need help. With Amy, at least. It's not a comment on your character to accept some assistance. Think of it as a perk.'

'Daddy, come and see my room. It's got toys and everything.' Amy appeared and grabbed him by the hand, tugging him away from Kaja and any chance of a meaningful conversation.

'We got a few things in to make your stay more enjoyable. I'll arrange transport over to the hospital when you're ready. Amy is welcome to help herself to the toys.'

'I appreciate you going to all this trouble for us.' She'd gone to a lot of effort to make them comfortable. Some might say too much. He couldn't help but think it was due to a guilty conscience and was beginning to wish they'd booked into a hotel instead.

Kaja excused herself and left the room. With the door closed behind her, separating her from Seth and Amy, she let out a long, ragged breath. Seeing him again was never going to be a straightforward meet and greet when theirs had been much more than a professional acquaintance. She'd known that. Yet, she hadn't been prepared for the tumultuous emotions seeing him again would churn up.

Her entire adult life seemed to flash before her eyes in the short time since they'd been reacquainted. All the mistakes she'd made, the regrets, and, almost worst of all, the good times she'd had with Seth, came flooding into her brain. Cuddled up together back then, there'd been none of this awkward formality she'd adopted to protect her status in her home country and her heart.

When she'd heard he had a daughter he intended to bring with him it was undeniable evidence that Seth had been in another serious relationship. A marriage no less. Except Amy, the spitting image of her father, was completely adorable and Kaja had fallen in love with her the second she'd taken her hand.

Now it was going to be doubly hard not to get personally involved with her house guests. The sooner she got Seth settled at the hospital to oversee her father's kidney transplant, the better. Then her whole focus would be on her family's survival.

'Is everything all right, ma'am?'

'Yes, Fatima. I'm going to retire to my quarters now. Perhaps you could bring me some tea.'

'Right away.' Her faithful lady-in-waiting was more of a friend and a confidante, the only person Kaja could talk to, but when it came down to it, Fatima was paid to listen. Just as Seth was being paid to be here. It appeared the richer she was, the higher status she had, the lonelier she became. She didn't want to be alone in her ivory tower any more and would give anything to be back in England where she'd had work colleagues, friends, neighbours and a loving boyfriend. But she'd given it all up to do her duty to her country and could never go back.

Even here in her own home she couldn't simply take a duvet day for some time out of her duties. There were always people coming and going, expecting an audience with her without offering any real, personal interaction. She also had an image to maintain, if only in the presence of the palace staff. Sometimes she wondered if Seth was the only one who'd ever truly known her but she hadn't been honest with him either about who she was or where she'd come from.

Now he knew the truth, Seth would see right through her to how unhappy she was in this life she'd left him for. It was karma, she supposed, for what she'd put him through. Not only had she lied to him but she'd abandoned Seth and the life they'd had together as though it were nothing. The truth was it had been everything.

# CHAPTER THREE

'FATIMA'S GOING TO mind you while Daddy's at work. I'll see you when I get back, okay?' Seth kissed his baby on the top of her head then joined Kaja at the front door.

'She'll be fine, Mr Davenport. Amy and I have this whole house to play in. We can make some cookies for everyone to enjoy later too.' Fatima separated the clingy youngster from her father's trouser leg.

'You'll enjoy that, Amy. Fatima makes the best cookies in the country.' When she had free time, Kaja helped Fatima bake too. It took her mind off matters outside the kitchen and she got to comfort eat afterwards.

While it didn't help maintain her trim waistline, whipping up a few biscuits went a long way to clearing the clutter from her mind. Worries, memories, regrets— it was better to bake them in the oven than spend another night locked away in a room with them.

'I'll see you later, sweetie.' Seth gave Amy one last hug then Fatima distracted her with one of the new toys they'd bought so she wouldn't fret after him—a bright yellow convertible car to drive her dolls around in was just the thing to draw her attention.

'If there are any problems, call me. You've got my phone number, right?'

'Yes, Mr Davenport.' Fatima was smiling but she probably just wanted them to leave so she could get on with taking care of her charge. She loved children and helped raise Kaja and Bruno. They'd preferred her company over any of the nannies their parents had ever employed and she'd become like their second mum. As someone who'd devoted her life to looking after others, the prospect of spending the day with an excitable four-year-old was undoubtedly preferable to her usual housework routine.

'Don't worry. The Royal Alderisi Hospital is only five minutes down the road.' There were some advantages to ruling such a small country and having access to the best health care money could buy was one of them.

She led Seth outside where the afternoon sunshine cast a golden glow on everything it touched, illuminating the immaculately manicured gardens and showing off her country in the very best light.

'Can't we walk? It's a beautiful day and, well, I'm finding everything a little stifling in there.'

Kaja understood. Between the staff, and their history waiting patiently to be unpicked, it was claustrophobic. There was barely room to breathe despite the size of the place. However, when you were royalty simple things such as a walk alone weren't possible. Another thing she missed about England, where people were too busy, too involved in their own lives to be concerned with hers.

'Sorry.' She shrugged, continuing to apologise for the way she ran her life here. 'It's a security issue. With the amount of preparation it would take in advance, it's quicker and easier to take the car. Perhaps we can work something out for tomorrow.'

Seth sighed and approached the limo already waiting for them with the doors open and the chauffeur readied. He'd obviously tired of the regime after only a couple of hours but seeing it might help him understand why she'd left in the first place and moved to Cambridge.

'It doesn't matter. I'm being a nuisance. It'll take a bit of time to get used to things here, that's all. You don't have to keep apologising for everything.' He gestured for her to get into the car first and once the door closed she wished that walk were a possibility. Now there was no escape from confronting their troubled history.

'Don't I?' If she said sorry every day for the entire time he was here it wouldn't be enough to cancel out the wrong she'd done him.

'It's your life. You shouldn't have to apologise for the way you live. I'm only here in a professional capacity after all.' He'd sat at the opposite end from her on the back seat. For all her worry about being enclosed in here with him, now she wanted to close some of that emotional distance that had settled between them.

'That's not strictly true, is it? I got you here to carry out my father's kidney transplant because I know you're the best, but it would be remiss of me not to address what happened five years ago.'

'I don't want to drag that up and cause any ill feeling that might impact on the job I'm here to do.' Seth's attempt to evade the subject only succeeded in making Kaja feel worse by admitting there was lingering resentment on his part. She didn't want to create a toxic environment at the hospital, or in her home, but neither did she want to keep acting as though they were strangers. In her opinion it was better to get things out and clear the air instead of tiptoeing around each other faking congeniality.

'That's why I thought it best to tackle it now and explain myself. It's the least you deserve.'

He didn't argue any further, proving her right. She

took a deep breath and settled her hands in her lap in the hope they would stop shaking.

'I should have told you about my family from the start. I am sorry about that.' Along with everything else, but apologies couldn't alter history.

'Why didn't you, Kaja? We had a life together. I thought I knew who you were.' When he did look at her the pain shining so brightly in his eyes took her breath away. All this time she'd convinced herself he'd got over her was rendered a convenient lie when he was clearly still so affected by her actions.

'You've got to understand, Seth, I went to England to escape my life here. I never envisaged anything beyond that. After graduating high school I was expected to take on my own royal duties and projects. A scary prospect for an eighteen-year-old who wanted to be like everyone else. I persuaded my parents that getting a medical degree would be useful to my position when I returned. That I could put it to good use in the community. I told them England was the best place to study. Where no one knew me. Selfishly, I chose it because it was so far away I reckoned I was beyond their reach. They couldn't make me go back. As time went on I created a life there and I met you. I lived, studied and worked there so long I didn't think my heritage mattered any more. I didn't tell you the truth about who I was because I was in denial myself. I had no intention of coming back.'

'Until I asked you to marry me. Then you disappeared without a trace.'

She hung her head, not knowing how she could begin to make amends for her cowardice. 'That was my wake-up call. My reminder that I was living in a bubble with you. You weren't asking a lot except for a normal, family life. Something you would've found with anyone other than me. There's nothing normal about my family or my life, as you can see, but you're right, I shouldn't have gone like that. You deserved better.'

'Yes, I did.' He clearly wasn't going to make this easy for her.

'Your proposal made me realise I was fooling myself in living out this fantasy I could marry you and simply be Mrs Davenport. I had obligations at home that would have caught up with me eventually and I thought it best to end things before I entered into a marriage based on lies.' The right thing to do, evidently, when she couldn't have helped him realise his dream of becoming a father either.

'You could have told me that. I'd rather have talked things over than wake up to find you'd gone.'

'I panicked, didn't know where to begin explaining myself and thought I could do it better from a distance. I intended to get in contact but then my mother died and I was swept away in a tidal wave of grief.'

'You could have at least got a message to me.'

Even with the air conditioning on Kaja was feeling the heat, shame burning her from the inside out. 'I was a mess, Seth. I was grieving for my mother, and feeling guilty for everything I'd put everyone through. Believe it or not I thought by leaving I was somehow saving you from getting hurt too instead of stringing you along pretending to be someone I wasn't.'

Seth's soulless laugh disputed her warped sense of logic. 'How did you work that one out when you didn't explain any of that to me? Didn't you think I'd be worried that something had happened to you when you vanished without a trace? For all I knew you could've been abducted or had some sort of accident. I called everyone we knew and the hospitals and police. Of course, when they heard you'd rejected my marriage proposal they decided it was your way of dumping me. It took me a little longer to work things out.'

'I'm sorry.' Her voice came out as small as she felt right now. She'd never meant to humiliate him but she was guilty of thinking only about herself. In her attempt to avoid a confrontation or get talked into staying, she'd jumped on the next flight without thinking about the impact her disappearance would have on him.

He didn't need to know that her fertility issues had helped her to maintain that distance since. There hadn't seemed a need to reach out to him when there was no chance of a happy-ever-after and so she had only done so when her father's survival was at stake. It was a private matter she didn't have to share with anyone because she had no plans on repeating past mistakes. Getting involved with anyone would only bring heartache and pain when she could never live up to expectation. She had reconciled herself to never having children, perhaps never being in another relationship, because experience had shown her it wasn't feasible. That didn't mean she didn't yearn for both of those things. More so now that Seth was here, representing everything she wanted and couldn't have.

'When I saw you on the news at your mother's funeral I thought I was hallucinating. Never mind that you'd told me both your parents had died a long time ago, there you were walking behind your mother's coffin with your father, the grand duke.' He shook his head as though he was still trying to come to terms with it all.

'What can I do to fix things between us, Seth? I don't want you to hate me.'

'I could never hate you, Kaja, that's half of the problem. What's done is done, I suppose. We can't change what's happened so there's no point in dwelling on it. I don't think I'll ever forget but I can learn to forgive.' The smile he gave her was devastating on so many levels it made her want to weep. The fact that this man she'd obviously wounded deeply had been willing to fly halfway around the world to help her family and forgive her showed the strength of his character compared to hers.

There were other questions she had about his life but this was more than she could ever have asked of him. Anything else she needed to say to him could wait. It was more important that they started out on this journey on amicable terms when these next few days were going to be tough. A kidney transplant was no small operation. It came with risks to everyone involved. She was putting her faith in Seth to get them all through this and that would be easier to do with the knowledge he didn't hold a grudge against her.

'Thanks.' It seemed inadequate to express how grateful she was for everything he was doing for her when he would've been within his rights to refuse to even take her call. For now, it was the best she could give him. It probably wouldn't improve relations between them if she burst into tears and told him leaving him was the biggest mistake she'd ever made in her life.

They were going to have plenty of time together as her family members went through this huge procedure and, hopefully, she'd be able to show him just how sorry she was about ending their relationship. Maybe then they'd both find some closure.

Seth was glad the journey wasn't too long between the palace and the hospital. Kaja's attempt to call a truce so they could move on had actually caused them to lapse into an even more uncomfortable silence. One only broken when they reached their destination and she advised him on the proper protocol for meeting her father. He found it disconcerting being in this alien situation when she'd been a huge part of his life for so long. A woman he'd been so comfortable around once upon a time.

With their conversation slipping back onto more familiar, albeit rockier, ground he'd almost forgotten he was dealing with royalty. He suspected etiquette would be more scrutinised by her father.

As it was, he was glad he hadn't tried to gain access to the hospital, or his patients, alone. A stranger's face didn't seem welcome as they were met with imposing guards at every corner.

'Isn't this a tad OTT? As far as I'm aware your country doesn't have a high crime rate, never mind a history of assassination attempts. I thought your family was more of a figurehead than a political party?' He'd done his homework. Not only did the country have a ban on personally held firearms, with the exception of the military and police, they had one of the lowest crime rates in the world. From everything he'd read the population was pretty content here since most residents had their own wealth and status. It was a tax haven for the rich and famous after all, as well as those born into a booming economy.

The royal family appeared popular even if the articles he'd skimmed concerning Kaja's love life were less than complimentary. He knew she'd abhor the constant attention and the patronising, cruel nickname the press had awarded her.

She spoke in her own language to another of the guards who'd attempted to block their access down the corridor. Another reminder he no longer knew the woman beside him when he'd been unaware English wasn't her mother tongue. He could only assume the gist of the conversation was something along the lines of, 'Don't you know who I am?', given Kaja's stern body language and the chided guard stepping back to let them pass. He continued to glare at Seth as they passed, perhaps unconvinced about his credentials rather than his companion's.

'We can't afford to take any chances. The whole world knows where my brother and father are. You can't expect us to let people swan in and out as they choose.'

Apart from the extra staff, it looked like any other private hospital Seth had worked in. It was clean and airy, with the extra touches of artwork on the walls and aquariums lit up with brightly coloured marine life setting it apart from the facilities attended by lesser mortals.

In his experience the added luxury of comfortable beds in private rooms or in-house chefs serving up specially tailored meals didn't mean a lot in the grand scheme of things. It wouldn't matter if the walls were made of pure gold or the floors were encrusted with diamonds. At the end of the day he was employed to do the same job he did everywhere else. Money couldn't buy a clean bill of health.

Kaja knew that. Perhaps that was why she was so on edge. She could fly someone out with the best surgical reputation in the world to perform this transplant but the rest of the recovery was down to fate. There was a possibility her father could reject the new organ. As always, Seth would do everything he could to prevent that happening but there were no guarantees in this life. He'd found that out for himself the hard way.

Another guard outside her father's private room greeted their arrival with a curt nod of the head, followed by a conversation on his walkie-talkie before they gained admittance. Seth assumed his face was on an all points bulletin by now, his whole background undergoing a thorough check if it hadn't already. He prayed his recent site visits to research the country—the ones about their princess in particular—wouldn't come back to haunt him if they looked into his online search history.

'Father, this is Seth Davenport. The surgeon who's carrying out your transplant.' Kaja stood in the centre of the large private room announcing him to the frail gentleman swamped in his bed by pristine white cotton sheets and plump pillows.

'Ah, come forward, young man. My eyes aren't what they used to be. Along with the rest of me.' The grand duke sat up, immediately adopting an air of authority, which forced Seth to advance from the doorway towards the bed.

'I'm honoured to meet you, Your Royal Highness.' Seth dipped at the waist into a bow as prompted by Kaja, secretly hoping he wasn't expected to do this every time he walked into the room. It would become tiresome when he had a job to do.

The grand duke waved a dismissive hand. 'We can dispense with all of that nonsense. Call me Olov. I fear it is I who should be bowing to you. I can't thank you enough for coming to our little corner of the world to help me. My daughter tells me you once worked together and that you're the best there is.'

His excellent English was heavily accented compared to Kaja's. Seth assumed it was the time she'd spent in Cambridge studying that had made her sound more like a local.

It was clear she hadn't shared their personal history with her family. The grand duke might not have been so humble and welcoming if he'd known Seth had lived in sin with his only daughter for years, or that he'd had the audacity to propose marriage to her. Now he'd seen her life out here and the people she was surrounded by it was becoming clearer why she wouldn't entertain the idea of marrying a commoner like him. What more could he have possibly offered her that she didn't have already? Nothing except his love. Which hadn't been enough for her to even stay in the same country.

'That's correct, sir.' He wasn't going to be modest about his credentials when that was the reason he was here. Kaja's father would expect confidence from the man who would have his life in his hands.

'Good. At least something positive came out of Kaja's time away.' The focus of both men's attention lowered her head. Seth didn't know if it was in deference to her father or because she couldn't look at him.

Goodness only knew what she'd told her father about her career or her personal life during that time. It was a punch in the gut to think that their life together was nothing for her to be proud of when they'd been some of the best days of his life. Along with some of the worst after she'd gone.

'I've read up on your medical history and your ne-phrologist's recommendations. As far as I can see the procedure should be relatively straightforward.' Seth adopted his professional persona, determined not to linger on anything liable to distract him from the upcoming surgery.

'Glad to hear it. The last thing I want is to find out there could be more complications or setbacks. Time's running out for me.'

Seth didn't argue with him. He'd read the files and agreed that the transplant was the last option available given his condition. If he'd been any older or less fit than he was, a transplant might've been deemed too risky.

'This kind of operation comes with its own risks. We can't predict how your body will react to the transplanted organ. Obviously, we'll be monitoring you very closely and will do everything we can to prevent rejection. I'll need to meet with the rest of the team to discuss contingency plans to cover every eventuality.' Although he was the medical lead he wouldn't be able to do this without a team of other professionals with the same goal of making this operation a success.

'I can organise that for you.'

He'd forgotten Kaja was in the room until she voiced her intention to help.

'I'd appreciate that.'

'Is there anything else you need me to do?'

Seth knew only too well how it felt to be powerless as your world continued to spin out of control and there was nothing you could do to halt it. Yet, her suggestion to contribute fell flat when it had been made clear to him it was only the present that interested her. With no real consideration towards him or their history.

'Not at the moment. If that changes I'll let you know.' He turned his back on her, doing his best to block her out of his head so he could think straight.

'What do you require from me, Doctor? Apart from my kidney?' Another male voice entered the fray. Followed, of course, by another shadow figure who was quietly dismissed at the door.

Even if the new arrival hadn't been wearing an identical hospital gown to the one Kaja's father was sporting, the family likeness was uncanny. All three Alderisis had the same sea-green eyes, aquiline nose and height befitting royalty.

He held out a hand towards Seth. 'Bruno. Pleased to meet you.'

'Seth Davenport,' he countered as strong fingers gripped his in a handshake.

'This is my big brother. Bruno, this is the surgeon

who'll be carrying out the transplant.' Kaja introduced them in case there was any doubt about their identities.

'Ah. So you're the man who'll be cutting me open and rummaging about in my insides?' The dark humour he employed wasn't unheard of in these situations. A lot of patients joked to cover their fears. Bruno did seem relaxed about the impending operation considering the sacrifice he was about to undertake to save his father.

'Bruno, I wish you would take this seriously.' Kaja chastised him with a clip around the ear.

'Don't tease your sister. You know how she worries,' the elder Alderisi scolded.

It was clear this was a family who cared deeply for one another. He had no idea why Kaja had found it necessary to keep them hidden from him during the course of their relationship. Yes, her heritage had come as a shock but he would've got over it given time.

'I am taking this seriously. Trust me, giving away one of my kidneys isn't something I would do on a whim.'

'If it's any comfort, donors have the same life expectancy, general health and kidney function as anyone else.' He said it as much for Kaja and Olov's benefit as Bruno's.

'See, Kaja? I trust my new best friend here not to botch this when he comes so highly recommended. I'm going to be under anaesthetic so I'm not the one who'll be doing the worrying.' A meaty hand slapped Seth on the back. He liked this guy. His whole attitude and demeanour was a refreshing change from the earlier heavy-hitting conversation he'd had with his sister.

'We will need you to fill in the consent forms and other necessary paperwork before we proceed.' If anything did go wrong, it was necessary to have everything down in writing to protect all those involved. They all knew the risks but Seth would be the one primarily shouldering responsibility or blame if necessary.

'No problem. It's not as though we have much else to do while we're waiting. We've exhausted the whole board-game collection and I don't think Father is up to a game of table tennis just yet. Maybe in a week or two when he's fully recovered with a new lease of life, thanks to my young, highly sought-after vital organs.'

Kaja rolled her eyes and groaned. 'I give up.'

'I'll arrange everything once I've had a meeting with the team. The paperwork, that is, not the table tennis.' Seth exchanged grins with the handsome prince, satisfied they were both on the same wavelength. It was a serious procedure but a positive one if everything went to plan.

'Good stuff. I can jot kidney transplant into my diary for this week, then?'

'I don't see why not once we have everything in place. I'll go back and check on my daughter and return later to go over any questions you think of in the interim.' He was keen to find out how Amy was getting on. He'd be spending a lot of these next few days at the hospital and wanted to spend as much time with Amy as he could now.

'I'll call for the car and get Isak to take us back to the palace.' Kaja motioned for the attention of the guards at the window.

'If you don't mind, I'd rather walk. I'm sure I don't need an entourage to keep me safe and I'd much rather get some fresh air.' Along with some distance from Kaja and the memories he couldn't quite manage to shut out altogether.

# CHAPTER FOUR

'I LOVE YOU, BRU. I love you too, Papa.' Kaja struggled to say goodbye and leave them in the hands of the surgical team even though she knew it was for the best. They were the only family she was ever going to have.

She couldn't bear the thought of losing either of them but her father's age and health were against him. Despite that, she managed to stem the emotions welling up inside her. The last thing they needed to see was her crying before they went under the anaesthetic.

'You'd think we weren't coming back to hear you, sis.' Trust Bruno to be making jokes even at a time like this. Her father simply raised his hand to give a wave as though he were simply popping to one of his lengthy state dinners.

'Don't worry. They'll be back on the ward before you know it.' Seth met her at the door, already prepped in his surgical scrubs. It was the most he'd spoken to her in days, his time split between his patients and his apartments. He hadn't sought her out at all.

Of course, he had a lot of meetings with the rest of the transplant team to occupy him, but she thought he'd gone out of his way to avoid her since his introduction at the hospital to her family. Perhaps it was being faced with the reality of life here and the patients he'd agree to take on or down to her completely disregarding their life together in England as purely work-related. Although she didn't think either of them would have wanted to bring up their painful romantic history right before Seth performed the transplant. There didn't seem any need.

The truth was she'd never spoken to her father about her life in England. She didn't think it was necessary to rehash it all and detract from the work she'd come back to do. He didn't need to know about her disastrous love life now she was back in her rightful place at the palace. Except of course it wasn't that easy for her to forget.

It might have been different had her mother still been alive. She would've had someone to confide in, a female shoulder to cry on. As it was, she only had Fatima and she'd had to draw a line somewhere between friend and employee.

'This is going to be a very long day. As the donor, Bruno will go into Theatre first for the laparoscopic donor nephrectomy.'

'It's a less invasive procedure than the old method so that means a quicker recovery period, right?' Despite her own medical knowledge, she needed Seth's reassurance that they weren't taking unnecessary risks by going ahead with this surgery. He was the expert and could be more objective on the matter when it wasn't his own family he was dealing with.

'Yes. There'll be a few tiny incisions and we'll remove the kidney with the scope camera and miniaturised surgical instruments. It's a straightforward procedure I've been involved in on many occasions.'

'I know this is the best thing for my father but I can't help worrying about them both and what this means for the future.'

'A kidney from a living donor does give better long-term results and from a family member there are lower risks of complications or rejection. We hope for a better early function this way. You know all this, Kaja.'

She could detect his frustration with her, perhaps taking it personally that she had doubts about this transplant being a success. It wasn't Seth's abilities she was wary of but that possibility of losing another family member.

'I'm just trying to get things clear in my head. Perhaps I could watch you carry out the transplant?' She needed to do something to feel part of what was happening. If anything did go wrong then she would know she'd done her best too. She couldn't live with the extra guilt if she failed anyone else she loved.

'Honestly, I don't think that's a good idea. My advice would be to leave the hospital grounds for a while and find a distraction.'

'I couldn't do that. They need me here. I could just stay here—' She tried to go back into the room where her brother and father were keeping each other company before they went for surgery. Seth caught her none-too-gently by the elbow and pulled her back.

'Kaja, will you please just leave and let me get on with my job?'

Her mouth flopped open and closed at the audacity of Seth basically calling her a nuisance. Telling her she could be no help to her family and only a hindrance to him. It illustrated how far apart they'd drifted in the space of a couple of days. There was no way he spoke like this to any other anxious family members he encountered at work or she would've heard about it a long time ago. Colleagues had only ever said good things about him. It seemed this level of brusqueness had been reserved solely for her and it wasn't an honour she was enjoying.

As if she weren't tense enough already, Seth's sudden bout of control-freakery set her teeth on edge and her blood pressure rising.

'I'd prefer you kept our personal issues out of this, Seth. This isn't about you, or us, for that matter. You have no right to deny me access to my own family.'

'I don't want to call security to have you removed from the premises for being disruptive but I will if I have to.' Seth didn't acknowledge the accusation that he was exercising his authority in a vendetta against her. Which riled her even more.

'Disruptive to whom?' As if she didn't know.

'We'll phone you to let you know when they're out of surgery so you can visit. Okay?' He seemed to soften a little towards her even if he wasn't backing down.

Kaja nodded. There seemed little point in arguing further and causing a scene. Especially when this was the man carrying out the transplant. She didn't want him going in to surgery distracted. They could hash this out at another time.

She hurried back to her waiting car giving no thought to Gunnar running to keep up with her, or Isak, who'd been snacking in the front seat. It didn't matter a jot she had to open her own door when she simply wanted somewhere to hide her tears, emotions catching up with her all at once.

'Take me home,' she commanded shakily and pushed the button to raise the privacy screen between her and her staff.

Only then was she safe to demonstrate her fragility. The tears didn't take time to fall once they started, streaking down her face as though someone had released a pressure valve and years of upset and turmoil had finally been allowed to be expressed. It was grief for her mother and the relationship with Seth she'd lost. Worry over her father and brother. Most of all it was sorrow for the life she'd been denied with Seth. If circumstances hadn't conspired against her she could've had a lifetime of being his wife instead of the half-life she had here as The Unlovable Princess no one wanted.

Seth wasn't proud of the way he'd spoken to Kaja but he needed her to be away from him while he operated on her father. He had to concentrate on what he was doing rather than worrying about what she was going through waiting for him to finish. As her anxiety had increased so too had his want to comfort her. That would have undone his efforts to put some distance between them these past few days and only brought them closer.

He'd succeeded in alienating her now and would be lucky if she forgave him for his behaviour at all. Regardless that he'd thought sending her home would be best for both of them. Kaja sitting here watching, worrying and waiting wasn't going to help anyone. Seth was the one who had the success of this procedure resting heavily on his shoulders.

As a living donor Bruno had to have routine checks to ensure he was suitable—health screening, physical exam, X-rays to check for signs of any kidney disease. His father also had to have pre-transplant tests to check for any signs of infection. The transplant couldn't go ahead if there was any problem with either the new organ or the patient.

Bruno's operation had already been completed, with the kidney safely removed, and by all accounts he was recovering well with no sign of infection or unusual blood loss. Although the kidney was able to survive out of the body for up to forty-eight hours, the optimal time from removal to transplant was four hours. A factor always on Seth's mind when the operation itself could take anywhere from ninety minutes to six hours depending on the complexity of the situation.

With the duke's bloods and urine tests satisfactory, Seth scrubbed into Theatre along with the anaesthetists and other attending medics. He'd carried out this operation countless times over the course of his career but there was even more pressure on him today to be the best at what he did. This was Kaja's father and the leader of an entire country.

Watching his progress on the monitor, Seth made several small surgical cuts under Olov's ribs. Each one a reminder that he had the responsibility of this man's life in his hands.

This keyhole technique, while delicate, aided speed of recovery when there were smaller incisions to heal. While there was no need to remove the damaged organs, he would have to hitchhike the blood into the new kidney.

He wished he could apply a similar procedure to his relationship with Kaja so they could live with the damage from their past and use the good parts to jump-start a new working relationship. He couldn't continue banishing her from the hospital to avoid their personal issues. Once this surgery was over he needed to hold out an olive branch and hope she didn't use it to whip him.

Now he'd consigned himself to making reparations with Kaja, he focused on his patient, whose body was lying open to him.

'Clamp, please.'

He isolated the renal vein, and iliac artery and the new kidney was retrieved from cold storage ready to be transplanted.

It was a demanding, technical operation but there was

satisfaction seeing the kidney turn pink and come back to life as it was warmed up with a warm saline solution.

Seth wondered if his relationship with Kaja could ever be resurrected in a similarly healthy fashion.

Once he was certain everything was working as it should, they began closing. Only then was he able to relax a bit, content he'd done his job to the best of his abilities. Equally important, he could tell Kaja the transplant had been a success.

'Miss Kaja! I don't know what to do. I know you are very busy with your poor brother and father…' Fatima crossed herself as she ran into Kaja's room.

'Fatima, what's wrong?' She didn't have the time or energy for any more dramatics. She was exhausted. Drained by the emotions and intensity of the day so far. Not only because of her worry about her family members but she was trying to fathom the reasons behind Seth's sudden personality change. He'd never spoken to her so abruptly before and she wasn't sure what she'd done to deserve it other than be concerned for her family's welfare. Whatever his reason, it was clear he'd wanted her out of the way.

Unfortunately, with all of that running through her mind she hadn't been able to shut her brain down even for a few hours' sleep. Despite Seth's insistence, being at home hadn't made her any less anxious.

'I had a phone call…my sister needs me. She's had a fall and been taken to hospital. I must go and see her but what about you and Miss Amy? I can't leave you alone.' Poor Fatima sounded as though she was about to have some sort of breakdown as she wrung her apron with her hands.

'Yes, you can. Take as much time as you need to look after your sister. Now, where's Amy?'

'She is sleeping. Are you so very sure you can manage without me?' Seeing Fatima's distressed face, Kaja was tempted to say no to assure her she was indispensable. She had managed alone for the longest time but Fatima was a comfort to her when she needed it. A mother figure providing some sense of belonging where she no longer felt she had any.

'We will do our best to cope while you are away. Don't worry about us. Go, be with your sister. Family must take priority.'

'Thank you.' Fatima kissed her on both cheeks and the gratitude expressed for a few days' leave humbled Kaja. She'd become so engrossed in her own world and problems she'd selfishly forgotten Fatima had a life outside the palace. The woman she took for granted was needed and loved by her own family too. It would do them both good to be reminded of that.

'Take as much time as you need and let us know how your sister is keeping.' Although it might have sounded like an afterthought she was genuinely concerned and decided taking an interest in Fatima's personal affairs was long overdue. It might stop some of this continuous self-pity she'd been indulging in for too long.

It was only when she waved her devoted companion off that Kaja realised what she'd agreed to. She was taking charge of Seth's daughter in Fatima's absence. Without his knowledge or permission.

Kaja couldn't relax. She couldn't focus on the book she was attempting to read, the words blurring every time she looked at the page as her mind wandered. There was too much going on for her to sit on her plush plum velvet banquette surrounded by plump cushions pretending she didn't have a care in the world.

Despite any appearance of her as a princess lounging around waiting for her prince to come and rescue her, her nerves were shredded to ribbons. She was on high alert, ears straining for the sound of the telephone call from the hospital, or a sign of Amy stirring in her bedroom. The afternoon was a fraught one as she waited for it to be disturbed. Even more so now she had to come up with some idea of how to entertain a four-year-old. She had little experience of children, save for those she'd treated in a medical capacity. It was important to get this right for Amy because if she was upset, Seth would be too. More so than he apparently already was with her.

Not only did she want to prevent Amy from becoming bored and starting to miss her father, but she had to prove to Seth she was capable of taking care of his daughter. If she let him down again he'd never forgive her.

Kaja didn't know how long she'd been sitting here in Seth's apartment waiting to be useful to someone. Every tick of the brass clock on the mantelpiece seemed longer and louder than ever, echoing around the empty lounge. With only Seth's personal effects for company.

His jacket, clearly redundant in these current temperatures, was slung over the back of a chair. A pair of trainers sat by the door ready for his early morning jog around the palace gardens. The one she watched from behind her bedroom curtain and which had steadily become the highlight of her days. There was a stack of crime thrillers sitting perilously on the side table by her seat and a trail of Amy's toys stretched across the carpeted floor. It already looked like a family home. Lived in. She was sure he'd dismissed any member of staff who'd offered to tidy and clean the rooms, regardless that he was too busy to do it himself.

These were signs of a man content with who he was, without a need to impress anyone else. She envied him that freedom along with that one huge responsibility who demanded his time and attention.

Kaja lifted one of Amy's pink plastic teacups from the floor. Father and daughter had obviously been having a tea party together before he'd gone out to do his other job as a life-saving surgeon. It was such a simple indulgence of his daughter but the image it conjured up brought a smile to her lips and a pang in her heart. That was the kind-hearted, warm man she remembered. Someone who'd never be too busy to play with his child because he understood the gift he'd been given. Not everyone was lucky enough to be a parent.

Seth might have appeared a distant stranger to her in comparison but there was one thing that continued to niggle her. If he remained resentful about their past relationship, or as indifferent to her as he'd have her believe, why on earth had he come here? He had plenty of work at home and clearly no desire to tread old ground on a romantic level so what had prompted him into helping her? Seth didn't owe her a thing. It was the other way around. She couldn't help but think that the only reason he had for coming out was the unfinished business between them.

A shiver of excitement tickled the back of her neck. He must have forgiven her to some extent to have considered her request to help her father. Perhaps his love for her hadn't simply died the way she'd believed after hearing about his subsequent nuptials. He'd practically told her he'd done that on the rebound.

Kaja tried her best not to get carried away by the idea. Given recent events, she had a long way to go to get him to even talk civilly to her again. Besides, even if their feelings for one another hadn't evaporated completely, their circumstances wouldn't be any more compatible now. They were still worlds apart and he had his daughter's feelings to consider along with his own. She stared into the plastic receptacle wishing it could tell her fortune, map out her future for her when she couldn't do it herself. As much as she had wanted Seth to look at her the way he used to, she was afraid awakening old feelings was a wasted exercise.

Kaja was plagued by the confusion over what it meant to have him back in her life. She still couldn't be the woman Seth needed her to be.

It was exhausting being in her head. When she heard Amy's little feet patter across the floor it was a relief to have something else to focus on.

'Hello, sleepyhead. Fatima had to go home to her family for a little while. Her sister's very poorly.'

The four-year-old was still rubbing her eyes when she wandered in, her clothes and hair in disarray. 'Like your daddy?'

Kaja's heart lurched, surprised that the child had picked up on what was going on in the adult world around her.

'Not quite, but she's in hospital and Fatima has gone to visit.'

Amy thought for a moment. 'Can Daddy fix her too?'

'Your daddy is very busy but Fatima's sister will have a doctor like him to take care of her.' That seemed to be enough to satisfy her curiosity as Amy climbed up onto the settee and tucked her legs beneath her.

'I'm hungry. Fatima said we were going to make cookies and play hide and seek.'

'I guess that's what we're doing, then. Let me get

changed and I'll take you down to the kitchen.' That took care of how she was going to keep Amy occupied for the afternoon. Only time would tell if Seth would be appeased so easily on discovering Fatima's replacement.

# CHAPTER FIVE

'LET ME KNOW when they're ready for visitors,' Seth instructed the staff in the intensive care unit before exiting the hospital.

At this moment he was regretting telling Kaja to send away her chauffeur and stretch limo. His job might not involve heavy manual labour but it was exhausting just the same. The intense concentration, knowing the fatal consequences if he messed up, along with the hours spent on his feet took their toll mentally and physically. He was sorry he didn't have someone to pick him up outside and deliver him to Kaja's door.

The short stroll he undertook suddenly became a marathon when his whole body was crying out for rest.

It wasn't only shunning a bit of luxury he was kicking himself for either. He'd been short with Kaja today. Not at all supportive at a time when she needed it because he was too wrapped up in his own issues. If he'd been dealing with the family of any other transplant patient he would've been more sympathetic. He hadn't been fair treating her differently at such an emotive time. If this had been either of his grandparents, or, heaven forbid, Amy, he would've been beside himself with worry too. Sending her away hadn't been his call to make.

He had no right to be rude to her simply because he

was afraid of getting too close again. Behind all the glamour and privilege, he could see she was still the same woman he'd wanted to marry. The problem with that was she'd already rejected him once before. After a divorce, losing his gran and with all of the baggage his mother had left him with, those shutters around his heart should've been on lock down. Yet he kept thinking of the good times he and Kaja had once shared, scuppering any chance of remaining impervious to her charms.

Since Kaja wasn't party to the complicated web of thoughts causing him to act so unreasonably, he wanted to deliver the news about the surgery in person rather than let her hear it in a two-second phone call where he was desperate to get off the line. It was an effort of reparation on his part and would give her a chance to voice any question she might have. This wasn't about him and Kaja, it was about her and her family. That was why he was here. If she tore strips off him for the way he'd spoken to her today he'd have to stand and take it. It was the least he deserved in the circumstances.

'Seth Davenport.' He waved his ID at security as he'd become accustomed. Regardless that they knew him by sight now he had to wait until they waved him through and some unknown entity opened the gates.

As after every other tense shift, he was looking forward to some downtime with his daughter. He needed some normality more than ever. An uncomplicated period where nothing was asked of him other than loving his daughter. Something he didn't need to work at when she was the only person he could guarantee wouldn't want him out of her life.

'Hello?' His voice echoed around the hall, eliciting no response. It was so different from the usual homecoming he received when Amy launched herself at him, pleased to have him to herself again. Here, everything seemed flat, lifeless, lonely. It was impossible not to pity Kaja if this was what she came back to on a regular basis.

Despite his weariness Seth jogged up the stairs to his apartments, eager to get to his daughter and that familiar sense of home, family and being loved.

There was no sign of Nils, which wasn't surprising since he'd told him in no uncertain terms he didn't need assistance. Fatima was a different story. Seth wouldn't have been able to work without her looking after Amy and the two had already forged a bond, which he took as confirmation his daughter was content. That was all that mattered.

He was surprised the two of them hadn't come haring straight at him the second he'd come through the door. Along with Amy's demand for his attention he'd become used to the older woman constantly trying to feed him up.

'I'm home!' The sound of an excited squeal reverberated around the entire floor of the building but his daughter remained elusive.

He frowned, a tad put out but also too tired to go child-hunting just yet. Instead, he gave into exhaustion, kicked off his shoes and sank into an armchair, which was surprisingly comfy for something that resembled a golden throne. It was something he suspected had been chosen only for the aesthetics. Amy was clearly enjoying herself wherever she was and as long as she was happy he could afford to close his eyes for a moment.

He was about to nod off when the sound of bare feet slapping on the tiled floor and a familiar voice called him back from oblivion.

'I didn't realise you were home.'

He opened his eyes to see Kaja skidding to a halt in front of him and was momentarily lost for words. Like his daughter standing beside her, Kaja's face was splattered with either mud or chocolate, or both. The elegant princess had been replaced with a ragamuffin. Her sleek, perfectly coiffured glossy hair had been tied up into a messy ponytail. Loose tendrils, which had escaped during her obvious exertions with his daughter, clung damply to her rosy cheeks. However, it was her choice of outfit that made him do a double take. She'd swapped the chic trouser suit he'd seen her in this morning for something more practical.

With one swipe she transferred most of the chocolatey mud onto the sleeve of her—his—oversized grey sweatshirt.

'I think I recognise that.' He nodded towards the hoodie she'd teamed with a pair of loose tracksuit bottoms.

Kaja's cheeks pinked a little more. 'Um…yeah, I think this one's yours. It was the only comfy thing I could find. My wardrobe isn't exactly conducive to childminding.'

Seth could only imagine the carnage if her expensive silks had been plastered in the same way as his old university sweater. She looked like the old Kaja standing there wearing her favourite item of his clothes. He wondered if it had accidentally found its way into her suitcase when she'd fled or if she'd packed it as a reminder of him. His bruised ego and wounded heart hoped it was the latter and that she'd thought of him, might have even missed him over the years. As he had her.

He decided not to reference her clothing any further or attach any significance to it aloud. Not when she'd essentially told him she'd only worn it because it was dispensable and it didn't matter if it got dirty or torn.

'Why are you minding Amy? Where's Fatima?' He didn't know if it was more surprising that the officious older woman had abandoned her post or that the previously stand-offish Kaja had enthusiastically stepped up in her place.

'Fatima had a family emergency. I'm afraid she's had to return home for a while. I hope you don't mind but I've been looking after Amy in her absence.'

'Not at all. Thank you. I hope everything's okay with Fatima.' How could he object to her stepping in when she was doing everyone a favour? It had simply come as a surprise to see Kaja like this, playing with his daughter and looking more carefree than he'd seen her since he arrived.

'On the subject of family…' Kaja was toying with the elasticated cuffs of her sweatshirt. Fidgeting was always an indicator of how anxious she was about something and there were no prizes for guessing what that was today. It wasn't fair to keep her in the dark any longer.

'Amy, why don't you go and wash your face while I have a talk with Kaja?'

'Will you play hide and seek with us after?'

'Sure. Now go. Shoo.' He clapped his hands and Amy scuttled off with a giggle.

'You sure have a way of getting people to do what you want.' Kaja's sardonic tone was to be expected after their last encounter.

'I'm sorry for the way I spoke to you earlier. I was out of line.'

'You think?' She folded her arms across her chest, fending off his attempt to apologise.

'It wasn't my place to tell you to leave the hospital but I promise I was doing it with the best of intentions. I didn't want to think of you sitting in the corridors all day fretting about something you had no power to control.' That was the main problem. He was worried he'd be distracted by thoughts of her so close by while he was busy saving her father's life.

She waved away his explanation with the hand she'd now untucked from her defensive position. 'All that aside, you didn't call. Does that mean something went wrong? Are Papa and Bruno okay?'

'Everything's fine. I just wanted to tell you in person. The transplant went as planned and they're both recovering now. Someone will page me when they're ready for visitors and we can go and see them together.' He waited for Kaja's exclamation of relief, braced himself for her enthused gratitude, certain she'd forgive him now, but she remained stock-still and wide-eyed.

'Kaja? Did you hear me? They're going to be all right.' He wished she would say something, even if it was to swear at him. Instead she'd gone into some sort of shock. Seth was contemplating shaking her out of her stupor when she suddenly burst into tears. Her whole body appeared to collapse into itself as she finally took in what he was saying. A tsunami of all that emotion she'd apparently been holding back.

'Oh, sweetheart.' Any resentment he might have subconsciously harboured over their break-up dissipated along with the notion that theirs should remain a strictly professional relationship when she was so clearly in need of a hug.

It was pure instinct that drove him to catch her in his arms and provide that comfort and support she must've been lacking to fall apart in front of him. She didn't rail against his compassion, instead, crumpling against him in emotional exhaustion. He dreaded to think what it would have done to her if she'd had bad news.

'Let it all out.' Seth held her close, his arms wrapped tightly around her to keep her upright and let her tears soak through his shirt. That protective need to take care of her hadn't left him. Even though these were tears of happiness he knew she needed someone to lean on who understood her. Someone who knew she hated showing any weakness and would hold her until it passed without thinking less of her. She needed him. That superseded his, probably futile, endeavours to emotionally detach himself from the only woman he'd ever truly loved.

'All clean, Daddy.' Amy burst in again reminding them that time and their relationship had moved on and comforting Kaja was no longer in his job description.

'Good girl.' He praised his daughter and ruffled her hair, giving Kaja time to wipe her eyes and take a step away from him.

'What's wrong with Kaja?' Quick to notice all wasn't well, Amy frowned at him as though he'd obviously done something to upset her. Seeing the thunderous look on her face, he had a hunch she'd take her new friend's side if she had to choose.

'I'm fine, honey. Your daddy just gave me some really good news.' Kaja's eyes and smile shone a bit too brightly as she faced Amy, making Seth inclined to hug her a little longer.

'Is your daddy all better?' Amy's frown evened out into a smile and, though it would be easier to let her think everything was all rainbows and unicorns, he preferred to be honest with his daughter.

'We hope so. He needs to stay in hospital for a while to make sure.'

Amy digested that new information before asking her next question cautiously. 'Does that mean we can keep playing hide and seek?'

'I don't see why not.' Kaja pulled her into an embrace, making Seth proud of the child he'd raised who'd consider someone else's feelings before thinking of herself. Unlike her father this morning.

The squealing and running about that had woken him made more sense now. Hide and seek always made Amy excitable, though her hiding places required a high level of acting on his behalf to pretend he couldn't see her feet sticking out from beneath the curtains.

'Good. I'm it this time. You and Daddy go and hide.'

Seth and Kaja looked at each other with the same expression of horror before stumbling over each other's excuses to avoid being paired for the game. Regardless that he'd lent her his shoulder to cry on, there were several layers of unresolved tension between them, which weren't conducive to playing happily together.

'I'm sure your daddy needs a rest after working all day—'

'You and Kaja were having plenty of fun without me—'

Amy ignored their protests, putting her hands over her eyes as she began to count. 'One, two, three…'

His daughter had a habit of getting him into all kinds of predicaments but this one topped the lot. Playing hide and seek with an ex-girlfriend who probably despised him more now than when she'd dumped him wasn't awkward at all.

He looked at Kaja but she shrugged her shoulders, apparently unwilling to help him find a way out of this. When she took off running his competitive nature rose to the fore with his pride at stake if he couldn't outwit a four-year-old.

At the adorable sound of Amy trying to count, sometimes stumbling over her numbers, missing a few, and repeating others, he did his best to find a suitable hiding place. It wasn't easy at his size but Kaja hadn't had a problem since she'd disappeared completely from view.

He dived under his bed only to be met with a painful roadblock, forgetting he'd stashed his suitcase there.

'Ready or not, here I come!' Amy sing-songed with glee.

Crawling back out from his failed hiding place, Seth searched frantically around his room for a last-minute alternative. He yanked open the wardrobe door and jumped inside as Amy's footsteps echoed down the hall.

It was only when he closed the door it became apparent he wasn't alone. Before his eyes managed to adjust to the dark he heard the distinct sound of someone breathing next to him. He batted his way through the row of hanging shirts seeking the source.

'Kaja?' he whispered. 'I hope to goodness it's you in here and not some creepy stalker hiding in my closet.' It was disorienting in the cramped dark space. Not to mention unnerving knowing he wasn't alone.

'Do you get many of those?'

'You'd be surprised.' He didn't care that she was making fun of him if it took her mind off everything else that had gone on today.

'Where are you? It's disconcerting hearing a disembodied voice in the dark.'

'Tell me about it.'

He heard her shift position, then felt hands patting across his chest and up to cup his face. 'Ah, there you are.'

She inched closer until he could see the twinkle of her eyes shining in the shadows as she toyed with him. The soft touch of her hands on his skin made him temporarily forget to breathe. All he could do was stare at her beautiful smile and remember how it used to be to wake up next to it in the morning.

'Kaja… I really am sorry about the way I behaved at the hospital today. I didn't mean to upset you.' When they were here, so close to one another, it was impossible to maintain that detachment he'd been striving for. He wasn't fooling anyone, least of all himself.

'I was too full on, fussing around Bruno and my father when you were just trying to get on with your work.'

He reached out and brushed his fingers along the side of her cheek. 'It wasn't your fault. This is on me.'

'Well, you've apologised, more than once, and held me while I cried like a baby.'

Seth saw the sheen of tears in her eyes again and he had no choice but to reach out to her so she knew she had some support. 'That's nothing to be ashamed of when you've been dealing with so much. I'm always available for hugs should you need them.'

'I'm going to hold you to that.' She sniffed as she leaned her head against his chest and wound her arms around his waist with a sigh.

His attempts at being emotionally closed off from Kaja were short-lived when her every tear was a hit to his solar plexus. He couldn't bear to see her hurting and when she was clinging on to him like this, trusting him to provide her with some comfort, he could almost forget they'd ever parted. A treacherous path to venture down with someone who'd almost destroyed him once before.

'Come out, come out, wherever you are…' Amy's Child-Catcher-like song encouraged Kaja to giggle. A sweet, welcome sound in the aftermath of today's stresses.

When she looked up at him he placed a finger on her smiling lips. 'Shh!'

They locked eyes in the darkness, their bodies still entwined with only the sound of their synchronised breathing to be heard. Although, he was sure it had become more ragged over the course of the past few minutes. This wardrobe had suddenly become their whole world. Population two.

Kaja's mouth parted beneath his touch, her breath hot against his skin. He remembered the honeyed taste of those lips and the way they moulded perfectly to his even though it seemed so long ago now. Tentatively, he drew his finger down, slowly uncovering her delectable mouth. He wanted, needed to kiss her when she was looking up at him with equal longing, drawing him down towards her, encouraging him to act on his urge.

'Found you!' Bright light infiltrated their cosy cocoon once Amy discovered them, flinging both doors open wide. Kaja's arms fell away from the embrace, leaving him bereft. It had been so long since he'd felt that intimate interaction it came as a shock to be reminded he wanted it. That beneath his roles as a father and a doctor he was simply a man with needs of his own. Her touch had reawakened feelings he'd put on hold in the pursuit of being the best parent he could be for his daughter. Only Kaja had the ability to do that.

Since she was an ex who'd rejected his marriage proposal and he was currently treating her family members, he knew exploring that route would only lead to trouble. Especially when they were living under the same roof and now sharing his daughter's care. Renewing their relationship would be a bad move for all manner of reasons, primarily that she'd already broken his heart and he couldn't go through that again. Nor would he inflict that pain on his daughter when she was growing closer to Kaja by the minute. As far as Amy was concerned, once his patients had recovered they'd be flying home. He wanted to keep it that way rather than let her think

Kaja was going to be part of their lives only to have her run out when it all got too real.

Seth stepped out into the real world leaving Kaja in the land of make believe where a kiss was possible and wouldn't cause a multitude of problems.

'You are too good, Amy Davenport. I think you deserve a prize for finding us so quickly. Why don't I take you out for a special treat?' He put his hand on his daughter's back and ushered her out of the door. Thankfully, she was so jubilant at having found them she hadn't picked up on the tension between the adults. He wished it were going to be so easy for him to put the incident out of his mind and dismiss what could have ended up as their second first kiss.

Kaja was tempted to close the closet doors and slink back into the shadows. Seth was making it clear he didn't want to spend any more time with her. He couldn't even look at her. She knew why. A moment together, unguarded and isolated from their responsibilities outside this room, and old feelings had been given space to breathe. Another second alone and she knew they would have given into temptation to kiss, to touch and taste one another again.

She'd been on her own for too long. Well, she'd been living with her family and the entourage of staff her father insisted upon, but she'd been short of actual company. Why else would she have turned to an ex in her hour of need? Clearly, she was confusing her gratitude for the surgeon who'd saved her father's life with desire.

She'd known from the start having Seth here was going to be difficult, but she'd thought putting her father's health above her failed romance should take precedence. That was until she'd become aware that the physical attraction between them hadn't lessened over the years.

She'd wanted him to kiss her and if Amy hadn't busted them she was pretty sure he would have.

'Can Kaja come too?' Amy's plea for her to be included put a stop to any thoughts of slinking away unnoticed. It also prevented Seth from leaving the room as quickly as he'd intended.

Realising it would look strange if she continued to hide in the wardrobe, she had no choice but to step back out into the spotlight.

Gone was the passion burning in Seth's eyes for her, replaced with a look of frustration. He didn't want her hanging around with him and his daughter. Whatever that moment had been between them, it was over.

'I'm sure Kaja would rather wait here until the hospital rings with news.'

'I'm not really dressed for going out, Amy.'

'Right, and it would take ages to organise cars and security.' Seth was quick to add to the list of excuses why she couldn't go with them but they both knew the real reason he didn't want her tagging along. They'd almost kissed in there and he wanted to put some distance between them so they'd forget it had ever happened. It stung to have him reject her so casually when the moment had literally made her go weak at the knees. There hadn't been anyone since Benedikt. She hadn't even been tempted. Until now. Probably because she knew the passion of Seth's kisses, wanted them and was surprised he still looked at her with that same burning desire. After everything she'd done to him, she knew he would never hurt her and for a lonely divorcee that was the greatest aphrodisiac of all.

'We don't have to go out, Daddy. Me and Kaja made cookies. Can't I have some of those for my treat?'

Amy always had an answer for any obstacles preventing her from getting what she wanted. It was a credit to Seth how smart she was, and determined. He'd raised a strong daughter and Kaja bet there was never a dull moment in the Davenport household.

'I…er…'

'I did promise Amy we could sample some once they'd cooled.' She watched with increasing amusement as Seth tried desperately to come up with another counter argument and failed. They were only going down to the kitchen to scoff a few biscuits. It wasn't as if they were on their own and about to act out some erotic scene from the contents of the fridge. Not unless he asked her to…

# CHAPTER SIX

'THEN I SUPPOSE we have no choice…'

Amy was Seth's conscience as well as his get-out clause. He had tried to use her to run away from his re-surging feelings for Kaja. He'd wanted to kiss her and he'd come close to it. When they'd been fooling around, the only thought in his head had been that need to be with her again. The time he'd spent worrying where she'd gone, what he'd done wrong and how he was going to live without her dismissed all too easily. Worrying when she had the power to make him feel as rejected and unwanted as his mother had by her absence in his life.

What he didn't understand more than his own reaction was why Kaja had been leaning in for that kiss in the first place. Not only because he'd been abrupt with her today, but she was the one who'd ended their relationship. While he might have unresolved emotions and issues, Kaja had made her feelings pretty clear five years ago. She didn't want him. What had changed in their time apart? Nothing as far as he knew. It was possible she was simply lonely out here and had been confused by his company and their romantic history.

He wasn't going to mistake his feelings towards Kaja for anything other than a want for her, which apparently hadn't died simply because she'd left him. More than that, left him open to be hurt all over again.

They were different people now but the problems that had taken Kaja away from him in the first place remained. He didn't belong as a permanent feature in her life any more than she did in his. She lived in a different country, moved in higher social circles, was born royal. Their backgrounds couldn't be more different or incompatible. Rejection had been an all too common feature in his life and he'd sworn not to put himself in a position to let it happen again. If this trip had been the ultimate test of that vow, he was failing miserably.

Thankfully, Amy's appearance snapped him back to his senses and made him willing to forget the incident ever happened and redouble his efforts to protect his battered heart. Except Kaja apparently had bewitched his daughter too, preventing total escape. There was no way he could forbid contact between them simply to prevent himself from making any further potentially disastrous decisions. It wouldn't be fair to either Amy or Kaja and would give them both cause to despise him.

Tensions were already running high around here without doing anything to upset either princess in his presence.

Despite his resolve to remain unmoved by his reacquaintance with Kaja, he was persuaded into the kitchen by two aspiring, giggling chefs to taste their goods.

'What about this one?' Amy, sitting on a high stool, was force-feeding him the misshapen biscuits she'd made. The crunchy brown lumps weren't appetising in either appearance or taste but she was so proud of them he couldn't refuse.

'Delicious,' he managed to utter through a mouthful of crumbs.

'I thought you preferred these?' Kaja popped a delicate shell-shaped cookie into his mouth with a mischievous grin.

'No, he likes mine better.' A laughing Amy wedged another lump into his full mouth and Seth realised he'd become the butt of their joke. They weren't competing for his praise, they'd joined forces until his cheeks were bulging like a hamster storing sunflower seeds, and he was in danger of going into a sugar coma.

It had just been the two of them as a family for so long it was a new experience to have someone else join their fun. Paula had never been part of Amy's life so the only mother figure she'd known was his gran and he doubted she remembered much of that time, being so little. Watching her with Kaja was a bittersweet experience. In different circumstances perhaps this could have been a real family scene between them. Something he'd always wanted and, judging by the delight on his daughter's face, something she would like too.

He was a good father but that couldn't make up for the lack of a mother in her life. Someone she could confide secrets to that she didn't want to share with her father and someone to gang up with and play pranks on him. He'd pictured this life with Kaja. It was a shame she hadn't wanted it. She'd given up their future to return to her duties as a princess. He hadn't been enough incentive for her to stay when she'd made her choice five years ago. That was something he'd do well to remember instead of believing it could still be possible.

'Stop! I'll sick if I eat any more, you rascal.' He tickled Amy, incapacitating her with laughter so she couldn't do any more damage to his waistline.

'Nonsense. I know you, Seth. I'm sure you haven't eaten anything all day.' Kaja dipped one of her golden-brown morsels into a bowl of melted chocolate sitting on the worktop.

She knew him too well. With a day of surgery ahead of him he hadn't stopped to refuel since the breakfast Fatima had provided this morning.

Kaja made sure hunger raised its head again as she bit down, the chocolate coating her lips, keeping Seth mesmerised as she licked it off with her pink tongue. Somehow, he'd turned another playful moment into an erotic display in his lustful mind. It didn't help matters when she dipped another cookie into the chocolate and offered it to him. He couldn't resist, even though he knew it was bad for him.

The confection was sweet on his tongue but nothing compared to the taste of Kaja as he sucked the remaining chocolate from her fingers. His eyes didn't leave hers, watching until they darkened and a small gasp sounded from her lips.

'Where's my chocolate?' Once again Amy saved him from himself, demanding to be included in this new game.

'Last one before dinner.' He half coated another and gave it to the appreciative audience before washing away the chocolate on his fingers at the sink. Anything to get away from temptation and a woman with whom he seemed determined to tread old ground.

'I'll put the rest away for later.' At the other end of the kitchen Kaja busied herself parcelling up the remainder of the treats, but he could see her sneaking glimpses at him when she thought he wasn't looking.

This push and pull between them was torture. Especially when he already knew how good they were together on a physical level. It was geography, class divide and a lack of honesty that had been their downfall. If her reason for leaving him had been not loving him, or that they'd no longer been attracted to one another, living under the same roof wouldn't have caused the same intense level of tension simmering between them. It might have been better for his peace of mind if she'd stayed mad at him.

'Your Highness, I'm so sorry I was gone for so long. Please forgive me.'

'Fatima?'

Kaja's faithful aide bustled into the kitchen as if from nowhere. She untied the headscarf keeping her curly brown hair in place and struggled out of her heavy coat, which made Seth sweat simply looking at it. He supposed she was accustomed to the climate but, as a visitor more used to inclement British weather, he found the temperature and humidity stifling.

Kaja seemed more stunned by her arrival than her outdoor wear. 'I wasn't expecting you back so soon. How is your sister?'

'She hurt her back but it's nothing serious. I telephoned her daughter and she's driving over to be with her. Now, let me get back to work and clean up this mess you've left in my kitchen.' After hanging up her coat she pulled a floral apron from a drawer and tied it around her waist, then herded them out of her territory.

Seth's phone vibrated in his pocket with a text message.

'That's the hospital. You can go and see your dad and Bruno whenever you're ready.' He halted their procession down the hallway to tell her immediately. Now there was no doubt about where, or with whom, he'd be spending the rest of the day.

Kaja dithered when he'd half expected her to race off at once. 'I need to change but, er, would you come with me?'

'To get changed?' She made it too easy for him to tease her but joking around was safer ground than those hot, loaded looks they kept exchanging.

She rolled her eyes. 'To the hospital.'

'Can I stay with Fatima?' Amy had already turned on her heel and was running back towards the kitchen before he could answer. Clearly, she hadn't been spoiled enough today. He couldn't begrudge her some attention from an alternative female role model than an ex they were both growing dangerously close to, however.

'Yes, Kaja, I'll accompany you to the hospital. I have to check on my patients anyway. Yes, Amy, you can stay with Fatima, if that's all right with her.' Seth addressed each of them in turn telling himself it was the right thing to do for all concerned.

'Okay, I'm ready to go. Sorry for the wait.' While Kaja wanted to sprint immediately to the hospital to see for herself that her family was safe, it wasn't as simple as that.

'No problem.' Seth rose from the armchair he'd been sitting in waiting for her to make herself presentable for the outside world.

It was easy for him. A quick shower and a change of shirt and he was ready. As handsome as ever. She needed a bit more assistance to be camera-ready in case she was snapped on the way. The chances of that happening were high with the press camped outside the front of the hospital waiting for news.

Her car was out front, engine running. Seth graciously helped her into the back seat before climbing in next to her. The photographers were there at the gates too, wanting to catch her reaction, some sign of what had happened to her father during surgery. It was draining having to keep up a façade when any display of emotion was deemed unbecoming for a member of the royal family. That was why she'd wanted Seth to accompany her. At least when she was with him she no longer had to keep that stiff upper lip. She'd already broken down in front of him, clung to him for support, and the world hadn't ended because she'd let someone in. Although it still could if she got too used to having him around.

'Thank goodness for tinted windows. They give some illusion of privacy even if the press always manage to sneak a picture somewhere along the way.'

'Don't you get sick of all this? Wish you could just run away from it all and live a normal life?' There was pity in Seth's eyes and she found it worse than the pain she'd seen there most of the time when he'd looked at her.

She didn't really deserve anyone's sympathy when she led such a privileged life. Regardless that she found it trying at times. People had been hurt worse than her in her pursuit of normality. Seth for one.

'I tried that, remember? I made my escape to England but running away doesn't solve problems. Everything catches up with you in the end. I'll never regret our time together, Seth, but I was living a lie. I'm sorry you got caught in the crossfire while I figured that out.' Her love for Seth had been genuine but coming back here only proved it could never have worked out. Protocol impinged on basic things most people took for granted, such as privacy. Something she knew Seth was struggling with in his short stay here so far.

Neither of them would want that kind of intrusion for Amy either. Playing together today, having fun like any other normal family, only served to increase her sense of loss. Being a mother was never going to be possible for her. The more time she spent with Amy, the more she realised what she was missing out on. Despite appearances, Seth was the one who had everything.

Perhaps she should've stayed single rather than ever getting involved with anyone. Then no one would have been hurt. Including her.

'I wish you'd told me that before I flew all the way out here.' There was that sad smile again, which wouldn't have been noticeable to someone who didn't know him as well as she did.

'Why?' There had been a couple of unguarded moments between them but Seth had been quick to stamp out any flames when heat sparked between them. She doubted rekindling their romance was the reason he'd agreed to help her father in the first place.

He sighed and leaned back into the leather. 'I think that's what I was doing by accepting your request to treat your father. After Gran died I was lost. Coming here has been a distraction from the reality of her no longer being around. If what you're saying is true, the grief will be waiting for me on my return.'

She fought back the sudden and surprising disappointment as he confirmed his motive had nothing to do with her and reached out to squeeze his hand. Seth glanced down at the fingers clasped around his, then up at her, his eyes misted with unshed tears.

There were similarities that had brought them to where they were now. She was apparently mourning their relationship and her chance to be mother to someone as wonderful as Amy as much as he was grieving the loss of his grandmother.

'It's not easy facing up to the things that keep you awake at night. I don't know how many times I rehearsed that call, dialled your number and hung up before I asked you for help. I know it's not the same but you'll feel better when you deal with your fears once and for all.' She'd thought of Seth often over the years, wanting to make amends but convincing herself to shove it all to the back of her mind and pretend to move on. When, in truth, she'd never got over him. Her heart hadn't let go of him simply because she'd thought it the right thing to do.

'Did it work? Do you think you've exorcised some demons by seeing me again?' He was searching her face for answers, making it difficult for her to lie to him.

Her blush would give her away anyway. She had no business dishing out advice when her life had been such a car crash up until now. Plus, if she was going to be honest with him it meant confessing she still had feelings for him. News that might not be welcome after everything she'd done.

'I'm glad I called. For my father's sake and I, um, I'm pleased I got to see you again. It gave me the chance to explain why I did what I did.'

'But… I get the sense this hasn't played out the way you imagined?' He was able to read her way too easily. Perhaps after being burnt so badly already he watched her more carefully these days.

She glanced out of the window trying to get her bearings. Why did this journey seem to take longer when she was in the car with him?

'I, uh…' she cleared her throat '… I didn't expect that we'd, uh, still have that spark.' Or that she'd be faced with the reality of her infertility issues again. Babysitting Amy reminded her what she was missing out on and even if circumstances made a relationship possible with Seth, she couldn't give him everything that should come with that.

The ensuing silence was interminable as she waited for him to confirm or deny her observation.

Then Seth said quietly, 'Nor me.'

There wasn't time to analyse what that meant for them other than it hadn't been all in her head as the car pulled up outside the hospital.

'Before we go in, I need you to be prepared. Remember, they've just come out of surgery. You know they're going to be weak and groggy.'

She nodded, not concerned about anything behind those doors other than seeing her family again. Despite her fears her father might not get through this, she'd always had faith in Seth's abilities. There was a long way to go until they could say her father was in good health but at least the transplant had gone to plan so far.

'I'm here for you,' he said, resting his hand gently on her arm.

She bit her lip to stop from begging him to hold her again as he'd done earlier. That connection with someone who expected nothing from her in return was invaluable. Something she hadn't appreciated as much as she should have when she'd had it.

Then there was that rush of arousal he still managed to incite with a mere look. Her heart, and body, were crying out for his touch but they couldn't do anything in public without causing an uproar.

Instead, they exited the car separately, ignoring the cameras and the microphones being thrust in their direction as security hurried them inside.

'Oh, Papa.' Kaja rushed to her father's bedside battling for space amongst the attachments and machines assisting his recovery. He had drips going into his body, drains coming out and a morphine driver for pain relief, but he was here.

'Kaja…my daughter,' he rasped through dry, cracked lips under his oxygen mask. The effort of opening his eyes to look at her proved too much and they fluttered shut again. He was obviously still tired. She'd never seen him so frail. He'd refused to let them accompany him when he'd been having dialysis and had always put on a brave face afterwards, even though he'd spent the rest of those days in bed. One to always defy his age and keep himself busy with the running of the country, now he was in his hospital gown without his tailored suits there was no hiding the truth. He was as vulnerable and mortal as everyone else.

His paper-thin skin was almost translucent, except for the lurid red and purple marks where his body had been through the wars. It was clear there would be a long recovery period.

Seth, who'd been talking to the other doctors about his meds to prevent rejection of the new organ, came over when she kissed her father's forehead.

'We should let you get some sleep, sir. I hate to drag you away again so soon but he needs as much rest as possible, Kaja.'

'I know. I just wanted to see him for myself. Can I look in on Bruno quickly too?'

'Sure. He's still next door.'

'I'll come back and see you again tomorrow, Papa,' she whispered before following Seth into the adjoining room.

'Hello, sis!'

'Bruno!' Seeing him sitting up in bed looking so well considering what he'd been through, she wanted to hug him so tightly. She saw the fleeting panic cross his face as she ran to him and reined herself in before she caused him any further pain.

'How are you feeling?' She settled for giving him a peck on the cheek instead.

'Sore,' he said with a grimace. 'How's Dad?'

Seth stepped forwards then to put his mind at ease.

'Everything went to plan. He's understandably tired but doing well.'

'He's awake?'

'Only briefly. He knew I was there at least.' Kaja would've hated for him to have woken up and found himself alone in a strange room.

'That's good. Maybe I'll get to see him tomorrow when I'm back on my feet?' Bruno looked hopefully at Seth to authorise the visit.

'We'll see how you both do overnight.' Seth apparently wasn't going to be swayed by sympathy when it came to his patients' recovery times. He was the kind of doctor who'd do whatever he could to buoy his patients' spirits. It went a long way to aiding recovery. She'd seen for herself how much having beloved family members around helped people get better quicker compared to those left languishing alone with no visitors to boost their mood.

'Is there anything I can bring you from home, Bruno?' She wanted to do something, anything, to make her brother more comfortable when he'd sacrificed so much to save their father. The fact she hadn't been a match had put paid to any idea of her being a donor even if either of them would've let her do it. As a result, her conscience insisted she needed to pay some sort of penance because she wasn't the one lying in a hospital bed recovering from an operation.

He shook his head. 'I think I'm all set. I have books, magazines, puzzles and a phone somewhere.'

'Has Missy been in?'

'Where do you think I got the supplies from? I'm sure she'll be back later. I asked the staff to let her know when I was awake too.'

'In that case, I'll let you recharge your batteries. You've got to look your best for your sweetheart.' Her brother was still head over heels about his long-term girlfriend and vice versa. They made an adorable couple but she couldn't help but envy them their future together.

'Thanks for calling in, Kaja. Hopefully, next time I see you I'll be on my feet.' He flicked another glance at Seth.

'We'll see.' Her visiting companion refused to be drawn any further on the subject despite Bruno's plea. She knew her brother well enough to predict him ignoring all medical advice to try and get on his feet before he was ready. When they were out of earshot, where she couldn't be accused of being a tattle-tale, she'd tell Seth to keep an eye on him for that very reason.

'Get some sleep. I just wanted to call in and say hello.' She kissed her brother on the cheek for a second time, content to leave now she'd been assured he was his back to his mischievous self.

'In that case, hello and goodbye. I'll see you tomorrow and don't forget to bring my running shoes with you,' he teased one last time before lying back down and closing his eyes.

'He seems in good spirits.' Seth echoed her thoughts aloud as he closed the door behind them.

'It would appear so. Although my brother wouldn't be inclined to tell me if he was in any pain.' She couldn't resist another peek through the window, finding him already fast asleep.

'All the reports so far are positive so I don't think there's any real cause to worry.'

'Not that that will stop me,' she said with a self-deprecating grin.

'It must be nice having a sibling. Even if it is one more person to fret over on a daily basis.'

'We weren't always this close but, yes, I'd be lost without him now. Do you think you've missed out on something by being an only child?' Bruno had been another casualty of her selfishness during those years she'd spent incommunicado in England but he hadn't held a grudge. He'd welcomed her back with open arms and told her how much he'd missed his little sister. Kaja hated herself for the estrangement but it was in her brother's good nature to forgive and forget. She had a much harder job forgiving herself.

Perhaps if she'd been honest with Seth, he and Bruno would have been friends from the start.

'I was never lonely when Gran and Gramps were alive but now… It would be nice to have someone to lean on. You know, someone who understands what I'm going through.' He let out a sigh and Kaja knew how truly lucky she was to have the family she did. At least when her mother had passed away she hadn't grieved alone. Her father and brother had lifted her up when she'd been at her lowest. Seth had no one except his young daughter.

'I know it's not the same but you can talk to me, if it helps?'

'Thanks, but, um, this is only short term, remember?'

How could she forget when he was always so desperate to get away from her?

'I know Amy's a comfort to you but you know where I am if you need a listening ear.'

'She is, but it's made me realise I want more for her. Given the chance I'd like to settle down with someone again and give her a stable family life. Perhaps even give her a brother and sister. Although, I suppose you need a partner before there's any chance of that happening.'

Kaja faked a laugh to accompany his, ignoring the lead weight that had dropped into the pit of her stomach. The family he wanted wasn't something he'd find with her. A quiet, ordinary life was something she'd sacrificed long ago because it had never truly been her destiny. Seth, on the other hand, could still have it all. Without her.

'Where is my driver?' she demanded from the nearest security officer, the effort of hiding her heartache becoming too much to sustain on top of an already emotional day.

'I'll check for you now, ma'am.' The burly shadow clone began issuing orders over his walkie-talkie.

'Are you in a hurry to get back?'

She momentarily stopped pacing the corridor like a caged animal.

'Yes. No. Well, there's no point in hanging around here getting in the way.' As she was wont to do when reminded of her inadequacies, she wanted to lock herself away from the outside world and hold herself a pity party.

'I think Amy and Fatima were expecting a bit more time together. We could do with a timeout too. Between the stress of the op and, I'm sorry to say this, but the oppressiveness of that house, I think we need a break.'

'What are you suggesting? I'm all for a change of scenery but you know I have to run it past a lot of other people first.' He'd intrigued her but protocol spoiled any notion of spontaneity.

'That's my point. You need some breathing space and a distraction from all this stress. It's not good for your mental health to be cooped up all the time like a trapped bird. You need to spread your wings once in a while. Come on, while he's not looking. Let's bust out of this joint.'

Kaja glanced at the guard walking down the corridor in the opposite direction with his back to them, then at Seth's hand, which was wrapped around hers.

'I can't just disappear. All hell would break loose.

They'll think I've been kidnapped, for goodness' sake.' She resisted as he tried to pull her away.

Seth narrowed his eyes and she could almost see his brain working overtime to come up with a solution. Then he turned back towards the door to Bruno's room. 'This should do the trick.'

He lifted the marker pen tied to the whiteboard, where someone had scribbled *Bruno Alderisi—No Food*, and added his own message in bold letters.

*Taking a mental health day on doctor's orders. No need to look for us. Back soon.*

He handed her the pen. 'Well, they're not going to take my word for it.'

She let out a titter in disbelief he was serious about this. They weren't merely ditching class like a couple of naughty schoolkids, he was asking her to go against all the rules in place to keep her safe.

'You're a grown woman and one who has worried herself sick all day. Surely, an afternoon off isn't too much to ask for?'

It wasn't, unless you were part of a royal family being constantly scrutinised under a microscope. She thought about what Seth was offering, what he represented. A freedom she hadn't had since she'd left England, and him.

She took the pen off him, ignoring his triumphant grin, and signed her name to their sick note.

'I guess not. What's the worst that could happen?'

# CHAPTER SEVEN

'WHAT ARE WE waiting for, then?' Seth tugged her by the hand again and this time Kaja let herself be led astray.

This naughty side of Seth's made him appear years younger than the serious surgeon dealing with her brother only moments ago. It was impossible for her not to get caught up in the moment. For a little while at least it would be nice to pretend they were the two young, carefree people they used to be. Except it wasn't as straightforward as giving her security the slip.

'Wait. I'm going to be recognised the second I set foot outside. We're not going to get very far with me looking like this.' She could hide her jewellery in her pocket and tie up her hair but the expensive, brightly coloured clothes were going to draw attention.

'We'll figure something out. For now we need to put some distance between us and your human shield there.'

Kaja chuckled as they hurried down the corridor hoping their escapade wouldn't be suddenly cut short or that they would cause too many problems for the staff. She simply wanted to have some fun for a change.

'This reminds of that time on night shift together. Remember?'

'How could I forget?' The husky tone of Seth's voice and the memory itself warmed Kaja from the inside out.

She didn't know why she'd chosen that particular intimate snapshot from their history together to share when it was a million miles away from who and where they were today. Even in her thin layers of silk she was burning up thanks to the images she'd conjured up in her head.

That night had been during their first flush of love when they'd wanted to spend every second together. Preferably in bed. Work and conflicting schedules had made it difficult to get that quality time. So, when they'd found themselves working together on an unusually quiet night shift they'd made the most of it.

'In here, quick!' He opened a door halfway down the corridor and pulled her inside.

'What are you doing? I didn't mean for us to recreate that night together. I have to be more discreet about these things now, Seth,' she spluttered as he shut them into the tiny store room.

He tried to stifle a laugh, then reached out and cupped her face in his hands. Kaja held her breath, convinced he was about to kiss her. The adrenaline spiking through her body indicated how much she wanted him to.

'As much as I would love to, that's not why I came in here. I thought you might want to get changed.' He directed her gaze to the rows of freshly laundered scrubs hanging on the rails above them. She'd been so concentrated on Seth and the thought of his mouth on hers she hadn't noticed their surroundings.

'Oh. Yes. Of course.' She turned away, breaking physical contact so he couldn't see her turn scarlet with mortification. Now he knew exactly where her thoughts had gone to he might change his mind about spending the rest of the day with her.

'I'll grab one of the lab coats.'

With her back still to him Kaja lifted down a plastic-wrapped set of scrubs, swearing to launder and return them as soon as possible. She slipped out of her purple jumpsuit and shimmied into the less flattering, baggy outfit. The thin gold rope belted around the waist of her discarded clothes doubled up as a makeshift hair tie as she caught her tresses up in a ponytail and she used a fresh towel to wipe away her make-up. Now she was no one remarkable at all. If only she could disguise her true self from Seth too, she might be able to stay out of trouble.

Seth slipped his arms into the sleeves of the crisp white coat despite the sweat already clinging to his back. He was all too aware of Kaja standing behind him stripped to her underwear. It had been a spur-of-the-moment decision to duck in here when she'd been looking for excuses not to take some time off. As had the notion of running away in the first place.

He wanted to make up for his behaviour this morning along with easing some of the sadness Kaja had been cloaked in since the day he arrived. Five years was a long time to hold a grudge when he had a successful career and a daughter he doted on. She was the one in pain now, a wild exotic bird trapped in a gilded cage here, and he wanted to do something to set her free again.

It had come at a cost. The reminder of their passionate encounter on that nightshift was something he couldn't get out of his head. Especially now she was so close, half naked, with her familiar perfume filling the air.

The sensual memory of the last time they'd been locked in a storage room, clothes in disarray, getting hot and heavy up against the wall, blazed brightly in his head. Even though they'd tried to be quiet Kaja had made those little moans that drove him crazy.

*Damn, they had to get out of here fast.*

'I'm ready when you are.' Kaja's quick change came not a moment too soon.

'Great. Once I'm sure we're all clear out there we'll head for the fire exit.' Seth's relief was short-lived when he spun round only for her disguise to steal his breath away. The fresh-faced, beautiful surgeon he'd fallen in love with at work was standing right before him.

'I'm not sure these go with the outfit but beggars can't be choosers.' She lifted her trouser leg to show off the purple, open-toed sparkly heels she was wearing.

Seth reminded himself he wasn't a Regency hero who should be bowled over by a well-turned ankle. 'As long as you can walk in them I think we should be fine.'

They were going to have to stop cosying up in tight spaces if he was to resist temptation for the duration of his stay. The way Kaja continued to look at him with that reflected longing was severely testing his restraint and rendering his broken heart a distant memory.

He cracked the door open a fraction and peered out. 'Corridor's clear. Let's go.'

Kaja followed him out and the few staff they passed didn't bat an eyelid.

'So far, so good,' she whispered with a hint of excitement in her voice. She really had been locked away in her princess tower for too long.

'Don't speak too soon.' He grabbed hold of her and pretended to study the chart pinned to the wall as another guard charged past them.

His heart was thumping so hard he swore their pursuer would hear it. It was crazy to have suggested this. More so to have acted upon it. Kaja was royalty and for all these guys knew he could've abducted her. If he wasn't careful he'd find himself locked up for kidnapping their precious princess. She was no longer a mere work colleague he could blow off some steam with when the mood struck.

It was only the sound of heavy work boots continuing on past that let him breathe again and stop him imagining the rest of his days doing hard labour.

'It's amazing what a change of clothes and a make-under can do,' Kaja tutted.

'Indeed.' He withdrew his arm from around her shoulder, aware he'd broken all sorts of etiquette today. Both royal and personal. However, he had more serious matters to deal with. If he wasn't careful he'd find himself taken out by a SWAT team.

Moving swiftly away from the commotion building elsewhere, Seth led her towards a side exit next to the ambulance bay. Heads down, they walked past the paramedics unloading a gentleman in a wheelchair, doing their best not to raise suspicion.

'Where are we going? Kaja was tottering along in her spiked heels struggling to keep up as they tried to get as far from here as quickly as possible.

'I have no idea. The only parts of this country I've seen are the airport and the palace. Both of which I'm guessing will be on lockdown by now.'

'This is your great plan? To bust me out of the hospital and what? Take me on a day trip around the car park? I'd have been better off at home.' It was no wonder Kaja was ticked off at him. He really hadn't thought this through. This level of risk should've had a reward at the end to be worth all the trouble. If he'd planned this properly there would've been chilled champagne and a gourmet picnic waiting for them on a secluded beach somewhere. He wasn't good at spontaneity when the unknown presented a threat to his well-being.

'Hey. It was a spur-of-the-moment decision. Give me some credit for trying to shake things up around here.'

'In case you missed it, we've had enough drama recently to last a lifetime.' She hopped along on one foot while trying to dislodge her shoe from the other. Once completely barefoot she stomped silently towards the patch of grass at the back of the car park.

'Look, we've managed to get some time away from rent-a-hunk. We can spend it discussing my inadequacies as a member of the resistance or we can make the most of it.' He cocked his head to one side and fluttered his dark eyelashes.

It had been a long time since he'd had to employ that move to win her over but he was pleased to see it had the same desired effect as she failed to hide her grin.

'Okay, okay. I'm glad you took the initiative. I've forgotten what it was like to play hooky every now and again. You're a bad influence, Mr Davenport.' The faux scolding only confirmed the decision had been the right one. For both of them. How long had it been since he'd had a break from being Mr Responsible too? They needed to cut loose for a while. If only to remember the people they used to be before life got in the way.

'Now we've established this is entirely my fault if anyone asks, perhaps you'd like to have some input? This is your country after all. I would've thought you'd have some idea where to hide out for a couple of hours?' Back in England they could've disappeared easily with open fields, forests or seaside towns a mere train stop away. He knew nothing about the hiding potential here and with their history they needed somewhere with plenty of space around them.

Kaja knew she was taking out her bad mood on the wrong person. It was herself she was mad at for agreeing to this when after a couple of minutes alone in a locked room she was back to having lustful thoughts about Seth. Now, to all intents and purposes, they were on the run. As if they needed this romanticised any more when he was the man who believed he was giving her some freedom back.

In a way he was, when every moment she spent with him made her feel like the Kaja who'd spent those years in England living a normal life.

Something she shouldn't be reliving when she was doing her best to live up to her family name.

'There is a place not too far from here where Bruno and I used to sneak off to when we were kids.' It was her time to take the lead, carefully picking her way barefoot down the grassy incline away from civilisation.

'Won't Bruno rat us out? Surely that'll be the first place he'll think of if he hears you've gone AWOL?' The more cautious Seth began to re-emerge as he jogged down the slope to join her. His fancy, dress shoes weren't coping on the wet grass any better than her bare feet. Despite today's warm weather it must've rained some time during the night, ensuring Seth's every other step was more of a slide. Adding even more of an element of danger to their outing when there was the extra risk of him falling onto his backside at any given moment.

'First off, Bruno is probably asleep and the chances are no one is going to wake him up after donating a kidney to tell him his kid sister has gone for a walk. Secondly, he'll have forgotten about this place by now. If it even exists any more. Besides, he knows how exhausting this whole royalty deal is, better than anyone. Who do you think found this place and planned our escape days in the old days?' Before Seth, her brother was the only person who'd understood her need to get away. That was before duty had called him away from their childhood games and she'd realised the reality of the responsibilities of royal life when he'd no longer had time for her or anything else.

The unmistakable squeak of smooth leather losing its grip on wet grass sounded nearby, followed by muffled curses.

'Take your shoes off, Seth. Your socks too. There's something very liberating and earthy about being barefoot in the countryside.'

He leaned against a nearby tree to do as she'd suggested and rolled up the bottoms of his trousers so they didn't get wet.

'If this is what getting back to nature feels like, it's slimier than I imagined.' Any Austen-esque notions about romantic walks in the country were obliterated thanks to Seth's unpoetic observations.

'Man up. For someone who spends his days elbows deep in other people's innards you shouldn't be this squeamish.'

'I tend not to walk barefoot through the operating theatre,' he said with a heavy dose of sarcasm. 'So, where does this slimy green road lead to anyway? A technicolour world with flying monkeys and grass-resistant ruby slippers for all?'

'Tobel. It's a derelict medieval village. If there's anything left of it by now. It's far enough from the usual tourist routes to hopefully avoid detection.' To be honest she'd forgotten all about the place until now. It had been relegated to the back of her mind as merely a childhood fantasy. A mythical land she'd imagined exploring in the mists of time.

Now, treading familiar ground, there was a bloom of excitement coming to life at the prospect of seeing the place again and reliving those carefree days.

'Forgive me but it doesn't sound like the ultimate escape. What's the fascination with some old ruins and how far away are they?'

'It was a place for us to hang out without being studied like lab rats. We just played hide and seek, had a moan to each other about how unfair life was, drew chalk pictures on the walls… You know, the usual kid stuff.'

'You're breaking my heart here, Princess. Some of us only had a back yard to play in. Not a whole abandoned village.'

She stuck her tongue out and teased him right back. 'I know, I know, and all you had to play with was a stick and a hoop…'

'You cheeky—'

For a second she thought she might have actually offended him as he halted their woodland walk. When he started after her, tossing his shoes aside, she let out a squeal before taking off at high speed. It was exhilarating running through the forest, branches whipping past, her heels discarded in her desire to escape Seth's false indignation. His deep laugh was sweeter than the sounds of the chirping birds watching them from high up in the treetops and she began to wonder why she was running at all.

Fate stepped in and plonked an exposed tree root in her path, causing her to trip.

'Are you okay?' Seth caught up with her in time to see the inelegant display as she landed face down on the ground.

She rolled over and sat up, dusting the dirt and leaves from her hands. 'I'm fine. It's only my pride that's taken a knock.'

'Let me give you a hand up and I swear I'll say nothing about karma.' He held out his hand to help her back onto her feet but the smug grin on his face demanded payback.

She slapped her palm against his but instead of letting him pull her up, she yanked his hand, unbalancing him so he too fell victim to the trip hazard.

Seth stumbled over the root and landed on top of her.

'S-sorry. Clearly I don't know my own strength.' She swallowed as his chest pressed so hard against hers she could feel his every rapid breath. His hands were either side of her head, braced on the ground giving him every opportunity to lever himself off her if he chose to. He didn't.

Instead, he dipped his head lower, his eyes not leaving hers, waiting for her to stop him. She couldn't find the words, or the inclination, to do so. He hesitated for a heartbeat, lips hovering so close to hers she could almost taste him. That need to kiss him suddenly consumed her body and soul. The soft pressure of his mouth on hers immediately gave way to something more passionate, more intense, more than a mere kiss.

Kaja closed her eyes and surrendered to the thrill of having Seth all to herself again. She wound her hands in his hair, revelling in the silky curls beneath her fingers, pulling him towards her to deepen their connection. Mouths and tongues entangled, breath hot and ragged, it was clear they'd both giving up fighting this powerful attraction defying their separation. For once, she didn't think about anyone else. Seth was everything. They could've been locked back in that stock room on the night shift again or tangled up in the sheets of their old double bed when the need for one another was just as great.

She shifted position, parting her thighs so Seth's body was hard against her right where she needed him most. He groaned.

'Kaja…what are you doing to me?'

The second he spoke she knew the spell had been broken.

He stopped kissing her and pulled away. She lifted her head and tried to coax him back into that blissful abyss of blood-rushing lust with kiss after kiss. Pride and dignity took a back seat in her desire to fall back into that fantasy world where only the two of them existed. Seth's touch made her forget everything bad in her life to focus on the way he made her feel. Damn good.

'We can't do this.' This time he did push himself up off her, leaving her hands empty and her body cold.

'It was only a kiss,' she said, trying to claw back some dignity as she hugged her knees to her chest to find some comfort. Aware she had been the one trying to turn it into something more.

He fixed her with his heavy-lidded eyes and gave a coy half-smile. 'Kaja, you know with us it's never going to be only a kiss.'

Seth didn't appear ashamed of succumbing to his desire, only afraid of where it would lead. Kaja understood that fear when it was exactly the same reason she should be resisting. Their circumstances might be different now but they still faced the same obstacles. Only now with added complications.

Less defensive now she knew it wasn't her he was rejecting, but the implications if they took things any further, Kaja got back on her feet. It was only then she realised she'd hurt her ankle as it buckled under her.

'Ow!' She grabbed for Seth, afraid she was about to fall over again.

'What's wrong?' He moved quickly, wrapping his arm around her waist to support her.

'I must have twisted my ankle. I can't put any weight on it.' She tried to take a step forward, which resulted in a sharp pain shooting up her leg. The adrenaline rush Seth had caused with his mouth-to-mouth technique must have temporarily blocked out the pain. She would've asked for a repeat prescription if she'd thought he'd oblige.

'You can't hobble around on that all day. We probably need to get it strapped up. Maybe we should head back?'

As well as wanting to spend more time with Seth, Kaja wasn't in a hurry to go back with her tail between her legs, or, in this case, her ankle in a plaster cast.

'We're closer to the site now than the hospital. I'll be fine.' She brushed off his concern and tried to walk on, grimacing through the pain but not yet ready to let go of her human crutch.

Seth huffed out a sigh. 'Sit down.'

He manoeuvred her over to an upturned tree trunk and made her sit while he wandered off. After a few minutes of sitting there on her own Kaja began to panic that he might have gone to get help. Visions of search teams swarming the woods looking for her made her regret this outing even if she had finally been able to kiss Seth again. She could only hope he wouldn't find himself in trouble when he reported back.

The sound she expected to hear next was helicopters or blaring sirens, not the rustle of leaves as Seth trudged back towards her swinging her heels in one hand.

'I'm not sure they'd suit you,' she said, trying to hide how inexplicably teary she was to see him, grateful he was going to help her find a way out of this mess she'd got herself into. He could easily have handed over responsibility to any one of the entourage paid to look after her.

'I'm not sure they go with a twisted ankle either but I brought them back for you.' He whacked them against the edge of the tree until the heels came off, making them into a pair of flats and leaving her wincing at the sacrifice.

It took everything she had not to squirm when he knelt down to take her foot in his hand. She was ticklish at the best of times but Seth touching her bare foot was too much to take. How often had he taken advantage of that weakness until she was screaming with laughter and they'd fallen into bed in a tangle of limbs? Except this time he was deadly serious as he examined her, showing no memory of those fun times that had always led to something more passionate.

'Can you move it? Good. It's a bit red but not too swollen. You probably need to rest it.'

'How am I going to do that? Hover?' Okay, her ego was as bruised as her ankle if he'd forgotten her little quirk so readily.

He turned around and crouched down. While he was giving her a good look at his tight backside, she wasn't sure what he was expecting her to do.

'Right, jump on.'

'Excuse me?' It was true she wanted to climb him like a tree but he'd made it abundantly clear that wasn't an option.

'You can't walk and taxis are scarce out here. Think of me as your trusty steed.' He whinnied and pawed the ground with his foot. Boy, she missed his silly sense of humour. It hadn't died after all. He must have buried it along with his feelings for her but the more time they spent together, the more she got to see flashes of the old Seth.

'You're kidding, right?' He couldn't possibly expect her to climb on his back and let him carry her not inconsiderable weight to their destination.

'Not at all.' He slapped his backside and crouched down a little more until his trousers were stretched tight around his peachy behind. 'Now climb on before I can't get up again.'

'Only if you're sure. I don't want us both lying crocked out here waiting for a rescue team to come and find us. Think of the scandal!' She shook her head, wondering how she'd found herself in such a ludicrous position. Kaja climbing onto the back of her father's transplant surgeon, barefoot and covered in grass stains, was a million-dollar photo op. Seth Davenport was making her reckless and she'd be lying if she said that wasn't the biggest thrill she'd had in years.

# CHAPTER EIGHT

SETH'S PLAN TO break out of Kaja's claustrophobic existence with her in the hope it would provide some space had backfired spectacularly now she was clinging onto his back like a baby monkey.

'Are you comfy back there?'

'I wouldn't say "comfy", exactly, but you're saving my ankle. I'm not so sure about your back though.' She shifted her position to sit higher and strengthened her hold around him.

With the soft mounds of her breasts rubbing against him, legs wrapped territorially around his waist and cheek brushing against his, his back wasn't the part of his body he was worried about.

'Don't you worry about me. You're light as a feather.'

'Liar!' She slapped him playfully on the shoulder but made no attempt to disengage herself. Seth was simply glad he could do something to help. This whole sorry debacle had been his idea and now, not only were they probably causing mass panic back at the hospital, but she was hurt. Something he'd never seen coming. Along with that kiss.

He didn't know where he'd found the strength to end it but it had saved them both from making any further mistakes. Getting together again could only end in a mess and more heartache when he inevitably returned home to England. Perhaps that was part of the reason he'd agreed to come to her country when he knew he'd be the one leaving this time. Ensuring his departure meant there was no way she could hurt him. He hadn't counted on causing his own self-destruction by kissing her.

Now they'd crossed that boundary and let passion take over it was going to be difficult not to let it happen again.

The pilgrimage to her childhood hangout wasn't an easy one without a well-worn path to follow. There were dips and hills, rocky outcrops and streams to navigate along the way. As a reasonably fit adult man he would've struggled even without his Kaja backpack. It would've been even more of a trek for two young kids from the palace. He could only imagine the pressure of their heritage, which had driven them all the way out here on their own. It showed the strain she was currently under when this was the first place she thought of to escape to for a while.

'Oh, no. It looks like we're not the only ones visiting today.' Kaja pointed up ahead. Right beside the site of the crumbling grey ruins of a once bustling village was the juxtaposition of a bright red, super modern hatchback.

'Best case—they don't know who you are and we can hitch a lift back with them. Worst case—you let them take a few selfies and they give us a lift.' They'd had their adventure en route, rolling around in the grass together.

'I suppose so… In that case I should probably walk the rest of the way. We wouldn't want to draw any more attention than necessary.'

She had a point. Regardless if these other visitors knew they were in the presence of royalty or not, the sight of two people in medical attire piggybacking in from the woods was going to seem a little strange.

He crouched down to allow her to step away.

'Do I have to book a time slot for the tour or can we do it now?' As keen as he was to get Kaja back for medical attention and prevent any further concern as to her whereabouts, he was curious about the place. From the day she'd left him it had struck him that he'd never known her at all. He'd learned something of her background having lived it himself these past few days, but hearing more about her childhood might provide him with better insight into what had made her who she was today.

'There's not much call for my services. I can't tell you a lot about the history of Tobel. I'm sorry to say that wasn't important to an impetuous nine-year-old. However, if you'd like to see the very spot where I first beat my big brother in an obstacle race, or hear about the time I befriended a stray dog and kept him as my secret pet, then I'm your girl.' She limped ahead of him, apparently eager to revisit this place that held such treasured memories for her.

'Sounds perfect.' This was what he'd wanted for her all along. A chance to forget everything going on at the hospital and simply enjoy herself.

Thankfully the occupants of the car were more interested in the picnic they'd spread out on the outer wall of the old village and didn't see them approach. Seth made a note to do the same with Amy when he got the chance. Perhaps not here, but he was sure she'd love a picnic out in the countryside.

Seth's stomach growled with hunger as they made their way along the cobbled street towards the tumbledown houses of yesteryear. He could see Kaja's foot already beginning to swell. Stumbling over this uneven ground with her foot wedged into broken shoes wasn't going to help. She'd be lucky if she could walk on it at all by the end of the day. Although, as she hovered in the doorway of one higgledy-piggledy building it was obvious she wanted to do some exploring before they thought about making their way home again.

'Is it the same as you remember?' There was a certain kind of beauty about a place where wild flowers were springing out of the glassless windows, the pale lemon and blues providing some colour against the grey stone. Nature had taken over from the last inhabitants and decorated accordingly. Even the weeds and moss that had set up home in every crack and groove of the crumbling structure had a certain aesthetic charm.

'A little more overgrown perhaps, but basically the same.' She ducked her head under the arched doorway and ventured inside with Seth following close behind.

'Smaller than I remember.' They walked through the remains of someone's house with only partial walls separating each of the rooms. 'I think the elements have taken their toll too.'

Seth could hear the tinge of sadness in her voice as she traced her hand over the faded mural barely there on what remained of the plaster. There were some flourishes and cornices left from what must have been a decorative abode at one time. Definitely a place where one could let their imagination run wild.

'Sometimes we look back on things with rose-tinted glasses. Reality doesn't always match up with the memories we might have embellished over the years.' Though, if this had been abandoned centuries ago he couldn't see it was in much better condition when Kaja and Bruno were here as children.

The look she gave him made him feel as though he'd taken her favourite childhood toy and set fire to it.

'I'm sorry if meeting me again has been such a disappointment to you, Seth. Speaking for myself, I have no regrets about anything we've done. You met all the expectations I had based on my memories.' With that, she flounced out, leaving Seth scratching his head about what had caused the outburst. It took a minute too long for him to realise the misunderstanding.

'Wait… Kaja… I wasn't talking about us. I don't regret what happened between us back there either. If anything, being with you, kissing you, is even better than I remember.' He followed her into the next almost-room, her upset at believing he was unaffected by their tryst totally understandable.

She had her back to him, arms wrapped around her waist in a gesture of self-comfort that caused him physical pain on her behalf. He placed his hand on her elbow and gently turned her to face him.

'Hey, I was talking about the village, not us.' He gave her a soft smile, trying to coax one back in response. 'I didn't want to stop kissing you. That was the problem.'

Her mouth formed a perfect 'O'. 'Honestly?'

'Honestly.' He knew he shouldn't do it, yet Seth couldn't seem to stop himself from reaching out and tipping her chin up to make her look at him. The beautiful sad eyes and the pouting pink lips were too much for him to ignore.

He rested his lips on hers. Only for a second. Enough to comfort her and satisfy his need to feel her mouth against his one more time. He closed his eyes and blocked out the forsaken terrain around them, the soft touch of Kaja's lips transporting him to paradise instead.

It wasn't supposed to be a replay of their time on the forest floor, yet when Kaja sighed and let her arms fall away from their defensive position he wanted her closer. He pulled her body flush with his and that comforting kiss developed into a passionate display of his feelings for her.

It was pointless denying it any more when he'd known from the second he'd set eyes on Kaja again he'd never stopped loving her. With Amy to take care of he'd been able to deny that fact and convince himself his heart only had room for his daughter. Now he was confronted with the person he'd so desperately wanted to share his life with and slowly rediscovering the woman he loved, those feelings refused to remain hidden.

They might not have a future together but he was willing to fully embrace the present.

Kaja was a fool. Why did she ever think she could live without this man and how had she managed it until now? It was only having him here in her world she understood what she was missing when his kisses were giving her life. She didn't care how stupid she'd been mistaking his comments about the ruins as a narrative on their relationship when it had prompted him into confessing his feelings for her. At least he still had some even if they weren't as strong as before. With her hands she reacquainted herself with the contours of his body while reuniting her tongue, her lips and her heart with his.

Seth held her, warming her back yet still managing to make her shiver. He was here, he was real, and, for now, all that mattered. When he slid a hand up inside her scrubs she held her breath, his palm grazing her ribs and reaching further to cup her breast. She let out a shaky breath as he brushed his thumb lightly across the silky material of her bra, bringing the sensitive peak of flesh to attention.

She wanted his touch, to feel skin on skin so badly she was practically begging him with her body. Grinding against him, she could feel his arousal standing proud and ready through the thin layer of clothing between them.

Seth groaned and in one swift move lifted her off her feet, hitched her legs up around his waist and carried her over to the recess at the window.

'Seth...we can't do this here.' Somewhere at the back of her mind beyond the rushing blood and carnal thoughts she remembered they had company outside.

'I know,' he said before claiming her again in another frantic coupling of mouths and tongues. Confirming he knew they couldn't get carried away any further than they already had but was as powerless as Kaja was in fighting this tidal wave of desire. Now it had broken free she didn't know how they were going to stem it again.

A loud rumble reverberated through the room, so strong it seemed to shake the very ground beneath them.

'I didn't know trains ran this far out.' Seth broke off the kiss, apparently as startled as she was by the loud sound suddenly approaching.

'They don't. There aren't any tracks out this way.' Come to think of it, the dirt roads out here wouldn't usually be travelled by any vehicles larger than the car parked outside.

It was only when the very walls of the building seemed to move with them that it dawned on her what could be causing the noise.

'Earthquake,' she shouted over the grinding noise coming from the earth below.

The warning came too late to get out of the seriously precarious structure as the underground monster roared its arrival. The ground undulated and warped as though they were on a roller-coaster ride they couldn't get off. Where once Kaja and Seth had been in the midst of a passionate embrace, now they were clinging to one another in an attempt to stay upright.

'Aren't we supposed to go and stand in the doorway?' he shouted, trying to pull her in that direction.

She resisted, shaking her head. 'It's not stable enough.'

With that, the world seemed to cave in around them. Walls were collapsing, including the arched doorway, their only means of escape. Plaster began to fall in chunks around them. Seth covered her head with his hands and pulled her down onto the ground with him, using his body as a shield to protect her from the falling debris.

Kaja had never been in an actual earthquake as there hadn't been one here in living history but she had a vague recollection of what to do should one ever occur. She thanked the heavens she had Seth with her providing comfort in a terrifying situation. He was the only stable thing she had to hold onto at a time when she couldn't even rely on the *terra*-not-so-*firma*.

She scrunched her eyes shut, her head against Seth's chest. Unfortunately, she couldn't turn off the sound, every dull crack and thud as debris rained down reminding her how very small and fragile they were. There was every chance that neither of them would come out of this when there seemed no end in sight to the destruction happening right on top of them.

'We are going to get out of this, Kaja.' He kissed her forehead, providing a moment of calm tenderness in the midst of such overwhelming chaos. Then he added, 'We have to,' with such a determined look on his face she believed him.

Amy. He was thinking about his daughter, of course he was. With that came the horror of what was happening to all of their loved ones: her father, Bruno, Fatima. There was no time to descend into hysterics and what ifs as another crash of rubble sounded. Along with a sharp curse from Seth.

'Are you all right?' She'd felt him tense at the same time as the new fall of debris and poked her head out of her Seth cocoon to make sure he was all right when he was bearing the brunt of the blows to save her.

'I'm fine.' He was much too abrupt to convince her.

Sure enough as she reached up to brush the dusty swoop of hair from his face, her fingers encountered a sticky patch of blood at his temple.

'You're bleeding.'

'I'll live.' He kept turning his head and trying to put her off but she could see the cut and wasn't going to rest until she examined it. A head injury wasn't something to simply brush off. Thankfully there was only a trickle of blood so it likely didn't need stitches.

'You'd better.'

As quickly as the world seemed to erupt around them, the upheaval subsided again, the roar fading along with that sensation of being at sea. It couldn't have lasted for any more than a minute but it had been an eternity waiting to find out if they'd live through it all.

'Quick, let's get out of here in case there are any aftershocks.' Paying no heed to his injury Seth grabbed her hands and pulled her to her feet.

Her legs wobbled as though she'd spent months on the ocean and had just set foot on land again. It was difficult to see, darkness having descended along with a curtain of dust, but when it cleared the state of the devastation was obvious.

'The door's gone.' The archway, along with most of the walls that had been holding up what was left of the building, were a mound of slate and brick. Looking around, she could see how lucky they'd been in the grand scheme of things.

They could have been buried alive. She shuddered

when she recalled how Seth had cradled her with his body. She would never have forgiven herself if he'd died sacrificing himself to save her.

Unfortunately, they discovered none of the original exits had survived. They'd literally been entombed in her favourite childhood playground. The angle one of the beams had fallen and thankfully created a pocket of air around them so they had space to move.

Seth began shifting the biggest obstacles, kicking and pushing until there was a large enough gap for them to break out of their stone igloo.

'C'mon!' There was an understandable urgency in him as he reached back for her. They had to get out into an open space before any further ructions erased any chance of them escaping.

Kaja followed through the tunnel he was burrowing through the rubble, incapable of speech until they saw daylight and Seth pulled her through to safety. They collapsed in a heap on the grass outside, breathing heavily from a combination of physical exertion and fear.

'I don't even know where we are.' It was disorienting when nothing looked the same as when they'd first arrived. Most of the old buildings were now reduced to little more than a pile of rubble amidst a cloud of dirt and debris. She didn't know why she wasn't a hysterical mess screaming and crying after the trauma of what they'd been through. What they might still go through. She was clearly in some sort of shock, trying to process what had just happened.

Seth stood up and paced around. Even he didn't look quite as steady on his feet as usual. Kaja wasn't sure she could even stand again.

'Come over here and let me look at that head injury.'

'It's nothing.'

'Let me be the judge of that,' she insisted, unwilling to take any chances in the circumstances.

He reluctantly came back to her, not wanting a fuss but bending down so she could make a closer inspection of the wound. Using the hem of her top, she gently dabbed at the blood, cleaning the site enough so she could see the extent of the cut. 'It's not too deep. I think it'll heal itself. No need for improvised stitching.'

'Good. Can we focus on something more important now?'

'There's no need to be tetchy. I just want to make sure you're safe.'

'I know. Sorry. I think we came out the back of the house. We should be safe out here away from any more falling wreckage.'

Kaja glanced back at the way they'd come. From this vantage point on the hill she could see plumes of smoke in the city and now the thundering sound had stopped she could hear sirens going off everywhere. They were isolated with no idea what had gone on in the rest of the country or who was hurt. It was part luck, part Seth that had saved them, but there was no way of knowing what was happening elsewhere to everyone else or how bad the devastation.

Seth had the same thought as he pulled his phone from his pocket. They both waited as the call rang out until they eventually heard Fatima's voice.

'Are you and Amy okay?'

'Yes, Mr Davenport. We hid under the dining table. No one got hurt. How are you and Miss Kaja?'

The line went dead and Seth tried again and again to reconnect without success. 'I don't have any signal. At a guess I'd say all lines are down and the power's probably out.'

'At least we know they're all right. Fatima will keep Amy safe. What about Papa and Bruno…? Seth, what'll happen to them?' Her heart was in an ever-tightening vice as she thought back to all the machinery monitoring them. Her father especially, who was so vulnerable after the transplant.

Seth walked back to her and took a seat on the grass again. 'Hey, they'll be fine. Surely the hospital will have emergency power for a situation like this?'

She knew they would, yet it wasn't any consolation. Logic wasn't getting a look-in when emotions and her imagination were running wild. 'We have to get back.'

'Don't you think I know that?' he snapped. 'My daughter is miles away, frightened, without her daddy but we can't go anywhere. We'd be taking a risk going back through the trees if there are further aftershocks. The same if we take the road. We could get hit by all sorts of debris and there's always a chance the roads themselves could open up. That's if you hadn't hurt your ankle and were capable of walking back. We're going to have to wait this out. No matter how hard it is not knowing what's happening to our loved ones.'

He was trying so hard to be strong for her but Kaja could hear how choked up he was about Amy. The way he'd protected her and dug them out of that house with his bare hands…she knew he'd have done the same for his daughter. This separation had to be so much worse for him.

She reached across and squeezed his hand. 'Fatima will take care of her and the palace is one of the safest places to be. When it was remodelled for our family it was extensively renovated to withstand any eventuality.'

'It's just…there's so much in that house which could fall on her. The heavy furniture, the chandeliers…she's only a little thing.' The catch in his voice threatened to undo them both. Kaja needed him to stay strong or she'd lose it altogether too.

'Fatima knew to take cover as soon as the earthquake hit and they're fine. I'm sure the rest of the staff will be taking care of them too.'

'You're right. If we start thinking the worst we'll go around the bend. We need to focus on us for now. Until we can get back and do something to help.'

Good. Seth was taking back control. That made it easier for her to hold it together too.

'That siren sounds awfully close.' She couldn't help but hope someone knew where they were and had sent the emergency services to their rescue.

Seth scrambled to his feet. 'It's a car alarm.'

'The tourists. Maybe we can get a ride back with them.' The notion that they had a solution right here galvanised her back into action too. She tried not to think about the pain in her ankle returning now that the adrenaline had worn off. With any luck she wouldn't have to walk much further.

They followed the blaring noise and the flashing lights back to where the car was parked. The windows were smashed, glass everywhere, but it was still standing.

'Where did they go?' She looked around but there was no sign of the family who'd been sitting nearby. It felt as though the roller coaster went into free fall again, leaving her stomach somewhere on the ground.

'What if they're in there?' Seth voiced her fear as he looked back towards the empty skyline where the village had once stood.

Neither of them wanted to venture back there for their own sake but they were both medics and knew it had to be done.

# CHAPTER NINE

'YOU STAY HERE. I'll go and look for them.'

'Like hell. I'm coming with you.' There was no way she was going to let him go back in there alone. If the past few minutes had shown her anything it was that they needed each other to survive and she wasn't going to stand back and let him put himself in danger.

Seth opened his mouth to protest and she folded her arms across her chest and pursed her lips. He wisely closed his mouth again and headed back towards the devastated village they'd literally just crawled out from.

'Hello? Is there anybody here?' he called as they walked into the courtyard that had once been the centre of the village. Now it was simply the epicentre of the destruction.

Any bright colour nature had once displayed had been obliterated by layers of grey as far as the eye could see. Glancing at what little was left of the buildings, Kaja realised how incredibly lucky they'd been. The house they'd wandered into was unrecognisable as a structure at all, her beloved mural now nothing but a few painted bricks scattered here and there.

'Maybe they ran off when it started?' Optimistic, perhaps, but she really didn't want Seth putting himself in jeopardy again for anyone.

'They wouldn't have had time to get very far and there's no one to be seen for miles out here.' Undeterred by the resounding silence, he kept walking further into the danger zone.

Kaja took a deep breath, refusing to let him go it alone but not without some trepidation. The next time the earth shook they mightn't be so fortunate.

'Hello? Can anyone hear us?' He put his hands to his mouth to amplify his plea for signs of life. With the car alarm still blaring in the background it was difficult to hear anything else. The place had a distinct Pompeii vibe. How Kaja imagined it after everything had been wiped out by Vesuvius.

They climbed up what felt like two storeys of wreckage listening for anything to indicate there was someone here who needed their help.

Kaja thought she heard movement where the row of houses opposite the one they'd been inside had once stood.

'Seth! Over here.' She moved closer to investigate and beckoned him over. They began excavating the site on their hands and knees, certain there was someone beneath the remains.

'We're going to get you out,' Kaja called out, trying to provide some reassurance to whoever was trapped.

They heard whimpering far below and Seth became a man possessed, tearing away boulders with his bare hands, sweat trickling down his face. Both of them were covered in dirt, skin and nails torn to shreds before they made any progress. The small gap they managed to open up provided a peephole where Kaja could see the tear-streaked face of the little girl who'd been picnicking with her family staring back at her.

She sat back on her heels, stunned at the sight of the

frightened child buried alive. It took Seth a heartbeat too before he resumed scrabbling at the rocks in desperation and she knew he was thinking this could easily have been his daughter.

'We'll get you out, honey. Is there anyone else with you?' Kaja kept talking, getting the child to focus on her as the rocky world around her shifted once more.

The little girl nodded her head. Not a good sign. There had been a family, parents and a child enjoying the afternoon sunshine, and now only silence.

Kaja had to look away so the little girl wouldn't see her welling up. She was bound to be terrified enough without having an adult making things worse.

All of a sudden Seth stopped digging and sat up.

'What is it? What's wrong?'

'Shh! I thought I heard something over there.' He pointed to a spot close to him and they took a breather, listening until they heard a faint cry for help.

Seth glanced at the place where the little girl was waiting to be rescued, then back to where they'd located a new survivor.

'Go. I'll get her.' He'd already done most of the heavy lifting and the little girl was okay as far as they could tell. If there was someone else buried here Seth could rescue her and Kaja would concentrate on the child.

He didn't waste any time debating the subject, having the same confidence in her capabilities as she had in his.

Kaja cleared the obstacles as quickly and as deftly as she could. Hearing Seth murmur to the woman who was stuck down there was comforting and she believed every word he said about getting everyone out safely.

She was lying across the rubble now, stones and bricks jabbing into her ribs and every other part of her body in contact with the jagged floor beneath her.

'Here's my hand, honey. Can you grab it? Good girl.'
Her cheek was practically embedded with part of the
village landscape as she reached down through the gap.
Even if she couldn't get the girl out right away she could
assure her she wouldn't let go of her until someone did.

'Okay, sweetie, hold on with both hands and I'll pull
you out of there.'

Although she was only a little thing, Kaja was sure
she was going to dislocate both shoulders with the strain
of wrenching her up through the hole alone.

'If you could put your foot on that rock…good girl.'
With one last heave she pulled the child free and collapsed on the uneven ground, panting for breath.

Once she managed to control her breathing Kaja
turned to check on the little girl. 'Are you hurt anywhere?'

She shook her head. Eyes wide with fear, face stained
with dirt and clothes torn, she resembled a Victorian
street urchin. Not someone who only a short time ago
had been having the time of her life with her family.
Kaja's heart went out to her, hoping she'd be reunited
with them soon.

She remembered the child had indicated someone else
was down there with her but Kaja hadn't seen or heard
anything other than the debris continuing to fall.

'Is there someone else down there?'

She nodded.

'Are they awake?'

She shook her head. Kaja understood she was in shock
but she could really use some help to establish who was
down there and in what condition. With Seth still bull-
dozing his way through the adjacent site it was down to
her to locate any further survivors and get to them as
soon as possible.

If there was someone else stuck down there she wasn't going to be able to get them out herself. Then again, she couldn't call Seth away from his task until she knew what they were up against.

'I'm going to go down and see if I can help. I need you to run over to that man there and he'll keep you safe until I come back up. Okay?'

Another nod. If anything happened while she was down there she knew Seth would get this little one to safety. There was a slight hesitation but Kaja assured her she'd join her soon. She took a deep breath to steel herself before she climbed into the gap they'd made in the rubble. It was a tight squeeze but the discomfort as she shimmied down was bearable. Whoever was down here had surely endured worse.

She dropped onto the ledge accessible through the new skylight they'd installed. From there she had to pick her way carefully down the loose stones and step down onto the ground. 'Hello? Is there someone down here? I got your daughter out. She's safe. Can you make a noise so I can find you?' The only sound she could hear was Seth's nearby excavation work.

It was dark and ominous in the depths of the devastated building. There was every chance the whole lot could come down on her at any time as she moved from room to room, climbing over mounds of rock. Her ankle screamed every time she jarred it on an uneven surface but she persevered.

When she came to the area of the building that seemed to have suffered the brunt of the damage, making it largely inaccessible, she was ready to give up the quest. Except as Kaja went to leave she spotted a flash of colour breaking through the grey. She bent down to take a closer look and there, buried in the landslide, was the very definite shape of an adult male whose bright Hawaiian shirt might have just saved his life.

'Can you hear me?' Kaja began to move the rocks around the rest of his body, careful not to knock anything more on top of him. His face was turned away from her but when she checked his wrist she could feel a rapid pulse beating against her fingers. It was a relief to know he was still alive but a fast heartbeat could also be an indication of serious injury. She needed a better look but he was unconscious and there was no way she could move him on her own when he was pinned under several large boulders.

'What the hell do you think you're doing coming down here on your own and scaring me half to death?' Seth's disapproval boomed around the enclosed space and gave Kaja such a fright her heart nearly popped out of her chest. Any more surprises today and she'd find herself in a hospital bed along with the rest of her family.

'There's a man trapped under the rocks.' She ignored his irritation at her to concentrate on the important matter at hand.

He came over to help but not without muttering about how stupid she was for putting herself in danger. As though he wouldn't have done exactly the same thing.

'He hasn't gained consciousness since I found him and his pulse is too fast for my liking.'

'We're going to have to get him out of here.'

'What about the woman you were helping?' She was almost afraid to ask in case the latest rescue attempt hadn't been successful.

'She's fine. A few cuts and bruises but she's with her daughter now. It was her who directed me over here. When I couldn't find you…' His face was dark. He was angry with her and it was only now she could see what it would've looked like when she disappeared. The last time he'd seen her she'd been digging in the rubble. A few minutes later she'd vanished, with only a hole remaining where she'd once stood.

'Sorry. I wasn't thinking about anything other than helping.'

'Right, well, no more disappearing acts. I don't think my heart can take it.'

It was a throwaway comment but the sentiment behind it meant the world. He was worried about her. As he'd so gallantly displayed during the earthquake, he cared. She wasn't going to let that slip through her hands again but they could talk about that when this crisis was over.

'First things first, we need to move him.' This guy was twice her size and she had been foolish to think she could do that on her own. It remained to be seen if they could do it now.

It would've been preferable for them to stabilise him with a neck brace and a back board until he had his injuries assessed properly in hospital. There was a danger of paralysis but life came before injury and getting him out of here was crucial to his survival. They couldn't risk another rock slide in here in case it injured him further. Crush injuries could prove lethal unless promptly treated.

Kaja pulled her ponytail loose and used the hair tie to apply a tourniquet above the injury site prior to moving the rock. 'Hopefully that will prevent the release of toxins into his bloodstream.'

Once she had limited the blood flow to the injured leg, Seth jumped over to try and shift the weight hampering their progress. Working together like this was reminiscent of those busy nights in A & E when their paths had occasionally crossed during an emergency. It was the same rush of adrenaline and understanding of each other's roles that made them such a good team. That didn't always happen with fellow surgeons and was probably more to do with their genuine affection and respect for one another.

'I'm…not…sure…I…can…lift…it.' Regardless that Seth was bound to be exhausted she could hear the effort he was putting in attempting to dislodge the obstacle.

'If you can shift it a fraction, maybe I could drag him out from under it.' Kaja grabbed the shoulders of the gawdy shirt and got ready to pull him free.

Seth manoeuvred himself between the man and the boulder and with a huff of breath braced his back against the rock to lever it off. His legs were shaking and his face was a violent shade of red with the strain he was putting on his body.

'I've got him.' Kaja hauled him out while Seth took the weight of the rock. Once he was free Seth let out a grunt and dropped the boulder as gently as he could without dislodging any more stones.

'His pallor is a little blue. A direct trauma to his chest during the rock fall could have fractured his ribs and punctured his lung.' Kaja had done her best not to jolt the man too much as she'd wiggled him free but there was no way of telling how much internal damage might have been caused during his ordeal. If air had collected in the space between the layers of tissue lining his lungs it would prevent them from expanding properly.

She put her ear down to the man's chest to listen to his breathing and the short, gurgling breaths did nothing to relieve her anxiety. 'We could be dealing with a traumatic pneumothorax. If we don't release that pressure he could suffocate.'

'We don't have the luxury of medical facilities to help him or even access to a chest tube to help drain the air.'

'We'll have to improvise. I don't suppose you've got a pen on you?' She was only half joking, having seen this scene dramatised in a number of TV programmes. In real life it was a risky move with too much room for error. However, in these circumstances they were out of options.

Seth emptied the contents of his trouser pockets into his hands. While there wasn't a pen, he did have a mini pocket knife. Literally, a lifesaver.

'What's in this?' Kaja pointed to a small metal tin he held.

'It's a reusable metal straw. Amy's very insistent on using it instead of the plastic ones, which could find their way into the ocean and choke a turtle or something.'

'Good girl. That has to be an improvement on an empty pen barrel. Although, I think you might have to buy a new one after this.'

'No worries. I keep it scrupulously clean so it should be sterile enough to use.' The tin contained the tiniest brushes Kaja had ever seen so she didn't doubt him.

'Okay. I'm going to make a small incision with the knife for access and insert the straw to let the air out. That should let the lungs expand again and help him breathe.' These weren't the ideal conditions to work in with so much dust and dirt but they were far from help and if they did nothing, this man wouldn't make it. Neither she nor Seth would stand and watch him die without trying their best to save him.

Seth opened up the man's shirt, exposing the torso so Kaja could work. 'You can do this.' Seth urged her on as the butterflies in her stomach threatened to fight their way up and out.

In England she'd thrived with every emergency that came through the hospital doors. Although she did her best to keep her hand in at the hospital here, this felt as though it was the first time she'd really been tested on her home turf.

She could do this, she knew that deep down, but she was thankful for his encouragement. Any other capable surgeon might have tried to muscle their way in and take over. It was reassuring that he believed in her as much as he always had where her job was concerned. They worked as easily together as ever, happy to let the other take the lead when necessary. Much like their relationship. Seth had never put any pressure on her to do anything, letting her do everything at her own pace so she was comfortable. Including moving in with him, which had taken her some time to agree to as it had seemed such a huge step at the time. Seth had always believed in her and, despite everything since, that had never changed.

Kaja felt her way along the patient's torso until she was sure she'd located a gap between the lower ribs. A deep breath to steady herself and she plunged the tip of the small knife in, allowing the trapped air to escape. Seth passed her the metal straw to insert in order to keep the airway open.

'Ideally, we'd have some surgical tape to keep that in place.'

'Sorry. I don't keep that on me but it's a foldaway straw. Perhaps if you retract it as much as possible there's less chance of it falling out.' He held the base of the straw steady in the site, letting her push it down as far as it would go.

Kaja tried to be as gentle as possible when there was no pain relief available but their patient remained unconscious throughout.

It was vital they got him to hospital as soon as possible so surgeons could use the appropriate equipment to repair the injuries but how? They were both running on empty, he was a big guy and there was no way they could carry him back up the way they'd come in.

'We need to find a way to keep him lying flat and stretcher him out.'

'Easier said than done, Seth.' If they'd had access to the emergency services that wouldn't have been too much of a problem. However, this emergency rescue rested solely on their shoulders.

'We should be able to tunnel our way back out to the main courtyard.'

Kaja didn't know if he was trying to convince her or himself. Even if they managed to get him out there were still risks of him suffering from infection, inflammation or fluid developing in the lung. At worst, cardiac arrest. For everyone's safety they needed to get out of here before they were hit by any further complications.

'Should we enlist some extra help from outside?' The only other available pairs of hands belonged to the two they'd just dug out but they had run out of options.

'Good idea. I'll go back out, try and pinpoint where we need to go and get his family to start working from the other side. At least that way we might cut down on the time.' Along with the effort required.

She waited for Seth to climb back out of the hole above and listened for him on the other side. Eventually, she heard him shouting. 'Kaja, let me know when we're close.'

'Kaja?' Seth shouted again, closer this time.

She moved as close to the outer wall as she could. 'I'm here, Seth.'

That all too familiar sound of scraping and tumbling rocks began again and she waited for those on the outside to clear a path to them. It was hard manual labour in the heat as well as stressful. She was beginning to wonder if the nightmare would ever end. It seemed as though they'd been living on the edge of hell for hours now when in reality it was probably only a matter of minutes.

After a while she could see a chink of light through the gap made in the outer wall. It grew steadily bigger until Seth was visible on the other side working alongside the woman he'd rescued from nearby. Even the little girl was helping to move the rocks aside.

Once there was enough room for Seth to pass through he joined her inside and between them they lifted the incapacitated man. Seth grabbed him under the armpits and Kaja grabbed his legs. He was heavy but they were careful not to knock out the straw chest tube, carrying their patient until he was free from the danger of being hit by any more falling debris.

'Do you have the keys to the car?' Seth asked the woman crying over her husband's battered body, stroking his face and begging him to wake up.

'My husband had them.' She sniffed and searched his pockets. There was a collective sigh of relief when she produced them. They would never have found them if they'd fallen out along the way.

'We need to get him to the hospital for X-rays. He might have a punctured lung so we've put this tube in to help him breathe better. Can you drive?' Kaja asked the woman, aware that this car was the only available means to get back and they didn't even know if it was drivable.

She nodded, pulling her little girl close.

'Go and get the car and bring it back here. We're going to have to put the back seat down and lay him flat in the back to prevent as much movement as we can. You'll have to keep an eye on that straw to make sure it's not dislodged on the journey.' Seth issued the orders with so much authority no one questioned him.

It was a blessed relief when the car alarm was turned off. Once the car was reversed in as close as they could get it, Seth cleared the glass from the interior.

They lifted their patient again, Seth backing up inside the car so they could fit him comfortably on the passenger side lengthways.

Kaja gave the terrified wife directions to the hospital as she clutched the steering wheel. 'Try to avoid driving close to any trees or any other large structures in case there are any aftershocks.'

'I think you should squeeze in there too, Kaja.' Seth's last-minute suggestion threw her so much she nearly lost her professional composure.

'No!'

'You're hurt. It makes sense for one of us to try and get help. I'll be fine here. There's nothing to stop me walking back along the road.' He was being sincere but that only strengthened her resolve to stay with him.

'There's no way I'm leaving you behind.' She'd done that once too often.

'Kaja—'

She ignored his plea and put her own to the woman in the car. 'If you could let someone know we're out here and need transport back, we'd be very grateful.'

'I'll do my best. Thank you so much for everything.'

They said their goodbyes and wished each other luck before Kaja and Seth waved the family off.

'You didn't have to stay with me.'

'Yes, I did.'

He sighed, apparently getting the message she wasn't going to back down over that. She was done being selfish.

'You were amazing back there,' he told her, downplaying the lives he'd rescued too.

'All part of the day job. It felt good to be back in the thick of things. Although, I'd have preferred to have been working in a more traditional setting.'

'That makes two of us. Still, if we hadn't been here that family wouldn't have got out alive.'

The thought made her shiver but it also gave her a boost knowing she'd made a difference today. Her work as a surgeon was more important than anything she did in a royal capacity and infinitely more fulfilling. A matter she couldn't ignore now their close call with death was making her reassess the choices she'd made and the unhappy life she'd been living as a result.

# CHAPTER TEN

'YOU KNOW, YOU could've increased our chances of getting rescued if you'd told her who you were,' Seth said with a bemused grin.

Kaja wrinkled her nose at the suggestion. 'I wouldn't do that. In this situation we're all in the same boat. It wouldn't be fair to divert emergency services when they're needed much more elsewhere. We're not hurt, we're safe. If she passes the message on someone will get to us eventually.'

She didn't count her ankle as a serious injury when it was neither life-threatening nor caused by the earthquake. Even if it was throbbing like hell.

'My Kaja. Always putting other people first.' Seth put an arm around her shoulders and kissed her forehead.

She wanted to fall into his arms and pick up where they'd left off before nature had roared its disapproval but so much had happened since then. Seth's worry for his daughter, for all those caught in the quake, had overridden any discussion about their relationship. Even if there was some way of sustaining a long-distance romance the issue over her divided loyalties remained. They were both going to have to make big life changes to make it work. In her case there was one huge problem that couldn't be overcome with desire alone.

He led her outside the perimeter of the village back onto safer ground out in the open.

Kaja spotted some objects lying in the field behind the ruins of the wall where the family had been having their lunch earlier. They walked over to find a rolled-up blanket and the remains of their picnic in a cooler box.

'Okay, we've got a bottle of water, an orange and some breadsticks.' Seth discarded the half-eaten sandwich and the dubious-looking yoghurt back in the cooler. Hopefully they'd get picked up before they had to resort to eating any of that.

He spread the tartan rug out on the grass for them to sit on. The light was beginning to fade as the evening drew in but thankfully it was still warm. If help didn't arrive soon there was every chance they'd be spending the night under the stars.

'Do we need to ration the food or can we feast?' Kaja teased as she held up the meagre provisions they'd scavenged.

'I'm willing to take the chance we're going to get rescued before we resort to divvying out crumbs. We haven't eaten since breakfast and I think we deserve a little treat. Now, would madam prefer an orange segment or the bread course first?'

'Mmm, I think I'd like to start with some orange, thank you.'

It was ridiculous sitting out here in the aftermath of an earthquake joking and pretending that things were all right but Seth wanted to make Kaja laugh rather than have her dwell on things beyond their control.

He didn't want to think about what could have happened to her back there either, when he'd come close to losing her. For ever this time. Her stubborn refusal to go with the others and stay with him had been touching. If she'd been more concerned with her own welfare she would've gone to the hospital. It proved, along with their earlier kisses, that he was more to her than a house guest or simply here for her father's benefit. He didn't know what that meant for them but, for now, he was happy they were together.

He peeled the orange for her, the sweet, refreshing scent of citrus preferable to the earthiness and dust they'd been breathing in since the quake hit.

Kaja popped a piece in her mouth and closed her eyes. 'Mmm. That tastes so good.'

He had to agree. On a day like today one small piece of fruit had suddenly become the best thing he'd ever eaten.

'Could I also recommend our house water to accompany the dish?' He opened the bottled water and offered her the first sip.

Kaja waved the bottle under her nose, took a drink and swilled the water around her mouth before swallowing. They were being silly. A kind of hysterical reaction to the trauma they'd just been through. It didn't last and they fell silent as they devoured the rest of the orange. His body was becoming weary now and his muscles were aching after all the heavy lifting he'd been doing. He lay down on the blanket leaving Kaja sitting up, nursing what was left of the bottle of water.

Only moments after closing his eyes there was that ominous rumbling below the earth. He felt Kaja tense beside him, as the ground shook and forced them back onto that unwanted fairground ride. It was impossible to remain flat when every tremor was reverberating through his body. He sat up and hugged Kaja until the world stopped trembling. It was all he could do to protect her out here.

'I think that's it over for now.' It was little reassurance to her, he was sure, as they could still hear the sound of loose rocks tumbling nearby and see the new fissures opening up in the road ahead. 'Hopefully the family got to the hospital before the aftershock. Although I'm sure it won't be the last.'

Kaja was quiet. Too quiet. Then it seemed as though a mini earthquake of emotions began inside her. The shaking came first, her shoulders heaving beneath his arm, but it was the sobbing that took him most by surprise.

'Hey, we're gonna be okay. That one was quick.'

He cursed himself for being the voice of doom predicting more nerve-shattering aftershocks even though it was the truth. Usually Kaja preferred that kind of straight talking but perhaps under the circumstances she was a bit more fragile. From now on he'd be careful not to upset her. Not when he'd been drawing from her strength to keep going throughout this ordeal.

She leaned back into his chest, content to let him hold her. A cry for help in itself for someone who'd single-handedly waded into a collapsed building to rescue a man twice her size. Kaja was a strong woman who didn't accept help easily, as he'd discovered in those early days of working together when he'd tried to get closer to her. It took her a long time to trust anyone but he'd been persistent, willing to put in the time getting to know her when he'd been so entranced by the newest medic on the block. There'd been something so endearingly naive about her beyond the efficient, focused surgeon. Of course, now he knew why she wasn't as worldly wise as some of her counterparts and the reasons she liked her privacy so much.

He let her cry it out until they were both soaked with her tears and she was ready to talk.

'It's just too much to take in. We could've been killed. We still could.' Her face crumpled again as she contemplated their fate.

Seth didn't want to upset her but neither would he lie to her. There was no way of knowing how this would end for anyone. It was probably the shock setting in that was making them both so emotional. Without the drama and distraction of saving others they had time to replay events and think about their loved ones. If he let himself go down that rabbit hole and start catastrophising what was going on with Amy back at the palace he'd be sobbing too.

'We're still here,' he reminded her. 'Mother Nature has tried twice to take us out and failed. Hopefully she'll take the hint and leave us alone for a bit, yeah?'

She managed a half-hearted smile. 'Thanks for today. I know this wasn't what you had in mind when you suggested an adventure but I'm glad I'm with you.'

'Me too.' He snuggled in closer to Kaja, nuzzling his nose into the curtain of her hair. In the short space of time since they'd got to know each other again she'd quickly become an important element of his life once more. As if those intervening years had never happened and their life together had carried on where it had left off. Easy to do out here where there were no reminders of how different her world was or the relationships they'd had after their separation.

He breathed her in, her hair smelling of dust and earth but also the sweet floral perfume that was unmistakably Kaja. If he closed his eyes he could almost believe they were back in their house in Cambridge.

She turned her head so he was almost nose to nose with her now. Eyes open, lips parted, their breath mingling as they mirrored each other. Seth didn't know who made the first move, they were so in tune with each other, gravitating towards that kiss they both knew was coming.

Here, now, she was all that mattered to him. She was everything reminding him he was still alive. He kissed her as though it might be for the last time. Hard and passionate enough that he forgot to breathe. They fell down onto the rug still wrapped up in one another, hands tugging at one another's clothes, impatience erasing all logical thought. Seth wanted Kaja as he'd never wanted any woman before. He needed that reaffirmation that she was back in his life, that she hadn't fallen out of love with him after all and that she wanted him too. She was telling him that with her words and every stroke of her tongue against his.

He slid her top over her head but his shirt buttons proved more time-consuming. After fumbling with the first two she gave a frustrated groan and yanked the shirt open. The night air cooled Seth's fevered skin but not for long when Kaja trailed first her fingers then her tongue down his chest and lower. Now his breaths were coming in excited pants as she snapped open the buttons on his fly and left him in no doubt what it was she was expecting from him. Seth flipped her over onto her back to slow things down. He hadn't been with anyone since Paula and he needed to regain some control over his body as well as savour every moment with Kaja while he could.

Not that she was doing anything to help that vow as she wriggled out of her scrub trousers so she was lying beneath him clad only in skimpy black silk lingerie.

'You're beautiful.' The sentiment slipped from his lips. She didn't need the expensive clothes or the royal title to be anyone special when to him she was the most beautiful woman on the planet.

'And you're still dressed,' she purred as she grabbed

him by the collar and pulled him back down into another brain-melting kiss. If this was all she wanted from him for now he wasn't going to turn her down. This memory would be a more pleasant one than the last night they'd spent together. Only this time he'd be the one leaving and hopefully on better terms.

This was madness. Kaja knew it yet she didn't want her sanity to return any time soon. She'd never felt more alive than she did right now getting naked with Seth in the open air. They had all the reasons in the world not to pursue a relationship further but none that could convince her that sleeping with him here and now was the wrong thing to do. They'd been through a lot together and in the scheme of things it seemed silly not to act on these feelings they had for one another. Life was too short to deny themselves some pleasure. She didn't want to wait any longer.

Seth was taking his sweet time kissing the skin along her neck and across her clavicle, until Kaja was aching with need. She undid her bra and tossed it aside, revelling in the hungry look he gave her as she exposed her breasts to his gaze. He cupped her soft mounds in the palms of his large hands, kneading and kissing the sensitive flesh until her nipples were throbbing in anticipation of his touch. When he pinched them between his fingers and thumbs she bucked off the ground, that painful ecstasy only furthering her desire. He flicked his tongue over the taut tips, teasing her, the glint in his eye promising her so much more. When he took her in his mouth and sucked, he delivered on that promise.

Arousal swept away the very last of her inhibitions and patience. She pushed down his briefs and pressed her body against his engorged erection. It was the final straw for Seth too. He let out a primal grunt, pulled the last of her underwear away and plunged inside her.

Kaja's gasp was one of surprise and satisfaction that she'd finally got what she wanted. They paused for a second, their bodies both adjusting as they joined together.

His eyes searching hers. 'Are you okay?'

'Uh-huh.' She nodded, though she doubted she'd ever be okay again after this. It was such a wanton display of need and raw passion she knew nothing or no one else could ever surpass it. He kissed her softly on the lips then began moving rhythmically inside her, reminding her how good they could be together. She rocked her hips against his, losing herself in that full feeling every time he rammed her to the hilt.

'I've missed you so much,' he whispered in her ear, sending tiny shivers of delight up the back of her neck both from what he was saying and doing to her.

She was incapable of talking right now. Even if she hadn't been in the throes of ecstasy the sincerity of his words would've rendered her speechless. He should hate her for the way she'd lied to him, the manner in which she'd left him, but most of all for denying them a future together. Hearing him say those words, knowing he would've forgiven her and taken her back, made those bad-decision years all the more painful. At least she had him in this moment and she intended to make the most of their time together.

Kaja clung to him, never wanting to let go as he took her higher and higher on that wave of pure bliss. Why had she ever given up on this? On them? Especially when…

*Oh.*

All regrets and tears, any thoughts at all, were now simply background noise as Seth set off a fireworks display inside her. Lights flashed behind her eyelids as a succession of delicious explosions detonated in her body, all triggered by what Seth was doing to her. Her orgasm was prolonged and repeated over and over again as he continued working his magic, not letting up on his now frantic pace until she was limp and sated beneath him. Totally exhausted and completely satisfied. Only then did he give into his own fierce need, his climax seeming as overwhelming as hers when he cried out into the night.

When she was able to see straight and breathe again—albeit hindered by the gorgeous hunk currently sprawled across her body—she fully appreciated the beauty of the moment. '*Belle Crepuscolo*—it means beautiful twilight.'

A dazed Seth looked down at her, his hair flopping over his face and his eyelids heavy with exhaustion. He kissed her again and though she knew she was getting carried away by the romance of the moment she couldn't help it.

'This is madness,' she reminded them both.

'What, sleeping with me?' He genuinely looked hurt but her comment had absolutely nothing to do with sex.

'Of course not. You know that was amazing.' Despite everything they'd just done she felt her skin flush at acknowledging the mere memory. She wrapped her arms around his neck, pressing her chest to his and nibbling his earlobe. 'I mean the fact we're lying naked in the middle of a field.'

But she didn't care. Being with Seth was her happy place.

'It's certainly a night to remember,' he said with a grin.

'I wish it could be like this all the time. Only without the whole earthquake and danger-to-life thing.'

'I know what you mean.' He lifted her hand to his mouth and kissed it. A contented moment that should have been played out in the privacy of a bedroom but out here under the stars somehow seemed equally intimate. They knew they were alone and today's events had taught them to live in the moment in case it was their last; a feeling Kaja wished she'd be able to hold onto and carry back to real life.

She let out a wistful sigh and laid her head on his bare shoulder. Right now a simple life seemed very appealing. One where all she needed was a naked Seth and somewhere to rest their heads. 'How long do you think we'll be out here before someone comes to find us?'

'Hopefully a while longer.' One suggestive look was all it took for Kaja's body to wake again in anticipation of more mind-blowing, bone-melting sex with him.

He tangled his fingers in her hair and pulled her in for a long, sensual kiss reaching every nerve-ending in her body. She put up no resistance when he lowered her back onto the ground and showed her what it was he intended to do with the extra alone time.

There were some aftershocks through the night but they gradually decreased in intensity. Kaja was certain they weren't the only ones sleeping outside when most residents would be afraid of staying indoors tonight in case of further structural damage. Although she was sure she was the only one waking up with a smile on her face. She knew there would be a fallout back in the city. Not only would they have to deal with repairs and casualties and generally getting the country back on its feet, but their loved ones would take precedence over examining what was happening between her and Seth. For now she was content to remain where she was.

As the sun rose, the sky around them changed from the inky black they'd fallen asleep under, to a warming *ombre* of pinks and golds, the beauty only eclipsed by the sight of the man she woke up to. His dark stubble combined with his mop of unruly hair gave him a wild look in keeping with the animal passion he'd unleashed.

She shivered with memories of what had kept them awake most of the night.

'Are you cold?' he mumbled, still half asleep, misunderstanding the trembling in her limbs. He pulled her closer to his chest and threw his leg over hers to share his body heat.

The movement brought them into contact in the most intimate of places so she could feel his body waking to start the new day. His burgeoning erection pressing against her was the early morning wake-up call she missed. Making love with Seth was something she'd never tire of or take for granted when she'd been without him in her bed for so long.

Kaja shifted position until he was sheathed inside her and hooked her legs around him as he drove deep into her core. This was the only place she wanted to be right now. The only place she wanted Seth. Worrying about everything else could wait until they could do something about it.

Once the sun had fully risen and the morning had well and truly begun it felt too indulgent, as well as risky, to continue lying au naturel in the open countryside. With the last of the water drained and every breadcrumb consumed they hadn't enough sustenance to keep on with their energetic sensual reunion. Well, her mind was willing but her body needed a rest before they resumed relations again. Something she was looking forward to after a proper meal and, preferably, in a comfortable bed.

They got dressed in yesterday's dirty, torn clothes. Going home in these was the ultimate walk of shame although she hoped no one would guess what she had actually been doing all night. If the clothes didn't give her away the great big smile on her face might. Then she looked at the scene of utter devastation on top of the hill and quickly quashed the smug feeling. Residents had a lot more to worry about than her love life today. What was more, there would be a lot of people concerned about what had happened to her during the earthquake.

'Everything okay?' Seth glanced over at her as he pulled on his shoes and began tying his laces. 'You're very quiet.'

'I'm just wondering what we'll be going back to.' She was surprised to find her lip beginning to wobble as she spoke, the enormity of yesterday's events in full force now they would have to face the aftermath.

He shifted over beside her and helped her put her scrub top on, scooping her hair from inside the neckline to let it fall onto her shoulders. She leaned against him, gaining strength from simply having him taking care of her in such a small way. 'Whatever it is we'll face it together.'

'Will we, or are we just fooling ourselves, Seth? As much as I want a relationship to be possible, sleeping together won't magically make our problems disappear.'

'No, but it's a starting point. If we decide that's what we both want, surely we can work to make it happen?'

'It'll mean big changes for all of us.'

'Something I would be prepared to make as long as I know you're in it for the long haul this time.' He wasn't making a jibe at her; she could see he was being totally serious and with good reason. The last time he'd been planning a future with her she'd taken off and left him to pick up the pieces. Kaja knew she'd made the wrong decision at the time but there was one thing she was still holding back from Seth that could affect them as a couple.

She was hesitant to make that promise to him now without being completely honest with him. In doing that there was a chance he wouldn't want to be with her at all and she wasn't ready to end things before they'd really begun.

'It's a big decision for me to make. Not because I don't want to be with you but there's a lot of stuff I would have to sort out before that could happen.' She knew it wasn't the answer he wanted but it was all she could give him for now.

He studied her quietly for a moment then said, 'I'll wait.'

It was such a comfort knowing he intended to stay by her side until she dealt with the issue that could end their relationship once and for all. She hadn't had that level of understanding for a long time, not since the day she'd left England. Now it was down to her to decide the next move.

In the distance she thought she heard the sound of a car out on the road. 'Seth, is that—'

He was already on his feet and running towards the first sign that they weren't out here alone. Kaja should've been elated but a heavy cloak of sadness settled around her shoulders, preventing her from getting up to follow. Once they left this place the fantasy was over and a selfish part of her wanted it to last for ever. The part of her who'd had this happy life with him once and thrown it all away. Only now did she truly realise how stupid she'd been.

'It's a police car,' he yelled back, jumping up and down trying to attract its attention.

'Great.' Kaja had to psych herself up to go and join him rather than lying down and praying she'd remain undiscovered.

If this was someone come to rescue them it was time to put her game face on. They were no longer two lovers stranded together enjoying some quality time, but a princess and her father's transplant surgeon, who'd been displaced during the country's worst earthquake in living history.

She could see the flashing lights on the car roof as it pulled into the car park and her stomach rolled at the prospect of being recognised in her current state or, worse, having to explain it. Without a mirror she didn't even know how bad she looked but she was guessing a day rescuing people trapped in the rubble of an earthquake and a night sleeping rough weren't going to make a pretty picture.

When she attempted to put her shoes on again it became apparent the swelling around her ankle would make that impossible. She had to limp barefoot towards the approaching police vehicle but held her head high, attempting to maintain some modicum of decorum.

Seth was leaning in through the open window of the car when she got there, shaking hands with the officer in the driver's seat.

'Kaja, this is Constable Bailey, the white knight riding to our rescue.'

She winced at the casual use of her name, which suggested an intimacy between them that, while true, was no business of this complete stranger or those he would later retell his tale to.

'Good morning. Thank you for coming.' She was always self-conscious meeting new people but she had more reason than usual to worry about being judged. Especially when the young officer was openly gawping at her. Too late, she wondered if she had any grass stuck in her hair after rolling about in a field with Seth for most of last night.

'Oh, my goodness... I didn't realise...we were so busy

with calls last night…they just said there were people stuck out at Tobel. No one said it was you!' He got out of the car and opened the door to the back seat, giving a little bow as he did so.

He hadn't known who he was coming to rescue. Whether he'd recognised her immediately or only when Seth had tossed her name into the conversation wasn't clear, but he knew who she was now and that was what mattered. It was important for her to try and claw back some respectability when she was at her most vulnerable.

'I'm sure you had more pressing matters to deal with last night. If you'd be kind enough to take us to the Royal Alderisi hospital we'd be very grateful. Mr Davenport, perhaps you'd like to ride up front with Constable Bailey here.' She wanted to reduce the chance of further impropriety to gossip about by separating them but if Seth's glower was anything to go by he wasn't impressed by the idea.

'Of course, Your Highness. I know my place.'

Kaja had hoped he'd understand her need to keep up a front even in these circumstances, but as he gave her a mock bow and jumped in the passenger seat she realised she was asking too much. Even more so when they were all settled in the car and he put in a request to their driver.

'If you don't mind, could you drop me off at the palace first? My daughter is there. She's all I have in the world and I want to make sure she's safe.' Seth's words cut deep. She understood his need to see his daughter as she also wanted to check on the welfare of her own family, but he was making it clear to her that things said or implied last night had simply happened in the heat of the moment. She was no more a priority in his world than she had been yesterday.

'Sure.'

'Do you know how the hospital and the palace fared in the earthquake?' Kaja kept her voice measured although her heart was cracking open, those old wounds she believed healed now ripping apart the old scar tissue.

The police officer spoke to her in the rear-view mirror. 'Yes, ma'am. The palace, as far as I know, wasn't too badly affected. All hospitals, as you'd imagine, are busy with the casualties, although no fatalities reported so far.'

'Thank goodness.' Despite all the reassurances she'd given herself and Seth, she exhaled all her fears for her loved ones in a long breath with the confirmation. She could see some of the tension released in Seth's shoulders in the passenger seat though he remained facing away from her.

'What about the people who reported our location? There was a man with serious crush injuries. Do you know anything about his condition?' Seth kept the questions coming and while Kaja genuinely wanted a progress report on the family she was glad it was keeping the focus off what they had been doing all the way out here in the first place.

'Sorry, I don't know. I just got the call to do a welfare check. I'm sure if they'd known it was you they would've had someone out here sooner.' He was twisting in his seat to apologise face to face but Kaja didn't want to risk an accident on her behalf.

'It's fine. We can make some enquiries when we get to the hospital. I'm sure Mr Davenport can use his influence to get that sort of information.'

'Oh, I don't know. I think Princess Kaja is pretty good at getting what she wants out of people.'

Officer Bailey glanced at each of them in turn. Seth wasn't exactly being discreet and neither was the heat steadily rising in her face. The atmosphere in the car was almost more unbearable than the one in the aftermath of the earthquake. She and Seth needed to talk, clear the air and lay down some ground rules. He couldn't play around with her reputation like this. That was, if they were going to have any relationship at all. At the moment the vibe he was giving her certainly wasn't all hearts and flowers.

'We're nearly at the palace. Perhaps I should get out here with you, Mr Davenport, and check things are all right at home?'

He met her gaze in the mirror with a steely glare of his own. 'No, I don't think that's a good idea. You should go on to the hospital. After all, you've sustained an injury and I don't think I'd be very popular if I prevented the country's princess from getting the necessary treatment.'

She couldn't swear to it but she thought the young constable put his foot down on the accelerator when he heard that. Kaja knew there was no point in arguing that it was not likely to be anything more than a sprained ankle when Seth would come back with some other smart answer. He wanted to be with his family and that didn't include her. She got the message loud and clear.

Kaja slumped back into the seat. There was no point arguing. It wasn't going to make her feel any better, only push Seth further away. If that were possible.

As they drove through the city, the car bumping around craters in the road, the sight of now derelict buildings spouting pillars of smoke and fire made her chest ache for all those affected. The desolate wasteland replacing the once vibrant country was an accurate depiction of her emotions over the past twenty-four hours.

Last night she'd been on top of the world thinking this was the beginning of a new life together for her and Seth. Now they were back to the real world where she didn't have him by her side.

She watched as the residents of the worst-affected houses set to work outside, banding together to clear away debris and salvage what was left of their lives here. If there was one thing she and the inhabitants had in common it was that survivor spirit. That ability to pick oneself up and get on with things though you'd lost everything dear to you was something she'd mastered. At least, she was good at pretending she had.

When Seth got out of the car and slammed the door she knew what they'd had was over before it really began again. So why did it hurt so much more this time around?

## CHAPTER ELEVEN

SETH STORMED UP to the house gates. If he'd been thinking clearly he would've let Kaja come on up as she'd suggested so he wouldn't have to go through the security rigmarole.

'I need some ID,' today's sentry demanded.

He flashed his hospital pass. 'You know who I am. You've seen me often enough. Now can you please let me in so I can see my daughter?'

The guard waved him through and Seth uttered a begrudging thanks.

This was typical of the nonsense in Kaja's world and he was sick of being reminded he wasn't part of it. Even in emergency situations they couldn't give him a break. Regardless of the fact that he'd probably saved the grand duke's life, he was never going to be accepted as Kaja's equal. She'd made that very point herself when she'd segregated herself in the back seat of the police car from the lesser mortals.

He hadn't come out here with the intention of getting back together with Kaja but it had happened last night and it had been glorious. What he hadn't been prepared for was the fallout of being rejected again.

There had been no class distinction lying out there naked entwined in one another's arms. They had just been two people who'd needed each other. That had changed the second they'd been in the public domain and she'd acted embarrassed to be seen with him, reminding him once again that their lives weren't compatible and she could turn her back on him at any given moment.

The only person he should be concentrating on spending time with was his daughter. Especially as he hadn't been there at a time when she'd needed him most.

The interior of the palace remained relatively the same. It did look a tad more minimalist than he recalled, devoid of a few of the ornate—and perhaps fragile—furnishings. It wasn't immediately obvious if they'd been broken during the earthquake or hurriedly stored away but the place had been cleaned and tidied back to its original state. He could only guess by the absence of the huge chandelier in the hallway that they hadn't got away totally unscathed. Things could be replaced, loved ones couldn't. So when Amy came running at him he had to stifle a tear or two of relief.

'Am I glad to see you.' He crouched down so she ran straight into his arms and hugged her as tight as he could.

'Daddy, you're squishing me.' She pushed him off, then came back for a second, less squishy hug.

'Are you okay? Were you hurt?' He brushed her curls away from her face, checking for any signs of injury.

'It was scary, Daddy. The noise made me cry.' Her bottom lip trembled and Seth could feel his going too. He'd been afraid so he could only imagine what had gone on in her head in a strange place, so far from home without her father.

'I know, sweetheart. I'm so sorry I couldn't make it back to you.'

'She is fine. This was the safest place for her. A little noise, some shaking, but no one hurt. What about the princess? She is not with you?' Fatima was frowning at him as she wiped her hands on the apron tied at her waist. The thought that they might have been baking again made his stomach growl and remind him he hadn't had anything to eat other than the picnic leftovers last night.

'Thank you for taking care of Amy. I took Kaja out for a walk to clear her head after seeing her father at the hospital. I didn't know we'd get stuck out there all night. She's gone back to the hospital to check in with him.' Something he'd be sure to do too once he'd spent some time with Amy. As well as whatever upheaval had been caused by the earthquake at the hospital, they'd need a progress report on the grand duke's recovery post-surgery. There was a good chance of Bruno getting released today too if he hadn't had any complications overnight.

'I hear on the news the hospital is very busy. A lot of people hurt yesterday. We were all very lucky.' Fatima crossed herself and thanked the heavens they had all survived the experience.

'I should probably head down there too and see if I can be of any assistance.' It would be all hands on deck in the emergency department to get through the wave of casualties coming in. They probably didn't have the staff numbers available with this kind of nationwide incident.

'You can do that after you have a shower and I make you something to eat.' Fatima steered him towards the staircase but it seemed selfish to be thinking only of himself during a crisis.

'I don't really have time—'

'Nonsense. You will be no use to anyone if you die of hunger first. Go, get washed and changed. I'll cook.' Fatima wasn't going to take no for an answer.

'Yeah, Daddy, you stink.'

'Charming,' he mumbled as he trudged up the stairs, dejected and rejected all at once.

'If you are going to be seen with the princess you really need to look the part. You don't want to shame her.' Fatima wasn't to know Kaja was equally grimy and unkempt but he supposed that would only earn her some fans to be seen mucking in with the rest of the community.

'No, Fatima, I would never want to shame her.' He would never do anything intentional to hurt her. That was why it was so galling when she could be so cruel to him without seeming to give it a second thought.

As expected, the hospital was a hub of activity. There were people, staff and beds everywhere as Seth walked in—unimpeded this time, although he was sure there were still guards posted outside the royal hospital rooms.

'Seth Davenport. I'm a surgeon. Can I do anything to help?' He'd been directed towards the co-ordinator in Reception, which was now serving as a triage area.

'We need all the help we can get. It's mostly stitches and broken limbs in here. The seriously injured were seen to first. You should have been here last night.' She snorted a humourless laugh as she handed him a stack of files before calling her next patient.

Seth could tell from her stained uniform and the bags under her eyes that she'd been here long past the end of her usual shift. 'Sorry, I was…stuck out at Tobel.'

She stopped shuffling files long enough to stare at him. 'You weren't the one who saved that family out there, were you?'

He wasn't sure he deserved praise next to someone who'd probably been on her feet since yesterday. 'I didn't do it alone and I'm sure the staff here did more than we did at the scene.'

'I was here when they came in. That straw trick was a stroke of genius for the punctured lung. The father's on the ward now if you want to go and see him?' It was a magnanimous offer when she was clearly under a lot of pressure to attend to the waiting patients but Seth was keen to see for himself how the man was doing.

'Would you mind? I swear I won't be long, then I'll come back here and get stuck into these.'

She held out her arms for him to offload the patient files. 'Don't worry, they'll still be here when you get back.'

Seth thought he'd take a quick look at the man's notes, maybe have a word with whoever was treating him, then he'd come back and set to work on that waiting list in the emergency department.

He hadn't counted on running into Kaja visiting at the same time.

'Hello. I wasn't expecting to see you here.' He should have been. She was always going to check up on a patient as well as setting to work to help everyone else who needed it. It was a foregone conclusion they were going to meet up at some point in the same building.

He hovered at the doorway, uncertain if he was going to stick around now when relations between them had turned sour.

'I just ducked in to see how he was doing while I was in between patients. He had emergency surgery when he came in but he's sleeping it off now. The surgeon said he'll recover. In time.'

'Good. What about the others?'

'Mum and daughter were a bit shaken up but they're okay.'

'And you? How's the ankle?' They were acting like strangers or, at most, colleagues with a patient in common, but it was safer than tackling what was really on his mind when it would only bring more pain.

Kaja lifted the bottom of her trouser leg up to show off a fresh bandage and an unattractive white clog. 'I think being seen in these shoes is more painful than the sprain. They could probably do with a little bling and more of a heel to fit in with the rest of my wardrobe.'

'They're not very you,' he agreed with a smirk. She was definitely more at home here in the midst of this organised chaos with barely enough time to breathe never mind care what she looked like, than swanning about in a palace.

'I shouldn't complain. The staff were very kind to lend me a change of clothes and patch me up. This is nothing compared to some of the injuries that have come in through the doors.'

'Speaking of which, I said I wouldn't be long. I promised to help out with the walking wounded.'

'Me too. I'll walk down with you.'

They left their sleeping patient and tiptoed out of the door. Well, Seth tiptoed. Kaja kind of squeaked across the floor.

'Did you manage to get anything to eat? Fatima wouldn't let me leave until my stomach was fit to burst.'

'Some of the locals have been fuelling us with coffee and cake. I'm glad Fatima made you take a break. You worked so hard yesterday; you deserve a rest.'

He didn't miss the coy look and guessed her mind had wandered to their energetic relations last night, and this morning, as well as the physical labour they'd put into rescuing the family. The way his had.

She cleared her throat. 'I see you had a chance to clean up as well. You look good.'

In trying to avoid using the elevator in case of any

further power outages, they'd taken the stairs. It was the one relatively quiet area in the hospital but it also seemed to amplify their awkwardness around each other, along with their voices. Seth decided to address what had happened this morning rather than ignore it and let it fester. There was nothing worse than drifting apart from someone without having a chance to understand what had gone wrong.

He waited until they were halfway down, pausing on a landing to broach the subject. 'Kaja, are you ashamed of me?'

'What? No. Whatever gave you that idea?' Her frown gave the impression she was being honest with him but with evidence to the contrary he couldn't be certain.

'After last night I was willing to give things a shot. To the point of setting my ego aside until you decide if I'm enough for you. Then the policeman turned up and you went cold on me, making sure I sat up front with the other "civilian".'

'Seth, it wasn't like that at all. I don't know, I panicked when he recognised me and I was worried he'd guess what had happened between us. I don't want people gossiping and speculating before we even figure out what's going on between us. Last night was special. I'm certainly not ashamed about what happened.' She rested her hand lightly on his arm, imploring him with those big eyes to believe her.

'Nor me, but I need to know where I stand. I'm not going to set myself up for another fall, Kaja. Not when I've got Amy to consider in all of this too. If we're going to make a go of things we both have to be on board one hundred per cent. I'm not convinced you're ever going to be.'

'That's not fair, Seth.'

'I'm being honest. Something I think you need to be with yourself too.' He was no longer willing to leave room for confusion. It was all or nothing; he wasn't going to risk his heart again.

The silence as Kaja contemplated what he was saying went on for an eternity before she broke it. 'I've been thinking about that and I would like to go back to medicine.'

'So what are you going to do about it, Kaja?'

'Pardon?'

'There's nothing to be gained by simply thinking how you could improve your life here. You have to actually do something to make it happen and fight for what's important to you. What is it you want, Kaja?' It had to come from the heart if she was going to be honest with herself and him.

'I want… I want…'

'What?'

'I want the life I had in England.' She blurted it out, surprising them both, judging by the shocked look on her face. Seth had no intention of leaving it there.

'Why, when you gave it up to come back here?'

'Because I was leading my own life. I had a job I loved and…and… I had you, Seth.' When her voice cracked he had to swallow down the urge to hold her and comfort her. This was make or break for him.

'Five years ago you didn't want any of that.'

'I did, I swear, but I thought I had to give it all up because none of it was real.'

'What's changed now?'

'I'm miserable here, Seth,' she sobbed. 'I came back to do the right thing by my family but it cost me everything. Being with you last night was the first time in a long time that I was actually happy. I want that to last.'

'So, I'll ask you again. What are you going to do about it?' He rested his hands on her shoulders, resisting the full-on embrace he wanted to give her.

'I'm going to speak to my father about stepping down from my royal duties. I'll tell him I want to go back to medicine full time. I don't know how we're going to do it yet but I also want a life with you, Seth. If that's what you'd like too?' She looked up at him, so full of hope, his heart soared. Everything was out in the open now. No more secrets preventing them from forging ahead. She wouldn't have the conversation with her father if she wasn't serious about making the changes it would take for him to risk his heart on her again. It was his turn to take a leap of faith and prove his commitment to their relationship by forgiving her for her earlier slight.

'It's all I could ever ask for.' They could work out the logistics later. For now it was all the confirmation he needed to go with his heart.

He leaned in and laid his mouth gently upon hers just to experience that connection once more until they had a chance to get some quality time alone again.

'So, we're good?' Kaja broke away to check but Seth didn't want to stop kissing her now that the obstacles to true love had apparently been removed.

'We're good.' He smiled against her lips. Just one more kiss and he'd get back to work.

They heard the squeak of a door being opened at the top of the stairs and he remembered to cool it. Kaja was right, they didn't need to have their every move analysed or have bystanders commenting on what they thought of their relationship. They had to figure things out for themselves.

'Can we pick this up again later?'

'Just give me the word and I'll come a-calling.'

That demure, lowered-lashes look she was giving him, unaware of how completely under her thrall he was, would ensure he came back time and time again.

'You are such a dork.' She slapped him on the arm, her laughter every bit as intoxicating as her kisses.

'You're such a princess,' he teased back, and to the female visitor coming down the stairs behind them they probably looked like two friends engaging in a bit of banter, which was exactly what they wanted people to think.

Now he understood her need to protect their relationship he wasn't going to take it personally. This way it kept Amy out of the spotlight too. It would be such a change in their family dynamic for him to have a partner it was something he'd have to lead into gradually with her. She didn't need to see their faces splashed all over the newspapers with the gossip columns listing all the reasons this single, divorced dad wasn't a good match for the country's princess. He didn't need reminding when he felt it so acutely every time he looked at her.

He bounded down the remainder of the steps, much lighter for having set the record straight with Kaja and with something to look forward to at the end of his shift.

They worked on into the night assisting where they could, patching people up so they were able to go home as soon as possible. Occasionally Kaja caught sight of Seth behind a cubicle curtain or walking by with his next patient as she treated hers.

After their talk on the stairs she hoped this was the start of a new life together for them. But there was still something she'd kept from him and if they were going into this with a clean slate she knew she'd have to tell him about her infertility issues. Her stomach tied itself in knots every time she thought about the last time she'd told a man she couldn't have his child, but Seth was nothing like Benedikt. Hurting anyone on purpose simply wasn't in his nature.

She could hear him now, his deep voice soothing the screams of a small child obviously in pain.

'I know it hurts, Lottie, but I need you to keep still so I can take a good look at that eye. Mrs Gallo, perhaps you could help hold your daughter still for me.'

Kaja had a few minutes to spare and small children were never the easiest patients to wrangle. Perhaps she could provide a suitable distraction for the little girl to enable Seth to do what he had to.

'Hey. Sorry for disturbing you, Mr Davenport. I'm in between patients at the minute and wondered if there was anything I could do to help?' There was a fine line between offering assistance and being seen as interfering.

If anything, he seemed relieved to see her.

'Thank you. I think Lottie here might need a little more persuading to sit still for me.'

Her mother was trying to stop her from rubbing her already red eyes with her bunched-up fists.

'Did you get something in your eye, Lottie? They must be very sore.' Kaja took a seat at the side of the bed as the little girl nodded and sniffed.

'I think she might have some grit irritating her. We need to get some fluorescein stain in to check.' He was as reassuring to an infant with a sore eye as he was to a fully grown woman trapped under rubble. It didn't matter what background he came from, Seth's caring and understanding nature was the mark of a true gentleman. He was pure class as far as she was concerned. A prince amongst men.

'The doctor needs to see what's hurting you, Lottie. We need you to keep your eye wide open so he can do that. Do you think you could be a big girl and tilt your head back for me?' There was no more reason to trust her than the handsome man trying to help her, but Kaja was hoping that by teaming up they would manage to persuade her.

If there was something stuck to the cornea it would explain the red, watery reaction. It could also be something more serious, such as a piece of metal. That could require surgery.

Kaja gently eased the girl's hands away from her eyes. Although Lottie let her, she did let out a pitiful whine and tensed her whole body.

'I couldn't see anything in there but I did try to give her an eye bath with some hot water. It didn't help.' The mother fretted from the other side of the bed as she brushed her daughter's hair away from her forehead.

'That's fine. We advise people not to try and remove any foreign bodies from the eye themselves in case they do further damage. You were right to bring her to us.' Seth's assurance she'd done her best eased the anxious look on the woman's face.

Kaja stood up alongside Seth so the child was looking up at her, keeping her hands tightly in hers so she wouldn't suddenly lash out. 'You just keep watching me, Lottie, while Mr Davenport takes a look in your eye.'

Seth held her eyelids open so he could have a look and the little girl squeezed Kaja's hand.

'I can't see anything in there so we're going to have to use the dye.' He clearly didn't want to distress her any more than necessary but if there was something irritating her it could cause conjunctivitis or lead to scarring.

'Lottie, the doctor is going to touch your eye with a small piece of paper. You just keep looking up at me, okay?' Another hand squeeze and whimper in response.

'I need you to blink on this for me, Lottie,' Seth coaxed, then addressed her mother to explain the process. 'The blotting paper contains an orange dye, which, when used in conjunction with a blue light, detects any foreign bodies or damage to the cornea. Blinking helps spreads the dye.'

He did the test as quickly as his patient would allow then whisked the paper away again.

'You're so good, Lottie. Now I'm going to shine a torch on you. There's nothing to be afraid of. It's a very special torch.' Seth turned the torch on so she could see the light for herself, shining it on her hand then on the ceiling so she could see it wasn't harmful.

'Is it magic?' Lottie was captivated now, the tears giving way to childish curiosity.

'Well, hopefully this will help us make you feel better again. Just keep your eye open for us, Lottie.' It was down to Kaja again to reassure her while Seth inspected the site. Any problems on the cornea would show up green under the blue light.

He had to look under the eyelid first, causing Lottie to tense up again. 'Okay... I think I can see something on the surface. I'm going to put some special eye drops in to stop it hurting, Lottie.'

It was difficult to make sure she didn't blink out the local anaesthetic drops but Seth persevered.

'I'm sure we'll have people of all ages coming in with the same problem given the air quality after the earthquake. It will be full of dust.' Kaja kept talking as Seth used a cotton swab to remove the grit.

Every adult in the room breathed a sigh of relief and when no one else was looking, he gave Kaja a wink. Confirmation if it was needed that they made a good team.

'All done. I'll put a dressing over that eye just to make

it more comfortable for a day or two. Try not to rub your eye if you can help it, Lottie. It shouldn't give you any more trouble but if it does Mum should make an appointment with your GP to get it checked out.'

'Thank you, Doctor.' Mrs Gallo waited until he'd taped a dressing over the eye before enthusiastically shaking his hand. Then she bent down and gave her daughter a kiss on the top of the head before they disappeared out of the cubicle, leaving Seth and Kaja alone.

'I'm glad we didn't have to refer her to the surgical team to cause any more trauma. Thanks for the moral support too. I'm sure it would've taken me twice as long if you hadn't been here.'

'It's never easy with the young ones and nearly always a two-person job. It's not the easiest task to perform either. I presume you've done that a few times to take on the job yourself?'

'Once or twice during hospital placements. You weren't so bad yourself, with the kiddie-whispering. She was putty in your hands once you gave her some attention, much like Amy. It seems no one is immune to the princess's charms. At least, no one under the age of six.' Beyond the complimenting was that teasing that made her blush and bluster at the same time.

'Then your daughter is a good judge of character, even if her father's opinion of me wavers from time to time.' She wasn't going to let him completely off the hook about earlier. Although she hoped she'd put his mind at rest by telling him about her plans. It wasn't going to be an easy conversation with her father, but one that was overdue.

'My opinion on you is rock solid.' He wrapped his arms around her waist before gently fitting his lips expertly around hers. Seth was the tonic she needed for her increasing tiredness but it couldn't last when there were more patients piling in by the moment.

'The next shift is here to take over.' Seth poked his head into the cubicle to notify her that it was the end of their working day.

'I'm just finishing up in here and I'll be with you in a minute.' She'd been so busy she hadn't had time to think about taking a break but every part of her poor body was aching.

Resisting the urge to leave with him there and then, she turned back to the young man sitting on the bed with his hand in a cast. 'If you make an appointment out at Reception for the fracture clinic, we'll see how your fingers are healing in a few weeks' time.'

'Okay, thank you, Doctor.'

Even though most of the people through the door had recognised her at some stage, or had been made aware of her identity, once they were in their doctor/patient roles it didn't seem to matter. She preferred it that way, being accepted and respected for her medical expertise rather than her family background. It gave her a sense of purpose and, if she was honest, more self-respect to be of some use to her country rather than merely tabloid fodder.

The earthquake had put life into perspective for a lot of people and most of those affected were only too glad to have an extra pair of doctor hands available to care about who she was outside the hospital doors.

With her last patient discharged she went straight to find Seth. 'I could get used to this freedom, you know.'

He looked at the people still waiting to be seen in the reception area. 'I'm not sure your colleagues would be keen to be so "free" every day.'

'You know what I mean. Haven't you noticed?' She

leaned in to whisper in case saying it aloud would some-how jinx it all. 'No bodyguards shadowing my every move.'

It brought Seth up short and she could see him check-ing for any ninja-like security hiding in the shadows, waiting to pounce. 'What happened to them?'

'I told them they weren't needed. They weren't around yesterday when my personal security was threatened and I survived. I couldn't very well work efficiently in the midst of the emergency here with them getting in the way or vetting every single person I came into contact with.' That conversation with Gunnar had been the first step in reasserting herself. She had a long way to go, decisions to make and conversations to have, but Seth had shown her she should be enjoying her life, not simply existing.

'Good for you. If I'm not careful your father will have me thrown out of the country for being a bad influence on you.' He laughed but Kaja suspected there was a smid-gen of real concern mixed in there too.

'Don't worry, Papa is well aware I know my own mind.' She knew he was still groggy when he'd agreed to get security to back off but he was the same man who'd given into her desire to leave the country and study in England all those years ago. That hadn't been down to anyone's influence other than her own, even if Seth had been the main reason for her extended stay.

'I think you've proved your medical worth here today, if that was ever in doubt. You are so much more than a pretty princess, Kaja, and it's time the rest of the world knew that too.'

Kaja could virtually feel her skin smouldering under his intense gaze. They had to get out of here if they intended to keep their love life under wraps. Eye-sexing each other in the middle of a busy hospital wasn't being discreet.

'I…er…mightn't have given up all of my royal privileges. I hope you won't think any less of me but I've texted for the chauffeur to come and pick me up.'

One step at a time. Perhaps some day she'd start driving herself but not all changes were going to happen overnight.

He didn't say anything as they left the reception area and she braced herself for criticism about her sense of entitlement or, at the very least, a look of disapproval. Instead, he turned to her once they were outside and simply said, 'Thank goodness. I don't think I could walk after the past twenty-four hours and I'm not the one with a dodgy ankle.'

She wanted to kiss this man and, in keeping with her new vow to be true to herself, she did just that. Albeit at the side of the entrance where there was no lighting or prying eyes. Small steps. Big smooches.

When she saw the headlights approaching the front of the hospital instead of parking around the back with the normal visitors she had to let go of him again. At least he knew now it wasn't a rejection of him but of those around them knowing their business. When they were ensconced in the back seat of the car, Seth reached for her hand and she took it gladly. With him in her corner she knew she could make it through whatever challenges were thrown at her. In her uncertain world she was sure of one thing. Her love for Seth Davenport.

# CHAPTER TWELVE

'NEXT TIME YOU go walkabout in the middle of an earthquake give me a heads up, will you?' Bruno lit in on Kaja as soon as she walked in through the door, but his tentative hug said he was more pleased to see her than angry at her.

'I can't promise you anything but I am sorry I didn't get to see you before you were discharged.' He looked so good considering he'd just had surgery the day before, better than she did after a long day on the front line of emergency medicine.

He shook hands with Seth. 'No worries. I think you had more important things to deal with. Good to see you again, too. Thanks for keeping an eye on my little sis yesterday. I knew we didn't have to worry too much if she was with you and since you both disappeared at the same time…'

Her brother wasn't stupid. There was no way he could know exactly what they'd got up to but the wink he gave them implied he was aware something was going on between them. Thankfully he was too polite to ask them outright.

'Daddy!' Amy made a flying leap at her father, confident he would catch her. Which he did, holding onto her legs as she wrapped them around his waist and hung her arms around his neck. She was always so overjoyed to see him Kaja was almost moved to tears. The way Seth hugged and made such a fuss of Amy his love for her was unquestionable. She tried to ignore that tug on her heart telling her she would never have that bond with a child of her own so it wouldn't spoil the moment.

'Oh, Miss Kaja, you're so filthy.' Fatima scuttled over, hands up in horror as she took in the spectacle of her working clothes. An unknown concept in the Alderisi family wardrobe.

'I did get stuck out there during an earthquake.' She laughed to cover her embarrassment when everyone else was so clean and tidy in comparison. Thank goodness she'd had at least one change of clothes since yesterday.

'I know, I know, Mr Davenport told me. You're so brave and compassionate to go and help those people without thinking about yourself.'

'I don't know about that.' Kaja shied away from the praise. It was circumstance and a desire to be useful that had driven her to act.

'What other princess would do that? Tell me. Who?' Fatima demanded from Bruno and Seth and they were stumped to come up with an answer. Which, it turned out, was the correct response. 'See? Only Miss Kaja.'

'Seth was there too—'

'Yes, and when he came home I made him shower and eat too.' She took Kaja's hand and tugged her towards the staircase.

'I wouldn't try arguing if I was you.' Seth was openly laughing at her as he swung Amy around so she was hoisted on his hip.

Not even her brother was in her corner. 'We've all had the same treatment. It's your turn.'

She stuck her tongue out at him when Fatima wasn't

looking, just as she had when they were kids. Like then, Bruno simply laughed it off.

'You need a nice relaxing bath. I could arrange a massage if you want?'

'That won't be necessary, thanks.' For a moment she truly believed Fatima was going to accompany her upstairs to bathe her. As much as she appreciated the concern Kaja drew the line at that.

'Well, you need to take it easy. And eat. I will make you something. Yes, I will make dinner for everyone.' Hands on hips, Fatima decreed that was what was going to happen. A sit-down, home-cooked meal.

'Thank you, Fatima. That would be lovely.' Kaja was exhausted, usually this sort of thing would prove even more draining, but as she looked around she realised there was no one else she'd rather be with tonight than the people around her right now. They weren't all blood relations but they certainly felt like family to her.

The bath had gone some way to helping her relax. She'd used some perfumed oils and lit some candles and the stresses of the day had begun to melt away. It was only her still-throbbing ankle, now an attractive purple and yellow hue, reminding her of yesterday's trauma.

She threw on Seth's old sweatshirt—freshly laundered— and her tracksuit bottoms so she could properly relax for the rest of the evening.

The sound of chatter and the smell of freshly baked bread led her down to the dining room. Amy darted out in front of her just outside the door, almost causing her to trip.

'Be careful, Amy, that floor can be slippery.'

'Okay, Kaja. I'm helping Fatima.'

'Good girl. Remember to walk, don't run. We don't

want any accidents or you'll end up like me.' Kaja showed off her freshly bandaged ankle and watched as the excited child skipped off so full of self-importance at whatever task Fatima had assigned to keep her out of mischief.

She hadn't intended to eavesdrop but when she heard the men talking she couldn't bring herself to interrupt the conversation. It would be good for them to get to know each other better if Seth and Amy were going to prove a more permanent feature in her life.

'Amy's a real whirlwind. You're very lucky, Seth.' Bruno's voice rendered her immobile.

'I know. I couldn't imagine life without her.'

'And her mother? I haven't heard anybody mention her. Sorry if that's insensitive of me to ask.'

She could imagine Seth shaking his head to ease her brother's conscience that he might have inadvertently offended him in some way. 'Paula left not long after Amy was born. We're divorced now.'

'Sorry to hear that. I'm looking forward to marrying Missy and having a family of my own one day. What about you? Do you think you'll ever do it again?'

'Absolutely. I'll make sure to pick the right woman next time. Joking aside though, I can't wait to settle down again and have more children. I adore being a dad.'

It took a while for the reality of Seth's words to sink in, Kaja's heart plummeting when she realised his plans for the future included an extended family she couldn't provide him. Her heart couldn't take disappointing him month after month.

Seth was a fantastic dad. It was clear in every second he spent with his daughter and even today when he'd treated that young girl so compassionately. It wouldn't be fair to deny him the chance of settling down with someone who could give him everything he wanted. More children and the chance to experience it all again. Amy would make a great big sister too. It was Kaja who didn't fit into that picture-perfect happy family.

Just because she was forced to suffer a childless future it didn't mean he had to.

Seth was a good man who deserved better than a barren princess who would bring him nothing but pain. Perhaps they should stick to the original plan and let him go back home without her. She shouldn't expect him to disrupt the life he had with Amy for her sake. Not when she still couldn't be the woman he needed. Even if she gave up her royal title, her loyalties no longer divided, she was failing him in the most basic fashion. She'd been selfish in not telling him before now simply so she could have him in her life a little longer.

Ending things now had to be better than waiting until he resented her for not giving him a baby. She'd been there before with Benedikt and knew how this panned out: disappointment, accusing fingers and crying herself to sleep every time she didn't meet expectations.

'What are you doing out here? Food is on the table going cold. Go, join the others.' Fatima, closely followed by her little shadow, Amy, both carrying baskets of bread rolls, harried her into the dining room.

Seth and Bruno were pleased to see her and she didn't think it was merely so they could finally tuck into their dinner. It was unfortunate she was going to have to spoil the evening for one of them.

'Much better.' Seth approved of Kaja's new attire. It was funny how he found an old baggy sweatshirt on her just as attractive as the expensive couture she wore in public. Probably because it reminded him of the previous life they'd had. One he hoped they'd have again. This time with an alternative ending.

She flashed him a subtle smile and took a seat beside her brother on the opposite side of the table. Amy jumped up on the seat beside Seth, on the cushion they were using as a booster seat so she could see over the table. It was how he imagined a medieval banqueting table would look in terms of the amount of food and the length of the actual table, although the assortment of shining cutlery and obviously expensive china created an altogether more regal experience. He wasn't used to all this pomp and ceremony for dinner. Usually, if Amy had already been fed by the childminder, he settled for dinner on a tray in front of the TV.

'I was just telling Seth the hospital rumour mill was working overtime today.' Bruno poured Kaja a glass of wine so she could catch up with the one they'd already downed waiting for her.

'Oh?' Seth noticed the wary look in her eyes. She probably assumed the worst, the way he had when Bruno had mentioned it to him too, but she didn't need to worry. Their al fresco tryst remained a secret as far as he knew.

'Yes, you impressed quite a few with your dedication, pitching in with everybody else. I mean, I know you were there too, Seth, but people don't expect to see anyone from the royal family getting their hands dirty in the midst of a crisis.' Bruno was very matter-of-fact about the way his family was viewed by the public. Unlike his sister, he didn't seem to care a jot what other people thought of him.

It was always different for men, of course; they weren't judged as much as their female counterparts on their looks or their relationships. However, Seth got the impression Bruno wouldn't compromise his sense of self for anyone.

'It wasn't anything I hadn't done before. Just because you haven't been down at the coalface, big bro, doesn't mean I haven't.'

'Well, I heard you had to staple a man's scalp back together.'

'True.'

'And the kid impaled on the handlebars?'

'Also true.'

'What about the baby you single-handedly delivered in the back of the ambulance.'

'Not true. There were three of us.'

Seth scooped some of the pasta dish Fatima had made for them onto Amy's plate before serving himself while the siblings discussed some of the patient stories that had circulated about Kaja's time at the hospital. He devoured the cheesy, creamy comfort food as though he hadn't eaten all day. If he stayed here much longer letting Fatima fatten him up he might have to invest in some trousers with an elastic waist. Goodness knew how Kaja kept her svelte figure. Stress, he supposed. It was impossible to enjoy a hearty meal properly if your stomach was constantly in knots with worry.

Even now he noticed her picking at her dinner, not eating more than a forkful or two. He'd have a chat with her later to put her mind at ease that no one had mentioned the possibility of a romance between them in his presence. After Amy and the others went to bed he was looking forward to having some alone time again with Kaja. Libido aside, they needed to figure out how they were going to make this work between them. If she was as unhappy as she appeared here and so keen to get back to work, he hoped it wouldn't take too much to persuade her to return to England with him once her father was fully recovered.

'No more hospital talk, please. People are trying to eat.' After hearing one too many surgical procedures Fatima held her hands up to her ears, although she was the only one who seemed bothered. Amy was more concerned with getting a second helping of pasta than any hospital drama.

'Sorry, Fatima,' Kaja and Bruno chorused, sounding nothing of the sort. He could imagine the two of them as mischievous children running rings around her when she was the only one giving them any attention without their parents around.

'I told Dad what you'd been doing. He was very impressed.'

'I don't know why. I am a qualified surgeon. I worked in England for a long time in the emergency department and I do the same here once a week, as he very well knows.' Kaja stabbed her pasta.

'He's very old-fashioned when it comes to our roles. Perhaps it's different now he knows it's not some vanity project you're running. It could be that he's going through some sort of epiphany. After all, he's received a second chance at life.'

'Thanks to you.'

'Thanks to all of us. If it weren't for you, we wouldn't have got Seth here involved, and Fatima has been the one keeping us all going. Not to forget Amy, who is a ray of sunshine here and I'm sure will play a part in Dad's recovery.' Bruno held up his glass of wine. 'To us.'

'To us,' the rest of them toasted along with him. Including Amy with her beaker of milk.

Kaja set down her glass and her cutlery, abandoning

any pretence she was eating. 'I've decided to go back to medicine full time.'

'That's a big deal, sis. There will be a lot of logistics to consider. People to consult.'

'I'm aware of that but I can serve the country better that way.' For the first time since bringing up the subject she looked at Seth.

'You're staying here?' He didn't care that no one else was aware there was a different option available to her if she chose. She did. He'd really believed this was going to be their second chance. If she was expecting him to fall into line with her decision and relocate here permanently, uprooting Amy from everything she knew, she really should've consulted him on the matter first.

'Yes.'

'Oh, Miss Kaja, you are a very honourable woman. Your mother would be so proud.' Fatima, close to tears at the news, rose from her seat and threw her arms around Kaja's neck in a hug. Bruno remained seated, his gaze travelling between her and Seth.

Seth couldn't move even if he wanted to.

'You're really going to give everything up here for the stress and drama of an emergency department?'

'Give up what, Bruno? I don't have anything I'm not willing to drop to give my life some meaning.' She didn't look at Seth but every word was a thousand daggers plunging into his flesh. There were so many reasons for him to take offence in that one simple sentence. Apparently he was nothing.

That wasn't what she'd told him hours earlier when they were planning a future together. She'd told him she was giving up her position to do what she wanted in life. Now, suddenly he wasn't a part of that? If she'd changed her mind and decided he wasn't worth giving up her position for after all, there were kinder ways to do it. She could've broken it to him in private, for a start. There was no way she wouldn't have known how hurtful those words would be and she had to have a reason why she'd wanted to wound him so deeply. By doing this to him in company she was denying him the chance to call her out on those empty promises she'd made. Not that it mattered now, when the damage had already been done.

He was mad at himself for falling for her all over again and believing her vow to speak to her father. She'd probably only said it to stop him hounding her when he'd been pushing her so hard to give him the answer he wanted to hear. Now she'd had time to think it through, a life with him wasn't any more attractive to her than it was five years ago.

'I think we should leave you to discuss family matters in private. Amy, it's bedtime.' Seth tossed his linen napkin on the table and pushed back his chair, desperate to escape the room and this conversation.

'I'm not tired, Daddy.' Amy folded her arms across her chest and pouted in an uncharacteristic bout of petulance at the worst possible time.

'It's getting late and I've had a very trying day. Let's go, Amy.' He was pleading with her in his head not to cause an even greater scene when he was already at breaking point. It wasn't his temper he was worried about losing, rather control of his fragile emotions. In the space of a few minutes his dreams of becoming a family with Kaja had been shattered, only to be faced with returning to his lonely life back in England. And he had no idea why.

Thankfully his daughter gave up on her sit-in and climbed down off her chair. 'Night, night, everybody.'

'Night, sweetheart.' Seth had to wait not so patiently while Kaja came to give her a hug, closely followed by Fatima.

He managed an abrupt, 'Goodnight,' before taking his daughter by the hand and leading her away from the family they'd both begun to feel a part of. Returning home was going to break both of their hearts.

There was no way he was sleeping until he confronted Kaja about her comments tonight. Once Amy had brushed her teeth and settled into bed he crept out onto the landing separating their apartments from Kaja's. He made sure to leave the doors open in case she stirred while he was waiting for answers.

When Kaja appeared he was sure he saw her take a deep breath as she met him at the top of the stairs.

'Do you mind telling me what that was all about down there?' He practically spat the words at her.

'I told you I'm going back into medicine permanently.'

'But you're staying here?'

'Where else would I work? This is my country. My family are here.'

'What about Amy and me? I thought we meant something to you.'

'You'll always have a special place in my heart, Seth. Amy too. But I've had some time to think and I want to focus on me and my career. I can't do that if I'm playing house with you and your daughter.' She was so calm and cool as she devastated him Seth thought it was worse than having her simply disappear from his life, seeing firsthand of how little significance he was to her.

'What's changed in the space of a few hours? Earlier we were making plans to get together again, then you dump me halfway through dinner. It doesn't make any sense.'

'We want different things. I heard you talking to Bruno, telling him your plans to get married and have more children. That's not going to happen with me.'

'That's what all of this is about? A snatched bit of small talk between me and your brother?' He wanted to laugh at the absurdity of it. 'In an ideal world, yes, I'd like to settle down again. That's not so bad, is it?'

He moved towards her, wanted to hold her again so she could remember how it felt to be wrapped up in each other's arms and forget everything else.

Kaja stepped back, reluctant to let him touch her. 'What if I told you I can't have children, Seth? I can't give you that family you want. Would you still want to be with me?'

That bombshell rendered him speechless. It was such a huge thing for her to have kept from him all this time and he was trying to process what that meant for them. He'd pictured building on their family but now he had to adjust to the idea of a future without further children.

Unfortunately, Kaja took his pause as he processed this news as the rejection she'd been expecting.

'I'll take that as a no. Just as I thought.'

'That's not what—'

She rejected his attempt to placate her with a wave of her hand. 'Forget it, Seth. I've made up my mind.'

'And what? That's the end of it? No discussion?'

'Exactly. What's the point of pretending there's a future for us? My career is all I'm interested in now. It's the only thing I have going for me.'

'What am I supposed to do? Forget anything ever happened between us and carry on living here and treating your father?' It had been hard enough to do that first time around but now, with such new and erotic memories of their time together, it would be impossible. Not to mention painful, with the knowledge she wasn't going to fight for them this time either. It seemed Kaja was ready to walk away every time they faced an obstacle and that wasn't a stable foundation for any relationship. Perhaps she was right after all. This was never going to work between them.

'I wouldn't expect you to do that. That's why I think you and Amy should go home. You were flown in to do the transplant and you managed that successfully. We have a team of surgeons and consultants who can oversee the rest of his recovery. If there are any complications they can't handle I'm sure they'll be in touch.'

'You have it all figured out, don't you?' He wondered if this was the royal equivalent of ordering a taxi for a regrettable one-night stand the morning after. She couldn't wait to get rid of all traces of him.

'I don't see the point in dragging things out.'

'Thanks for being so honest with me. It makes a change.' He was lashing out now, wishing to cause her some of the pain she was currently causing him, but she didn't flinch. Only one day returned to her world and that cool princess was well and truly back in charge. When she offered no defence against his jibe he knew the battle was lost. She didn't even feel strongly enough to argue with him any more. He walked away defeated, knowing he wasn't wanted enough for anyone to fight to have him in their lives.

Kaja opened her bedroom curtains, the morning sunshine unreflective of her current disposition. She'd slept later than she'd intended. Mainly because it had taken her so long to get to sleep, her guilty conscience replaying her harsh words and the image of Seth's crestfallen face on a loop in her head. She knew she'd hurt him. Again. This time, she told herself, it was for his benefit, not hers. It was completely different.

Five years ago she'd run from their relationship, realising she couldn't make a lifelong commitment to him when she wasn't being true to herself. Now, she was saving him from doing the same. It didn't make her feel any better. He wanted to be with someone who could give him a family and he could pretend otherwise to be with her but they both knew it was the truth. Her body had failed her and the man she loved.

Unwilling to face anyone this morning, she made the decision to go straight to the hospital and assist where she could once she washed and dressed. There'd be time later for her to deal with her brother's questions, Fatima mourning the inevitable loss of her young companion and, worst of all, being faced with Seth's look of betrayal. Unfortunately, the pain in her own heart couldn't be avoided so easily. The best she could do was try and work through it.

# CHAPTER THIRTEEN

'I'M GOING TO take a break and go and check on my father.'

'No problem. It's quietened down a bit for now. Thanks for your help. You've really gone above and beyond over these past few days.' Cecilia, the woman who'd been co-ordinating all available staff in the emergency department, threw her arms around Kaja and hugged her. It was unexpected on a number of different levels. Kaja hadn't been working here to garner praise of any kind, but she had enjoyed being seen as part of the team rather than simply for novelty value. Cecilia was hugging her as a colleague, perhaps even a friend, without thought to her royal status.

The simple gift of a hug had her too choked up to bat away the compliment or offer any response. Instead she gave her a squeeze back and walked away before she made a fool of herself bawling in the middle of the corridor. Of course, when she came to her father's hospital room she had to erase all traces of that vulnerability. If she was asserting her right to work and step back from her royal duties it was necessary to show confidence in what she was doing.

'Kaja.' Her father struggled to sit up when she came in through the door.

'There's no need to strain yourself, Papa. I just wanted

to see how you were today.' She walked over and kissed him before helping him into a more comfortable position. He had more colour in his cheeks today and appeared brighter than he had in months.

'Sore, but I'll live and that's the main thing.'

'Yes, it is.' It seemed he'd inherited her brother's dark sense of humour along with his kidney, but that wasn't altogether a bad thing. If he'd stopped taking everything so seriously it might make it easier for her to discuss her plans for the future without the dramatics she'd been expecting.

She pulled a chair over so she could sit by the side of his bed and took his hand in hers.

'Papa, I've been thinking a lot about my life and I'm not happy with where I am right now. Some things have happened while you've been in here, which have made me reassess what I'm doing and what sort of legacy I'm leaving behind.' She mightn't be able to secure the royal line with children of her own, but she could make a difference by saving lives.

'It's about time.'

It certainly wasn't the response she'd anticipated. 'Pardon me?'

Her father rested his other hand on top of hers. 'Kaja, you haven't been happy since you came home from England. I had hoped marriage would give you something to focus on rather than whatever it was you'd left behind. I wanted you to have the love and happiness your mother and I shared. I'm sorry that didn't happen with Benedikt. What he did to you was unforgivable. I've been waiting so very long for you to find something to make you smile again.'

If she didn't have so many questions Kaja might have been stunned into silence. 'You don't mind if I go back into medicine full time? What about all your talk about family traditions and keeping up appearances?'

'All I ever wanted was for you to be happy, my darling. Without your royal duties these past five years I was worried you wouldn't leave the house at all, you were so miserable.'

'You never said any of this before. I thought I was a disappointment.'

'Never. I know I may not have been the best father over the years, consumed by my responsibilities elsewhere, but I was always proud of you.'

'Why didn't you reach out to me when I was in England?'

'Your mother thought we should give you space and you'd come back to us when you were ready. You did. We both just wanted the best for you. Then you met Benedikt and I thought you were focusing on the future.'

'I tried, but apparently I never did get over my past,' she muttered more to herself than for her father's ears. She'd never loved anyone but Seth and in hindsight it must've been obvious to her ex that she was on the rebound and not fully committed to their marriage. Looking back now, she couldn't completely blame him for seeking affection elsewhere. He could've discussed it with her, of course, rather than humiliating her with his affair, but they'd been doomed from the start when she was still in love with another man.

'You seemed to over these past few days.'

She wasn't entirely sure what he meant by that when he didn't know a fraction of what had been going on outside this room, but he was right. With Seth back in her life she had been able to put a lot of their bad history behind her. Mainly because he'd forgiven her, but also because she was happier simply having him around. Both of which were moot points now that she'd hurt him all over again and told him she didn't want him in her life.

'Are you telling me that all the decisions I've made have been based on my own paranoia?'

'I can't say that. I don't know what goes on in your head but please understand I don't want anything to stop you living your best life. Do what makes you happy, not what you think other people want you to do.'

She thought back to last night's painful conversation with Seth. He'd been quiet when she'd told him she couldn't have children but, instead of letting him digest the news, she'd jumped to the conclusion he wouldn't want to be with her. The same way she'd assumed her father would prefer to have her as some kind of waving automaton rather than a contributing member of society without ever talking it over. She hadn't let Seth answer or discussed any option other than splitting up. She really was her own worst enemy. It was Seth who made her happy and she was only punishing herself by pushing him away.

'I've been so stupid. I told Seth we didn't need him here any more.'

'I know; he told me when he visited with Amy.'

'When?' An overwhelming sense of dread crept through her. The house had been awfully quiet this morning and Seth would never have brought Amy to work with him.

'On his way to the airport. He said there was no point in him staying any longer when I was doing so well and I'm in the hands of the best team. I don't think he wanted to disrupt his daughter's life any more than was necessary.'

Kaja barely heard what he was saying beyond that first revelation. 'He's gone?'

She might have said the words prompting that departure, told everyone including herself it was for the best, but being faced with the possibility that she would never see him again was too much. To her horror she burst into a flood of tears. That careful composure that had weathered all storms until recently slipped again. She wasn't wearing her heart on her sleeve, it was tripping down her face and splashing onto the floor.

'I thought that was what you wanted?' Her father arched an eyebrow at her, questioning her tears but with a hint that he knew the answer already.

'No. I want him to stay.'

'I could see it in his eyes that's what he wanted as well. If you're quick you might be able to catch him at the airport. If that's what you want?'

That was the million-dollar question. This was her decision and if she made the wrong choice she couldn't blame anyone else this time. She'd have to live with the consequences of what she did next for the rest of her life.

'Thanks for being our chauffeur, Fatima.' Seth hugged her before opening the boot of the car to retrieve the bags. He hadn't wanted the hassle of getting the limo and he had a hunch Fatima's offer to take them in her jalopy was so she could spend as much time as possible with Amy before they left.

'It was my pleasure. I wish you were staying.' Tears welled in her eyes and he prayed she wouldn't start crying in earnest or she'd set Amy off, and him. Neither of them really wanted to leave but Kaja wanted him gone and there wasn't anything he could do to change her mind.

He shouldn't have to. If she felt the same way about him as he did about her she would never have said the things she did. He wasn't going to hang around and prolong the agony. Leaving this way, without any fuss or dramatic showdown, left him a smidgen of dignity. He was even beginning to see why she'd walked out on him without a word five years ago. It wasn't payback, he just didn't think he could face her without giving her a good shake or breaking down in front of her.

'We have to get home.' He went to open the car door to help Amy out but Fatima grabbed his arm.

'Miss Kaja has always been afraid to do what's in her heart in case it's the wrong thing. As a little girl she had a lot of pressure put upon her. Don't give up on her.'

'She's a grown woman now and for my sake, and Amy's, I can't do this any more. How did you know about us anyway?' They thought they'd been so careful not to let anyone know they'd ever been romantically involved, never mind that they'd rekindled their affair. It was part of the reason he was leaving so soon after being rejected. If he stayed it would become obvious to everyone how much his heart was breaking at not being able to be with her.

Fatima shrugged. 'I have known her for a very long time. She can tell me so much without saying a word. I saw the same look on her face when she came back from England as I did last night before she went to bed. I may be old but I'm not stupid, or blind. If you didn't love each other it wouldn't hurt you both so much.'

'There's nothing I can do about it now. We've made our minds up.' He opened the door and unstrapped Amy from the car seat, knowing they wouldn't carry on this conversation with her around. Fatima could call him a coward if she wished but he had more than just himself to protect this time around.

'Can't we stay a little longer, Daddy? Please?' Amy's quivering lip and big, pleading brown eyes almost made him agree to anything rather than hurt her, but he knew she'd be fine once they got home and she was back in her old routine.

'You can phone Fatima any time you want to hear her voice.'

Fatima nodded through her watery smile.

'You have my number and you're welcome to visit us in Cambridge any time.' It was unlikely this loyal mother figure would ever desert her post at the palace but he thought he should at least offer, as she and Amy had grown so close. In other circumstances he would've cultivated that bond, when they seemed to draw so much comfort from each other's company, but as things stood it was impossible.

'I won't come in with you. I'll say my goodbyes here.' She leaned down and hugged Amy as though she never wanted to let go. When she finally did, Seth saw her wipe away the tears before Amy noticed. 'Now, you be a good girl for your papa and I'll talk to you soon.'

'Thank you for everything, Fatima.' He kissed her on both cheeks, then led Amy towards the airport building, dragging their suitcase, and his heart, behind them.

'Stop the car!' Kaja's heart was hammering as she grabbed for the door handle. She'd recognised Fatima's car on the road from the airport and put two and two together. That was why the house had been unusually quiet when she'd got up. Even Fatima had gone AWOL. It was clear whose side she was taking if she'd personally driven Seth and Amy away without telling Kaja.

Fatima pulled over and wound down her window. 'I did my best to get him to stay.'

Her face crumpled and Kaja could feel her pain as acutely as her own at the loss. What had she done?

'Is it too late?' Her voice was a mere whisper, caught in her throat at the thought that she'd lost Seth and Amy for ever.

'I left them at the airport. I couldn't bear to go in and watch them fly away.'

'There might still be time. They still have to check in and go through security.' She was clutching at straws but without hope she might as well lie down on this road and weep. The talk with her father had made her realise it was up to her to take action and fight for what she wanted in life. That was Seth and Amy. She was the only one who could get them to stay and even that wasn't guaranteed.

'I tried telling him it was fear which had made you reject him. I think we both know you still love him.'

'Apparently everybody—except us—does,' she said as she got back into the limo intent on giving chase. All she needed was for Seth to believe it and be willing to give her a third chance.

They drove to the airport, lights flashing, horn blaring at any traffic so they'd let them pass. She made as many phone calls and asked for as many favours as she could en route in order to slow Seth's departure. It might make for a frustrating wait on his part but it would buy time for her to get there.

Security met her at the airport entrance after she'd called ahead and asked for their help to jump any queues. She'd purchased a flight ticket online in case she had to get on that flight to convince him she loved him. At this moment she was prepared to do whatever it took to win him back.

'Excuse us.'

'Make way, please.'

The human cordon around her moved as many travellers out of her path as they could. Kaja didn't usually take advantage of her position for her own benefit but on this occasion she was willing to use all available resources to get her man. When she got to the departure gate and saw it was empty save for the attendants at the desk, a cold sweat broke out over her skin. If she was too late she might never see him again.

'Do you have your boarding pass? The plane's sitting on the tarmac. You might just make it if you're quick.'

One last ember of hope burned a little brighter. It only took the woman a moment to scan her ticket but it might as well have been days when every second was so crucial. There was no time for niceties and Kaja snatched the boarding pass back once she was finished with it. Security hovered, uncertain of the protocol.

'I can take it from here,' she told them, then started running.

She didn't care if anyone caught a picture of her racing across the runway like a lunatic; Seth was more important than anything. It was the thought of him flying back to England and the life she'd have to endure without him that kept her legs pumping even when her lungs were fit to burst. They'd been happy together. Not just for that brief time when they'd shut out the rest of the world, but for years living together when she hadn't worried about anything except being in the moment. She wasn't going to let that simply go to waste when they might have a chance of being happy. Together.

'Wait!' she shouted at the member of the cabin crew who was getting ready to shut the door.

In her years of attending photo ops, ceremonial openings and giving public speeches she didn't remember having so many faces staring at her as she did once she stumbled on board. The whispering and gasps started off as a low rumbling, but by the time she'd made it halfway down the plane it was building up to a roar. People were turning their heads and leaning over the backs of their seats to get a better view.

'Kaja!' It was Amy who grabbed her attention first, standing up on her seat to wave while Seth gawped at her, mouth hanging open.

She rushed to his seat and knelt in the aisle. 'Seth, I'm so sorry about what I said. I didn't mean any of it.'

'Kaja, what on earth are you doing? Everyone can see you. This is going to be all over the news by the end of the day.' He was looking at all the heads peering around to see what she was doing, camera phones at the ready, not taking in what she was saying.

'I don't care. I want you to stay. I love you and I want to be with you.' It was on record now. For ever. She just didn't know if it was enough to counter all the mistakes she'd made along the way.

'You love me?' He frowned and leaned in closer for some degree of privacy. 'Only last night you told me to go. You keep blowing hot and cold, Kaja, and I'm sorry but I need stability for Amy. For my heart.'

'I'll move to England with you if that's what it takes to prove to you that I'm serious.'

'You did that once before. It didn't work out too well, remember?'

'This is different. I'm different. I thought you'd be better off with someone who could give you the family you want and I'm sorry that I can't. All I can offer you is me.' She grabbed him with both hands and kissed him full on the lips to a plane full of whoops and cheers. This was her way of showing him she meant every word and he was all that mattered. When he kissed her back and the cheers faded into the background she knew she'd finally made the right decision.

At least Seth remembered where they were before things got too heated. 'How on earth did you manage to get here on time? I thought you were at the hospital.'

'I was. I went to see my father about going back to work and I realised I've been the one holding myself back from being happy. No more. You and Amy are my happy place. In case you didn't hear it the first time, I love you. Nothing else matters to me.'

'Then we'd better get off this plane because all I need is you. I love you too. I always have and I don't care where we live as long as we're together. Besides, I've never seen Amy so happy as I have out here. It already feels like home.' Seth took Amy by the hand and followed Kaja back down the aisle. She held her head high as the cheers rang out from the other passengers, uncaring about what they thought. All that mattered was that she was being honest with Seth and true to herself. It was all that was needed to make her happy.

This princess had never needed a prince to save her. She simply had to do it herself.

# EPILOGUE

*One year later*

'WELL? WHAT DOES it say?' Seth was waiting for her the second she came out of the bathroom.

'We have to wait a couple of minutes.' Kaja understood his urgency when she'd been wishing away the time all through her shift in the emergency department to get to this moment. She loved her job almost as much as her husband and her stepdaughter of six months, but the anticipation had been killing her.

She'd kept the test until she got home so they could see the result together. Although that hadn't stopped Seth texting and phoning her all day once she'd told him her period was late.

Do you feel pregnant?

When do you think it happened?

Can't you take a quick break and come home?

She hoped they weren't getting their hopes up for something that might not ever happen. It seemed too good to be true after all those years she'd failed to get pregnant. Perhaps her baby had been waiting for Seth too.

'Is it time now?' Seth leaned over her shoulder, watching the window on the pregnancy test with rapt attention.

'You're worse than Fatima,' she said with a laugh. Although Fatima hadn't said anything to Kaja directly, according to Amy she'd taken to knitting lots of dolly clothes recently, 'And she doesn't even have a dolly, Kaja!' Perhaps there was something to her claims of having 'the gift' after all if she'd known something before Mother Nature.

Seth was beaming now as much as he had on their wedding day at the palace. One good thing about having such a huge family estate was they'd been able to get married in private. The ceremony had been held in the gardens with only family and friends from the hospital where they both worked in attendance. They'd only made the announcement public after their honeymoon in England, where she and Seth had been able to reminisce about the old days and tie up loose ends before he and Amy moved over for good.

'Sorry. I'm just excited.'

'I know. Neither of us thought it was going to happen.' She'd been honest with Seth that another child might not be a possibility but he'd been insistent that he still wanted a future with her. Now it seemed those impossible dreams might be about to come true.

PREGNANT

The word filling the tiny LED screen made them both gasp and stare at each other like loons.

'It's true? We're going to have a baby?' He was practically vibrating with excitement as he grabbed her into a hug.

'Yes. I'm pregnant. You're going to be a daddy again

and Amy's going to be a big sister.' It was the icing on her perfect year after marrying Seth and becoming stepmother to Amy.

'You're amazing.' He held her tight and the feel of his strong arms around her was reassuring at a time where she was a little out of her depth.

'I didn't do it all on my own, you know.' The passion for one another hadn't ebbed since they'd married or moved into their own place away from the palace. Especially now they had some privacy. After the initial furore when they'd got together, the press had lost interest in a busy working mum. A happily married medic wasn't very glamorous but it was exactly the life she wanted.

'I'm going to have to book in with a midwife and organise antenatal classes. Then there's all the things we're going to need for the nursery.' A to-do list getting longer by the second popped into her head as the reality of the situation began to sink in.

'Hey. We're in this together, Mrs Davenport. I can handle all of that. I don't want you worrying about anything.' He tilted her chin up with his finger and the sheer love she saw reflected in his eyes, felt in every pore in her body, was everything she'd ever needed. Their marriage was a shared partnership and, good or bad, they would go through everything together.

'Love you, Mr Davenport.'

'And I love you. You'll always be my princess.' He kissed her on the lips, sealing the promise, and she knew when the baby came they'd be the happiest little family in Belle Crepuscolo.

\* \* \* \* \*

# RECLAIMING
# HER ARMY DOC
# HUSBAND

SUE MacKAY

**MILLS & BOON**

Dedicated to my wonderful friend, Vicki Rule,
who has a fantastic shoe collection
and is one of the kindest and strongest women I know.

# CHAPTER ONE

'COLE, IT'S ME. I need to talk to you urgently. Please, sweetheart.' Vicki Halliday pressed her phone so hard against her ear it hurt. 'We've got a problem.'

She'd miscarried. Their baby was gone. Their dreams and excitement were over. Maybe her dream more than his. He'd seemed a little distant since learning about the pregnancy.

'Please leave a message after the beep and I'll get back to you as soon as possible,' her husband's strong, don't-mess-with-me voice intoned. Not the voice she adored, went to bed with to have sweet nothings whispered against her skin. Not the man she hugged and kissed in return because of the deep sexiness that was the love of her life.

She pressed 'off' and leaned forward over her knees, her hands clenched around the only link she had with her husband. Damn, how she missed him. Would give anything for him to be here so they could get through the loss of their baby together.

Not that there was anything unusual about his absence. Twelve months ago he hadn't been around when she'd had to have their spaniel Benji put down after a car had hit the beloved pet that had helped her through the lonely days when Cole was offshore. Neither had he been around two months later when her mother had been having chemo and Vicki had thought she would lose her too.

He *had* surprised her by turning up for her thirtieth birthday. One night of passion, then he was gone before she'd woken up. Gone without a word of when he'd see her next, without waking her to say he loved her. As always, he'd had to follow orders. Fair enough. He'd gone into the job willingly. But she hadn't. Now he was in East Timor with his army unit. Not here. Where he was needed the most. Where, for once, he could put his own needs aside and help her through this tragedy—together.

'Cole, you have to answer your phone pronto.'

In desperation she tapped his number again. Again heard his impersonal message.

The pain and despair combined to fling words out of her mouth with no thought of consequences. 'Just for once, answer your blasted phone, Cole Halliday. I've miscarried our baby,' Vicki shrieked through a burst of pain. 'I've miscarried,' she repeated, quieter this time.

The words clogged her throat and she threw the phone onto the couch beside her as she sprawled lengthways in a wasted attempt to ease the ache in her abdomen. And her heart. 'This can't be happening,' Then again, why not? Nothing had gone right in their marriage for a while, so why would believing she'd see their pregnancy through to full term be any different? Except this time the pain was unbearable, and that wasn't the physical.

*I've lost our baby.*

'It's so unfair,' she cried through clenched jaws.

*I think I've lost my husband, too.*

'Still no answer?' Molly rubbed Vicki's back.

'Obviously not,' she vented at her friend, then instantly regretted it. None of this was Molly's fault. Molly had strapped her baby twins into the car and driven halfway across Sydney to pick her up the moment Vicki had said what was happening.

*Also*, as much as she wanted to, she couldn't really blame Cole for the fact she was losing their baby. But he should be here, cuddling her, or rubbing her back when it ached instead of Molly sharing her grief because it would be his, too. No matter how hard her friend tried, it wasn't the same as having the man she loved with her during this crisis, giving the emotional support he all too often failed on. Because he stood tall, he thought she could too.

Instead she was used to having a loving family at her side through everything, so these past years in Sydney away from them, and with Cole coming and going, had been hard. He didn't get it. Didn't understand how much she needed him to listen to her worries and take them on board. Like Molly was doing now. She dragged herself upright. 'Sorry, ignore me.'

'It's okay. I get it.'

'True.' If anyone did, Molly did. Years ago her friend's ex had put her through a horrific miscarriage via a fist to her stomach. For Molly, it had been the final straw in a violent marriage, and she'd left him for good. Eventually, she'd found happiness with Cole's best friend, Nathan.

'I only wish you weren't going through this.'

Vicki gave a sick sigh. Right this moment she struggled to find the strength to see it through without her man. 'You and me both.' All the excitement of having a baby, of believing that she and Cole would be a proper family with a child to nurture and love, had gone down the drain, almost literally. Angry tears burned down her cheeks. Her broken heart continued doing its job from under a weight of despair and sadness. She was a mixed bag of emotions, not one of them good. 'Cole's not here to see it. To hold my hand. To tell me silly stuff like I'll be all right. That we'll try again.' If he wanted to.

'Here.' A box of tissues appeared before her. 'He'll feel terrible when he gets your message.'

*When* he got it. Who knew exactly where he was and for how long? Not her. He never told her when he was going on a mission, or what happened on the forays the unit engaged in. Not that she wanted the details, they'd only give her more graphic nightmares worrying if he was safe.

'You reckon?' Vicki couldn't help the bitterness tainting her question. Was she being unfair? Selfish? Sure she was, but today she didn't care much. She needed Cole. Right here. Now. Not in another country looking out for people he didn't know. It was important to him, and some would say she was selfish, that other army wives coped with disasters.

To hell with them. Watching her mother, after her close shave with cancer, begin to understand how much she'd sacrificed for her family, Vicki had started realising she was going down the same track by forfeiting her own needs to keep Cole happy. She liked making others happy, or helping them get well. It was one reason she'd become a nurse. When she and Cole had got married her own dreams had gone on hold, but over the past year she'd begun resurrecting the idea of owning a nursing agency. Maybe she should've done it when Cole had first signed up and then perhaps she wouldn't be so at odds with him now.

She hadn't known where to start. It didn't come naturally. Cole didn't understand how important it was to her to create something for herself, so she'd vacillated between what she had and what she wanted. When she'd become pregnant, the future had become clearer—in a different direction. She would raise her child with all the love she was capable of, while still being there for Cole, at his side, loving him. Putting herself on the backburner. Just like her mother had done with her father, and now regretted.

Watching her mother blossom over the last months as she followed her artistic aspirations had been an eye-opener, and had made Vicki take a long look at herself. It was scary. Following through on her own dreams might mean losing Cole. If that happened, then maybe she'd fallen in love with the wrong man. *No.* She loved him so much, that wasn't possible.

Whatever the truth, all the hopes and plans and excitement of a family were now finished. Gone. Poof. No more. Through no fault of her own, or Cole's. Miscarriages happened—often. She just hadn't figured she'd be a statistic. Neither had she'd started her pregnancy thinking how it might go wrong. That was unhealthy. Yet she was already grieving for her baby.

Where should she go from here? She could go back to work tomorrow, get on with living like nothing had happened, stiff upper lip and all that. It was a role she had played every time Cole had left her for another army excursion. Taking days off would only add to her loneliness. Her friends would be at work or, like Molly, busy with their little ones. To head home to the family in Cairns where she'd be wrapped in love and comfort would make it even harder to return to Sydney and the empty apartment at the end of her break.

Molly hadn't finished playing the diplomat. 'You know Cole will be gutted. He was so excited about the pregnancy, and he loves you to bits.'

'Then why do I come second to everything?' The army was like another wife, a more demanding one who had to be obeyed at all cost. Right from the start of their relationship Cole had warned her he was going to sign up after finishing his medical degree. Because she'd been so much in love she'd thought she'd manage as long as he was in her life. Going along with his plans without question made him happy.

Unfortunately, she hadn't *known* what living alone while married really entailed. Hadn't understood the relentless loneliness when he was away for months on end. An isolation that encroached even when he was back in Sydney and they were sharing army digs. Sharing a bed, spending their days and nights together—when he wasn't working—was what she craved when he wasn't here and worked at making wonderful when he was.

Yet being a soldier wasn't like any regular job. Not even a medical registrar's frantically busy position had taken him away from her so much. Often lately, even when he was home with her, he wasn't really *with* her.

Regret for not getting on with the agency years ago hit hard. She'd have been busy, focused, not trying to fill in the empty hours. Deep down, she'd been hoping the baby would change everything, bring Cole home to her permanently so he'd share their lives beside her, not from a distance. *And* give her strength to revisit her plans. But her baby was gone. Raw agony slammed into her again. There was nothing to smile about.

'You're staying here with us tonight, no argument.' Molly locked her newly learned formidable gaze with hers, which was no doubt pathetically sad at the moment.

'You didn't used to be so bossy,' Vicki muttered through an overwhelming gratitude that she'd met this woman and they'd become firm friends.

'That's a yes, then.'

'Didn't think I had any choice.' She had nothing to hide from Molly. 'Okay, thank you. I don't want to go back to the apartment and stare at the walls while trying to absorb what's happened.' Yes, happened, as in no going back. No changing the outcome. The bleeding had begun sometime before she'd woken that morning and was all but done now, though the occasional painful cramps still underscored what had occurred. As if she needed reminding. The weight on her chest, the emptiness in her heart, the incessant tears—all tells of her loss. *Our loss.* Just because she hadn't spoken to Cole didn't mean his world hadn't irrevocably changed too.

She straightened up, swung her legs over the side of the couch. She needed to be doing something, not lying around waiting for the next hit from life. 'I'm going to walk to the end of the lawn and back.' Stop and stare out over the Tasman Sea from the clifftop, and draw up some strength to move forward.

'Want me to come with you? I can bring the baby monitor. It works from as far as the fence.'

Vicki shook her head. 'I'll be fine. You stay near those two cuties.' Her lip trembled.

Molly wrapped her in a hug. 'I'm glad you called me.'

'So am I. It would've been an even longer day if I hadn't.'

She'd phoned in a panic when she'd realised what was happening and, while it wasn't essential she go to the emergency department, they'd agreed it was better if she got checked over at the hospital where she and Nathan worked and let him talk her through the medical details—which she knew from a nursing perspective—before Molly brought her back to their house.

She was so grateful for Molly's company, though it was hard when the babies cried, or needed feeding or changing. That was supposed to have been *her* future. If Cole had been around she wouldn't have needed anyone else to hold her, talk when she wanted a distraction, listen to her vent about how unfair life was. He would have understood everything.

Before heading outside, she picked up her phone to tap Cole's number, knowing he still wouldn't answer but needing to hear his voice. 'Cole, sweetheart, answer me.'

'Please leave a message…'

She banged 'off', tossed the phone aside. So much for needing to listen to his voice. The message was not solely for her, it was generic. It wasn't special, or sexy. She choked, the tears a waterfall soaking into her crumpled tee shirt. 'Where the hell are you?' she yelled.

Nathan appeared in the doorway. 'Vicki? It's hard, that's what it is.' He crossed the room to hug her. 'Cole will call as soon as he can.'

'I know that. But it'll be too late.' She sniffed, soaked up some of her friend's warmth and leaned back to look directly at the man she'd known almost as long as she'd known Cole. 'I need him *now*.' Already the emptiness from losing her baby was taking over, more destructive because her husband wasn't here to share it, to console her, to let her comfort him. They could've cried together, held each other, got through the days ahead a little easier. 'I really do.'

'You'll get through this. You're tougher than you think.' Nathan squeezed tighter, then released her, a grim expression on his face.

Tough? Yes, she could be. But today she'd run out of tough. She wanted to be selfish for a while. Curling up in bed, pulling the covers over her head, and ignoring the world going on around her was a priority right now. Which was why she'd go outside for a few minutes. Acting tough? Sniff. *I suppose*. But, no, she really had had enough.

The phone rang. She stared at it. Was it Cole? No, it wouldn't be. Hope rose, fell, rose higher, like a wave in a storm. Reaching for the instrument, she picked it up, stared at the screen. Her heart soared. Cole. Pressing the button, she banged the phone against her ear. 'Hey, I'm sorry. So, so sorry.' Like it was her fault. Who knew? Maybe it was.

'Sweetheart, is it true?'

'Why wouldn't it be?' As if she'd make up something like that.

'I didn't want to believe your message. Are you all right? I hope you're not alone.'

Her eyes widened. Cole wasn't exactly spilling his heart with support and love. Was she all right? 'No, I'm not all right,' she snapped through her tears. 'I'm with Molly and Nathan, at their place,' she added.

'That's good. They'll take care of you.' He really was a barrel of comforting words.

'They can't replace you. It's your arms I long for. It's you I need to hug and cry with, not our friends.' Didn't he get it? They were a couple. They shared everything.

'Unfortunately, there's not a thing I can do about it. The CO won't let me go at the moment. There's a mission starting tomorrow we've been preparing for that requires everyone on board,' he explained. 'It will take all our resources to pull it off.'

'Cole, I've miscarried. I don't care about your mission.' Had they drifted so far apart that they couldn't connect over this? She didn't want to believe that. She loved Cole more than anyone, anything. Yet nothing about their relationship felt safe any more. It was as though she lived in a dark box and only came out when he was back in Sydney, when it suited the army to let him have time off. He'd chosen to sign up, never really explaining why, always fobbing her off when she asked, which irked, but as usual she'd let it go rather than start an argument.

'Hang in there, sweetheart. I am getting out at the end of my contract.'

*That's for ever.*

She swallowed the bitter taste in her mouth. She'd have to find it within her to see out the days and weeks. 'Are you certain?' Because if he changed his mind she'd never cope. 'You don't always tell me everything.' There were things he never discussed, especially about his youth. Sometimes, when it got too much for him, he'd spill his anguish over some of the tragedies he'd seen with the army. She'd listen, try to console him, and he'd pull himself together. Once he'd told her she was the strongest woman he knew for taking him on. Maybe it had been Cole's love for her speaking, because she hadn't been that tough, though over the past year she'd tried to improve. Or so she'd thought. Today she was floundering.

'I'm telling you I'm leaving the army. I will not have a second crack at it. I've done what I set out to do. I want to be with you, Vicki. More than occasionally.'

Her heart swelled with love. That was what she'd waited to hear for so long.

'We just have to get through the next year.'

Her relief deflated like a pricked balloon at that reminder. It seemed so long. Time interspersed with occasional visits when they'd make love and laugh. Not a lot of talking happened, and then she'd go back to that box. 'Then what will you do?'

'It's too soon to decide.'

Once again he wasn't telling her anything. He must have been considering his next move. Cole didn't make major changes without thinking everything through thoroughly. Fresh pain engulfed her. Where was his love?

Not in his voice or words. All hope of him comforting her was deflated; left her cold and drained.

Her mouth dried as she whispered, 'Cole, I don't think I can do this any more. I married to be with you, not the wife in the background, available whenever you have a few hours or days to spare. To me, marriage is about having you around whenever my world flips upside down. To be there for you when yours goes haywire. To share everything.'

Oh, hell, what did she mean? Was she walking away from him? For good? Was that what she wanted? No, it wasn't. She loved him. But she couldn't continue with the way things were. It *was* only for another year, but then what? More Cole ideas she was supposed to fit in with? Her patience had gone from thin to non-existent. But? But could she leave Cole? Tough, remember? Lonely, remember? Alone, not lonely. Yeah. Lonely *and* alone.

'Vicki, don't say that.' Panic flared in his voice. 'Please, don't, sweetheart. I know you're going through hell right now, but I'm here for you. You know that.'

'No, you're not. You haven't been here anytime I've needed you.'

*Stop it, Vicki.*

This was a conversation for when they were together, not over a phone. Therein lay the problem. When would they be together again? 'The miscarriage is the last straw. I cannot live always waiting for you to show up. I need fixed plans to work towards, and to follow some of my dreams as well.'

'Wait, Vicki. We'll talk. I have to finish this duty. I don't know when I'll return to Sydney to see out my time but it will happen.'

'We'll talk? Over the phone? That's great when it's something as important as our future, as us. As losing our baby.' Tears flooded down her cheeks. 'I can't sit back and wait for you to come home for a face-to-face discussion. I need to see you *now*.'

'Sweetheart, you know that can't happen. It's impossible.'

'Exactly.' Life as she knew it was over. What she had to find out was how to make it unfold in the future. But not today. Today was raw enough without adding to the agony.

Cole winced as the line went dead. Vicki had hung up on him. After saying she doubted she could carry on with their marriage. Without talking about the miscarriage. A dull throbbing started behind his ribs. Vicki was the love of his life, his first reason for waking up every morning. She could not leave him. She didn't mean it. She was broken-hearted about their baby. That's what this was about. She was trying to cope in any way possible.

The pain in her voice had been like nothing he'd heard before, not even when her mother had been so ill no one had believed she'd pull through. Vicki's pain had got deeper and stronger as she'd talked, adding to his guilt, creating a sense of failure for not being there with her. She needed him. More than anyone. And there was nothing he could do about it. His own pain scudded across his lips in a sigh. Once again he'd hurt one of the most important people in his life.

*We've lost our baby.*

Sharp agony squeezed hard, taking away his ability to breathe. Why was he here, and not with Vicki?

He had chosen this life to meet a promise he had made to his mother when he was seventeen. Along with two close mates and his girlfriend, he'd been accused of the theft of thousands of dollars from a local charity after a fundraising event. Not even his parents had believed him when he'd said he knew nothing about the robbery. All he did remember was the four of them going to the local park late that night where he'd had two beers while cuddling with his girlfriend. The next thing he recalled was waking up alone in his car outside his family's home.

Many months later, one of his mates had confessed that the girlfriend had put a date drug in Cole's beer to make him sleep, then had taken his car keys and driven herself and the other two guys to the charity building to steal the money.

The shame of not being aware of what had gone on around him that night and how easily he'd been used hadn't left him. Only his granddad had stood by him, saying what had happened had changed his life for ever, but he mustn't let it ruin his future. He had loved him for that more than anything. His mother had lost most of her friends and become stressed and anxious. His father, a criminal lawyer, had hidden behind his work, putting in ever-increasing hours and staying away from home. Even when they'd finally admitted they'd been wrong, his family had never returned to being their easy, loving selves. They'd let him down.

*As I have Vicki.*

His gut clenched.

*We've lost our baby. I'm not there for Vicki.*

But he had to be here. It was the promise he'd made to his mother before he'd been exonerated and she'd lain dying in ICU after a massive heart attack. Desperate for her to live, he'd have promised the moon if it would've helped. Instead he'd said he'd make her proud by joining the army after he'd become a doctor, which had always been his aspiration. Granddad had been a highly decorated soldier, and Cole had also wanted to show him he was worthy of his belief in his grandson.

That night his mother had passed away, never to see him fulfil his promise, leaving him with a load of remorse nothing would shake. Had the stress from what had happened caused her death? The guilt and shame had stuck to him like glue.

And now this. The baby was gone. Unbelievable. Even to his doctor's brain it didn't make sense. It was so unfair. Cole couldn't find any words to describe his feelings at this moment. In trying to do right by his mother and granddad, he'd let his wife down so much. If only he had a red cape and could fly to her side, hug her, kiss her, promise they'd make it through this latest tragedy—together.

His life had become compartmentalised after he'd been exonerated. Adelaide—the good, bad and downright ugly. Sydney—adulthood, medicine, new friends. Vicki. The army—meeting his promise. Vicki. His love. He groaned. Vicki. What he wouldn't give to be with her. Right from the beginning of their relationship it had been good having someone believe in him, love him, without having to expose the frankly awful time of his past. Though deep, deep down lay a seed of doubt about that decision not to tell her. But he hadn't wanted to bring the past into the future with her.

Nathan was the only person he'd told the whole truth to when he'd demanded to know why they couldn't go to Adelaide for a break and get together with Cole's friends from school days. Because Nathan held nothing back from him, he'd finally explained. It had been a test of their friendship, one that had never faltered.

Yet he still hadn't found the courage to tell Vicki. She was a fresh start he hadn't wanted to taint with the past. She was the precious jewel in his life. He loved her so much sometimes it was almost too much, made him fear he couldn't get enough of her. Yet here he was in East Timor while she was back in Sydney, needing him desperately.

*She's thinking about leaving you.*

She couldn't. He'd talk to her as soon as he returned to base. She was hurting. Big time. He understood. But leave him? No. She didn't mean it. She needed time to come to terms with the miscarriage.

*Which is why I should be with her, not here.*

There wasn't anything he could do about it. Except go AWOL, and the consequences of that would be worse. So he'd phone every day. It wouldn't be enough, but it was all he could offer. It would help him to get through this ragged pain caused by the miscarriage. He'd signed up for the army without a backward glance, ignoring the sadness in her eyes, only saying it was a promise he owed. Whenever he'd been home and she'd hinted that it was getting lonely living in their apartment in the middle of such a large city, he'd worked hard to put a smile back on her face and made love to her so she knew he was on her side. And every time he'd gone away *again*, following orders, using them as an excuse for the life he was living. He'd been utterly selfish.

As he and the men headed back to barracks from their last training exercise before tomorrow's job, he stared out at the passing scenery of never-ending dirt and dust and crowds of people trying to get by in this area, trying to absorb everything Vicki had said, failing to ignore the ache under his ribs. The miscarriage. Her pain. The life he'd chosen to follow that kept him away from her. The army was like nothing he'd ever known. With the way everyone had to fall into step, dress the same, eat the same, be prepared for anything horrific any time, he didn't enjoy the life, but once he'd fulfilled his promise he'd be able to get on with the next phase of his life without looking back.

The marriage vows he'd made to Vicki needed acknowledgement. To love and cherish and be there always, through the wonderful and the awful.

*Vicki, I am so bloody sorry. We've lost our baby and you need me. I need you.*

He'd signed up for that, too. Vicki was his future, the army the final nail in his past.

His stomach tightened into a painful ball. Their baby was gone. It had been amazing to learn he was going to be a dad. He'd been stoked, couldn't wait for it to be born. He'd already imagined playing football, going fishing, having family picnics at the beach with his son or daughter. Family was what it was all about. A loving, caring, believing family. And Vicki, the most amazing woman to have kids with. Now it wasn't happening.

'You okay, Captain?' The driver of their truck had turned to look at him as they drove along the main road out of a village.

*No. I've never felt worse.*

'All good,' he lied through gritted teeth. Something large and dark hurtled across the road directly at them. A laden ute. 'Look out, soldier,' he snapped.

The driver swore as he wrenched their lumbering vehicle to the right. His reaction might've been fast but the other vehicle was faster.

Cole's butt left the seat, his head punched through the windscreen. Fear tightened his belly. Not now. Not when he needed to be at home. His body was airborne. Air stalled in his lungs. Landing was going to hurt. Or worse, he thought. His fingers gripped his phone as though his life depended on it.

*Vicki! I love you. Wait for me.*

# CHAPTER TWO

'JACK, BEHAVE. Water will soak that moonboot if you don't hurry up and get in the car,' Vicki growled at the man she was trying to help into the passenger seat while he fiddled with the window button, opening and closing the window.

The umbrella she held over them both wasn't working. Water had found its way through the back of her shirt. At this rate, by the time she returned inside the medical centre she'd be soaked.

'You're worse than most toddlers I've worked with.'

'I was one once,' the middle-aged man grunted, and finally sank onto the seat and lifted his damaged leg inside. 'Quite the nuisance, I've been told.'

'You don't have to sound proud of it. You're not doing yourself any favours thinking you're one of the world's heroes who has to be out amongst it all the time.' Vicki dredged up a smile for the fireman who was temporarily off work thanks to having rolled a quad bike down a slope on his rural property a couple of weeks previously. 'You've got to take things easy.'

'Boring,' Jack mock-yawned.

'You think?' She shook her head in admonishment at her brother's friend, before nodding to his wife. 'Try and keep him out of mischief until those ribs and fractured thigh have had time to knit.'

'Give me something easy to do.' Barbara laughed. 'The moment I turn my back he'll be heading for his shed and the other quad bike.'

'I figured.' She shrugged. 'Men, eh?' Hell, she missed hers so much she hardly slept at night after following through on her decision to walk away from her marriage. It hadn't been easy. When she hadn't heard from Cole for more than a week after the miscarriage she'd closed in on herself and tried to deal with the agony of losing their baby alone.

Quitting her job at the hospital, unable to stand the sympathy in everyone's eyes whenever she turned up at work, she'd packed up the apartment and headed north to Cairns and her family, to be surrounded in their care. And the tears kept on coming. She'd never known it was possible to bawl her eyes out so much. There shouldn't be that much fluid in a person's body. Still the agony hadn't abated. Not for her baby or her marriage.

Nothing filled the void that had once been her excitement over being pregnant. Or the empty air between her and Cole. When he'd finally begun phoning, their conversations had been stilted, and the silences, longer every time, had become full of all the things neither seemed able to voice. Eventually, she'd told him they were over and had gone to stay with her sister in London while she made decisions about the future. As if she could decide with all the distressing emotions tugging at her heart.

Cole had gone quiet again. As in not a word by phone or email. The hurt grew. It was so typical of him not to talk about the important stuff. It was the main reason she'd left him. There'd be no more waiting around, ready to put everything on hold whenever he came home, and then go back to a kind of single life when he left again. That was over. Even when he got out of the army she'd still be that wife, trying to keep him happy all the time and putting herself on hold for the foreseeable future. Like her mum had done, first for her dad and then for her and her siblings.

Warmth stole through Vicki as she remembered presenting Mum with an easel and painting equipment. Mum's shock, the delight followed by excitement had said it all.

'You wouldn't want a wuss for a husband.' Jack grinned at Barbara around a groan as he settled further onto the seat.

Vicki shivered. *She* hadn't had one either. Cole was a tough guy who never showed pain or hurt. Too much so. If only he could've relented a little and stopped being so strong, they might not be about to spend the weekend together, finalising the dissolution of their marriage. His attitude was a mask he didn't drop even for her. Which wasn't right.

There weren't supposed to be any secrets between them, yet more and more she'd started seeing there were. He'd never explained why he'd needed to sign up for the military, just muttered something about keeping a promise. She'd asked for more information—often—and been fobbed off every time.

But were they really over? It felt like it. It had done for months, if not longer, when she thought about how she hadn't recognised the loneliness and need to fill her time with anything for what it really was.

The recent months spent mostly travelling while trying to side-track herself from the mess that had become her life hadn't been easy but at least now she was working to find her feet again, beginning with making the goal of her own nursing agency a reality. The idea held the promise of something exciting, something to hold onto and gain strength from her efforts.

Her fingers clenched the umbrella. First there was the weekend to get through. Time with Cole. How would she cope? Seeing him, breathing in his smell, being stuck in the house together—the thought had her heart racing already. As long as they didn't get angry at each other or upset one another too much. Tears were already threatening, and he wasn't due yet.

'See you on Monday when I bring Jack back to have his dressings changed.' Barbara revved the engine, then stuck her head out the window. 'If you feel like a coffee any time, just drop in.'

'Thanks. I might do that when I've run out of ways to annoy Damon.' Her older brother was a fireman at the same station as Jack, and everyone there had been super-friendly since she'd arrived back in Cairns from London three weeks ago.

Her other brother, Phil, was a local cop, and he too seemed intent on keeping an eye on her by including her in every social event he went to—usually for a pint at the pub. She loved them both, but they could be a little suffocating.

With Cole coming, their protective instincts were on high alert. In the past she'd relished their support, but now she needed to do this without them interfering. Her spine *was* getting straighter, tougher.

Ducking under the overhang at the medical centre entrance, she saw a taxi pull up over the road. She had two patients to go before she packed it in for the weekend and headed to the airport to wait for Cole. Scratching her palms, she swallowed hard. Air slowly seeped from her lungs. Nothing about the weekend was going to be easy.

It wouldn't take forty-eight hours to come to an arrangement about whether to sell the Sydney apartment or get Cole to buy her out. That was the sum of their marriage now. Her stomach had been a tight ball all day, and she hadn't eaten a thing, replacing food with endless mugs of coffee, and now was so jittery her teeth clacked.

Closing the umbrella, she shook the water off before dropping it into the tall pot standing in the corner. Despite the incessant monsoon rain the air was still warm and humid. There was nothing like Queensland temperatures to make her feel right at home again. Except she wasn't. These past weeks she'd been unsettled about whether to stay here permanently or return to Sydney and her friends down there. She presumed Cole would live there once he returned to civilian life, which held her back on that choice.

If—when—they divorced she'd want to live somewhere without all the memories. Sometimes, in the middle of the night, she'd admit she wanted to be near him. But that wasn't being strong. And strong was what she had to be, otherwise why go through this agony of finishing her marriage to the man she'd given her heart to?

Cole was out of the army early. He hadn't said why. Typical. Her heart thumped hard. Despite everything she'd said in the brief phone conversations in the past months, he still hadn't recognised how much she needed to share his life, to understand his thinking; not to be standing on the sidelines, waiting for him to give her some attention.

Footsteps on the path.

Her skin prickled. No, it was too early. Cole's flight from Sydney wasn't due for three hours. The goosebumps tightened, the hairs on the back of her neck lifted. She wasn't ready to confront him, needed more time to get her game face on. Although, she had to admit it, she'd never be ready. But—but this weekend wasn't going to go away without her spending time with Cole. Only one person turned her into a blithering wreck just by being near him. He was here.

Another wet step. 'Hello, Vicki.' Two words, soft, endearing, and full of memories that threatened to make those tears spill. Blink, blink. She loved that voice, heard it in her sleep, held it to her whenever she needed her man. Every day and night. Thump-thump, banged her heart.

*Be strong.*

Which was easier said than done.

'Cole.' That taxi must've dropped him off. 'Hello,' she muttered through suddenly dry lips.

The rate of her heart lifted. The ends of her fingers tingled. Cole. The man she adored. The man she had to hold out on for a more secure future. The man she'd once done anything to make happy, and now couldn't. *Wouldn't.* Her breathing went out of whack.

'Vicki.' He paused, waited, finally asked, 'How are you?'

He had to ask? The brave face slipped on. She didn't bother forcing a smile. Straightening her back, she slowly pivoted around on her heels to stare at her handsome husband. Except— The ground moved beneath her feet. Putting her hands out for balance, she struggled to stay upright. 'Cole?' She gasped. This was all wrong. 'What's happened? Are you all right?' Stupid question. He looked terrible. Worse than terrible. 'Obviously not.' Her instinct was to rush to him, wind her arms around that body she knew so well—not like this, she didn't—and never let go. To take away his pain, make him better.

*We're over, remember?*

She drew in air, clamped down on her emotions, clenched her hands at her sides, and remained fixed to the spot. Not that her feet could've lifted off the porch. They were as heavy as rocks. Studying him, her heart pounded harder, the tingling in her fingers tightened. He was far too thin. There were lines on his face that hadn't been there before. When he stepped closer his left leg dragged. There was fierce concentration on that lined, grey face, as though he was determined she wouldn't see how much it hurt to move. But there was no hiding the pain reflected in his eyes. 'Cole?' she whispered through pain of a different kind. 'Please tell me you're all right.' Please, please.

'Vicki. I'm all right.' Two more steps and he stood before her, looking stunned. Lifting his arms as though he was going to hug her, he hesitated, dropped his hands to his sides. 'Hello, sweet—' He stopped, staring at her, swallowing non-stop. 'Damn,' he muttered.

Vicki jerked backwards, away from his tempting body. Tension sparked between them like forked lightning. Anxiety blindsided her. She couldn't do this. He'd nearly called her sweetheart. As normal, as though nothing was wrong.

*I love him. Totally. Nothing has changed.*

Her heart was coming out of her chest, her head spinning out of control.

*I love him as much as ever.*

Forget all the doubts since the miscarriage. Forget her own needs. Cole meant everything to her. Memories of him holding her, his hands strong, and warm, and, well, right. They fitted her. Slowly, she raised her head to gaze into his dark blue eyes.

*I love you.*

Had she said that out loud? He hadn't reacted, so hopefully she hadn't. The moment for telling him would never come if they didn't reach some understanding. They had to. He meant everything to her, was her life, the future.

*Fight for what you want.*

This weekend was about finishing their relationship, or possibly getting back together with different ideas of how to go ahead.

She froze, one muscle at a time. Gritted her teeth to keep words back. Words like, 'Hello, darling, I've missed you so much'. She wasn't going to be that woman again. Had no intention of returning to being the woman who was more concerned about keeping Cole happy before all else. She would eventually shrivel inside, turn bitter, or unhappy and sad as her mother had become before she'd woken up to what she needed to do. It was time to fight for herself, not give in to this gripping love.

Remaining still, she denied the warmth and longing warring in her veins. Fought the desire to touch Cole, to lean in against that altered yet familiar body. To let him hug her tight and close. To hug him back like there was no tomorrow. But there was. Give in now and she might as well walk down the drive and go back to Sydney with him tonight, no conversations, no plans or changes made. Forget her hopes for the future.

'You're early.'

*Lame, Vicki.* But she was fighting for survival. Anything went.

'I didn't want this weather bomb to prevent me making it to Cairns so I changed my flight.' His gaze bored into her with a hunger she hadn't expected since their infrequent phone discussions had been so awkward.

It was good to see his reaction; despite everything, it warmed her throughout. It had to mean there was hope.

What was she hoping for? A lightning bolt moment where Cole understood what she needed? After all these years?

'I could not miss seeing you for anything,' he added.

Now Cole stood before her, she realised she'd been holding her breath for days in case he changed his mind about coming. Not that he would've. That wasn't his way. But, still, their relationship was unrecognisable. They had to do this, sort out everything before they could move on separately. Not together. He'd wouldn't have changed that much. Nausea rose.

*Give in, carry on being the pleaser you're so good at being. Kiss him, hug him. Buy a ticket on the next flight to Sydney. Make him happy.*

No. She mustn't. Because eventually something would happen to drive a wedge between them again, or she'd sink into an abyss where she'd given up on herself. But she still loved Cole. There was no denying that. Which only made everything so much harder. 'I've still got nearly an hour before finishing up here.'

He nodded curtly, wincing as he shrugged his shoulder where a small pack hung against his back. Like it hurt having any weight pulling at him.

What had happened? 'Cole?' His name slipped across her lips before she could stop it. 'What—?'

He cut her off. 'Not now. I'll wait down the road at the pub.'

Nothing had changed. 'No. Tell me now.'

He shook his head as though clearing something away. Those piercing eyes she knew so well were filled with a pain she'd never seen before. They locked onto her, sending shivers of excitement right down to her damp toes. Damn him. 'Vicki, seeing you is the best thing to happen for a long time.'

As she made to stop him saying anything more that

might undermine her determination to keep him at a distance she once more had to fight the urge to throw herself at him and hang on tight. As usual he'd deliberately diverted her from her question. Nothing new there.

Cole held up his hand. 'Hear me out.' Then he couldn't continue. Vicki, his beautiful wife, stood there, the battle going on in her head showing through her eyes and on her face. All he could think was, *I love you*. Nothing else mattered. He loved Vicki. He always had and always would.

Something like relief floored him. His love hadn't changed, was as deep, as strong, as ever. Not that there'd been any doubts, but *knowing* helped, shoved away some of the dread that getting together might make matters worse, not better. Over the days leading up to this moment he'd despaired that they mightn't talk, wouldn't resolve anything.

*So tell her how you feel.*

He opened his mouth. Closed it. Last time he'd said it over the phone she'd gone quiet, then said she had to go and hung up.

He found his voice. 'We have a lot to sort out, and none of it's going to be easy, but I've missed you badly. More than ever. Seeing you tips me sideways.' And upside down, all around. He was not giving up without a fight. A hard one. With everything he had.

He'd started and was close to getting a job that involved staying in one place for the foreseeable future, which meant they could buy a house and settle down in Sydney. Try again for a baby. First he owed Vicki an apology. He'd given it more than once over the phone but face to face would go a lot further. She'd see his how genuine he was, not hear it over a bad phone connection.

'Cole, you're not making this any easier.'

She was definitely holding back, whereas he'd blurted out how he felt. He didn't do blurting. His gut churned. She hadn't reacted positively to being told he'd missed her. Were they really at an impasse? Please, not that. He hadn't said the three most important words. Should he? Would that break the barriers Vicki was clinging onto? Or would it put her on alert, make her warier than she already was? Because she was fighting to remain cautious. It showed in her rapid blinking, in the way the tip of her tongue poked over her lip.

He had to slow down. 'We've waited months to talk properly. We can wait a little longer. I'd rather be some place with just you, not out front of a medical practice. It feels rather surreal.'

'You can start by telling me why you're limping.'

This persistence was new, putting him on alert. He was in for a verbal hiding. And not as prepared as he needed to be. 'All in good time,' he said too forcefully, and suffered an unhappy glare coming straight back at him.

So they'd talk about whatever Cole chose, when he chose. 'How normal,' she muttered under her breath. From the moment she had sensed his presence she'd been struggling to stay grounded. Her head pounded in time with her heart. Parts of her body alternated between hot and chilled. This was the man she'd sworn to love for ever. It would be too easy to tell him nothing had changed, and then slip her hand in his and ask him to take her away, to forgive her for standing up for herself. But do that and she gave up *everything*. She'd go back to fitting in with his choices, ignoring her own. So… Deep breath.

'You're right. We will talk later. About everything.' Turning away, she tried to deny the ache in his eyes, worked hard at pretending this would all work out fine. Because it wouldn't. Cole loved her. She'd never doubted that. The problem was that it was on his terms, which he didn't recognise, and so she had to fight for her own.

That moment the rain became a torrent, pouring out of the sky as though a massive bucket had been tipped over the medical centre.

Turning back, she tried not to stare at Cole with hunger, or study the adorable face that followed her to sleep every night; tried to deny the heat unfurling in her belly. 'You'd better come inside while I finish up. You'll drown trying to reach the pub.' Cole was right before her, and she couldn't leap into his arms for fear of never stepping out of them again. She'd missed him so much it hurt with every breath. Somehow she was managing to hold back, fighting against herself for herself. 'Come in.'

'Thanks.' He stepped up behind her, putting all her senses on alert, making her skin tingle with a familiar need.

Pushing open the door, she quickly stepped inside and surprised herself by smiling. This was a temporary job; filling in for a nurse on her final month of maternity leave. She was in familiar territory, with family and friends to call on when everything got on top of her. Since starting to look into start-up plans, the reality of owning and managing an agency hit hard at unguarded moments. This being strong didn't come naturally. Doubts crept in. Was it worth giving up her marriage to own a business? She'd lost count of how many times she'd told herself that wasn't what this was all about, that she was looking out for herself. And Cole, if he accepted what she was doing. Because if she was happier then surely he would be too.

One of the practice doctors approached.

'Vicki, I've been listening in on the emergency frequency. There's flooding north of the city, nothing major at the moment, but who knows what'll happen if this rain continues to get heavier over the coming hours, as it's forecast to do.' Joe paused and glanced behind her.

She turned to make the introductions. 'This is my...' *Stop. Start again.* 'Cole Halliday—Joe Burrows.'

Grief flared in Cole's eyes, blinked away as he reached to shake hands with her current boss. 'Pleased to meet you. I got here just in time. They were talking about closing the airport when my flight landed.'

Joe nodded. 'I'm not surprised. The reports are getting worse by the hour.' He looked to her. 'You'd better get home while you can, otherwise you might find yourselves holed up somewhere in town.'

At least then they wouldn't be stuck in the house, just the two of them, trying to be friendly while working through the problems they faced. Though hotel rooms weren't known for their spaciousness. Better the house. More rooms.

'I've still got two patients to come.' It wouldn't be fair to leave someone else to cover for her when everyone was anxious to go home as soon as they could.

'I'll see to them. If they turn up. The cancellations have escalated since lunch time.'

She couldn't find it in her to argue. 'Right, thanks. It'll be a slow trip as it is. Jack said more people than usual were heading out of town when he and Barbara came in. The schools closed at midday.' She couldn't put off spending time alone with Cole any longer. Did she really want to? In all honesty, no. The time had arrived to talk and make some decisions. 'I'll grab my gear.'

'Take one of the emergency kits in case you're needed

to help someone at Palm Beach,' Joe said, before turning to Cole. 'You're a doctor, aren't you?'

'Yes, I am, so no issues with administering drugs if required should we get called to an emergency.'

'Great. If there's an accident it might be a problem for emergency services to reach the scene in this weather.'

'There were a lot of frustrated drivers doing some damned silly things on the road in from the airport so anything's likely.'

Vicki interrupted the men. They were getting comfortable with each other. She didn't want that. This was her territory and Cole getting cosy only made it harder to keep him at arm's length. 'No need to take a kit from here. Dad's got a full drugs cabinet and the storeroom was topped up with everything you could think of before he and Mum left on their road trip.' These days her dad ran a small clinic at home when he wasn't tripping around in the campervan with Mum so she could take numerous photos for the paintings she hoped would re-establish herself as an artist. Right now they were in Western Australia. 'Keep yours here in case it's needed elsewhere.'

She rushed to the staffroom for her bag, said goodbye to the women in the office, and called to Cole. 'This way. Thanks for this, Joe.' Despite the tension in her stomach knotting tighter and tighter with each passing minute, she was grateful to him. To be stuck in town wouldn't be comfortable.

They dashed to her car, leapt in and slammed the doors, clothes soaked through in those few seconds. 'At least it's not cold,' she muttered. Inside and outside her pulsing body.

'How did you cope with the northern winter? I've seen pictures of England and Europe in blizzards and snowstorms. It's not exactly enticing to a Queenslander.' Cole adjusted the seat to give his long legs as much space as possible and clipped his seat belt in place.

If she hadn't been watching she'd have missed the tightening of his mouth as he shifted his left leg. What had happened? she asked herself again. Something terrible, by the way he looked and moved. Something more than a simple accident.

He hadn't mentioned anything during any of their infrequent phone conversations either. Anger started to boil at being left out of the loop—and his refusal to talk when she'd asked. She swallowed hard, forced it down. She'd demand answers when they were at home and she could watch his face. Right now she had to focus on *getting* home, and keeping the disturbing subjects on hold. 'You know me and any temperature below twenty degrees. Julie took me shopping for thick jackets and thermal tops the day I arrived in London.'

'How's Julie? Still enjoying living over there?' Cole and her sister had always got along, though now Julie was backing her determination to work out what she truly wanted with her future.

And her mother was setting a great example of being true to herself, even if it was thirty-five years late, by painting as though there were years of pictures stored in her mind waiting to be put on canvas. She was so happy and healthy. Dad was a different man too now that he understood there was more to gain than lose by supporting his wife in her endeavours. What were the chances of Cole doing the same if she explained again, more thoroughly? This time with more emphasis on how she'd still always be there for and with him.

'Julie loves London. If the company can arrange her a permanent work visa she intends staying on and buying an apartment. She's met a guy who might be the one.'

She was head over heels and had still taken a month off work to go away with Vicki to Europe, leaving her boyfriend behind. Setting an example of how a relationship should not be about one person keeping the other happy all the time. That was her sister.

Their brothers had always kept an eye on them both, too, even more so on Vicki lately. They meant well, but nowadays she preferred making her own decisions, right or wrong. It gave her a sense of self-worth. In a way their loving stifled her, and could explain why she'd fallen in line with Cole right from the beginning. They all meant well. It didn't mean they were right.

'What did you think of the countries you visited in Europe? Would you go back again? In the summer?'

'Maybe one day.' She far preferred melting in Queensland's humidity and heat any day. 'I'd like to return to France and Italy. Four weeks was nowhere near long enough. We barely got started. During my month in London I took short trips all over the north of England and Wales when Julie was at work, and at the weekends she showed me around London and the South.'

'You never once mentioned wanting to go over there.' Was that annoyance in his voice?

Too bad. When she'd needed to get away from Sydney it had been an instinctive reaction to head home but for the first time it hadn't felt right. Everyone had wanted to tell her what to do. Julie said she had to make her own choices, and supported her without overwhelming her. 'I really went to spend time with Julie. I'd have gone wherever she was.'

'Within reason, I hope.'

'No war zones, for sure.' Leaning over the steering wheel, she peered through the river running down her windscreen where the wipers were on full speed and not achieving a lot. 'This is crazy.' So was the way longing for Cole kept catching at her. It was diverting her from what this weekend was about.

'At least there's not much traffic about any more.'

He was right. 'Most of the shops are closed.'

'Is there anything we need to get?'

'No. I did the groceries last night.' Got in extra beer and wine in case the going got too awkward. 'You're on cooking the steak.' He was a dab hand at getting the sirloin perfectly medium rare.

'I figured.' Though still guarded, his voice had lightened.

Getting closer to old times. She didn't want that. It was a slippery path. Her head thudded. Tears threatened. *Don't cry.*

Then she'd need wipers on her eyeballs. She needed to get angry, not sad. No. Neither option was wise. Anger led to lack of control and that was one thing she couldn't afford to lose over the coming days. If only she could give in and pull over to the kerbside and wrap her arms around Cole and kiss him, long and deep, and filled with the love she had to deny. If only. A kiss might fix everything. Or nothing. But giving it a go would ease the tightness brought on by not throwing herself at him the moment he'd arrived at the medical centre as she'd always done in the past.

The desire became an ache in her heart, throughout her body. For the first time ever they wouldn't be making love the moment they charged into the house. Or kissing like their lives depended on feeling, tasting, pressing their mouths together. What had she done? Why hadn't she found the patience to wait until he returned from East Timor before she changed everything? Then she could've kissed him and wound her arms and legs around him, and shown how much she loved him all over again.

*And nothing would've changed.*

True. She'd started something there was no going back on. Fear hit her. What if this really was the end of everything between them? It was all very well telling herself she was doing the right thing and that they might be finished as a result, but Cole was her other half. She loved him, needed and wanted him.

*And I can't go back to being at his beck and call.*

Her foot pressed harder on the accelerator and the car shot forward. She braked sharply, and the wheels skidded on the wet tarmac.

'Take it easy,' Cole snapped. On his thighs, his hands were clenched, while his whole body was rigid.

What was that about? Her driving hadn't been dangerous, just a little abrupt.

'Slow down.'

She didn't reply for fear of shouting that it was impossible to take any damned thing easy with him sitting beside her, sharing the air, diverting her from what she should be concentrating on. Instead she focused on driving carefully through the numerous massive puddles covering the road at regular intervals, and hoped fervently that they got through to Palm Beach, while swallowing the longing and disappointment filling her. With every kilometre she drove her stomach grew harder, tighter, filling with stress over resolving everything in a way that worked for both of them, and fear that they never would.

'Dad sends his love.' Cole broke the tightening silence. Unable to cope any more?

Did Conrad know she'd left Cole? She should've kept in touch since the miscarriage but it was difficult. He was

Cole's father first and foremost. 'I phoned Conrad about the miscarriage. He was very upset, and supportive.'

Beside Vicki, Cole stared out the window, his fingers tapping a rhythm on his thighs as he recalled the day his dad had called to say Vicki had phoned about the miscarriage.

'You should tell her, son.'

His father's words had drummed inside Cole's head as he'd lain on his hospital bed in Darwin. 'Easy to say, Dad.'

'She has a right to know.' Dad hadn't given up. At least he'd promised not to talk to Vicki about Cole's accident until Cole had broached the subject first.

And that hadn't happened in a hurry. He hadn't been able to tell her until he'd known for certain he would walk again.

'Yes, she does. When I'm ready.'

He hadn't wanted to give her the chance to fly up to Darwin and see him attached to more medical equipment than he'd ever seen on any patient. It hadn't been the tubes that had worried him. It had been the reason for them. Not the splenectomy, or the three fractures to his left leg. It had been the pain in his back. The spinal damage was a concern, his orthopaedic surgeon had said. A downright nightmare, Cole had thought.

What if he never walked again? Until he could know for sure he would be able to get up and look after himself, he would not lay his problems at Vicki's feet. He had not wanted her taking him back because he was seriously injured. He couldn't have cope with that humiliation.

'She's got enough problems already.'

Neither could he have expected Vick to rush to his side when he hadn't been able to go to her, even before that vehicle had driven into the army truck. Not when she'd told him she couldn't take any more.

'You take care, son. I'll call again tomorrow.' His dad's voice had broken and he'd hung up before Cole could say any more.

'Damn it.' Cole had stared some more at the ceiling he'd been getting to know too well. 'I seem to have made a habit of upsetting those nearest and dearest without even trying.' Should he call Vicki and talk about that dreadful day? She wasn't going to happy whenever she learnt about it, which was a given, so he might as well wait until he was up on his feet. Because he would walk again. He *would*.

But what he wouldn't have given to have had the love of his life there with him; to hold her hand, feel her lips on his. Just to talk about them, the miscarriage, their future. A future they wouldn't have any more if she had meant what she'd said.

Giving in to the relentless agony in his heart, he had picked up the phone and hit the speed dial for Vicki. 'Hi, sweetheart. How are you today?'

'Much the same.' Her voice had had the familiar flatness he'd heard during the few conversations they'd had over the previous week. 'What about you?' It hadn't sounded like she even cared.

Resentment had risen. There he had been, incapacitated, in pain, afraid he might not walk again despite his determination he would, and she had been in a fog all of her own.

'Just great, thanks,' he had snapped.

'That's good. Did you want to talk about anything in particular?'

He hadn't even been able to wind her up, she had been

so down. The Vicki of old would've bitten his head off for the way he'd just spoken. 'Yes, us.'

Her sigh had resonated through the ether. 'Oh.'

Guilt had fought with a sense of loss and of being let down. 'What do you expect, Vicki? That I'm going to let you walk away without a fight?'

'I don't know what to think about anything at the moment, Cole. Losing the baby dominates my thoughts. I feel so sad, it's unbearable. It makes me feel useless.' The most emotion he'd heard from her since she'd told him she'd lost the baby had come at him.

He had let her down. Big time. He had known it. The guilt wouldn't let up. And yet what was he supposed to have done, even if he hadn't ended up in hospital, fighting for his life? 'It's going to take time, sweetheart.' All he had wanted was a little understanding that he couldn't always do as she needed, that the army was in charge.

*Tell her where you are. Let her come to you.*

It had been so tempting. As his mouth had opened, he'd heard, 'That's all just about everyone says.' Back to the flat tone. 'I didn't expect it from you, Cole.'

He'd got it wrong again. 'I'm sorry. I'm at a loss for words.' A hug would have gone a long way further, but wouldn't happening any time soon. The next day he would have to demand to be allowed to try and sit up and put his feet on the floor. The next day he would have to start getting his life sorted so he could work at making Vicki happy again. If she'd let him.

# CHAPTER THREE

'Idiot! Watch where you're going.'

Vicki's raised voice interrupted Cole's thoughts.

He looked around, saw a car skidding on the wet surface at the traffic lights ahead. 'Going too fast?'

'Definitely.' Vicki swore, braked slowly as she pulled to the side of the road. 'What the—?'

A kid on a skateboard shot across the road out of control, directly into the path of a car coming the other way.

Cole held his breath, watching with horror.

The board flicked sideways, throwing the boy in the other direction, where he landed heavily against the kerb. The approaching car skidded to a stop less than a metre from the boy.

'Phew.' Air rushed out of Vicki's mouth. 'That was close.

'It sure was.' Cole was already clambering out of her vehicle. 'Better make sure he's all right.'

The kid was lying in water, looking stunned. 'What happened?'

He squatted down. 'You lost control. What did you think you were doing out on the road?' Did he not know how dangerous his actions had been?

'It's cool, skating in the water.' The boy moved, tried to sit up and let out a yelp. 'That hurts.'

'Where?'

'My arm.' The left one was at an odd angle.

'Let me look. I'm a doctor.'

Vicki joined them. 'I'll help you sit up. What's your name?'

'Evan. Is my arm broken?'

'Could be,' Cole replied as he felt gently along the already swelling forearm. 'You're going to need an X-ray.'

'What the hell were you doing, Evan?' a woman shouted as she stamped across to them. 'I could've killed you, you little brat.'

Vicki turned to her. 'I'm sure he's sorry. He has to go to hospital to have his arm checked.'

'Serves him right. I panicked when he crossed in front of me.'

'You deserve a medal for the way you kept control of your car and avoided him.'

'Didn't feel like I had any control.' The woman was quietening, her stance softening. 'What if I'd hit him?'

'You didn't. That's what matters.' Vicki looked down at him. 'Cole? How's it looking?'

'Definitely broken. Mind diverting to the hospital?' It would be quicker than waiting for an ambulance.

'No problem,' she answered.

The woman was shaking her head. 'I'm Evan's teacher. I'll take him to his mother. She works just along the road,' the woman said. 'Then I'll drive them both to hospital. No argument from you, young man,' she added.

'Thanks, Mrs Waring.'

'I've got a small cotton towel in my car to use as a sling and keep that arm up.' Vicki went to get it.

Cole carefully helped Evan to his feet, and kept an arm around him when he began wobbling. 'Easy. You've had a shock.' He explained about the sling and held Even's arm away from his body when Vicki placed the towel underneath and then tied it behind his neck.

Within minutes Mrs Waring and Evan were heading up the road.

Cole turned to Vicki. 'I can't believe how lucky he was.'

She nodded. 'Doesn't bear thinking about.' Her gaze was on the disappearing car.

'We're soaked more than ever.' At least the rain wasn't cold. He was watching Vicki. Her blue eyes were clear and her mouth soft. 'Vicki?' he croaked.

Turning towards him, she looked into his eyes and smiled. 'Some things are out of our control, aren't they?'

'Sure are.' Being with her, after attending to the boy, sent a buzz of need throughout him. Hesitantly, he placed his hands on her shoulders, and when she didn't pull back he leaned forward to brush his lips across hers. Instantly, the need intensified, and he pressed closer, feeling her lips under his, her mouth opening slightly.

*Oh, Vicki.* He breathed deeply, drew in her familiar scent. *Vicki, my love.*

She was kissing him back, returning the pressure, drawing him in, relaxing her body into his.

Toot, toot. 'Get a room,' someone yelled out.

They jumped apart, staring at each other, their chests rising and falling fast.

'Damn.' Vicki swung around and leapt into her car.

Damn, all right. She wasn't happy. While he wanted more. Not that she'd been trying to avoid kissing him. No way. She'd been fully into it. As he had. He swore. This was all wrong. They were husband and wife, and had always had a great relationship, and now they couldn't kiss? His lungs expelled the air they were holding, and he trudged across to the car and dropped into his seat, gasping as his leg protested at the sudden movement. When he was breathing normally again, he turned to face her. 'I'm not apologising.'

Her beautiful mouth quirked, giving him some hope they'd not drag this out. 'Okay.'

He nearly laughed. But he was fresh out of laughs right now. He was hurting; in his leg and his heart. This was nothing like how they acted together. But there was the threat of their failing marriage hanging over them. 'I've never worked with you medically before.'

She turned the ignition on. 'We didn't do a lot this time.' Her voice had a quiver in it. She didn't know how to handle the situation any better than he did.

His love soared. She could tell him whatever she liked but he loved her, and that was that. Vicki existed, hadn't disappeared off the face of the earth, which had been a recurring nightmare in the dark days and nights he'd lain in a hospital bed, drugged to the eyeballs with heavy pain relief. Even when he'd stopped taking the drugs the nightmare had been a constant companion.

His apprehension over this weekend remained. Maybe he had to prove to Vicki how he felt, because she didn't believe him any more. Or believe *in* him.

She drove off, keeping a vigilant eye on traffic movement and not saying a word.

The atmosphere got more uncomfortable with every kilometre they went. Finally, he couldn't take it any more and came up with something mundane to break the silence. 'I spent last night with Nathan and Molly.'

She nodded. 'I talked to Molly yesterday. The little ones are growing fast. She sends me lots of photos.' Sadness hovered between them.

At least she'd spoken to him. Gazing at his beautiful woman, his gut clenched. The loss of their baby had taken the spark from her sapphire eyes and the ready smile he cherished. The jaunty way she held herself had been replaced with a heaviness he'd never known before, shocking him. Was she suffering from depression? She hadn't mentioned it. But then she'd told him little in their terse phone calls. It was so unlike his Vicki. Nathan or Molly hadn't said a word about her being depressed, but then they hadn't told Vicki about his injuries either. Those two knew how to keep their noses out of other people's problems and only give support when needed.

'They are little rascals, into everything,' he told her as he scoped those amazing legs that brought back some wonderful memories. Suddenly Cole smiled, despite the pain in his chest. Her purple, low-heeled shoes matched her lilac uniform perfectly, except they were classy, not drab like the shapeless outfit covering her curves. Vicki remained a shoe-aholic. It would take a lot to change that. Something about shoes had her reaching for her bank card all too often. Their wardrobe floor had always been chock-full, with no space for a single pair of his shoes, let alone his boots and sports gear.

He heaved out a breath tinged with relief. At least one thing was still the same. There had to be others. Maybe he could let the hope in a little bit further. Or was she buying more than her normal number of shoes to fill in the gap left by the baby? By him? Probably. By signing up for the army, he understood he had let her down. Especially because he hadn't explained why he'd done it. At first there'd been no regrets. They had come later when he'd understood the price—too little time with his wife.

'Have you met the woman Conrad's started seeing?' Vicki asked, reminding him he was meant to be keeping a conversation going here.

'Not yet. Dad says he's taking it slowly.'

'He deserves some happiness.'

'True. It's been a long time on his own.' Something he might be facing if this weekend didn't go well. 'His habit of working long hours means she'll have to be patient if she hopes to spend lots of time with him.'

'I understand that.' Vicki's jaw tightened.

Ouch. He'd walked right into that one. But he understood where Vicki was coming from. What if he had tried harder to be with her whenever he'd been on base in Sydney? What if he'd talked to her more about what made him tick so she'd understand where he was coming from? Cole shuddered. That mightn't come easily, but it was something he had to get over if their relationship was to work out. She did deserve the best from him.

At least now there'd be more time for her, for them together. *If* he hadn't left it too late. When he'd told her during their last phone call that he was back in Sydney, seeing out his contract, she hadn't been full of the joy he'd hoped for. Certainly hadn't given him anything to get excited about.

Since the scandal that had affected his family he'd become cautious about letting anyone into his heart. Nathan had eventually made it as a close friend. He glanced sideways to watch Vicki manoeuvre through the traffic along the water-covered road. This wonderful woman was the real exception. From the moment he'd met her he'd lost the battle to remain uninvolved. She'd had him by the short and curlies, and a whole more. She was beautiful, funny and serious all in one, cheeky, and totally into him. Unused to being accepted so readily and completely, he'd fallen hard.

He'd skimmed over what had happened all those years ago, hadn't wanted to tell her how shamed he still felt; and how his family had paid huge consequences for him blindly trusting friends. Now he had to tell her everything, bare his faults, if he stood a chance of winning her back. Frustration burst across his lips. Why couldn't he just touch Vicki? Feel her skin on his palm? Because he wouldn't be able to stop at that. That's why. Longing ran through his veins without any brakes. Only making love would calm him.

This weekend was too important to stuff up by coming on to her when she was obviously holding back. He'd love to return home to Sydney on Sunday with Vicki at his side. Or at least with a promise that she'd follow him as soon as she finished the job at the medical centre. From what he'd heard, the GP position at a family medical centre in Rose Bay, Sydney, was nearly his. One final interview on Monday and hopefully they'd move forward—together.

*Get real.*

From what he'd seen so far, nothing would be that straightforward. He had a lot of apologising to do, as well as a long-overdue explanation of why he had done the things he had. He needed to tell her why he'd become the man he was, but again the hesitation stalled him. He'd lost too much already because of those so-called friends. His mum to heart failure. His father to work as he'd tried to move on from his initial, ready acceptance of his son's supposed guilt. Now he was available for Cole in a sad, less involved way, except when it came to supporting Vicki.

Cole's life compartments—before the theft, during the repercussions, and afterwards were about keeping the past away from the future. Vicki didn't belong in the past, and yet she deserved to know, if only so he could bury it once and for all. So why was he afraid to tell her? Pride, probably. An emotion that got in the way of being open and sensible. Okay, he'd add that to the list of things to discuss this weekend. In the end, it might be the easiest of the lot.

A fire engine came towards them on the other side of the road, lights flashing, the siren ripping through the air. Vicki looked sideways as it passed. 'I imagine Damon's lot will be busy pumping water from buildings.'

'You haven't heard from him?' He liked Vicki's brothers, though where he stood with either of them right now was anyone's guess. This family was very loyal to each other, almost too much sometimes, and he might find himself an outsider now. 'What about Phil?' The police would also be out in force.

'Not a word from either of them. At least Mum and Dad's house is off the ground.'

'Looks like the power hasn't been affected.'

Just then lightning cracked across the sky directly in front of them.

'Did you have to say that?' Vicki smiled easily for the first time since he'd arrived.

His heart melted all over again, which it was prone to do whenever they were together. 'Of course I did.' It used to be one of their little jokes. Vicki reckoned he always tempted fate with his wisecracks. For a brief moment he felt good.

Then she spoiled it. 'Fingers crossed you're wrong.'

Vicki had hated the dark ever since, as a teen, she'd gone to the bathroom without turning on lights and sat on the toilet, only to get bitten on the backside by a carpet snake languishing in the water. Apparently, only weeks previously her friend had nearly died from a poisonous snake bite. She always kept a night light on in the hall when she went to bed. Out at Palm Beach it would be darker than in the city if there was a power failure with no generators to keep street lights going or emergency lights glowing from high-rise buildings. She wouldn't let him hold or comfort her tonight. She was too edgy for that. Apart from the odd slip she'd been holding herself tight, keeping away from him physically and mentally since the moment he'd said hello.

'I have been known to be,' he said quietly. About a lot of things. Especially about how he hadn't been there for Vicki at the worst times. But she hadn't always given him a fair chance, either. 'Why didn't you wait until I came home to discuss how unhappy you were? It wasn't going to be for ever. Hearing you say you'd had enough over the phone was awful.'

'It would've been nicer if you were standing in front of me?' she snapped.

'No, but it might've been easier to understand with you unable to hang up on me. That's when we could've talked about everything.'

'Like all the other times, you mean? Ten minutes between parade and going to the medical unit. Or in bed after making love and you falling asleep because you'd just done seventy-two hours nonstop on an exercise. Give me a break, Cole. You never took time to actually listen to what I said.'

'I heard everything. Every time. What about me? You know it was important to me to do the years in the army.' So much for waiting until they were at the house before talking.

'Didn't know why, though.'

The car's indicator was flicking, Vicki turning onto the road that led to Palm Beach and her parents' home. Her focus was totally on the street ahead. Her hands were gripping the steering wheel and her chin pointed forward.

The need to be out of this tiny, intense space began

overwhelming him. To be inches away from Vicki and not lay his hand on her thigh, or rub his shoulder against hers, was driving him insane. Not that spending the next two days and nights inside the house with only her for company was going to be much better. In this weather there'd be no getting away from each other whenever they needed to think and breathe properly and gain some equilibrium.

She turned into the driveway.

Time was up. Out of the car and into the fire.

Unless he could make her understand he'd never wanted to hurt her and that he'd do anything not to do it again—except walk away from her for ever.

Tugging the key from the ignition, she snapped, 'Come on, Cole. Losing the baby broke my heart. And you weren't there. From where I stood, it seemed you never had been when I needed you, and what guarantees did I have you would be in the future? Sure, I was sad, lonely and down. I reacted out of fear and desperation. But I've had time to think about it, and I would still do the same.'

'And you say I'm the one to let you down.'

'I'll take my share of the blame, if it makes you any happier.'

'Of course it doesn't.' He'd done wrong by her. Yes, he got that. So she had to give him a chance to make amends. And make some of her own. But he wanted to continue this conversation inside, out of this tiny, airless space.

# CHAPTER FOUR

DEEP BREATH. Long sip of wine.

*Say it. Ask him.*

Vicki swallowed hard. She had to know before anything else. Forget that spat in the car. They'd both been
venting pent-up emotions. This was her man, obviously
injured. How well had he recovered? Were there long-
term consequences to whatever had happened?

She carefully placed her over-full glass on the bench,
her shaking hand making the liquid slop from side to
side. 'Tell me why you're limping, and what else is causing you pain. Did something terrible occur while you
were overseas?'

Had he been caught in enemy crossfire? That had always been on the cards, and had often kept her awake at
night as she'd worried pointlessly over Cole being shot
or injured whenever he was overseas with the army. But
surely his CO would've informed her if that had happened?

Cole sighed, and rubbed his chin with his palm.
Returning to the table, he sank onto a chair, carefully
stretching his legs out to their long length. Reaching for
the bottle of beer, he rolled it back and forth between
those palms that could knead her into a frenzy if she let

him. Hot memories poured into her, awakening nerve endings some more.

Was that the way forward? Reconnect through love-making? Make the darker elements of their relationship easier to deal with? No. All that would happen was she'd give in with nothing changed. And have a wonderful time on the way. Her eyes focused on Cole's legs. Legs she loved having wound around her own as they slept. The open-neck shirt he'd changed into when ditching his wet clothes showed lightly tanned skin at the opening, making her hands itch to slip under the fabric and caress him, to feel his nipples tighten. Hers were tightening. This was hard. Impossible. He had to leave, give her some space, instead of cranking her up like a wind-up toy. Or she had to give in and tell him how much she loved him. And let go any chance of having meaning in her life that *she'd* created? 'No,' she repeated under her breath. 'No.'

He still wasn't answering her questions.

'Tell me,' she all but begged.

'An out-of-control laden vehicle ran into the light utility truck I was aboard with some of my men.' The bottle rotated back and forth faster. 'I was injured.'

'Where was this? While you were still overseas? Or after you came home?' Where had she been at the time? England? Italy? France? Or here in Cairns? 'When did it happen?'

'East Timor. Four months ago.'

He was still limping! His injuries must've been horrendous. Hang on. Four months! Around the time she'd had the miscarriage and had been trying to figure how to go on without Cole. 'You never told me. Why?'

Gripping the edge of the bench, she stared at him.

*I'm his wife and I didn't know.*

Opening her mouth, she let the words pour out. 'Did you think I wouldn't care? What happened to the "Together through the good and the not so good times" promise, huh? Cole?' She'd have been on the first plane out of wherever she'd been to get to his side. Forget everything else worrying her, Cole would've come first.

His mouth tightened for a moment. When he finally looked at her, those beautiful cobalt eyes were darkening with sadness. 'It's because I knew you'd come to me that I didn't tell you.'

'You didn't want me there?' Pain lanced her heart so hard it might stop any second. Cole hadn't asked her to be with him when he'd been injured. He hadn't wanted her with him as he recovered from those injuries. Here she'd been thinking she was the one who'd caused their differences.

Reaching for her glass to keep her hands busy in case she decided to throttle him, she stared at the man she'd thought she knew. Both hands gripped the stem to raise the glass. She took a big gulp, trying to drown the sense of falling into a deep quagmire of more pain and anguish. Their relationship was in a worse state than she'd imagined, had been for a lot longer than she'd realised. It was pointless to feel the slightest hope that they might find a way through their difficulties. It didn't matter that she loved Cole. Another large gulp didn't dissolve the fear starting to rise within her. They really weren't on the same page about their marriage, and it seemed they never had been.

'Vicki, no. You're wrong. Please, sit down. Hear me out.' His eyes were still locked on hers. 'Please?'

'I'm not sure I want to listen to you repeating how you didn't want me with you when you'd been injured.

Obviously seriously,' she added around the thudding in her head and chest.

Her elbows hit the bench, sending sharp pain up her arms, splashing wine over her fingers. Her legs didn't feel capable of shifting her to the table where Cole indicated. Staring at him, trying to read what he wasn't telling her, she held her breath. Hear him out? Sure. She had to know the worst, get it over with. But she wished he'd hurry up while she was able to listen without being ill. Her lungs rose as she filled them with thick, humid air. 'Explain that comment.'

Another anguished sigh fell between them. 'It happened the day you miscarried. Minutes after you finished telling me and hung up.'

'What? Truly?' Cole had been involved in an accident moments after she'd dropped her bombshell on him? Was it indirectly her fault for giving him the shocking news while he'd been on duty? She'd distracted him so he hadn't seen the other vehicle until it had been too late? Though he wouldn't have answered her call if he hadn't been in a safe place. Would he? She didn't really know him as a soldier, but she did as a man who was careful and brave. Or so she'd thought. 'Were you driving?'

'No.'

She staggered to the table and slid onto the chair he pushed out with his foot. 'Go on,' she whispered. He'd been hurt, badly, if that limp and his drawn face and less muscular body were anything to go by. She was a nurse, trained to read these things. Just hadn't expected to see them knocking her husband about.

*My husband.*

Yes, Cole was still her husband. They weren't together, were about to discuss divorce, but in the meantime…

Her heart sank. In the meantime what? She wanted to be with him.

*Hold on. Don't give in now. You've come this far. See it through. Remember your mother and all she lost by giving herself over entirely to her family.*

A deep breath, and then, 'I want to hear everything.' *I think.*

'My driver saw the truck too late to avoid the impact. I was thrown forward, through the windscreen onto the road into the path of a car that also failed to dodge the accident. It stopped on top of me.'

She was going to throw up. Images of what a car could do to a body filled her mind. She'd seen people in emergency departments who'd been run over. Not even Cole's strong, muscular body would've been a match for wheels attached to a heavy vehicle. Deep breaths. In, out, in, out. Cole had been squashed under a truck.

'Here. Take it easy.' His large hand splayed across her back, gently pushing her forward so her head was on her knees. 'I'm fine.'

'You don't look it,' she gasped between breaths.

'Thanks for the compliment.' His light-heartedness was forced, nothing like his usual banter. But then nothing was usual about tonight. Except that kiss. Intense, filled with love—*and* fear, which wasn't usual.

*Don't go there.*

Slowly, she lifted her head, sat back, shrugging his hand away when really she wanted to turn into his body and hold him for ever. 'Carry on,' she muttered around the longing filling her dry mouth.

Cole placed her drink on the table before returning to his chair, this time sitting with his elbows on his knees, his hands clasped under his chin. 'My left shoulder was dislocated, four ribs fractured, three fractures to my left leg. It could've been worse. My right side was spared. I also received a moderate concussion from impacting on the tarmac when I landed head-first.'

She wanted to cry, scream, be sick, to fling herself at him. Tremors rocked her, her fingers went rigid, and her mouth fell open. 'Are you telling the truth? You are all right?'

'Yes, I am. Not perfect, but functioning okay.'

Thank goodness. Relief poured in. Cole wasn't so badly injured he couldn't get on with his life. She should've been with him throughout his surgeries and rehab. He hadn't asked for her. The disbelief was still ringing in her head. 'You didn't ask for me.'

'No. I stalled the CO when he was determined to let you know what had happened and make arrangements for you to fly to Darwin to meet the plane I was medevaced out on.'

'I'm down as your next of kin.' The details were there in black and white on his contract. 'Did he call your father instead?'

Cole shook his head. 'No. I explained about the miscarriage and said I wanted to be the one to tell you about the accident when I had been operated on and my concussion was gone.'

'Obviously, he agreed.'

'Eventually. Mainly because I refused to have surgery until he did.'

'You were that determined.' It wasn't a question. 'Thanks a lot, Cole. It shows where we were even back then.' She tried to stand, had to get away from him, but her legs had other ideas, dumping her back on the chair, so instead she reached for her glass, took a small sip, and waited for the pounding in her chest to subside enough not to feel like a jackhammer was at work.

Cole tipped his head back and drained his bottle. Then he looked at her again. 'You're wrong. I knew you were unhappy, and that there were things I'd screwed up, but I've always believed our marriage was in reasonable shape.'

'Right,' she snapped around the bitterness tainting her mouth. Last time he'd come home she'd told him how she felt she was waiting in the wings instead of putting a life together with him. It was also when she'd become pregnant. 'You always expected me to be happy while I worked and waited for your short visits home.'

'I was wrong. I know that.' He watched her with such intensity it worried her. What was he about to say?

She remained silent, her fingers tapping the table top.

'There was nothing I wanted more than to have you with me. But...' He stopped.

Tap, tap, went her fingernails.

Finally, 'I injured my spine. At first the doctors weren't sure I'd walk again. You'd said we were over. I did not want you rushing to my side because you felt you had to take care of me.'

She stared at him, totally confused by his comment. And hurt beyond belief. Anger rose, unstoppable. She couldn't do this. Toughen up. She had to. Had to hear him out even if he never listened to her. Then she could go ahead with getting on with her life. But first she'd listen to the rest of his story, and try not to give in to the horror of his injuries and fall into his arms. Because that was really what she wanted to do the most. 'Go on.'

He went to the fridge, got another beer and brought the wine bottle over to top up her half-empty glass, though there was more on the table than had gone down her throat. 'Even as I was flying through the windscreen I held onto my phone so tight the indents on my fingers were there the next day. I would not lose my only contact with you.' He held up a hand as she went to protest. 'No, I don't remember your number off by heart. At least, I didn't then. I do now.'

*Too damned late.*

She said nothing. What could she say that wasn't full of anger and hurt and disappointment? And worry for Cole. Yet he'd had his phone all through whatever had happened after the accident and still hadn't called her.

'Vicki, I was desperate to talk to you, to hear your voice, to make sure you were coping, and get some comfort myself, but how could I expect anything when I hadn't been there when you were miscarrying our baby? The pain and grief in your voice tore me apart. How could I think I deserved you to come to my side after that? After the other times I'd neglected you? I won't use the excuse that I had no choice once I signed up with the army any more. I made that decision in the first place, so I manned up and took responsibility for letting you down, starting with not begging you to come to me when I was unable to go to you.'

'Which is it, Cole? You felt guilty? Or you were afraid I'd come out of a sense of duty, not love?'

'Both.'

She stared at this man who'd never once told her he could be selfish, never admitted he might've done the wrong thing by them when he'd signed up for the military. His answer was direct, and honest, and still filled with that stubborn pride so typical of him. Now what? Forgive and forget? The ball of anger and pain that had been with her for months was loosening, letting go a few of the strands that kept it wound tight. Could she let him off that quickly? That simply? Without explaining that she had a future of her own she wasn't prepared to put aside to follow him wherever he chose to go. No, she still had a battle on her hands, but at least the hope had returned to flicker behind her ribs. 'Were you admitted to a hospital in East Timor?'

'Only to have my spleen removed by an American army surgeon, before being flown down to Darwin for orthopaedic surgeries the following day. It was a little like flying in ICU, the number of wires and tubes attached to me.'

She closed her mind on that picture. 'Multiple surgeries?'

'Yes.'

'After a splenectomy.' This only got worse every time he opened his mouth. The pain he must've suffered being transferred before those fractures had been dealt with. Vicki shuddered. 'Cole, you should've told me. I would've been there as fast as possible, no matter what had gone down between us earlier. I'd have wanted to be with you, despite everything, not because I felt I had to.'

He nodded.

'You told Conrad everything?'

He blanched. 'Yes.'

Forget the fluttering hope. The flutter turned to lead. 'Did he race to be with you?' Honesty could be a bit much to swallow sometimes.

'He came to see me in Darwin.' His chest rose. 'I made him promise not to say a word to you. He argued with me, and I'm sure he picked up the phone to call you more than once, but eventually I won.'

'I bet he kept up to date with your progress.' This hurt so much. She was his wife. She loved him. 'You didn't even mention anything during those few awkward calls we had.' She might understand his restraint, but didn't accept it. 'That was wrong.' What he'd done made her angry, sad, and very frightened. 'I can't forgive this in a hurry.' If ever.

'Vicki, sweetheart, I'm being straight with you, not hiding anything this time. I am sorry I've hurt you. I will make it up to you, if you'll let me.'

Loud knocking on the front door interrupted her. Which was probably for the best. Who knew what would spill out of her mouth at the moment? She was hurting so much it blinded all common sense. Once spoken, words could never be taken back. Though right now she couldn't think of anything she'd want to withdraw once uttered. Had she ever really known Cole? As in really, honestly, truly?

'Vicki, you there?' someone called out.

She leapt to her feet. 'Helen?' Thank goodness for intrusions. She could put her whirling mind on hold, unless Helen only wanted a cup of sugar.

The neighbour from three houses down stood at the door she'd opened, water pooling at her feet. 'You're needed. Bill's fallen off his ladder onto the drive. He's unconscious.'

Hearing what the woman said to Vicki, Cole leapt to his feet, ignoring the pain in his leg, glad of a diversion. Seeing the emotions roiling in Vicki's eyes had decimated his already broken heart. What had started out as trying to do the right thing by her had turned into the biggest mistake of his life, and it had kept growing until now he had no idea if he'd ever be forgiven and allowed the chance to rectify things in their marriage.

'Cole, you hear that?' Vicki called out. 'Cole's a doctor,' she told the woman standing on the porch.

At least Vicki wasn't denying he had a role to play in what was obviously an emergency, despite her anger at him. Anger he'd expected, and deserved. Telling her the truth only made resolving their differences all the harder, but honesty had to be a part of sorting this mess out. If they ever did. Telling her about his injuries and how he hadn't called for her had been excruciating. Not least because he'd finally seen how wrong he'd been, how deeply he'd hurt her. That meant nothing was going to be as straightforward as he'd thought. Explain, apologise, and get on, that had been his hope. Not the reality, he saw now. Talk about being an idiot. Did he deserve her love when he could do this to her?

'Cole?'

He shook his mind clear of their problems. He was right behind her. 'Has anyone called an ambulance?'

Helen looked directly at him. 'Yes, but all emergency services are very busy. They'll get someone here as soon as the next ambulance is free.'

'That figures. I'll get the pack.' Vicki headed for her father's medical storeroom.

Cole was with her as she tapped in the security number to unlock the cupboard. 'Let me look at the drugs we might need.'

'All yours. Want the defib?'

'Might be wise. I'll carry it.' Thankfully, she didn't argue. It took only a moment to find what he might need, covering the basics for pain, shock, cardiac arrest. After hauling on a jacket and shoes, he rushed up the road with the women.

Vicki asked Helen, 'What was Bill doing up a ladder in this weather? He's at least seventy-five and not as stable as he used to be,' she added, for his benefit.

'Then some of his bones have likely broken on impact.' But it was the head injury worrying Cole most at the moment. The man was apparently unconscious. That wasn't good.

'His guttering was blocked with leaves and flooding the internal garage,' Helen replied. 'Stubborn old coot didn't think to ask anyone for help.'

'Where is he now?' Cole asked.

Helen glanced at him, quickly looked away. 'I know you're not supposed to move someone in this situation but he was soaked and with this weather we all thought it best to get him under shelter so we rolled him onto a blanket and slid him across the floor to the back of the garage where there's a modicum of shelter.'

There was no changing that so as they raced up the driveway, Cole said, 'You're right about getting him out of the rain.' Fingers crossed. Someone holding a large sun umbrella over the man might've been a better option, but these people were obviously not medically trained and couldn't be blamed for trying to do their best to helping a friend.

Gingerly lowering onto his knees beside the elderly man, Cole immediately began listening to his airway, and finally nodded. 'Breathing's shallow, but his chest's rising and falling regularly,' he told Vicki as she knelt on the opposite side of Bill.

'Bill? It's Vicki Halliday—Vicki Chandler. Can you hear me?'

The old man didn't move.

Vicki continued. 'Cole's here too. He's a doctor.'

No response.

She reached for Bill's wrist to take his pulse.

'Bill,' Cole said. 'We're going to check you all over. I don't want you trying to move at all. Okay?' He'd continue talking to him while finishing his primary survey in case the words got through. 'Pulse?' he asked Vicki.

'Low. He's sweating profusely.' She was placing patches from the defibrillator on Bill's now exposed chest so they could get a reading of his heart. Immediately, the rapid heart rate was apparent.

'Shock and probable internal blood loss.' Feeling Bill's abdomen, groin, listening to his chest, Cole found swelling, signs of haemorrhaging. 'The liver's taken a knock.'

'His arm was caught in the ladder and we had trouble removing it,' a man told him. 'It was jammed between his upper body and elbow.'

Why had they moved the man? Cole stared at the arm now lying beside Bill's body. More damage might've been done. His gentle prodding told him the elbow was shattered. He left the limb as it was, not wanting to inflict further injury. 'Right, now the head.' Gently touching the skull, he quickly found trauma that explained Bill's unconscious state. 'We need an ambulance fast.' He looked around at the people standing back, watching him and Vicki attend to their neighbour. 'Can someone call 000 and give me the phone when you've got the service on line?'

'On it,' a woman answered.

'There a neck brace in that pack?' Cole asked Vicki.

She gave him a quick glance before returning to watching the defib screen. 'Yes.'

'I'll find it.' Helen opened the bag and began removing containers of bandages. 'This what you want?'

'Thanks.'

The other woman handed him the phone. 'I've explained that we've already called this in so he knows where you are.'

He nodded and spoke to the dispatcher. 'I'm a doctor and I understand there're delays getting an ambulance but we have a GCS of two. Severe head wound, major fractures of ankle, knee and elbow, also internal bleeding.'

'I've contacted the rescue helicopter service. They're about to lift off. Can you put someone on so I can explain what we need done for the chopper to land safely?'

'Sure. And thanks.' Cole looked around. 'I need someone to take this. We need the road cleared for a helicopter.'

A man grabbed the phone and Cole returned his attention to Bill.

'BP's slowly dropping,' Vicki informed him. Calmly, she rechecked all the readings and noted them down on a pad, which Helen had found in the pack, to go with Bill to hospital. Nurse Vicki was in play. Not the woman whose heart he had broken. Or was breaking his. Even in nurse mode she was gorgeous.

His own heart squeezed. Damn, he loved her. He had to win her back. Had to.

'Have to get this collar on,' she reminded him, dragging his thoughts back to where they needed to be.

'Let's do it.' With practised ease they quickly had the collar in place. Even though Bill hadn't moved at all since they'd arrived, a sudden jerk could cause serious damage to his spine if there was any trauma.

Cole continued examining his patient, now checking the less urgent injuries. Blood stained the trousers around the knee area. There was a tear in the fabric that he used to rip down the leg to expose the damage. The bleeding was minor, the least of their worries. The right ankle was at an odd angle. Again, there was nothing he could do until the paramedics got here with splints and a stretcher.

It seemed for ever before the thumping of rotors suddenly slammed their eardrums from directly above the house. The rain had hidden the approach of the flying machine now hurling water in all directions outside as it descended to the road beyond the end of the driveway where many locals had come out with torches and lanterns to light up the area and stop any traffic that might come along.

Within moments paramedics were kneeling beside Bill, and Cole filled them in with his observations before stepping away, glad there were others to lift the stretcher. His leg was throbbing. The emergency crew was in charge now, and had all the gear needed to transfer Bill safely to hospital. There was nothing more he or Vicki could do. Time to head back to the house and that unfinished conversation.

Except what else could he tell her?

That he'd missed her more than ever while lying on his back for weeks on end, waiting for his bones to heal enough to be able to get up on crutches and start walking again. How the fear brought on by her words, which had kept ringing in his head throughout the sleepless nights, hadn't let up. Even when he'd been concentrating hard on walking and ignoring the pain of those broken bones, he'd kept hearing her desperation.

*I can't do this any more.*

As long as he lived he would hear the sadness, the anguish in her voice on that day. His darling Vicki believed he had let her down.

He had.

She'd been gutted over losing their baby. Her distress had vibrated through the ether to him. She'd needed him with her, not helping strangers. She'd needed him to talk about their loss. How *had* she got through those days and weeks afterwards? By talking to Julie? Her parents? Molly and Nathan? Hopefully, she'd had someone's support, otherwise there was still a lot of pain to be worked through. Not that it would've disappeared anyway, merely eased a little. He knew, because he held his own knot of pain deep inside. It would've been better for both of them if he hadn't been in another country at the time.

Never again. From now on he'd always be there for her.

If only she would give him a second chance to show how much he meant it. How much he loved her.

# CHAPTER FIVE

'I HOPE BILL makes it.' Vicki strode out alongside Cole as they headed back to her parents' house, aware that he didn't move as freely as he used to, despite saying he was fine.

He limped, ran, limped, ran. 'I can't lie. That head injury is a worry,' he agreed.

Quite likely Cole was still in pain from those fractures, especially when trying to run, as the impact when his foot hit the pavement would be sharper than when he was walking. She slowed a little, trying not to be obvious, ignoring the rain. There were plenty of dry clothes in the house. 'I can't believe he climbed a ladder in this weather.' Vicki let out a long, regretful breath. 'Actually, that's not true. He's a stubborn old man by all accounts, and apparently since his wife died last year he often says there's no reason to keep himself safe any more.'

'That's sad.'

'Terribly.' This was getting too glum, and for now she wanted to take a break from being down and angry and hurt. Nudging Cole in the arm, she said quietly, 'He had a good team on his side.' She held her hand up in the high five gesture, and felt happy when Cole's hand touched hers. Warm and strong. Lifting her spirits, reminding her not everything had gone bad in her life. Here she was, with Cole, tending to someone in trouble. Nursing satisfied a lot of her need to help others. Caring for Bill alongside Cole had been even better. They'd understood what each should do without hesitation. As they used to with most things.

'Not bad at all considering we've never worked together before today.' His smile was slow and filled with tenderness. The smile that had always made her feel special.

And, surprisingly, it still did. Butterflies beat behind her ribs. They might make this work. If they could get through the next two days without too many disagreements. 'First time for everything.' She returned his smile, not quite sure if she was referring to working together or something deeper.

Turning onto the path leading to the house, she said, 'Just because we've been along the road don't think you're getting out of cooking the steak.'

'I wouldn't dare. Anyway, I'm not letting you near it. I like mine rare.'

'You still not letting me forget the first meal I ever cooked for you?' It had been a disaster. She'd been so nervous, not wanting anything to go wrong, so of course the steak had been overcooked. Not to mention the onions and mushrooms. Inedible would be a kind description.

'Hell, no. I've had a lot of mileage out of that night.'

'True.' Unlocking the front door, she turned to him gleefully. 'Of course there were the daffodils you sent me at work.'

He held his hands up. 'Okay, we're even.'

She headed for the kitchen and a bottle of water. 'Plastic flowers last a lot longer than the real thing, but don't quite have the scent or happiness about them.' He'd ordered them online while he'd been away, thinking he was in touch with a Sydney florist, when it had been a Chinese warehouse and the box had taken ten days to arrive.

'You couldn't have kept real flowers to rub my face in for all this time, though. Still got them?' he asked, then stopped.

She admitted, 'Yes, I have.' She didn't want to get into talk about having packed up all her possessions from their apartment and bringing them with her to Cairns, leaving his gear and some photos behind. For the moment they were getting along and she'd like to keep it that way for a while longer.

'I didn't keep the steak.'

'Benji enjoyed it.'

Another touchy subject. He hadn't been around when she'd had to make the decision to put the dog down. Of course Cole couldn't have changed the outcome of the accident that had put Benji under the vet's care, but sharing the anguish of telling the woman to do the right thing quickly and painlessly might've been some comfort. The day she'd collected Benji's ashes she'd broken down, cried for hours, missing Cole so much her heart had ached for days.

They'd scattered the ashes together the next time he'd been in Sydney, sneaking out to their pet's favourite park at night so as not to get caught. Holding hands as they'd said goodbye had been some consolation, though the anguish of making the decision about Benji on her own had haunted her for some time.

She still missed the mutt. Might be time to get another one as part of moving forward. Her stomach tightened. Suddenly, she felt overwhelmed with a need to make the most of being together, to remember how easy it could be between them. Lately all she'd thought about was how they didn't get on any more.

'I'm getting out of these wet clothes and bringing the lanterns into the kitchen in case we do have a power outage.'

'I'll put the drugs back in the cabinet before I change. Want me to top up the bag as well?'

'Definitely. Not that we used much out of it.'

'Water or beer?' Vicki asked Cole when he returned later.

'Water.' He paused in front of the TV she'd turned on. 'The road's flooded north of here.'

'Nothing unusual in that. It happens every time there's a rainstorm. The council's geared up for it, but it does mean Port Douglas is cut off. The internal road to Cook Town is closed too.' She handed over a bottle of icy water as she watched the extent of the flooding being shown on the screen. 'They're saying the rainfall is heavier than usual for a monsoon. Bill might've been lucky the helicopter got here.'

Cole shook his head. 'No, even the smaller machines can fly through quite a lot. The deluge out there wouldn't stop them, only lack of visibility might have been an issue, but they did fine.'

'You'd have seen a lot of that overseas.'

'I did. Flew in a few too. Large suckers.' A pensive look came over his face. 'The last flight was when I was flown to the local hospital. Didn't see a lot on that one.'

'Were you conscious by then?'

'Yes, though not totally *au fait* with what was happening. The medic had filled me with enough painkiller to drop a horse. Or so it felt. I wasn't used to being pumped full of morphine.'

'Bet you are now.' She tipped water down her throat, and wiped her mouth on the back of her hand. If only she'd known. *Yes, Cole, you owed me that much.* 'You still get pain in that leg.'

'It's a bit shorter than it used to be. The fractures have healed but there're residual aches and pains, especially when I overdo things. It'll eventually quieten down. Or so I've told patients in the past. Guess I'll find out how correct my notes from training days really were.' Cole's tight smile went straight to her heart.

He'd have been determined to get back up and running in as short a time as possible once he'd known his legs would work. Damn it. He could've been a paraplegic. Yes, and she'd still have loved him. Straightening her shoulders, she refused to let his smile or his near miss with paralysis knock aside her resolve to fight for what was important to her, and thereby to them both.

'You want a salad with that or shall we have steak sandwiches? I bought some fresh buns today. There's chilli jam in the pantry,' she added, no longer in the mood for making a salad or cooking vegetables. Sleepless nights tossing and turning while thinking about Cole and this weekend were catching up.

'You've got me. Buns and jam it is. I'll turn on the barbecue. I'm starving.'

'It's getting late, for sure.' Where had the time gone? The landline rang. 'I hope that's not another accident.' Vicki picked up the phone. 'Hello?'

'Hi, darling. We've been watching the news and wondering if everything's all right at the house.'

'Hi, Dad. No problems here.' She hurried to put his concerns to rest. 'Lots of water, but no flooding around Palm Beach.'

'That's good. How's everything else? Cole make it?'

'Yes, just in time as the airport closed not long after.' She needed to divert her father before he came up with questions she had no answers for. 'We got called to help Bill. He'd gone up his ladder to clean the guttering and fell off. Did himself a lot of damage and had to be flown to hospital. He was lucky in that respect as the ambulances are in high demand right now, and it's taking them time to get anywhere.'

'That's not good. I hope he's going to be all right.'

'He was unconscious, has a few fractures.' Again she changed the subject. 'You still in Broome?'

'Yes, moving south tomorrow. I hope you gave Cole the key to the drugs cabinet.'

'Of course I did.' Why wouldn't she? 'It's handy having everything here. There might be more calls before this is over. The rain's not expected to ease till tomorrow at least.'

'Can you put him on?'

'Dad,' she warned, alarms bells ringing in her head. Her family loved her and would do anything to keep her happy, including interfering with her marriage if they believed they had the answers to solve her problems.

'I'm not going to tell him how to behave or to be careful what he says to my daughter. You're big enough and tough enough to do that yourself. This is about the medications in that cabinet.'

Relief sank in. Her dad was always ready to stick up for her, and while it was great to have her family at her back, she really did not want any interference this weekend. 'Thanks. Please mean that. I've got this.'

'You know what you want more than any of us, my girl. Just sort it sooner than later, all right?'

'I'm doing my best.'

'Vicki,' Dad growled lightly. 'I've learned my lesson after seeing how your mother held herself back for all of us, especially me. I don't want the same for you.'

'Aw, Dad,' she gulped. 'I need that.' His backing made everything a little easier to deal with. 'Here's Cole.' She passed the phone to her husband. Yes, whatever came about, he still *was* her husband. 'Dad wants a word.'

Immediately, wariness clouded Cole's face.

She put him out of his misery. 'It's okay. Nothing personal.'

'Marty, how's things?' Cole strolled out to the barbecue, which was sheltered by a plastic roof.

The lights flickered, went out, came back on. Vicki moved to the bench where the lanterns stood in case it happened again. Being left in the dark was the last thing she wanted.

Cole was back, phone still to his ear. 'Okay?' he mouthed, hand on her shoulder.

She nodded, glad of his company, trying to ignore the warmth his touch brought.

He smiled again. 'Good.' He'd know she wasn't being entirely honest, but it was part of the routine to say she was fine. 'Hang on, Marty, I'll go down to your office and check that.'

Vicki watched him walking out of the room, the limp not as noticeable in his long stride at the moment. Still as sexy as ever. Her heart lurched.

*Oh, Cole. I've missed you more than I'd have believed possible.*

What would he do if she followed him, wrapped her arms around his waist and laid her cheek against his chest? Or stretched up and kissed him again, showed him how much she still loved him? Made love with him?

*You think?*

The conversation still to come loomed between them, would taint any lovemaking.

She needed a distraction. Fast. After checking the

matchbox was full, she went to get a torch from the cupboard, trying to calm her racing heart. The dark was her enemy. Snakes could slither through the house and she'd be none the wiser unless they bit her on the way past.

Cole dropped the phone back on its stand. 'Didn't know anyone still used landlines.'

'It's Mum. She's prefers it to these modern new-fangled things.'

'That's Anna to a T.' He smiled—almost as though he knew how hard it was for her to pretend his smiles meant nothing any more. 'I'm glad you didn't get that gene.'

'As if.' She was right up to date with phones and apps, which made setting up her business simpler. With the help of a computer whizz she'd started playing with website designs. As she planned to continue nursing while hiring out staff to hospitals and medical centres, accessing files and messages anywhere was important and required a streamlined system easily used under pressure. A flicker of excitement warmed her. Her own nursing agency. The doctors at the centre where she worked at the moment had been very encouraging when she'd run the idea past them. There was a lot to do before she was ready to start seeking out placements and staff, but she'd get there.

'Those buns ready?' Cole called from the deck, where he stood under cover, cooking the steak.

'Nearly.' Letting out a frustrated sigh, she tried to shake away the thought that Cole was going to fight her on this one. He had to be told, regardless of the weekend's outcome. If, by some remote chance, they made up and decided to give their relationship another go, her agency would be an important factor. What worried her was her expectancy he'd say they'd be living in Sydney, not Cairns. An agency would work there too, yet the city was vast with a large population and she didn't think she wanted to try to set up there. She'd have more competition, or she'd have to limit the area she covered. Which could work, she conceded.

'Earth to Vicki. Rolls?'

Cole took the steaks inside and got two fresh water bottles from the fridge, handed Vicki one. 'You all right?' She'd been miles away when he'd popped his head around the door to check if everything was ready.

'Sure.' She pushed a plate with a buttered roll in his direction. 'Hungry as.'

There'd never been anything wrong with her appetite. It was one of the things he'd liked when they'd first met. None of that nonsense about only eating small portions and ignoring the foods she really enjoyed. But then they'd connected on so many levels right from the get-go. 'Me, too. The dry sandwich and bland coffee on the plane did nothing for my appetite.'

Exhaustion shaped her smile. 'You should've helped yourself to something when we first got home.'

His appetite had quietened down as he dealt with being with Vicki, treading carefully so as not to upset her any further. 'It's all good. I'm enjoying this.' He thought back to the night they'd first met. He'd been intrigued to find out who Nathan had thought might be his perfect match, and had gone along to the party fully expecting to have a laugh and maybe a good night with no follow-up and, wham, bam. Literally eyes meeting across the room.

When he'd first spotted Vicki he hadn't realised she was his date. His gut had told him nothing was ever going to be the same, while his head had mentioned he had to find Nathan to say, 'Forget who you've jacked me up with. I've found my match all by myself.' Instead he'd found himself owing his mate for bringing Vicki to the party to meet him. They certainly had *connected* that night, and never looked back.

Until recently. Not that he was glancing backwards, more like trying to figure out what was ahead. That kiss had rocked him to his feet. Kisses were part of them, as was lovemaking. Being stuck in this holding pattern turned the importance of enjoying each other upside down. They needed to talk, fully and frankly.

Yet it was difficult to start. Like where? What came first? At the moment they were awkwardly comfortable with each other, as though pretending the past few months hadn't happened. But they had, and they itched just below the surface. Explaining his failure to get her to fly to him after the accident had been difficult, but it was done. Maybe not quite finished, or accepted, but it was on the table.

He'd believed he'd been doing the right thing at the time, and hadn't wanted to add to her pain, or his. He'd learned to make quick decisions about difficult situations in the hope he didn't hurt anyone again. Had he been too quick?

Vicki said he was wrong to have decided for her. Hadn't she left him without so much as talking through the miscarriage and other problems first? Sure, she'd been hurting, but he'd deserved a chance to go over what bothered them both, too. 'How are you coping with the miscarriage?'

She put her fork down, and looked at him. 'The loss is huge still. I have times when the tears flow, my heart breaks, and I want to scream at the world. But that happens less often now. I'm getting there, I guess.'

'It's never a quick fix.'

'And you? How do you manage?'

'I had lots of time to think about it while lying on my back. Yes, the pain left me feeling raw, and wishing we had been together to face what had happened. I think I'm over the worst. Not that the sense of loss will ever go away entirely.'

'I agree.' She nodded slowly. 'It has been the hardest thing I've dealt with. I struggle talking about it still.'

'Might be best if we did.' When she didn't answer, he added, 'Whenever you're ready, I'll be here.'

*I love you, Vicki. Please don't ever forget that. Don't think I've stopped. I haven't. Won't.*

The steak refused to go down his throat. He chewed some more. What if he'd truly lost her? For ever? No. It couldn't happen. Could it? That blinding recognition of his feelings when he'd seen her racing to get out of the rain at the medical centre had told him more than anything else could how much she meant to him, and how nothing had changed. That short kiss had ramped up the stakes. Except now he was aware how quickly problems could escalate and would work hard to prevent them becoming a nightmare.

Vicki glanced up and locked wary, sad eyes on him. 'Thanks.'

He'd never seen her so unhappy. And he was the cause of most of it.

'Tell me again you're going to be all right, that those injuries are healing properly,' she said quietly.

He reached across the table for her hand and squeezed gently, felt the jolt that rocked her. 'Seriously, I'm going to be fine. Already am. Might not climb Everest any time soon, but there's nothing I can't do that I didn't used to be able to.'

Vicki returned the pressure on his hand before withdrawing. 'It must've been terrifying.'

That gentle squeeze softened the ache in his heart. 'It happened so fast I didn't have time to think.'

*Start being yourself. Be the guy you were before the theft ruined everything. The one who shared everything about himself, not just a select few issues that are easy to resolve.*

It had been so long he doubted he even knew that version of himself, might not be that guy any longer. 'Holding onto my phone was the only thought running through my head.' Sigh. 'And the thought that it was going to hurt when I landed.'

'So you were aware of what was happening all the way through?'

'Until I hit the road. I didn't see the vehicle as it ran onto me. It hurt. A lot. Mostly later.'

Vicki was blinking hard and fast. 'Thank goodness for small mercies. That'd be a picture most likely to stay with you for ever.'

His throat thickened. 'I remember being relieved when I came round and saw the medics beside me. It meant I was alive.'

'Now I understand your reaction when I braked too hard.'

'Instinctive, I suppose.'

'It seems weird that after all the time you served on active duty overseas you got injured in a traffic accident.' Those eyes were still blinking. 'Though you wouldn't have been there if not for the army, so I suppose it does make sense.'

*Don't cry on me. Or for me. I don't deserve your tears.*

His throat was closing. 'Them's the breaks.'

As she ate, she seemed to withdraw. Then, 'So where do you stand with the army now?'

'I'm on paid medical leave for another month while

receiving ongoing treatment, then I'm taking early discharge due to my injuries. There was another contract on the table but I never intended to continue as a career soldier. I wanted to come home. I'm a doctor and would like a full-time career as a general practitioner. A real job.'

'The army wasn't real?' Vicki snapped.

He huffed a low sigh. 'One where I'm fixing people, not driving around in armoured vehicles looking for trouble, and then picking up the pieces when we find it.' Serving his country was one thing, but soldiering had never been him. Sure, he'd been a good officer, had looked out for his men, but he'd done what he'd set out to do and kept his promise. Now he wanted to get back to his real passion—medicine. And Vicki.

'Don't regret what you did or it becomes worthless.' There was an accusation in Vicki's voice that stabbed hard, like a sharp knife under the ribs.

'I do have regrets, and they're all about you, me, us. But I can't change a thing. All I can do is go forward.'

'You want a hot drink?' When he nodded she got up to put the kettle on. 'That's true for both of us.'

What was she saying? That she didn't want to go back to being with him? Or, if she did, it was going to be different this time? Or that she had things to tell him he wasn't expecting that might blow his socks off? Here he'd been tentatively thinking the evening was progressing in a good way, and now the doubts were back. The edginess in Vicki's stance, in his thoughts, was tightening with every moment. 'Vicki?'

Sliding her hands into the pockets of her shorts she stared at the spot between her bare feet. 'I would've come to you, you know?'

'Yeah, I do.' Hadn't they dealt with this earlier?

'Whereas I couldn't fly over to you. I would've if it had been at all possible.'

The kettle switched off but Vicki didn't move. 'Which is one reason why you didn't believe you could ask me to join you. Not only the spinal injury. Do you know how that makes me feel, Cole?'

'Hurt.'

'Try angry. Try let down. Try disappointed. And hurt, sure. You were injured the same day I had the miscarriage. I would've joined you. No question.' She hesitated, drew a breath. 'It feels as though you were paying me back for something I have no idea about.'

It was his turn to be hurt. 'You're wrong,' he growled. 'I believed I was doing the right thing.'

Those sad blue eyes locked on him. 'By me? Or by yourself?'

'You said you'd had enough, our marriage was over. Would you have thanked me for guilting you back into it?'

Her eyes widened. 'Guilt wouldn't have had anything to do with it. Instead we could've talked face to face, fixed the problems pulling us apart, not made them worse.'

'Isn't that why I'm here now?' The divorce couldn't happen, not until they'd covered everything lying between them.

'It's too late.'

His heart plummeted to his toes. 'Why?'

'You've never really heard anything I've said about what I might want. Even now you can't accept I would've rushed to you, for you and us.'

He was not going to be forgiven in a hurry. If at all. His gut crunched hard. This wasn't going well. Not that he'd expected to be wrapped in another hug and kissed wildly, but just a little understanding would go a long way right now. He'd have sworn Vicki never held grudges. Seemed he'd got that wrong too. Or had she learnt to because of him? He could do with some levity before he sank too low. 'Can I ask you something?' Since when did he have to check before saying whatever was on his mind?

'That depends.'

'Can I have tea? Not coffee.' When her mouth started to flatten again he hurried to carry on. 'I'm not taking any of this lightly. It's hard, and I want to cheer you up. Though I guess that's expecting too much.' Not once in the years he'd spent with Vicki had he felt so useless, unable to say what he wanted without looking for implications he didn't mean.

With quiet efficiency, Vicki made two mugs of tea. 'Here, get that into you, though we'll probably end up sweating something awful in this humidity.' She sat down opposite him again and picked up the TV remote.

Obviously the conversation was over—for now. 'Thanks.' For the tea and backing off the hard stuff for a while. It didn't mean the problems had gone away, they were only on hold. Then the urge to pick up Vicki and kiss her long and hard, to make love tore through him. Flapping his hand in front of his face, he muttered, 'It's damned hot.' Every inch of his body was heated, pounding with need.

'That's Northern Queensland for you. I'm used to it and yet it still gets to me.' The news channel came up on the screen.

Could he get used to it? Move here if that's what Vicki wanted?

They watched in silence for a little while, then he said, 'Nothing's really changed from earlier. That has to be a good sign.'

'Or we're in the eye of the storm.'

Like their marriage. 'You're a box of cheer, aren't you?' he groaned, finally at ease again, though still a little tight in the groin. The need to kiss her wasn't backing off.

She yawned, and checked her phone. 'Blimey, where did the evening go? It's after midnight. I should go to bed, though I doubt I'll sleep.'

So much for kissing. She wasn't inviting him to join her.

'Might give it a try myself. It's been a long day.'

If only they were going to share a bed, he could deal with the ache that had taken over his body. But he'd been shown to the third bedroom without a hint of remorse on Vicki's part when they'd first got here. It was the first time they'd been in the same building and not slept together since the night they'd met.

His gut tightened in on itself. Talk about bringing home how far down the wrong track they'd gone. Would there be any turning around, getting back together? Behind his ribs, his heart slowed to a sad rhythm. Did Vicki see this weekend as their final time together? Was she going to tell him she didn't love him any more? That the divorce was a foregone conclusion?

'Or we could sit up all night and thrash out what's bugging us,' he said quietly, suddenly desperate to move on. Get this done one way or the other. No. He would not give up. He loved Vicki. There was only one conceivable outcome.

Vicki's head flipped up, her eyes wide and startled. 'No,' she gasped.

'Why not?' At least they could start the ball rolling so he knew what he was up against. He waited. And waited as she fidgeted with the hem of her shirt, looking everywhere but at him.

Finally, she raised her head and locked her gaze firmly on him. 'You're right.' She stopped, the heat in her eyes fading. 'Oh, Cole. This is crazy. Who'd have thought we'd come to this? I can't believe it.'

'It doesn't have to be all bad. We need to discuss everything that's worrying you. That's why I'm here.'

'Don't you have concerns about how we've blown it?'

'I understand you've got issues with the time I've spent away from you, and because I didn't ask you to come to me when I was in hospital.' He sipped his tea, staring over the rim of the mug at the woman he loved so much. 'I'm here to listen, to work with you to get our marriage back on track.'

'It's not that straightforward, Cole. There're two of us in this mess.' She fiddled with her fingernail, picking at it with her other hand. 'Why did you really join the military? You always avoided the question. I might've understood and coped better if you'd told me.'

The doorbell rang loud and sharp, cutting through the air like a laser.

Vicki scrambled to her feet, muttering, 'Go away. Can't you see we're busy?'

'Who's that at this hour? Have we got another accident to respond to?' This time he definitely did not want an interruption to their evening. Leaping off his chair, Cole followed her down the hall where a large shape loomed behind the thick glass panel in the front door. 'Careful,' he warned. 'Could be anyone.'

'It's safe around here.' Despite her words there was tension in Vicki's shoulders as she pulled the door wide. Then her shoulders returned to their normal position. 'Hello, Merv. What's up?'

The fireman at the door was saying, 'Hi, Vicki. There's been a hill slide that's taken out an occupied house. We need you and a doctor ready and waiting when the family's rescued. Damon says your ex is here. Is that right?'

Her ex! Cole's blooded heated in an instant. Not bloody likely.

*I'm still her husband, thank you very much.*

He stepped up beside Vicki who'd turned to him.

'Yes, Cole is here.' Even though they hadn't touched, she must've felt his anger because she laid a hand on his arm. 'Sounds like we're needed again,' she said quietly, as though trying to ignore her own annoyance with the man before them.

If only Vicki felt the same about him. She was the only person he wanted to need him.

He nodded abruptly. 'I'll get the emergency kit. Do you know what we'll be dealing with?' He stared at the man, trying not to dislike him for his blunder.

'I was only told to pick you up if you were available.'

Well, he was, despite his anger. Being a doctor came before most things. Just not before Vicki, and she was going with him so he'd settle down and do what was required of him. And then get back to that conversation they'd begun.

# CHAPTER SIX

'COLE'S FURIOUS,' Vicki acknowledged as Merv drove them towards the hills on the opposite side of the main road north.

*So am I. For being interrupted at a crucial moment and for that 'ex' comment.*

They hadn't made that a definite. Had Damon really called Cole her ex? Or was this man reading too much into whatever her brother had said about there being a doctor at his parents' home?

'Is Damon at the scene?' she asked the fireman. Because if he was, he was going to get an earful. He should not be talking about her private life to anyone.

'He was when I left. The guys are focused on stabilising the house to protect the family caught inside. Others, including neighbours, were trying to reroute the slip as small amounts are still coming down directly behind the property but it's not really feasible in these conditions, especially without a bulldozer and digger.'

'What state's the house in?' Cole asked from the back seat of the large four-wheel-drive vehicle. He sounded as though he'd got his anger under control, though Vicki knew he'd still be gritting his teeth.

'The back's stoved in. That's where the bedrooms are—were. The front rooms look normal, except for a dangerous lean, and the ceiling's down in places. When I left to collect you no one had been inside to check it out. It's too dangerous until we get joists in place.'

'Anyone been calling out?'

'A woman, presumably the owner, was heard yelling to get her children out,' Merv told them.

Worry rolled through Vicki. Children in a disaster area. They'd be terrified, and so darned vulnerable.

'I hope the kids don't try anything silly to get free.' Damon's bollocking was on hold.

'Two neighbours are talking to the children, though not getting any responses. They figure if they keep chatting it might help keep everyone calm.'

'If it's at all possible I'll be going into the back section as soon as we get there.' Cole wasn't questioning Merv, he was telling him. Officer mode in operation.

She smiled to herself, before announcing in a similar tone. 'So will I.' It didn't come out as strong and determined as she'd intended.

Naturally, Cole was onto her immediately. 'You wait outside and I'll bring those children out to you when possible. The firemen will help me.'

'The hell with that. I'll be needed there almost as much as you,' she snapped.

'Vicki, I don't want you in any danger.'

'Back at you.' Cole was not getting injured again. For one: he wasn't as fit as he used to be so recovery would be harder. For two: she loved him, and did not want anything bad happening to him. For three: ditto. She sighed. There was no doubt about her love for this man she'd always known to be her other half. Walking away would be nigh on impossible. Not that she wanted to.

*What?* Wasn't that what this weekend was supposed to be about? Not from the moment he'd said hello outside the medical centre it hadn't. She straightened up in the seat. So she had to explain her plans carefully so he'd understand what she hoped to accomplish, or their love would eventually crumple into a bitter heap.

'Settle, you two. No one's going in that building until Damon gives the okay,' Merv said. 'As for you, Vicki, I doubt you'll getting anywhere near those flattened rooms. We all know Damon won't let you get within range of any danger.'

True. Why did it have to be her brother's crew working this job? 'We'll see about that,' she grumped.

Cole tapped her on the shoulder. 'In, out, girlfriend.'

Unexpected laughter bubbled over her lips. He'd came up with it the first time he'd ever seen her lose her temper. Tenderness stole through her. This was what she'd missed. The small expressions of love they shared, as much as the big ones. A light touch was as important as hot sex. A look, a kiss on his jaw, his fingers massaging between her shoulder blades. Communications that belonged only to them. A personal language all their own.

*Why am I doing this? Holding out on Cole when he's my other, stronger half is crazy. And necessary.*

The doubts backed off slowly, to a point they lingered in the back of her head, not foremost for once. They hadn't talked enough yet and the first night was well on the way to morning. The next few hours were going to be taken up with other people's problems. Even if miraculously no one was injured, they'd still need checking over and given lots of reassurance that they were safe.

'Here we go. Hold on.' Merv dropped a gear and began driving slowly but purposefully into the torrent of water racing down the road in front of them. 'That flood marker shows the depth hasn't changed in the time I picked you up so we should be good.' Just then the ute lurched sideways and he deftly swung the steering wheel left, then right, then straight ahead.

Vicki gripped the edge of the seat and stared out the side window at the swirling brown water lit up by the headlights. Merv knew what he was doing. There was nothing to get stressed about, but this wasn't something she'd done before. 'Lots of logs and debris in there.'

'Also mud from the landslides further up, though no other house has bought it that we know of.'

'That's good news,' Cole said. 'What's the scenario with the rescue service? Are the helicopters still flying?'

'They were last time I asked, but if anyone needs hospitalisation we'll have to get them across this first. Can't have a chopper anywhere near the hill. The pounding from the rotors could bring down more land and trees onto other houses near the one we're going to.' Merv hadn't let up on the accelerator even when Vicki knew she would have. He was keeping the speed consistent, driving correctly for the situation.

'You're good at this.'

'Had plenty of practice over the years in the service.' Then the ute was climbing out of the torrent onto *terra firma*. 'Right, nearly there.'

Within minutes they pulled up beside the fire truck and bundled out into the rain. Cole retrieved the emergency pack, wincing as he slung it over his shoulder.

Vicki studied him for a moment. He hadn't mentioned an injury to his back or shoulder, but then a vehicle had parked on him so it stood to reason he had some muscular problems, and then there was that initial spinal issue. Again fear engulfed her for what might've happened to him. His injuries were bad enough, but what if they'd been worse? She might never have got the chance to talk to him again, might've had to live always knowing her last words to him had been terrible. 'Sorry,' she whispered.

He glanced down at her. 'Later, okay?'

Nodding, she slipped her hand in his, drawing on his strength as she walked alongside him to find out what was happening regarding those poor people in the house ahead of them. Or what was left of it. Nearing the hillside, she gasped, 'That's unreal.' The back of the house looked as though it had been built into the hill and then covered with soil until it could no longer be seen. 'How can anyone survive that?'

'Yeah,' Cole sighed, his fingers tightening around hers before he pulled away. 'You've got to wonder. Especially the kids.'

'Cole, Vicki, there you are.' Her brother crossed to them. 'So far we know there are three boys, aged six to ten, and their mother in the rooms at the back under that debris. We've talked to the mother and one of the kids, but nothing from the other two youngsters.'

One child talking was an improvement on what Merv had told them. But she wasn't relaxing yet.

'Can I get in there?' Cole asked.

Vicki restrained herself from snapping that she was going with him. She'd just do it. Best to listen to everything Damon had to tell them first.

'Yes, we've shored up some of the rafters and made a way in. Once you're inside there is a spacious cavern that used to be the bedroom on the far side. It didn't collapse as much as the others. Two men are in there, assessing the situation and trying to reach the two non-responsive children. They'll get you to the boys as soon as it's possible.'

This could turn out to be a dreadful situation. Vicki drew a deep breath. It was always hard dealing with seriously injured people, or worse, but kids knocked her sideways every time. They had to get to them fast, do everything within their power to save them. 'Let's go.'

Cole didn't even argue. Not a word. Just said to Damon, 'Lead on. We need to get in there.'

Her brother looked from Cole to her as though he was about to tell her to stay outside.

'Damon, Jack has heard a kid crying,' one of the firemen called.

Damon sighed. 'Come on, you two. Let's go save this family.' He started towards a group of rescue workers, then paused. 'By the way, the woman, Karen, is heavily pregnant, and complaining of pain.' He turned away and continued to the house.

Cole grimaced. 'It just keeps getting better and better.'

'Fingers crossed the pain is from shock or a hard landing when the house was knocked out around her and not labour,' Vicki said. 'No baby needs to be born in these circumstances.'

'Is it my imagination or did the rain just get heavier?' Cole glared up at the darkness above them.

'I doubt it could get heavier. I mean, how much water can clouds hold?'

'Thought you'd be used to this, having grown up around here.'

'I am, but doesn't make it any nicer to deal with. And I've been in Sydney for a few years so I'm out of practice.'

'A good reason to return there.' Cole nudged her gently.

The weather was the least of her concerns. 'We'll see.' They'd reached the side of the entombed house and she shivered. It was going to be just as wet inside. And dark. She'd try not to think about that. The fire truck had a pair of large searchlights focused on the house, but how much of that light was getting into the interior was an unknown at the moment.

'You can still stay out here,' Cole said quietly. 'I'm sure one of the neighbours would be happy if we used their home to see to any of these people when we bring them out.'

Then she wouldn't have to deal with the dark. Wouldn't be looking over her shoulder for snakes, even when it was unlikely there'd be any here considering the number of people tromping all over the place and banging at posts and house walls. In, out. 'I'm going with you.'

'Getting more stubborn by the minute.' His smile hit her hard, and deep.

And ramped up the sense she should just cave and hug him, hold on for ever. 'Better believe it. Let's get started. Those kids will be terrified.' She headed for Damon, who was waiting for them at the edge of the gaping hole they were going into. 'Lead on, brother.'

'It's going to be cramped in there.'

Cramped would've been comfortable. The bedroom they found themselves in mightn't have been completely crushed but the internal wall had been forced sideways and loomed over them, forcing everyone to hunch down to move around. How Cole managed, she had no idea.

'It's safe for now,' one of the men tried to reassure her.

'Let's do this fast as possible.' Cole nodded.

On the floor sat a woman looking shocked and scared. Her nightgown was torn at the shoulders and her neck and arms were smeared with mud. Blood stained her forehead and the side of her head above an ear. Someone had wrapped a blanket around her, but she was still shivering.

Vicki ignored the creepy feeling she was getting from the room where little light was making its way through from that fire truck. A large torch helped somewhat, but she couldn't stop herself from looking around for snakes.

Cole laid a hand on her arm, said quietly, 'All clear.'

He knew her failings too well. 'Thanks.' Then she crossed to the desperate woman and knelt down. 'Karen? I'm Vicki, a nurse. This is Cole. He's a doctor.'

'My kids. Where are they? Have they got them out?' Karen cried, snatching Vicki's hand and holding on hard. 'Where are they?'

'The men are working on getting them out safely. They've been talking to them.' Not saying only one had responded. That wouldn't help this distressed woman one little bit. 'Can you tell us if you're in any pain?'

'Leave me, go to the children. I can wait.'

Awkwardly, Cole hunched down beside them. 'Karen, I hear you but until the children can be moved out of their room we can't do anything for them. We can't get in there, and if we tried we'd be getting in the way of the men trying to make it safe for them. For now I'd like to check you over and see to any injuries you might have.'

'No, leave me, go to them. Now. Please,' she begged. 'Talk to them if you can't reach them.'

'As soon as I'm told I can get in there I will. I promise,' Cole told her. 'In the meantime, let's make sure you're all right so that when your kids are out you can hold them.'

Vicki held her breath. She totally understood this woman's need for her children to be dealt with first, but Cole had a point. Why waste time waiting for the children when Karen might be in need of help?

Finally, Karen nodded. 'All right.'

'How far along is your pregnancy?' Cole asked.

'Thirty-six weeks.'

Damn. After the trauma of having her house knocked from under her and her children stuck in their rooms, Karen was possibly in labour. 'Have you been having contractions?'

'I think so. Sometimes my belly tightens, and there's a pain like labour, only not so strong as I've had with my others.'

'How far apart?'

'I don't know. Not often.'

'Let's leave that until the next one,' Cole said. 'I want to check that wound on your head. Do you remember being hit?'

'Not really. It all happened so fast. There was a loud bang, lots of noise and then the wall was coming towards me and the bed slamming across the room.'

'Do you think you might've lost consciousness?' Cole asked as he gently probed the wound with a gloved finger.

'I don't know. Everything's a blur.' Karen blinked and tears slid down her cheeks. 'Except it's real.'

Vicki held her hand tighter. 'Everyone's doing whatever they can to get you all out. Are you hurting anywhere else?' The creaking and groaning of timber was scary.

'I didn't even realise I'd hurt my head until this man said he was going to look at it.'

'That's shock. I'm going to check your pulse and then we'll have a look at your body to see if there are any other injuries.'

'Cole.' Damon was crouched behind them. 'Can you come with me?'

Vicki's heart sank at the quietness in her brother's normally robust voice. One of those kids was in trouble. Had to be. Glancing at Damon, he was giving nothing away in front of Karen.

'Need me?'

'Stay with Karen.'

She felt certain this wasn't about her hang-ups over

being in the dark but about looking out for this frantic mother. Nodding, she said, 'No problem.'

Karen wasn't stupid. 'Have you got through to the boys? How are they? Is one hurt? All of them?' With each question her voice rose.

Damon drew a breath, tightened his shoulders. 'Karen, we've got through to the bedroom. The boys are talking so that's a good sign. Cole will take a look and help us get them out.'

'Thank you.'

They were all talking, or still only one? Vicki wasn't asking in front of their mother.

Cole stood up as much as he could. 'I'll let you know as soon as I've seen them.'

'Vicki, you must go too. I don't need you. My boys are more important.' Then she burst into tears. 'I wish their father was here.'

'Where is he?' Vicki asked.

'Arlo works in the mines in West Australia. Six weeks on, six off. He should be here, not over there where he's no use to us at all.' Karen stared around what used to be the bedroom she shared with her husband when he was home. 'I know he's doing it for our benefit, and that we are well set up because of the long hours he's worked, but he's missed out on so much with the kids. And me.'

Another man who wasn't around when he was most needed by his family. Vicki couldn't help glancing at Cole, and gasped. The stunned look on his face told her he'd been thinking much the same.

Dragging her eyes away, she took Karen's hand again. 'You're being very brave. Your children need you to keep focusing on that. Okay?'

*Hypocrite.* She'd been a wimp, screaming at Cole that he should be with her and not running around playing soldiers. But she'd meant it, had been hurting, had wanted no one but Cole with her at the time. Just as Karen wanted her husband here, and not on the other side of the country.

'Go to my boys, please. I want them to have all the help they can get.'

She nodded. 'I understand.'

'It's going to be darker in there,' Cole said softly. 'And a lot more crowded.'

'I'll deal with it.' She wasn't about to let Karen down. The boys needed her to step in for their mum.

'Agh…!'

Vicki spun around, whacked her head on the leaning wall, and swore under her breath. 'Karen?'

The woman was panting, gripping her stomach. 'A contraction. More like the real thing this time.'

'I'll stay with you. In fact, let's get you out of here.'

'No. Leave me. Go to the boys. It's been a while since the last pain. There's still a way to go. I hope.'

Spoken like a woman who'd already had three babies. 'If you're sure?' When Karen nodded, she added, 'Yell if you need me.' Then she followed Cole on hands and knees through to the remains of the boys' bedroom, and tried to ignore his sexy derrière. Like that was possible, even in the crazy situation they found themselves.

Cole's stomach dropped as he took in the sight before him. How could anyone—especially three little boys—survive the disaster that had only hours ago been a normal room? The walls resembled a mix of wood chips and wooden spears. The ceiling beams had crashed to the floor, one flattening a bed in its way. Under that beam lay the distorted body of a young boy. His eyes were wide open, filled with fear. His hands were clenched together over his chest. At least he was alive.

Where were the other two lads? Were they in a better or worse state? Karen had a point. The boys' father should be here, and yet he understood the man's reasons for being away. Which was more important? Giving his family a good start financially, or always being around, handing out love and joining in when things were to be celebrated or fixed? It gave him more to think about concerning him and Vicki. Not that he'd joined the army to get a better life. Far from it.

Vicki bumped into his butt, reminding him why he was there, and that he needed to forget about anything but saving these lads. He said to the boy lying in front of him, 'Hello. My name's Cole. I've come to help you. What's your name?'

No reply.

Cole waved his hand in front of the boy's face and got a blink in return. So he was aware, but too shocked to speak. 'I'm a doctor, and this is Vicki. She's a nurse.'

Nothing.

'Hello, young man. I'm going to hold your hand.' Vicki had moved up and now took one cold, tiny hand in hers and carefully laid a finger on the pulse in his wrist. 'You're a very brave boy, being so quiet.'

Blink.

Cole reached for the boy's legs and began carefully running his hands along the areas not held down by that beam. Judging by the odd angles, there'd be fractures below the knees. Looking over his shoulder at Damon, he said quietly, 'I'm going to administer morphine before your men attempt to lift that beam.' Checking for bleeding, he sighed with relief when he found none. Digging in the pack, he removed the drug and a needle, saw the fear grow in the boy's eyes. 'It's all right. Your legs are sore, so I'm going to make them feel better. That's good, isn't it?'

No reply.

Vicki took the vial he held out and read the date out before handing it back. Then she leaned closer to their patient. 'Okay, young man, how old are you?' When no answer was forthcoming, she continued, 'I think you must be seven.' Silence. 'Or are you eight?'

*Blink.*

'Ah—told you. Eight. Now, what's your name? What's a cool boy's name…?' She scratched her chin and stared at the floor. 'I'm thinking… Jack.'

A slight shake of his head.

Vicki pushed the sleeve of the boy's shirt up to expose his arm for the injection. 'Mickey.'

She was good. But then Cole knew that. He tapped the boy's vein.

Another shake of the small head. 'Callum.'

Bingo. She'd done it.

'Callum, eh? That's a great name for a brave boy.'

Cole slid the needle in and pressed down on the syringe.

'Ow!' Callum cried.

'Sorry, mate. But I've finished.' Cole pulled the needle clear. 'Vicki's right. You're very brave. Can you tell me where you hurt?'

'My legs don't move.'

'That's because there's a hunk of wood on them. The firemen are going to shift it away very soon and then we'll be able to take you out and have a good look at you. Okay?'

Callum nodded, then bit his lip, tears threatening.

'What's up?' Vicki asked. 'You hurting?'

'Where's Mum? She hasn't come to see if we're all right.'

'That's because she can't get through here with her baby tummy. It won't fit through the gap in the wall. She's all right, okay? You'll be able to see her soon.'

'I want her now.'

Cole's heart clenched for this brave wee man. 'You'll see her when the firemen carry you out of here. That all right?'

'I suppose.' Callum yawned as the drug took effect.

Cole glanced over his shoulder. 'Not long now,' he told Damon.

'The men are ready.'

Cole nodded. He wanted to ask Callum if he'd heard anything from either of his brothers, but that might add to the lad's distress so he turned back to Damon, said quietly, 'Where are the others?'

'Beside the wardrobe that looks like something out of a demolition site.'

Vicki crawled toward where Damon indicated, glancing left and right and sucking in a breath at the shadows darkening the corners. Nothing slithering and dangerous. She didn't relax.

Cole thought of the day he'd taken her to a snake sanctuary with the brainless idea that if she got to touch one, maybe hold it with a zoo keeper watching over things, she'd get past her paranoia, but that'd earned him a blasting and hadn't solved her problem. Once they returned to Sydney—he wasn't thinking if—there was less likelihood of her coming across her least favourite creature compared to up here in Queensland.

Two burly firemen squeezed into the small space. 'Hey, Callum. We're going to get this board off you and take you somewhere dry. Okay?'

The boy nodded. 'Is it going to hurt?'

Cole took his wee hand in his large one. 'You can't feel your legs now, can you?'

'No.'

'Then you won't notice the board moving away. I'll keep holding your hand, okay?' The little fingers were gripping his tight.

With a lot of straining the roofing beam was lifted enough for Damon and Cole to pull Callum free; they slid him onto the stretcher ready on the other side of the narrow opening.

Cole asked, 'Are there any leg splints in the fire truck emergency gear?'

'Yes. Want them now or when we're out?'

'Out. Callum's not feeling anything at the moment and it's best to move him somewhere safer.' It felt like an age since he and Vicki had arrived, but a glance at his watch showed it had only been ten minutes. One almost safe, two to go. 'We'll stop by Karen on the way and get her to agree to going outside with us. She's more help to her lads if she's out and safe.' His mind went to Vicki. He didn't want her in here either. Especially if that hill came down some more. But trying to talk her out of being with the lads was a waste of time they didn't have to spare. He called to her, 'I'll be back in a moment. You all right in there?' Not that she'd tell him, however afraid she was.

'Sure. Got more fractures here.'

Great. 'I'll hurry.' He had to make sure Callum didn't have any other, more serious injuries he might've missed in the semi-dark.

'No worries.'

He'd always worry when Vicki was in danger. No one had actually said that more of the hillside could come down on them. There was no need. With the torrential rain still persisting it was a given that anything was possible, so they had to work fast, yet carefully, to extricate this family. And get Vicki the hell away from here.

No matter where they were in their relationship, nothing mattered more to him than keeping her safe. Nothing. Not even this family he was helping.

*Sorry, guys, but that's how it is. I love her and will do anything for her.*

Hopefully, that meant getting back on side and staying there for ever.

# CHAPTER SEVEN

VICKI KNEW THE moment Cole returned, and not only because he blocked the light reaching her and the two boys, as well as the fireman who'd stayed in here from the moment the lads had been found. It was the way her skin tightened and her fear of darkness backed off. He'd always made her feel safe, no matter what the circumstances. 'They're taking Callum to hospital?'

'Merv's boating him across to the other side now. A neighbour's with Callum, making sure he's not moving around, and will go through to the hospital as well. An ambulance has got through and is waiting on the main road.'

'Hope they get another ambulance here ASAP.' She nodded at the boy sprawled on the floor in front of her. 'This is Lucas. He's unconscious, head trauma, BP low, swelling in the abdomen, irregular breathing. And this other little guy is Toby. He's as brave as his brother, Callum.' She smiled at the wee fellow. 'He's got a headache and a bloody nose, but no other injuries that I can find.'

'Hi, Toby. Where does your head hurt?' Cole asked as he did a visual appraisal of the boy.

'There.' Toby touched his forehead carefully.

'He fell out of bed onto his face when the wall crashed

into the room. I can't find any trauma on his skull. His speech is clear and distinct.'

'Good. Hold out your arms for me, Toby,' Cole instructed gently. 'That's it. Nothing sore?' When Toby shook his head, Cole said, 'Stretch your legs in front. They look fine.'

'He's got off lightly. Want me to take him out while you attend to Lucas? I'll be back in a minute. Hopefully with another stretcher.'

'Do that.' Cole was already working on the prone boy, listening to his breathing while fingering his skull and on down his body, looking for more injuries. Fast yet careful, he wouldn't miss a thing. This was a side of Cole she hadn't got to see in action, yet she wasn't surprised at how he dealt with urgent trauma.

Lifting Toby to his feet, she took his hand. 'Come on. Let's get you out of here. Watch your head on those boards.' She had to crawl along behind him to avoid banging her skull. Talking nonstop kept her moving, and Toby not looking around at the disaster surrounding them. She was relieved to see Karen had left, probably under protest, though she might've been willing to accompany Callum and try to make him relax more.

'Sis, who've you got?'

'Toby. No serious injuries, though best he goes to hospital for a thorough check-up. His case isn't urgent; he can wait for his other brother.'

'What's happening in there?'

'Cole needs another ambulance fast. A helicopter would be even better. Also a stretcher. Or a plank if there isn't one,' she improvised. 'Lucas is in a bad way.'

Damon nodded. 'I figured. I've talked to Search and Rescue and they're doing their damnedest to get transport here for the boys. The helicopters were temporarily grounded but they're about to fly again. Apparently, the rain's eased somewhat, though it's impossible to believe that from where we're standing.'

'Right, where do we put Toby while waiting for transportation? I need to get back to Cole and Lucas.'

'His mother's in that house down the drive. It's safe there, far enough away from any further slips, and not likely to be flooded. You take him down while I find something to carry Lucas out on.'

'Right.' It wasn't totally dark. She could manage. If she didn't think about slithering bodies on the ground. 'Lift Toby onto my back, will you? It'll be easier that way than if I have to keep looking out for obstacles for both of us.'

'Sure. And take this. I've got another.' Damon handed her a torch before swinging the boy onto her back. 'There you go, young man.'

As she started down the sodden track towards the house her brother stopped her.

'Stay down there, Vicki. I'll go in and help Cole with the last boy.'

She shook her head. 'I'll be back.' She wasn't going far from Cole for any longer than necessary.

'No, you won't. In the last few minutes there's been a couple of minor slips and we're acting on the side of caution. I don't want anyone else going into that wreck of a house who isn't absolutely essential to saving Lucas, and those in there are coming out fast, no matter what state the boy's in.'

The urgency in his voice made Vicki's stomach crunch tight. 'Why are you standing here talking to me then? Get in there now. Warn Cole, the others. No, I don't want you going in there either. It's dangerous.'

He wasn't listening to her, already facing the entrance the men had created.

She stood in the rain, her feet glued in the mud, her heart pounding and her breathing shallow. Hell, her body had been getting an internal workout since Cole had arrived. He and Damon were in danger. So were Toby's brother and one of the fire crew.

*Please be safe. Please. Please. Please.*

They couldn't have got this far with rescuing the family to have it go wrong now.

*Please.*

The sound of rocks rolling downhill broke into her pleas, sharpening her fear.

Someone scanned the hill side with a spotlight. 'Another small slip. That whole hill could go any minute.'

'What? *No.*'

'Hey, Vicki, that you? Get down to the house now. The boy needs to be out of the rain and safe. So do you.' Merv had returned.

'I'm not going anywhere until I see everyone come out of there.'

'Yes, you are. Think of your patient and what being out in this is doing to him. I'll make sure Cole joins you as soon as they're clear. We'll need to bring the third boy down there anyway. Now go.'

The thudding behind her ribs increased as she trudged through the water and mud, desperate not to slip, and turning every few steps to see if anyone had made it out yet. She wouldn't look at the hill, didn't want to see it come hurtling down on top of the ruin the previous slip had created. This time it would be on top of those she loved.

Banging on the open door of the house, Vicki called out, 'Hello. I've got Toby here. Is Karen about?' How was the woman managing with contractions and one son on the way to hospital and the other two hopefully follow-ing him soon?

'Come in. You must be the nurse. I'm Ester.' A middle-aged woman appeared before her. 'Here, let me take Toby. Hello, my darling, how are you?' She sent Vicki a ques-tioning look.

'He's fine, though we need him to go to hospital for a full check-up.'

'Toby,' Karen shrieked from the doorway. 'My boy, come here.' She scooped her son out of Ester's arms and hugged him tight, tears streaming down her face. 'Thank you, Vicki. I'm so glad you and Cole made it here. Who knows how we'd have managed without you.'

'Everyone's been working their butts off to save your family but, Karen, I have to warn you that Lucas has more serious injuries. Damon is working on getting him out of here and into hospital as soon as it's feasible. Cole also wants Toby to go with him, just to make sure he's as good as we think.'

Karen's knees sagged, then she drew a breath and straightened again. 'Can I go, too?'

'That will depend on the transport that can be ar-ranged.' Vicki ached for this brave mother. 'We'll get you there ASAP, I promise.' She changed the subject. 'How are those contractions coming along?' Fingers crossed they'd backed off.

'Picking up the pace.'

So her fingers were no use at all. 'It might be an idea if I examine you.'

'Soon. I want to hold Toby for a while.'

Heavy footsteps sounded at the front door, then Da-mon's voice called out, 'Hello, Ester. We're bringing Lucas inside.'

'Don't try and take your boots off. The carpet's a mess

already.' Ester rushed to make room in the lounge for the makeshift stretcher Cole and Damon were carrying in.

Cole looked around, his face tense until his eyes lighted on Vicki. 'Hey,' was all he said, but the simple word held a wealth of care.

He loved her. Nothing had changed there. She'd known that all along, even when she'd been trying to justify leaving and heading away while she came to terms with her life and what she'd do next. 'Hey, yourself.'

His face softened, and his lips turned up into a smile all for her.

She gave him one back, love warming her throughout. 'How's Lucas?'

The smile slipped.

That bad, huh? Her smile faded too. 'Damon, any luck with the helicopter?'

'It's coming, but will have to land on the other side of the flood waters, especially now there're more slips occurring. The houses further along have been evacuated but if we can avoid them being bowled over then we will. Merv's going to take the boys across one at a time in a motorised dinghy.'

'I'll go with them if they don't send a doctor,' Cole announced to the room in general.

Vicki saw Karen stiffen.

'I want to go,' the boys' mother cried out.

'There won't be room for anyone else in the chopper,' Damon told her briskly. 'I'm sorry. It's more important for a doctor to accompany the boys.'

'We've asked for the ambulance to come for you, Karen,' Cole said. 'But it could be some time off. There's a high demand for more urgent cases at the moment.

Vicki will stay with you in the meantime. And me, if I'm not required to go in the chopper.'

Again tears steaked down Karen's face. 'I tried phoning Arlo but got no answer. I need him. The boys need him.'

'Keep trying,' Cole said. But it wasn't Karen he was looking at. It was Vicki.

She felt it a punch in her chest. Longing soared. Likewise relief. Cole understood Karen's despair because he'd heard it all before. But did he really understand? Properly? Fully? Did he get that unless things changed and he discussed future plans with her, made sure they were on the same page, wanted similar things, they weren't going anywhere together? She deflated like a balloon stabbed with a pin. So far they hadn't achieved much when it came to resolving their differences, and it looked like they wouldn't be getting home where they could talk together any time soon. There was a badly injured boy in the room, not to mention a baby on its way. 'Karen's definitely in labour.'

Surprisingly, Cole grinned. 'Why wouldn't she be? It's the way the night's going.'

Karen grimaced at him. 'All very well for you to be cheerful.'

'I'm not really,' Cole said apologetically. 'But I'm grateful you're all out of that building and the boys will be taken care of in hospital. Is there someone you can call to be with them until you get there?'

'My in-laws. They won't hesitate. I'll phone them.' Then Karen's face scrunched up with pain, and she clasped her stomach with the hand that wasn't holding onto Toby.

Vicki was with her instantly. 'Breathe. That's it. You're

doing well. Hey, Toby, do you want to give Ester a hug?'
Thankfully, the little boy reached across to Ester's open
arms, giving his mother room to move.

'Tell me when it stops. I'm going to time the next
contraction.'

'They're about seven minutes apart,' Karen gasped.
'I don't believe this. Where the hell are you, Arlo?' She
stared at Vicki. 'Okay, it's going away.'

Glancing at her phone, Vicki noted the time. 'Think
I should examine you now.'

'Hang on.' Karen held her phone to her ear. 'Arlo, call
me as soon as you hear this. We've got problems. Big
ones. The house has gone. The boys are going to hospital. And the baby's coming. We need you. Love you.'

Vicki sucked in a breath, and glanced at Cole. She
hadn't ended her call to him that night of the miscarriage
with an 'I love you'. No, she'd said she'd had enough,
couldn't do it any more. Her gut churned. How soon could
they get away from here? More than anything else she
wanted to talk with Cole, explain her feelings and find out
more about his own needs, find a way out of this together.

An array of emotions crossed his face as he watched
her. Sadness, sorrow, disbelief all mixed up there. Similar
sentiments to those slamming around her skull.

Guilt battled with her sadness. She hadn't uttered
those three special words to him once since that night.
Not when he'd been listening, anyway. She'd been afraid
he'd see right through her attempt to stand up for herself. Though often in the middle of the night, when she
couldn't sleep and her pillow was drenched with tears,
she'd cried out how much she loved him.

In the beginning Cole had regularly told her he loved
her, but as the months had passed he'd said it less often,
until finally he'd stopped altogether.

Why hadn't she kept her mouth shut and held those terrible words inside? Or at least stopped long enough to think about what Cole had to be feeling about the miscarriage? Right from then they should've talked about it. It would've been easier without these past months hanging between them when she'd disappeared to the other side of the world, and he'd been fighting to get back on his feet while still occasionally talking to her as though she hadn't done something so horrible to him.

Yes, she had been selfish, and it had taken Karen's reaction to her husband not being there when she needed him so desperately to see that. Did that mean she'd go back to Cole without talking about their futures? Did it? No. She couldn't do that either.

'Are we going to get some time to ourselves?'

He nodded. 'Yes. Definitely.' He turned to focus on Lucas, though there was little to be done. A fully equipped operating room was required. In the meantime, Cole would do everything possible to keep the boy stable while they waited for the rescue flying machine to arrive.

'What are the chances of a doctor being on board the chopper?' she asked. Usually there would be, but who knew tonight when the rescue service was in high demand?

Cole answered without looking up. 'I told Damon one was necessary and Headquarters confirmed they'd send someone from the rescue centre. Otherwise I'll go with him and one of the paramedics might have to walk home.'

'That'll make you popular.' Disappointment flared. So far everything had worked against them.

'I figure, but too bad. This wee man comes before egos. Though, seriously, if they have to they'll probably squeeze all of us on board and it will be me walking back here. Not the other way round.'

'You could stay with my in-laws,' Karen said from the other side of the room.

No, he couldn't. He had to get back somehow. Vicki swallowed the expanding disappointment, and gave in to the urge to be *with* him. She was tied in knots of desire, and it was getting close to impossible to ignore them with each passing hour. Not that sex had been on the agenda this weekend. Not unless they suddenly made everything go away and were happy. They'd worked well together with all the injured people they'd been with, which went to show they were still in sync on some things, but it wasn't anywhere near enough. They'd be in sync in bed, for sure. The heat in her veins dissipated, replaced with sadness.

Cole was telling Karen, 'I'm here to spend time with my wife so I'll find a way back to Palm Beach no matter what.'

Her heart melted. Maybe giving in and following him wherever he chose to go next, get a job and have all the spare time available to spend with him—if he was around and not off on some medical project or working every hour available in a hospital or clinic—was the right thing to do.

Looking at him, she couldn't help but smile. He was gorgeous. The almost five years they'd been together hadn't changed her feelings. That physical attraction that had had her falling into bed with him the very first time they'd met still hummed in her veins. That instant rapport and understanding of each other still lit up her mind, and other parts of her body. Combine everything and no wonder she'd fallen head over heels in an instant and not once had come up for air—until the miscarriage.

She had lost a lot of time with Cole so he could follow his career choices, and mostly she'd coped by working long hours and surrounding herself with friends, not acknowledging that unsettling feeling she was missing out on so much. Until the last year when too much had gone so wrong and her world had rolled over. Julie had even asked if she was depressed, but she was certain she wasn't. Now Cole was here, and so far refused to let her walk away without a fight. Typical Cole. And one of the qualities she admired about him, she reminded herself.

'Cole?' she called quietly. 'We'll get time to ourselves, I promise.'

He grinned his special just-for-her grin. 'As long as nature backs off and gives us a break.'

'We'll hide up in the folks' house and ignore any more knocking or phone calls.'

'As if either of us would do that.'

'True,' she sighed. 'Let's hope—'

'Ahh…' Karen groaned, cutting through their moment. 'That hurts. Like a knife in my belly.'

Vicki nodded. Interruptions were the way of things tonight. 'I wouldn't know what that felt like.' Her smile dipped. She would if she hadn't lost the baby. Don't go there. Not now. There was enough drama going on without thinking about her own problems. 'Your contractions are now at six minutes. Long way to go yet.'

'Thanks for nothing.' Karen grimaced. 'Cole, how's Lucas?'

'No change. Which is better than him getting worse.'

'I can't complain about you not giving it to me straight,' Karen muttered. 'So what's taking so long with that helicopter?'

'There's a bit of a storm going on out there.' Cole leaned over Lucas and listened to his breathing. Hopefully, his mother didn't notice the unease creeping into Cole's demeanour.

Damon walked into the room. 'Right, we need to get Lucas and Toby across to the other side now. The chopper's minutes away. Cole, we want you to go with them in the boat. Merv will take you and both boys. It'll be a tight fit but the pilot doesn't want to stay on the ground any longer than he has to. Vicki, you okay holding the fort here?'

'We'll manage. Cole? If you end up going to Cairns Hospital with the boys, don't do anything risky to get back.'

*Get back quickly, so I know you're all right, but don't put yourself in danger.*

'We'll see that he gets a lift with one of the crews if necessary. Is Lucas ready?' Damon asked her man.

'Yes.' Cole stood up and crossed to Vicki. 'I'll be back as soon as possible.' His mouth brushed a light kiss on her cheek. 'Look after yourself.'

'You, too.' Her knees softened, and she stepped closer, felt his warmth and strength. Oh, Cole. 'Hurry back.' Be safe and sensible, *and* hurry back. She kissed him back, longer and deeper. Now who needed to be sensible?

Relief soared when Cole gingerly stepped out of the dinghy on the other side of the flood waters and heard a woman in dark blue overalls say to him, 'You Cole Halliday? I'm Bridget Ford, emergency doctor for the rescue services. I understand we've got a stat two patient?'

He'd get to spend the rest of the night with Vicki. 'I'm Cole. The seriously injured patient is ten-year-old Lucas. He was unconscious when the crew got to him, and there's been no change in the time I've spent with him. Suspected internal bleeding in the abdominal area. Fractured leg, and possibly ribs. Trauma to the skull.' Relief was still running through him. For Lucas and the medical help he desperately needed, and for himself because he wasn't flying to the hospital. Vicki's softening towards him had started a flutter in his chest that hadn't abated throughout the short ride in the boat watching over Lucas.

'Right, load and go,' Bridget said. 'We've got a stretcher ready at the back of the chopper. Bringing it to the boat meant getting it soaked and the boy already has enough to deal with.'

Cole held up a hand. 'There's also a second boy, Lucas's brother, Toby. He checks out fine, but I want him to go to hospital anyway.'

'We'll find room,' Bridget agreed.

Cole slung Toby onto his back and reached for one end of the makeshift stretcher in the boat. 'Ready, Merv?'

'Yes. On a count of three.'

Within moments Lucas was at the back of the rescue chopper and being swiftly but carefully transferred, and Cole waited until Bridget was ready to take Toby. Then he stepped back, letting the rescue medics take over and do their job. 'Good luck,' he called. Now he could return to Vicki. He'd be sharing her with a woman in labour desperate to get to her sons, but at least he'd be with her. His steps were jaunty as he turned back to the boat.

'Cole?' Bridget called. 'I've got a message for someone I think is with your lot. Karen?'

'Yes.' He nodded. 'The boys' mother. She's in labour.'

'Then you'd better pass this on.'

He listened carefully, nodded, and felt the familiar guilt kick in. 'That's great news.' News that Vicki would've wanted to hear the night she'd miscarried.

'You notice the rain's down to a drizzle?' Merv asked as they climbed back into the boat. He revved the motor and aimed for the lawn in front of the house they were using.

Cole looked up and laughed as his vision blurred with water. 'That was dumb.' He blinked the rain out of his eyes. 'But I think you're right. How long will it take for this new river to go down?'

'If we don't get another deluge I reckon less than twenty-four hours.'

'Now all we have left to do is get Karen out of here.' Cole looked around and was shocked to realise that the sky was lightening. The night was over. What a night it had been. Nothing like he'd expected when leaving Sydney yesterday. Yet he didn't feel any regret. This was why he'd studied medicine in the first place, to help those in dire situations. Okay, some regret, because he and Vicki hadn't had a lot of time alone together, and they definitely needed to. But it could be that just being together, working with their patients, had been good for them. They'd seen another side to each other. They hadn't argued, or withdrawn into themselves.

'Cole,' Vicki called from the house. 'Want to give me a hand? A baby's about to arrive.'

Wow. No matter how bad things got, there were the wonderful moments too. 'Coming. Those contractions sped up?'

'Karen suddenly had a huge meltdown. She needs to be with her boys, and wants her husband here, not in Western Australia. Then baby started getting on with the process, like it's got the message that Mum needs someone of her own right now.'

He couldn't help himself. He wound an arm around his wife's shoulders, hugged her lithe body in against him. Wonderful. Happiness rose, filled him. He was holding Vicki. She'd probably step away in a moment but he'd take what he could get. 'I've got news for her,' he said, breathing deep to savour Vicki's sweet fragrance. He'd missed talking to her, sharing jokes and laughter, and lying in bed with their bodies entwined. 'Good news.'

'Has Lucas come round?' Vicki asked, glancing up at him.

'I wish.' He also wished he could read total uncompromised love in those beautiful eyes. But he couldn't. Wasn't quite sure what he was seeing. Still with his arm around her, he took Vicki inside.

'Karen's in the first bedroom down the hall.'

'Right.' The moment he saw Karen, he said, 'I've been told to let you know that your husband is on his way from Perth right now. The reason you weren't getting through to him was because he's in the air, heading east. He heard about the flooding from his parents hours ago.'

'You're sure?' Hope flicked through her eyes.

'The message came via the rescue doctor from your in-laws. It's going to take time to get to Cairns as he couldn't get the flights he needed.'

'He's coming. That's all that matters. Thank you so much.' Some of the anxiety left her tight face. 'That's wonderful.'

Vicki slipped from under his arm, nodding. 'It is. Now you can relax and let this little one make a grand entrance, then you'll have something to show off to your man when he gets to town.' Her voice was clipped, filled with an emotion Cole didn't like. Sadness. And loneliness.

'I'm sorry,' he said quietly. 'It won't happen again.'

# CHAPTER EIGHT

'IT WON'T HAPPEN AGAIN,' Cole repeated under his breath.

He'd never meant anything so much other than telling Vicki he loved her. He used to tell her often, it hadn't been something to be reticent about. It was true, so therefore he told her regularly. Except not for a long time prior to the miscarriage, and definitely not during the last few phone conversations. The atmosphere had become uncomfortable, making him feel if he uttered those words once more she'd think he was deliberately trying to get her onside without going over what had pushed them apart in the first place.

Vicki was too busy taking obs on Karen to give him a smile. Deliberately too busy? Her focus was completely on her patient, though he saw worry filter through her gaze.

'Here we go again.' Karen stood awkwardly and reached for Vicki's hands, clinging to them as the contraction tore through her belly. 'Getting worse.'

'Getting closer.' Vicki smiled tightly. 'I need to re-examine you, see what's going on.'

'The baby's coming, that's what's happening,' Karen growled through gritted teeth.

'Then let's find out where he's at,' Vicki suggested in

a firm, don't-argue tone. 'What is it with you and boys anyway? Haven't you heard of girls?'

Karen relaxed a little and sank onto the bed that had been made available by Ester. 'Everyone asks me that, but I'm happy with my sons. It's never bothered me not having a daughter. It's easier having them all the same sex. Though Arlo would've liked a girl. He'd have spoilt her rotten. Oh, that's too soon.' Her face scrunched up in agony and her hands clasped together around her belly.

'Hopefully, this will be over quickly,' Cole said. 'Do you want me here, or should I go look busy elsewhere?'

'You can stay. Though Vicki's doing a great job.'

Vicki chuckled. 'It's you doing all the work and making things easier.'

'Lots of practice,' Karen grunted. 'I swear this is the last time. Four kids are enough.'

'When the contraction ends, can you lie back and let me see if baby's head's crowning?' Vicki slipped gloves on and handed Cole a pair. 'You up to date with deliveries?'

He was back in favour, as a doctor if nothing else. Then she smiled at him, and his heart turned to mush. More than a doctor then. 'Not a lot of those in the army, but who can forget the amazement of a new baby? I'll never forget the first birth I witnessed as a trainee. The most fantastic experience.'

'I know what you mean.' Her smile remained so she wasn't thinking about the baby they'd lost. 'Sometimes I wonder if I should've done midwifery, but then I think how much I enjoy what I do and it's all good. More variety.'

His heart did a happy dance. For now all was good in his world. 'You ready for this, Karen?'

'As long as you're going to tell me you can see baby.'

'We'll do our best,' he agreed. 'Have you and Arlo chosen a name yet?'

'We've always waited until we've met our boys before deciding on one. I don't know if it's about finding a name that suits or about not wanting to jinx anything, but that's how it's been from when I was pregnant with Lucas.' Mentioning her eldest brought the tears on, and her bottom lip was in danger of being torn by her teeth.

Vicki was quick to take her hands. 'Come on. He's tough. You told me that yourself. His grandparents are at the hospital and shortly all the boys will be there. Soon their dad will be too. The doctors will be doing everything possible to make Lucas well.'

'I—know,' Karen hiccupped. 'But I feel so useless right now. *I'm* his mother. I should've been able to save him from getting hurt. Same for Toby and Callum. Instead I was in the room that suffered the least damage.'

Cole locked a firm gaze on her. 'No one knew that hill would come down, let alone which building it would hit. Certainly, no one had a clue which rooms it would take out. Spare yourself this agony and concentrate on getting your new wee man safely out into the world. All right?'

'Yes.' She swallowed hard. 'I needed that.'

'No problem. We understand what you're going through, but the best thing you can do is stay focused on what's happening here. Once baby's born we can concentrate on getting you both to hospital to join your family.'

Vicki nodded, and moved closer to him, reached for his glove-covered hand, gave him a squeeze. 'You're right. About everything you mentioned.'

As in they both understood Karen's pain? Yes, they did. It had been a different scenario but the pain of not being there for each other had been real. He squeezed back, wishing he had time to hug Vicki tight. Unfortunately, there was a baby waiting to introduce himself to his mother and that really was as important right now. He gave her one anyway, smiled when she leaned into him briefly.

Vicki said to Karen, 'I'll take a look now.'

It didn't take a second to understand that baby was well and truly on his way, Cole saw. 'You're about to become a mum again. Push, Karen.'

'Strange but I haven't felt the need to do that yet.'

'Maybe not, but give it your best shot.'

He watched Vicki encouraging Karen to push harder. She was gentle and compassionate, yet not letting Karen off doing the hard work required.

Within minutes the room was filled with a delightful cry that tugged at Cole's heartstrings. One day he would be a dad. When Vicki had told him she was pregnant he'd been ecstatic. They were going to be parents, raise their own child, love him or her to bits, share the good and bad times, always be there to support him or her through everything the world threw their way. Believe in their honesty.

Then the dream had imploded. It was a common occurrence for parents-to-be, but not once had he realised how devastating it would be when it happened to them. He'd buried the despair while in hospital and only recently had he taken out the anguish of the miscarriage and thought it through. It hurt, but not as much as losing Vicki would.

'Let me hold him,' Karen squealed, holding her arms out to take the precious bundle he held in his large hands, making the tiny tot look even smaller.

He didn't want to let the baby go, wanted to feel the warm, wriggling body in his palms. Of course he handed him over, watched Karen snuggle her new son against her breasts. One day. He glanced sideways and saw the amazed expression on Vicki's face. Reaching for her hand again, he gave another squeeze. Definitely one day.

When she leaned close to lay her head against his shoulder he couldn't hold back a smile. Or the kiss he dropped on her forehead. This felt right, just like them, and encouraged him to think all was not lost.

'We know how to pick our weekend, don't we?'

Vicki dropped her sodden jacket on the laundry floor, then shucked out of her shorts. Not a good idea, if that gleam in Cole's eyes meant what she thought it did. Why would she be wrong, having seen it often in the past? Too late. She wasn't going to pull the pants back on. That would only make them both more aware of each other.

*Who am I kidding? I couldn't be more conscious of Cole if I tried.*

So she had to divert his interest. 'Here's hoping the rest of today and tomorrow are ours to use as we choose.'

Going by the way Cole's eyes widened, that wasn't working as a distraction. Seemed he had ideas about how he wanted to use their time together. 'Yeah, I'm hoping we've done our bit for the community. I'd like to spend time with you and no one else.'

'Me, too,' she admitted, remembering the gentle kiss on her forehead that had turned her toes to mush. 'But I confess I'm exhausted.' She'd had very little sleep the night before last, none last night, her nerves on edge for days over Cole coming, and there wasn't much oomph left inside her. Seriously? When the man of her heart stood before her? What was wrong with her? They still had a few problems yet to sort out. Her shoulders slumped. 'I'm going to have a shower, then some breakfast. Or lunch,' she added after seeing her mother's ancient wall clock showing ten forty-five.

'So am I,' he agreed, his eyes finally settling back to normal and a smile appearing. 'Let's go with brunch. Covers all the bases.'

'Sounds good.' Especially if Cole was cooking. Was she wrong to leave the order of things the same, or should she be stepping up more? The problem was she liked slipping back into their routine. It gave her confidence they'd work everything out in a good way. 'Where did the hours go?'

'Into boys and a baby, and hanging around waiting to get out of the place.'

'There was a time I started to wonder if we'd ever be brought back over to our side.' They'd waited more than an hour to be brought across the flood waters and driven home.

'You don't think Damon or Merv would've left you there any longer than they had to, do you?' Cole smiled. 'Not when Damon was on edge about you being anywhere near that moving hillside.'

'True. I suppose that second house getting swamped with mud and water ruined his plans for excavating us sooner rather than later.' Cole was still staring at her like he'd forgotten what her legs looked like. Grabbing a towel off the shelf, she wrapped it around her waist, and smiled to herself when he sucked a breath and looked away.

'I'm glad we were able to help those people, but I'm hoping that's the end of it this weekend.' Was it selfish to think she'd rather have spent time with Cole, sorting out their differences? Probably, but it showed she was human, didn't it?

'You're a confident nurse, and the patients respond well to you.'

Wow. A low laugh bubbled through her, followed by a wave of warmth that wrapped around her heart. 'I could say the same about you, Doctor. We did well in a tough situation. That house gave me the creeps. I kept hearing the walls and roof creaking and cracking, and expected it to drop on my head any moment.'

'The guys did a good job of shoring it up, at least for long enough to evacuate the family. Who knows what state the house will be in later today.'

'It's an insurance job, that one.'

'There'll be a few of those after this.' Cole ran his finger across her chin. 'I did enjoy being with you, despite the circumstances. We still fit well together.'

She locked her eyes with his steady, endearing gaze. 'You're right.' She swayed towards him, and couldn't find the brakes to stop. Lifting her arms, she wound them around his neck. 'It's been quite a night.' She had no idea where she was, other than holding Cole, being so close to him, needing him. Loving him.

His head came closer, his lips brushing hers before whispering, 'Vicki, love.' Then he was kissing her, deeply, lovingly.

Rising onto her toes, she pushed against his chest, kissed him back, her tongue darting into his mouth to taste. She had missed this, him, so much it had hurt. And heated her blood as she continued to return his kisses. 'Cole,' she murmured against his mouth as his hands spread across her waist.

He lifted her, sat her on top of the washing machine, pushed his hips between her legs, and continued kissing, continued ramping up her desire, turning her body into an inferno of need. This was them. This was how they'd got back together every time he'd been away.

This was bad timing. They hadn't resolved a thing

yet, and as much as making love would be wonderful, it might make keeping on track that much harder. Reluctance warred with need as she pulled her mouth away. She so didn't want to stop. But she had to if she was to be true to herself. Which she had to be. Or else lose everything. 'Cole.'

His eyes flew open, dark and excited with lust. 'Sweetheart?'

'I'm sorry.'

He blew out a lungful of air and stared at her, his disappointment so strong she nearly changed her mind. 'Me, too.' He didn't drop his hands from her waist straight away, stood there, holding her, watching her with such tenderness in his gaze she felt tears building up.

As she opened her mouth to apologise again, he placed a finger on her lips.

'Don't. You're right. We've some things to resolve first.' Then he brushed a light kiss on her cheek. 'But I'd be lying if I said I didn't enjoy that and wasn't hanging out for more.'

He knew how to make her feel better about what she'd done. She blinked, risked a smile. 'It's not just in the medical field we work well together.'

His eyes widened and he actually laughed. 'Never a truer word. Here...' He lifted her down. 'Go get out of the rest of those wet clothes and take a shower.'

'More water? Just what I need.' She grinned. Somehow she was comfortable, despite what had just gone down. 'See you in the kitchen soon.' She wasn't about to say that if she didn't make it to brunch he'd better look for her as she might be asleep in the shower. After that kiss, he'd be there before the water got warm, let alone cold again. She'd not be able to stop him. How she'd pulled away at all stumped her. She'd been ready for Cole to make love to her, to give back as good as she got.

Glancing outside, she saw that the sun was heading up the sky, peeking through gaps in the clouds, trying its best to turn the gloom into refreshing light. The rain had eased to a heavy drizzle, but Damon had warned the monsoon might not be over, could be gathering strength for a final deluge. There was water every darned where. Roads, parks and fields were drowned. Here at Palm Beach homeowners had been lucky so far. No buildings were flooded. Once the storm was over, it would take days for the area to dry out. Weather like this was one of the few aspects of living in Northern Queensland she hadn't missed when she'd headed south to Sydney.

Under a cool temperature in the shower she scrubbed mud off all her skin that had been exposed throughout the night, and some that hadn't. How had it got under her bra and waistband? When she shampooed her hair, brown suds filled the shower base. Hopefully, there was some softening element in mud that was good for skin and hair. Bending her head under the shower head, she leaned against the wall and let the warm water rinse her hair thoroughly. One yawn followed another, and another.

She would fall asleep if she wasn't careful. Then Cole would come to find her. That was not happening. Pushing the lever off, she reached for her towel. Had a moment where she imagined Cole handing it to her. Her eyes snapped open. Nope. She was alone.

Wrapping the towel around her, she dashed to the bedroom and thought about diving under the covers, but the smell of frying bacon coming from down the hall was too tantalising to be ignored. Pulling on shorts and tee shirt, she began brushing the tangled knots out of her hair. Hopefully, it would dry before she hit the sack because she couldn't be bothered getting out the dryer and styling the long, straight cut. If it looked too bad when she got up later she'd deal to it then.

'How many eggs?' Cole called from the other side of the bedroom door.

'Two.'

'Going on now.'

'I'm coming.'

Were they going to have a relaxed brunch? She hoped so. Spending time together working with people who needed their medical skills had done wonders to her stress levels. She could see herself living with Cole again with certain changes. Long talks with Julie had opened her eyes beyond the wake-up call her mother had given her. Until that time with her sister, Vicki hadn't understood why Julie had deliberately gone so far away so as not to repeat their mother's life.

*And now I have to stick to my guns and do the same.*

'Take a load off.' Cole pointed to a comfy cane chair in the covered outdoor area near the barbecue.

'I'll make some tea first.' That thick cushion looked tempting, but once she sank into it she'd not want to get up again.

'All done. Here.' He handed her a brimming mug.

'You must've had a quick shower to have got all this ready.' There was cutlery and plates, sauces and seasonings on the table. Bacon sizzled alongside the hash browns and tomatoes, eggs and mushrooms were coming up to speed on the second hot plate. She should've been getting everything ready while Cole cooked, not lazing in the shower.

Cole grinned. 'Thought I was going to have to come in with a bucket of icy water to wake you up.'

'That would not have won you any favours.' She

laughed, relaxing some more. Sitting, she sipped the tea. 'I suppose the next thing will be to get out and help people clean up the debris from yards where the waters have gone through.'

'That won't begin until the flood's receded. A couple of days away, I imagine. It's going to be a busy time for everyone.' Cole began filling a plate with the most delicious-smelling food she'd had in a long time.

'I've always been amazed at how quickly everyone gets back to normal. Except for those whose properties are damaged, of course. Still haven't heard from Phil. The boys in blue must be busy.'

Cole placed a laden plate on the table in front of her. 'Here you go. Get that into you.'

'Yummy. Thanks.'

'I have my uses.'

Her face heated. The number of times he'd said that to her over the years. It usually referred to time in bed, and nothing to do with sleeping. Concentrating on eating, Vicki managed to avoid looking directly at her husband until images of them making love finally faded. All she had to do was reach across the gap between them and entwine her fingers with his, and they'd be heading down the hall. Maybe getting up close and sexy would help, and they could laugh for getting so stressed about their marriage.

'Hey, don't go to sleep in your brunch,' Cole goaded her deliberately. 'Egg on face is not pretty.'

Sleep was the last thing on her mind. Unfortunately. She glanced across the table, and sighed at Cole's cheeky grin. 'Then you'd better wipe your chin.'

He did, then laughed when he saw there was nothing on the napkin. 'Wretch.'

'Don't you forget it.' She pushed her empty plate aside. 'Just what the doctor ordered.'

'Just what the doctor cooked, you mean.'

'And that.'

Cole wiped his plate clean and leaned back in his chair. He nodded in the direction of the lounge. 'I like that painting of the Daintree. It's new, isn't it?'

'It's one of Mum's. She's getting better with each painting. I can't wait to see what she brings back from this trip.'

'Anna's painting while on the road?'

'She's working on a series of coastal pictures. Mostly she's taking a million photos and notes to use when she's back home.' Pride filled Vicki. Her mother was already achieving recognition. 'The city gallery wants to put on a small show of her work next year and she's panicking about getting enough done. Says she'll lose her edge if she rushes the work. I don't believe she will. It's like a tap's been turned on and there's no stopping her.'

'I can't believe she's waited so long to get back into following her passion,' Cole commented.

*I can. And if I'm not careful I'll have the same regrets when I reach my fifties. Agency, here I come.*

'At least she's doing it now.'

Her contribution towards getting her mother started must've helped. The day she'd put that easel, those paints and brushes in the lounge, ready for when her mother came home, she'd waited with a beating heart, afraid of having done the wrong thing, and that her mother might tell her off for raising her hopes. But when her mother had picked up a brush, a look of wonder on her face, she'd known she'd got it right. Then denial had hit and instantly Vicki had stepped up and pressed the brush firmly back into her mum's hand and wrapped her fingers around the handle.

*You can do it, Mum. You have to. And so can I.*

'Why did she wait so long?'

'Four kids and Dad's demanding medical practice, I guess.'

*I know.*

'I get that, but couldn't she have found some time for herself? A few hours here and there between washing the dirty clothes and baking the biscuits?'

'Cole, that sounds like it was a hobby to fill in spare time. Mum has a special talent, and she did not want to give it a nodding glance. It was all or nothing, and because she'd committed to Dad and us it became nothing.'

'My mother was a bit like that too. Must be a generational thing.' He gathered up their plates and stood. 'Want more tea?'

'I'll get it, and clean up.' Wasn't that how she used to respond?

'Stay there. You look whacked.'

'Okay, thanks.' That was better. Whacked didn't describe how she felt. Behind the eyes there was a battle going on between falling asleep and telling Cole what she thought about his comment. 'It was quite a night.' Generational thing, like hell. He really didn't get what her mother had given up for her family. And if his mother had done the same, no wonder he'd thought it was normal. She hadn't done anything different to show she wasn't sitting around not getting on with her dreams either. 'So, back to full-time medicine, huh?'

A full mug appeared before her. 'Like I said, I'd like to go into general practice, leave the emergency scene behind. I've seen enough to know I'd prefer being in a position where I get to know my patients a little.' Cole began wiping down the barbecue. 'To have the whole picture, understand what drives them, how they live, where they work. Know the whole family. That sort of thing.'

'The complete opposite from working in ED then.' Her agency would hire out temps to his practice. Her mouth tipped into a small smile. This could work. She yawned. It was unbelievable how tired she felt. Another yawn. The tea warmed her even though she wasn't cold. Or was that Cole's presence? 'I've got some ideas for my career I'm working on that's different to what I've been doing, too.'

'Not retraining as a midwife? I didn't think you wanted to do that.'

'No. I'm looking at setting up my own nursing agency.' She held her breath, waiting for the quiz.

'You'd be good at that, organising people to do jobs, keeping staff busy and happy, getting them on board in the first place.' Cole nodded as he lowered the hood of the barbecue.

*Knock me down.*

'You were supposed be shocked and tell me I'm nuts.' Instead she was the one shocked.

He smiled. 'I figured.' Then he came over to drop into the seat opposite her.

'I've always thought about one day having my own agency, but I put it on hold when we married. Then one week last year when we were so busy at the emergency department, everyone doing extra shifts because there was a staff shortage due to a viral outbreak in the city, I started thinking about it again.'

'Don't the agencies already out there provide enough nurses?'

'It'll be a challenge, but it's one I want to do. I feel this is something I would be good at.' She stared at Cole. 'It's not a pipe dream. I've been looking into all the aspects a business like that requires. I can do it.'

'I believe you can, too.'

'Really?'

'Really.'

He still hadn't asked why she hadn't mentioned it before. Were they more alike than she'd realised? Vicki gasped. Yes, they were. Here she'd been getting upset because he hadn't told her about the accident and yet she'd kept the agency idea to herself after that one time years ago.

*That was slightly different.*

She hadn't started it up yet. The plans were coming together but she hadn't put anything in place to shackle him with. If she'd been open, would he have been more so about his accident? And other things? Something else she'd probably never have an answer to. 'You don't remember me mentioning it years ago?'

Looking baffled, Cole shook his head. 'No, I don't.'

Just as she'd thought. 'Maybe I should've reminded you.'

'Let's not argue over this. The important thing is I now know and can support you.'

Gulp. It was that simple? Go with it. 'Thanks, da— Cole.' She nearly said *darling*. Actually, now that she'd got the agency thing out in the open, maybe she should've. He wasn't running for the hills, or telling her it was all impossible because it wouldn't fit in with his plans. Things were looking up.

# CHAPTER NINE

VICKI HAD BEEN thinking about setting up her own agency? For that long? Cole shook his head to clear the surprise. He hadn't had a clue that she might want to do something different, especially starting her own business. She loved nursing, always said it kept her grounded in reality with the wonderful and awful cases she'd worked. 'What about nursing? If you're running an agency there won't be time for any of that.'

'At first I'll still be working. I'll need the money, and I won't be as busy as you're suggesting. It's going to take time to establish my name and get medical centres to call me instead of their usual source of temporary nurses.'

She wasn't acting overly confident, but seemed to have worked out some of the pitfalls at least. A good sign. 'Don't worry about start-up money. We'll sort that between us.' Why hadn't she mentioned it way back before they'd begun falling apart?

Embarrassment crept across Vicki's face. 'It wasn't a hint for you to help me out.'

'Didn't cross my mind you'd stoop to that. It's a genuine offer.' He wasn't asking if she wanted him on board with this, or with their marriage. He would continue to believe in them and act accordingly unless she put the brakes on. Then he'd fight tooth and nail for what they'd once had.

'Thanks.' The embarrassment deepened, her cheeks reddening.

'Vicki, we can make this work. I mean everything.'

She nodded. 'We were once strong together. Seems we've got a little lost this past year, but hopefully nothing we can't fix with a little patience.' She was drawing circles on the tabletop with her forefinger, getting faster all the time. 'I'm not going to change my mind about this agency, Cole. I want to achieve something for myself, something to be proud of.'

'Then you will. There's nothing stopping you.'

*Especially not me.*

Where did she want to set this up? Here in Cairns with her family nearby, or back in Sydney where they owned an apartment and their closest friends resided? Where they'd established their life after marrying? Except he hadn't been there often enough. What about the job he was close to obtaining? Nothing seemed straightforward.

Surprise replaced her embarrassment. 'You think?'

Ouch. 'Don't you know I believe in you?'

'I think it's more that I don't believe in myself as much as I need to.'

'Where does that come from? You're always confident. Look how you've managed in Sydney while I've been away. That took guts and strength.'

Her head came up instantly, and the eyes that locked on him were glittery. 'It did, and it wasn't enough.'

They were back at the beginning. At why they'd got themselves into this mess. Reaching for her hands, he gripped tight. 'You became lonely. I get that, though you did a good job of hiding it from me in the early years.'

She nodded. 'At first it was fine. I managed, I was

supporting you, and I had friends to spend time with. Then the wheels started coming off, and I couldn't seem to stop the bus.'

'Nice way with words.' He smiled, though his heart was stuttering. He wanted to believe they were moving forward together, but he couldn't help the sense of not quite understanding everything she was telling him. For every step forward there was at least another one backwards. 'Where's the bus now?'

She pulled her hands free and leaned back. 'It's beginning to turn around.' Then her face collapsed, tearing him in two. 'Oh, Cole. What have we done?'

'Nothing that can't be fixed, sweetheart.'

'I hope you're right.'

That was the first hint she might want the same as he did. He wouldn't let the hope get out of control. 'I'm damned sure of it.' Lifting her hands again, he kissed her white knuckles. 'Promise.'

At last a smile crept over her mouth. 'I'll second that.' She slumped in her chair, as though all the energy had evaporated out of her. Not that she'd been hyperactive since they'd returned from helping Karen and her family.

A phone rang. 'That's mine,' Cole said, and dug it out of his pocket, in need of a break while he digested everything Vicki had hit him with. 'Hey, Nathan, how's things down there?'

Vicki sank further into her chair, her eyelids drooping. As though now she'd let out about the agency she could relax. 'Say hi to Molly for me.'

'More like, how's things up in Cairns?' Nathan asked. 'Apart from wet?'

'Busy.'

*Not in the way I'd expected.*

'Vicki and I were called out to an old guy who'd taken

a tumble off his ladder late yesterday, then we spent all night working with a family trapped in their house.' He went on to explain what had happened, and watched Vicki's eyes slowly closing and her chin dropping onto her sternum. She was shattered. It wasn't like her at all.

'Suppose that means you haven't had time to tell her your plans for down here,' Nathan said when he'd finished.

Crossing to the window, he stared out. Those plans were up in the air now, apart from the interview on Monday that might mean he had a position in a very good medical centre. He huffed out a deep breath. 'There hasn't been much time to sit down and go through whatever's bugging Vicki, apart from me being absent so much. At least she knows that's over for good.' He wasn't mentioning her nursing agency while he was still getting his head around it. 'She says hi to Molly, by the way.'

'Moll wants to talk to her when we're done.'

Cole looked back at his wife. 'Not happening. She's fallen asleep in the short time we've been talking.' What was left of her tea was in danger of spilling over her thighs. He stepped across to retrieve the mug, hoping not to wake her. She didn't move, even when he lifted her fingers from the handle. His heart lurched at the unguarded expression on her face. She looked so fragile. There were so many sides to this woman, and he loved them all. Right now he wanted to hold her and promise she was never going to have to worry about him letting her down again.

After finishing talking to Nathan, he headed down to Vicki's bedroom to pull back the covers on the bed. Returning, he scooped her up into his arms, ignoring the tug on his spine where a niggling ache still made itself known. Back in the bedroom he gently laid her down on her side and pulled the sheet up to her chin. Still she didn't move.

He stood watching her, feeling his love ballooning, filling him, making him believe the future would be great. They'd replace the apartment with a house and fill the bedrooms with kids. Get another dog. He'd make her happy.

What if she wouldn't have him back? What if the agency was to replace him? Something to keep her focused because she didn't believe he was home for good? Sydney or Cairns? The niggling questions sent a cold fear through him. It might be a short-lived belief their future was safe. But they had so much to give each other.

'Cole?' Vicki muttered in her sleep.

So she hadn't stopped thinking about him while she slept. 'I'm here, sweetheart.' But he'd head off for a snooze so that he'd be on full alert later when they sat down together. To talk about things like how soon could she join him in Sydney? If she was prepared to return there? Why not set up her business there where there was larger scope of medical places to work with?

'I love you, Vicki. Always have, always will.' His chest expanded, ignoring the caution that he might be rushing this. That he might've got it wrong, and there was a lot more Vicki wasn't happy about. Apart from him being away so much, especially when disasters had struck, she hadn't said anything else had been wrong with their relationship.

Sitting on the edge of the bed, he let the memories come. Their honeymoon in Rarotonga. The excitement when they'd bought the apartment and moved in with only a bed for furniture. Meeting Benji for the first time, and instantly falling in love with his big brown, beguiling eyes. Those plastic flowers. They had history; good, binding, loving history. Too much to let go.

Vicki rolled his way, muttering, 'Cole…' again.

He lay down beside her, not touching her, barely breathing, needing to be close, afraid she'd wake up and yell at him to get away.

But suddenly her arm was wrapping over his chest, and she shuffled closer so her head was against his arm. Carefully, so as not to wake her, he slid his hand into hers and breathed slowly. Damn, how he'd missed this. Another of those simple acts that held so much love and understanding. He relaxed as her scent reached him, and listened to her steady breathing. And continued delving through those memories. Enjoying the good times and ignoring the nagging feeling there was more bad to come. That he'd missed something important.

Vicki smiled as she slowly drifted awake. Everything felt right with her world. Cole's arm was tucked around her waist, his chest and stomach pressed against her back, his legs touching hers, as his light breaths tickled her neck. She savoured the moment. As she became aware of his arousal heat flooded her body, brought her to wide awake in an instant. 'Cole?' she whispered.

His arm tightened around her, and he kissed the back of her neck, setting her skin tight. 'Hey.'

She tried to roll over.

'Don't.' His mouth trailed further over her neck and to her shoulder.

Reaching behind, her hand found his hip and slid beyond to his butt, where her fingers worked their magic on his sexy, smooth skin. Against her backside Cole's arousal hardened. Then she attempted to push between them to wrap her hand around him.

'No,' he whispered. 'Let me make love to you first.' His hand caressed her breasts, first one until it ached, then the other, her nipples almost exploding with tension.

Somehow she managed to remove her clothes. Then she was pushing at Cole's shorts and finally he paused briefly to get rid of them before he returned to circling her nipple while his other hand cupped her sex. And took her straight to the edge. Typical, she acknowledged happily.

'Now. Hurry. I can't wait,' she gasped through the haze of need clawing through her. 'I want you.'

*I've never stopped wanting you.*

'I'm here, sweetheart.' And he was, entering her, hard and fast, and they were as one in the best way imaginable. Moving with abandon, Vicki let go all the restraints and worries of the previous months and joined Cole in just being them.

Her face split into a wide grin as she rolled onto her back and regained her breath. Over before they'd begun. Giving, taking, knowing which buttons to push. It was always like this the first time they made love when Cole came home. Later they'd do it again, except they'd take time to touch everywhere with fingers and tongues, building up the intensity, letting it roll through them in soft waves that slowly built up and up until neither could bear not having the release they sought.

Reaching out, she ran her hand down Cole's chest, over his abs and beyond. Hang on. What was that? Running her fingers over his abs again, then further to the side, she felt a ridge. A scar? One of his injuries?

She sat up, her mouth drying. There was a scar where his spleen had been removed. Trailing her gaze downward, she took in more harsh purple lines on his leg. Leaning closer, she gently ran her fingers over each.

'Cole, darling…'

Then she couldn't say any more, her throat blocked with the tears she fought not to shed, her heart beating against her ribs. What if the accident had been worse? What if—? What if a hundred things.

'Stop, Vicki. None of it happened. I'm here, and in relatively good nick.' He lifted her hand away and kissed her fingertips one at a time.

'But—' She should've been with him. Would've been. If he'd told her, asked for her.

*Woulda, shoulda, coulda.*

They couldn't go back and undo a thing. What had happened had happened. End of. But it wasn't. The glow receded.

'No buts. Like I said, I survived.'

Swinging her legs over the side of the bed, she stood and picked up her clothes. 'Thank goodness for that.'

Cole sat up, and reached for her. 'Stop torturing yourself, please.'

She stepped back. 'I'm trying but it's not as straightforward as I'd thought.' There were so many reasons for walking into his arms and moving on. But she was held back by nagging doubts she couldn't define. 'Where do we go from here, Cole? You say you want to be a GP. It's great you've got plans for your career, as I have.'

'We can support each other in these choices.'

She was hearing the man who didn't tell her everything. 'Have you been looking for a position?'

He stepped into his shorts and zipped them up. 'Yes. It filled in time while I was incapacitated. Neither did I want to sit around filling in crossword puzzles when I could be making major decisions about my career.'

Anger won out. 'Come on, Cole. Tell me what's going

on. At the moment it seems like nothing's changed. You're making plans without involving me.'

There was reciprocal anger in the eyes that locked on her. 'And you haven't done the same?'

A strange sense of almost relief hit her. At last he wasn't trying to placate her about everything, might finally be beginning to show what mattered to him. 'To a certain extent I have, yes.'

'You either have or haven't, Vicki.' He stepped past her through the doorway and headed down the hall.

Following, she ended up on the deck where he stood, hands on hips, staring out to the road, chin thrust forward. Wanting to escape her? Not until he told her what he had done about a job, he wasn't. Because now she suspected he'd already found a position somewhere in Sydney. Which was fine, if only they'd discussed it first. She should have some say in where they'd live if they were to remain married.

Suddenly, he spun around. 'Which is it, Vicki?'

It was her turn to stare out. The rain had eased even more, but the yard still looked like a toddler's paddling pool. 'Having my own agency is not negotiable.' Guess that sounded like she was doing her own thing without involving Cole.

*Well, aren't you?*

Her stomach churned. To think a short time ago they'd made love like they didn't have a problem between them. There wouldn't be the follow-up long and slow lovemaking session. Not yet, possibly never. 'I've looked into the financial side of setting it up here and in Sydney. Likewise the feasibility of employing nurses, and the medical centres and emergency rooms that might use my agency.'

'Where have you decided on?' he ground out.

'I haven't come to a final conclusion.' This was where

she should be saying she'd been waiting to talk to him about it and make a joint decision about where they lived. But she was equally riled up now. 'Cairns would be a lot easier. I know a lot of people here, whereas in Sydney—well, the population's enormous.'

'Why is this so important now? Why not four years ago when I signed up for the military and you apparently told me? That would've kept you busy and left no time to be lonely.'

'We were newlyweds and I was busy making a home for us and being there for you whenever you came home. Don't forget we were living in the married quarters until you went offshore the first time and I chose to return to our apartment.

'You could've run an agency from anywhere. Still can.' He wasn't buying it. Also ignoring the reminder she'd given.

'At the time I had my dream job in the emergency department so thought I'd wait a bit.'

'You—'

She stabbed the air between them with her finger. 'Hear me out. After the miscarriage I couldn't face going into the department every day, pretending all was fine in my world. It was nowhere near. By then I'd been looking into this idea of mine more thoroughly. When I got pregnant…' *gulp* '…it seemed a great way to still be actively working while at the same time being a stay-at-home mum. For once I was thinking about doing what was important for me. As well as you.'

'That sounds like an afterthought. You working while raising a child when I can afford for you not to work doesn't add up to me, and doesn't tie in with any ideas we had when we talked about having a family.' Cole was still watching her intently.

'What about my own self-worth? Doing something that I get enjoyment from? I don't want to get to my fifties and realise I haven't followed my dreams too.' She nodded. 'I know I'd get that from being a mum if I carried a baby to full term.' She hesitated. That was a question she'd refused to consider before. But seeing Cole's bewilderment at her ideas made her face up to reality.

Instantly, his expression softened. 'Miscarriages are common, and most women go on to have normal pregnancies.'

'The nurse in me knows that. The want-to-be mum has doubts.'

'A perfectly normal reaction.'

Her smile was tentative. Were they getting back on side? 'So I'm normal. Thank goodness for something.'

'Did I say that?' Cole smiled back. 'Not too normal. That'd be boring, and the last thing you are is boring.'

This was all very good but once again they hadn't finished the discussion that had started with what Cole had done about getting a position in a medical centre. 'Where do you intend working?'

'I'd thought Sydney because that's where we live. Lived.'

Nice to have mentioned it. 'Have you applied for a place yet?'

'I've got a third and, hopefully, final interview at a medical centre near Rose Bay first thing Monday morning. The partners have intimated the position will probably be mine. It's quite exciting, and so different from anything I've done before. We could find a house in the area, and even have a boat since the harbour's on the doorstep.'

Bang. Exactly as she'd thought. It was like a fist to the heart. Sydney, whether they agreed or not. Discussed it or not. Added in her requirements or not. Where was the heads together, talk about the pros and cons discussion? 'Did you come here to tell me you're going to live and work in Sydney regardless of what I thought?'

'Jeez, Vicki, give me a break here. I came because I love you and want to get back together.'

'In Sydney. Near Rose Bay, to be precise.'

'Yes, because that's where I'll probably have a job.' His excitement was waning. Beginning to understand she mightn't be rushing to join him wherever he chose. That the divorce was for real.

'Did it never occur to you to tell me what you were aiming for? Before you went to your first interview?'

'We hadn't been talking a lot.'

'That's pathetic, Cole. You never even tried to tell me. No wonder this isn't working. You still expect me to toe the line. Sure, I can have my own business—it just has to be where you decide.' She stared at him, shaking her head in frustration. 'I don't believe this.'

Yet she should. Nothing had changed. Not really, despite everything he'd said this weekend about them being together.

'Here I was, waiting until we'd worked out if we were still together and then where *we'd* live before making my final decision on where to set up the agency, and all the while you've gone ahead with your own plans. That's not togetherness, Cole. That's me following you around again. Even if you're not going away any more, I'm a partner in our marriage. Or I was.'

*Stop. Right. Now. Too much.*

But it was how she felt. Hurt, disappointed, humiliated even. She wouldn't be accused of not telling Cole what she thought. Not now or later, if there was going to be a later.

Cole sank onto a chair and dropped his head in his hands. 'I thought you'd be pleased I was settling into a long-term job in the city where we've always been happy. It was supposed to make you feel sure of me and my motives. Look, I'm here for good, no leaving you to carry all the hard stuff on your own any more.'

The genuineness behind his statement rang loud and clear between them. It still didn't make the situation acceptable. Vicki pulled out another chair and sat down. Her legs were a bit wobbly and her head was spinning. They'd made wild love as only they could do, kissed until her body melted; laughed, talked, and worked together over the past twenty-four hours. Even argued, spoken of the past and the future, and yet here they were, stuck, unable to move in any direction.

But she wasn't ready to give up trying. Not yet.

'Cole, why do you make decisions that involve both of us without saying a word to me first?' The shock of finding out one day he'd joined the army still had the capability to rock her at times. He hadn't told her he was actually going to do that either, just mentioned in passing a couple of times that he was interested in finding out more about joining up one day.

He stood up, rolled his shoulders. 'Want a beer? Wine?'

May as well. Nothing else was working. 'Wine would be nice.' She was exhausted. Her body ached everywhere. The banging inside her head was worse than ever. It would be a darned sight easier to give up trying to make Cole see her side of this and just go with the flow. A lot simpler. And a lot more frustrating, which would eventually lead right back to this moment.

Cole returned with their drinks and a plate with Brie and crackers. The nibbles weren't so much a peace offering as something to quieten his rumbling stomach, which he hoped was caused by hunger and not despair of ever getting things right with Vicki again. Probably kidding himself there.

He didn't sit, instead leaned against one of the pillars holding the roof over the deck and sipped his beer. Vicki was watching him, waiting for an explanation. A long overdue one, true, and still difficult to deliver. More so because he'd shied away from it for so long. But this was the right time. Now or never, and never meant not being able to win Vicki back. 'I did tell you I was accused of stealing some money from a local charity in our town.'

Her gaze didn't waver. 'You were cleared of it. Or so you said.'

'I was.' And that was as much as he'd ever told her.

'I don't understand how you could've been accused in the first place. You're not the kind of person who'd do anything like that.'

Warmth filled him briefly. 'Thank you for that.' He sipped his beer before continuing. 'If only others had reacted the same way. The town was in an uproar, not because the amount of money taken was well over ten thousand dollars but that anyone would steal from the charity at all. That I would. The fact I came from a well-off family seemed to make it a worse crime in *everyone's* eyes.'

'As in your family and friends?'

He nodded abruptly, swallowed the bile that question had brought on. 'At first Mum and Dad accepted I was guilty. Then they began listening to me and finally admitted they'd been wrong. Dad tried to make up for it by ignoring those who believed I was guilty and burying himself in work more than ever. Mum became more withdrawn as the loss of her friends hit home.'

'How did you cope?'

*I became someone else.*

'My friends, or those I'd believed were friends, added to the misery. We were all together that night.' He explained what had happened. 'I didn't learn how they'd driven my car to the charity room until one of the guys admitted it all eight months later. I was embarrassed, then angry. My girlfriend had put a date drug in my beer. I'd always felt ashamed that I hadn't known what had gone on, and the truth actually increased my shame. I was used.'

Placing her glass back on the table without taking a sip, she again locked her gaze with his. 'That wasn't your fault.'

'True.' He shrugged. 'But how gullible was I to accept a beer that had been drugged?'

'No one knows they've been given date drugs until it's too late.'

'The whole incident taught me to be wary of who I chose for friends.'

'Why are you only telling me this now when it's obvious it's made you who you are?'

There was no holding her back on the tricky questions any more. It seemed the time he'd been away had made her tougher. Which he couldn't fault. At least that had kept her safe from making mistakes. 'It was a horrible time for me and my family, and when I fell in love with you I didn't want to bring it into our lives. It changed me so much. I became wary of trusting people and yet you I totally trusted instantly. It was something I didn't want to spoil. I had no issues with you believing me. It was more that I wanted to be accepted for who I was without all the bull dust attached.'

'So you've never told anyone since it happened?' The

hurt tightened her face, darkened her eyes. She didn't accept that he hadn't told her.

Now he was about to make it worse, because he wouldn't lie to Vicki. Not even if it meant she'd hate him. 'Nathan has known for most of our friendship.'

'I see.'

No, she didn't. But he wasn't going to grovel. He and Nathan had met when he'd still been raw from what his so-called friends had done and he'd wanted to test him. Quite the reverse to his decision not to tell Vicki. He should've done it the other way round, but then hindsight was all very well.

'Has this got anything to do with joining the army?'

His sigh was low and sad. 'Mum died before I was proved innocent. I always wondered if the stress killed her. In those desperate hours after her heart attack she apologised for not believing in me and said she was proud of me for being so strong.'

He swallowed as a picture filled his mind of his mother's drawn, white face as she'd lain there, crying and apologising.

'I was seventeen, and my mother was dying before my eyes. I couldn't face that so I promised to make her more proud of me.' A chill settled over him. 'I was trying to keep her alive by giving her something to hold out for. Granddad had been awarded a military medal for his part in active service and she was always going on about him so it seemed the way to go.'

'Why couldn't you have told me that?' Bleak eyes fixed on him. 'I didn't come into the picture at all, did I? How long was I supposed to sit back and wait until you were ready to include me in all aspects of your life?' Her questions were stabs at his heart.

'I got into the habit of not divulging things about myself, not wanting to bring my youth into my adulthood.' He should've known not to do that after the way he'd been treated over the theft. 'I'm so sorry, Vicki.'

She went on in a softer voice. 'To be fair, I did wait quietly in the wings. So I can't get angry at you for that. But I woke up after the miscarriage. I needed you then. More than I've ever needed anyone. That was our baby I lost and you weren't available. I know other women have been through a miscarriage on their own; I never expected it to be me. That was when I understood I do not want a marriage where we're not together most of the time. I grew up having family around me. I can't live without that. I'm sorry too.'

'It won't happen again, I promise. You'll always have me with you. I am not going anywhere without you again.'

'So you say, but you're still making decisions without talking through them with me. I'd thought we'd work this out. I was not expecting more shocks, Cole. I can't handle it. I need time to think it through. You may as well return to Sydney and your interview early.' She stood up and looked at him, sorrow written all over her face. 'I wish this had worked out how we'd both hoped.'

'What do you mean? Are you saying we're over? Our marriage really is finished?' He could hardly utter the words the pain was so horrendous. 'Vicki. Don't do this,' he gasped.

Tears streaked over her cheeks. His beautiful Vicki was hurting as much as him. He stepped forward to take her in his arms, only to be stopped immediately.

'No.' Her breast lifted on a deep breath. 'You need to stop proving to everyone else how strong you are and get on with living a life that's true to you.'

She was right. He had been hiding from so much.

Vicki hadn't finished. 'I'm sorry. I am not ready to return to being a couple. I don't believe we've really been one in the way I thought. So I guess I am saying we're still separating.' Then she turned and left him.

Cole watched her go, heading to her bedroom where they'd made love a short time ago. He could still feel her breasts against his chest, her moist warmth as he'd entered her. Would they ever do that again? Would she give him another chance? Pain lanced him into shreds. Vicki was his woman, the love of his life. It was impossible to accept she believed they were over.

He wasn't going to. Taking a step in her direction, he faltered. He'd said all he could. There was nothing more to add. Vicki had to believe him when he'd said he was always going to be here for her.

But she didn't.

Should he go and grovel? Beg for another chance? Or give her space and time to take in everything he'd told her? If he did that would she ever let him see her again? Ever talk to him again? Fear chilled him, lifted bumps on his skin, closed down the warmth of their lovemaking. They were so close, so far. This could not be happening. But it was.

Vicki believed he was wrong to make decisions without involving her. Maybe she was right, and he should've broached the subject of him applying for a position in Sydney. But he'd wholeheartedly believed he was doing the right thing by her, and himself. After all, she'd been making plans for her agency without telling him, and that had been going on longer than his application for the Rose Bay GP's job.

Staring through to the lounge, his gaze alighted on Anna's painting. It was superb. Filled with passion. As though by finally following her dreams, her heart had spilled out on canvas for everyone to share. A heart

that was devoted to Marty and their children—as well
as herself.

That's what Vicki had intimated she wanted. To follow her dreams with him at her side. He hadn't dis-
agreed. Neither had he said let's find the right place for
the agency and he'd find a job wherever that was, because
he was excited about his own possibilities in Rose Bay.
It could be perfect for them both.

*So could moving to Cairns.*

The lights flickered. Stayed on.

He'd head home in the morning and give her some
space so that hopefully everything would calm down
and then they could talk again. They had to. It couldn't
end like this.

# CHAPTER TEN

HAD SHE REALLY said that? Vicki lay on her bed, staring up at the ceiling, ignoring the tears filling her eyes. It had sounded selfish even to her, but if she wasn't going to look out for herself, then who was?

*Cole.*

The pain in his eyes, tensing his body as he'd listened to her, had whacked back at her. She'd caused that. Hurt them both. There was so much he'd not told her until now. Yes, he would look out for her if she asked. He might even have heard how she felt over his choices. But apparently he'd found his dream job and she doubted she could ask him not to take it. That would be like Cole asking her to give up the idea of her agency.

She could run it from Rose Bay. From anywhere really. Was she being too harsh? Expecting everything to go her way from now on? But that wasn't what she was doing. She just wanted to have the life that suited both of them, where they could be happy again and she could stop worrying about being left on her own during the times she really needed support. She wanted to follow her dreams, and Cole's. It could be done. If he was open to her ideas. He had sounded okay with the agency. Had he thought how it might impact on him, especially if they had a family?

The light flickered.

Vicki held her breath.

The flickering stopped, the light remained on.

She breathed.

They'd been lucky so far with the power still being on in Palm Beach. Damon had phoned earlier to warn her there were outages in other areas and it could happen here. Now that the rain was easing, perhaps there'd be no more.

*Flicker.*

Tempting fate, that was. Again she held her breath, again released it.

She was still in full, golden light.

Then she wasn't. Darkness filled the house abruptly. Black. Dense. Frightening. Sitting up, she waited for some natural light to filter through the windows so she could discern furniture shapes and the doorway.

'Vicki, you all right?' Cole called along the hall. Then he was in the doorway, his shape darker against the low glow from a torch he held.

'Sort of.'

'I've turned the barbecue on to cook the remainder of the steak. Want to join me?' He was keeping himself in check, speaking as he would to anyone, not with the verve and love he usually had for her.

She could do the same, friendly but careful. 'I'll make a salad or butter some bread.' Standing up, she slipped her feet into the turquoise sandals by the bed. She wasn't going around in the dark with bare feet. Next she tugged a lightweight jersey over her head.

In the kitchen, Cole started quickly emptying the fridge of everything they might need for dinner so that they wouldn't open it again and lose what cold air was inside.

Vicki tried not to get more uptight. The power could

be off for many hours with the electricity supplier already busy with other outages, and she going to have to get through the night without relying too much on Cole. That wouldn't be fair after what she'd said. Placing her torch on the bench, she reached for a lantern and struck a match to light it. After setting it on the table, she lit the second one. 'These'll make me feel cosier.'

'The rain's definitely lightened a lot. We might see the end of this by the morning.' Cole carried the oil and steak out to the deck.

Vicki followed him, and looked out over the yard. She shivered. 'Mum and Dad are lucky. The lawn will dry out fast enough, and the house hasn't been affected.' Cole would know she was trying to fill the threatening silence. Awkward. 'I'll make a salad.'

Inside, she went about preparing a green salad, taking regular peeks at Cole as he stood by the barbecue, waiting to cook the steak. What *was* he thinking? He probably wanted to get out of here as soon as possible but she doubted he'd leave while there was no power to light up the place. Despite being cross with her, he wouldn't do that.

After shaking dressing over the salad she pushed the bowl to the side. Done. Now to butter some slices of bread. Basic but good food. Her favourite. And Cole's.

The silence grew as they ate, and Vicki couldn't relax. Her skin felt cold, her head pounded. She'd told Cole to go back to Sydney, but here he was, sitting opposite her having a meal. So normal and yet completely abnormal. Should she try to talk some more about his plans for joining the medical centre? But what more could she say without repeating herself?

'Relax, Vicki. I'll be out of your hair first thing in the morning.'

Her fingers tightened around her fork. Now that he'd put it into words she wasn't so sure she wanted him to go. But he had to find out if he'd got the position, and think about what he really wanted before they could talk about *them*. If they did. 'Your flight's in the afternoon, isn't it?'

'Yes, but I'll try to change it. If I can't then I'll fill in the hours in town.'

He hated wondering aimlessly around shops, could only stop for a coffee for a short time before he became restless. 'I'll drive you in.'

'We'll see.'

It wasn't as though he had a lot of choices. Taxis were most likely thin on the ground with the weather bomb playing havoc with the roads. Refraining from pointing that out, Vicki said instead, 'I'll boil some water on the barbecue for tea.'

'Let me do that.' He was up and finding a pot before she'd moved.

'Fine.' She'd rinse the plates, and try to find something else to keep her busy. It wouldn't be the ironing or watching TV. Picking up her phone, she checked for messages. 'At least we've still got phone coverage.'

'What about internet?'

'Not strong, but it's there.'

Molly had texted.

You all right?

No power but otherwise okay.

She'd call tomorrow and fill Molly in on the landslide and their role in helping the family.

What about Cole?

Molly wasn't letting her get away with just mentioning the storm. He's returning to Sydney tomorrow. Which was sad, but necessary if he was to figure how to go forward.

Tapping another text, she replied to her mother's query about how the storm had affected Palm Beach.

Saturated and no power, otherwise unaffected.

Joe from the medical centre had also sent a message.

You all right up there?

Yes. Been busy helping injured people, but we're fine, thanks.

*Liar, liar.* Not telling Joe her position with her husband.

'Gumboot or strawberry tea?' Cole asked.

'Gumboot, thanks.' Her gaze wandered to the glass door leading onto the deck, and the red and yellow floral painted gumboots standing just outside, and she smiled. She loved them. They beat the plain old black variety most people wore.

'Here.' Cole placed her mug on the table and went through the pantry until he found a packet of chocolate biscuits. He joined her and checked his phone. 'Nathan's texted.'

'Molly did, too.'

They were good friends. Nathan had always been, and Molly had fitted in perfectly. She'd turned Nathan's life around, had given him a second chance at happiness, as he had for her. He'd won her over by showing her not all men were abusive, didn't use their fists to prove a point.

She was very happy for the pair of them. Across the table she saw Cole texting, his finger purposeful on the buttons, his mouth not as tight as it had been earlier. Hard not to lean over and wrap her hand around his. But she mustn't. He'd take it as an indication she was going to back off fighting for herself.

'Think I'll turn in. It's early, but what else is there to do?'

He paused his messaging and looked up at her, a sharp gleam in his eyes.

She had to ask that? In the past they'd have gone to bed all right, but there'd have been nothing to do with sleeping going on between the sheets. Hot memories roared into her mind and heat flowed up her cheeks. She spun away. 'See you in the morning before you go.'

Cole's heart was heavy as he watched Vicki sidle down the hall, a lantern in one hand, a torch in the other as she glanced left and right.

*Sweetheart, it shouldn't be like this. We love each other.*

The light on his phone faded, bringing him back to what he'd been doing before his heart had got sidetracked. He finished texting Nathan.

Internet's sporadic. Can you look up flights out of here early tomorrow for me?

He'd head home and drive around the Rose Bay area to get the feel of the place, try to look at it from Vicki's point of view. If she was determined to set up the agency it could be done from home, but she'd also want to take on some of the temp jobs that came in herself so a lot of travelling around the city would be an issue. Though that would happen wherever they decided to live, and the bay was only a few kilometres from the city centre, which was a plus. They could make this work, he was certain of it, and then they'd get back to normal. Maybe try for a baby again.

'What else is there to do?'

Her question reverberated in his head. Make love again, slower than before, touch, kiss, explore. Yeah, that one explosive moment had only been the beginning to what usually followed on when they got together after time apart. That and lots of hugs and sleeping spoon style, and waking up at all hours for more kisses and sex.

Vicki had been thinking of that too. Her face had reddened immediately after she'd asked that question, and then she'd hastily departed for the bedroom. But she'd been too late. He'd recognised her response and known the same himself. Unfortunately, it wasn't happening. He would not push the barriers. He'd lost too much ground already. For Vicki the marriage seemed over. But not for him.

Nathan came back with flight details and, given the thumbs up, changed his booking. Sadness enveloped him. He did not want to leave Vicki like this, but she'd made it plain she wanted nothing more to do with him at the moment. It was better to focus on sorting out what he could in Sydney than hanging around, trying to get her to see reason. If he did get the job he could relax, knowing he had work he wanted, and then concentrate on helping Vicki with her plans for the agency and anything else she might want.

Scrolling through his contacts, he found the number he wanted and sent a brief text. As soon as a reply came back, he pocketed the phone and, armed with a torch, he headed to his bedroom.

The landline rang as he passed Vicki's room. 'Want me to get that?'

'Yes. Hope we're not needed again.'

She can't have been banking on that hope, though, because when he returned moments later Vicki was dressed and tying the laces of her navy shoes.

'A supposed heart attack.' He gave her the address before ducking into Marty's room to get the first aid gear and defib.

'We'll take the car. It's a little way along the main beach road.'

Silence landed between them as Vicki backed out onto the road.

He waited as she drove carefully through the deep puddles. Then, when he couldn't bear it any longer, 'What's up?' Which of their problems was putting that strained look on her face that he saw in the glow from the dash? Which was top of the list?

At first he didn't think she'd answer, then she surprised him. 'I worry I'm being selfish.'

That he had not expected. 'Why would you think that?'

'I'm not used to putting my foot down over what I want. Not on the big issues anyway.'

'Okay with demanding chocolate ice cream instead of vanilla, but not where to live?' Yes, that was his Vicki. Now the ball was in his court. Had he taken advantage of her indecisiveness?

'In a nutshell. But why? I've never been a wimp.'

'You like keeping everyone happy.' Why hadn't he seen that before?

'Now I'm including myself.'

'So it seems.' He didn't know where that left him; if she still wanted him in her life or not. She'd told him to go back to Sydney and sort out his own future. She hadn't included herself in that picture. 'It's okay. Better than okay. You have to be happy before you make other people happy.'

She said nothing.

Frustration got the better of him. 'I thought you were happy with me. That we were so in love nothing could come between us.' He clamped his mouth shut. Too much, Cole.

'I was,' she sighed. 'It all went wrong. Just go back to Sydney, Cole. Sort yourself out, and let me know what you're doing if you still want to.'

The sadness taking over her mood caught at him, turned his gut into a roiling pool of longing mixed with his own sadness. Thank goodness they pulled into a driveway just then. He could focus on a patient, let his head clear for a while. Forget the elephant between them. Forget? Sure. Try ignore it for a brief time. That was as good as it was going to get.

The front door swung open and someone flashed a torch in their direction. Grabbing the kit and defib from the back seat, Cole headed to the house, aware of Vicki right behind him.

'Dr Cole Halliday,' he said to the man standing before him looking desperate. 'And this is Vicki Halliday, a nurse.'

'It's my sister. She's having a heart attack. Lots of pain in her chest. I've called the ambulance.'

'That's good. Show us where your sister is. What's her name?' Cole nodded down the hall.

*Hurry up. This is urgent.*

At last the guy moved. 'Sandra. She started complaining of pain an hour ago. In here…' He indicated a room where lanterns gave out an eerie light. 'That's my partner with her. Nadine.'

Why wait until now to get help? 'Hello, Sandra, Nadine. I'm Cole, a doctor, and this is Vicki, a nurse.'

'Hello, Vicki, how's things? Sorry to get you out in this weather.' Sandra was looking at his wife.

'No worries.' Vicki smiled at their patient as she reached to take the defibrillator from him. 'Had nothing better to do.'

*Thanks a bundle.*

'Where's this pain?' he asked.

Sandra tapped to the left of her sternum. 'Here. And here.' Her hand splayed across her upper abdomen.

'On a scale of one to ten, ten being the highest, how strong is it?'

'Five, though there are peaks when it's probably about eight.'

Vicki leaned over. 'You need to remove your top so I can attach the defib.'

Sandra gave her a wonky smile as she began lifting her tee shirt over her head. 'No problem.'

Cole studied the woman before him as he lifted her arm and felt for her pulse. Her colour was good, her eyes clear apart from the worry about her possible condition. Under his thumb her pulse was regular. Heart attack? Or indigestion?

Vicki had the pads on Sandra's chest and was connecting the lines leading to the defib. 'How long has the pain been going on?'

'At least an hour, maybe more. I first felt uncomfortable after dinner.'

Glancing at the defib screen as it came to life, Cole nodded. 'Eat in a hurry, by any chance?'

Nadine piped up. 'We all did. Wanted to get it out of the way while we still had power.'

Vicki glanced up at him, a smile lifting her mouth, relief in her expression.

Again, he nodded. But he wasn't done that quickly. There were things to check and note down. The steady beats resonating in the stethoscope said normal heartbeat. Sandra's even breathing backed that up. The temperature Vicki showed him read thirty-seven. Checking the line on the defib screen once more, Cole relaxed and gave the news. 'There's nothing wrong with your heart. I'd say you've got a bad case of indigestion.'

Sandra stared at him, struggling to take it in. 'Really?' she squealed. 'Not a heart attack?'

'No. See how even those peaks are?' he tapped the screen. 'That's good.'

'Really good,' Vicki confirmed. 'Cole wouldn't have you on about something so serious.'

Sandra let out the breath she was holding. 'I'm sorry to be such a nuisance. Especially in this weather.'

'Do we cancel the ambulance?' Nadine asked.

'Normally, they come regardless once a call has been logged,' Vicki said, 'You are still having pain, Sandra.' She looked to him. 'What do you think?'

*That I would like to go back a year—or more—and start over.*

'That we need to err on the side of caution. It is normal to send someone in this situation to hospital regardless of the results.'

'There you go. Decision made,' Vicki said. 'I'll leave these pads on until the paramedics arrive.'

She was onto it. Better safe than sorry. Although Cole doubted Sandra had a medical problem, he'd have done exactly what Vicki indicated. If there was an area where they were always in sync it was when they were working with patients. Funny how they hadn't known that before this weekend.

'The ambulance's here.' Sandra's brother stood in the doorway, hopping from one foot to the other.

'That was quick for the circumstances,' Nadine said. 'I'll feel happier with you going to hospital, Sandra.'

'Me too. My chest still hurts, though not as much as before.'

The drive back to Marty and Anna's house was quiet, though comfortable this time. The animosity had taken a hike, for a while at least. Shifting one way and another in his seat to ease the aching in his left leg and his back kept him busy for the few minutes before Vicki was pulling into the garage.

'Power's back on.' She stated the obvious.

'When did that happen? It was off at Nadine's.'

'Or they'd turned all the switches off and didn't realise the power was back.'

He supposed that was possible. Hoisting the pack over his shoulder, pain stabbed him. He gasped.

'You okay?'

'Fine.' Didn't have to tell her about every ache. 'Want a drink before hitting the sack?' he asked. It would be good to chill out together. They didn't have to talk about their relationship, could just be quiet, or chat about inconsequential stuff. If that was possible, given she'd told him to go.

'No, thanks.' She removed the defib from the back of the car before he had a chance.

Figured out he was hurting, had she? 'I'll take that,' he said stubbornly.

'I've got it.' Pressing the button to close the garage

door, she headed inside and down the hall to put the gear away.

As she went into her bedroom, he said, 'I'll be gone by sun-up.' He got no reply.

He didn't know if that was better than a goodbye or not. Collecting his overnight bag from the bedroom he hadn't used, he headed to the kitchen where he grabbed a beer before settling into the large comfy recliner chair in the lounge to wait out the hours until his taxi arrived. No point trying to sleep when there were so many thoughts battling for supremacy in his mind.

Just when he'd thought he had his future organised he'd learned he had totally screwed up. Apparently, his own career didn't fit in with Vicki's idea of owning a business. Working in the Rose Bay centre was a golden opportunity to get established as a GP in a good area for raising kids. He'd believed he was doing the right thing by them both. How wrong could a bloke be?

Slugging down a mouthful of beer, he stared into the dark corners of the lounge. Apparently, he hadn't listened to her.

*Well, sweetheart, you haven't exactly made yourself available for phone chats either.*

Anger was rising amongst the confusion and hurt. There were two people in this marriage, in this mess. Both were responsible for decisions affecting each other and themselves. The guilt he'd felt at not being there for Vicki when the miscarriage had occurred had never gone away, not even when he'd refused to call her to come to him after the accident. That had been a mistake. The fear of being a paraplegic when he'd first come round and couldn't move his legs had made him desperate for Vicki to be with him. When he'd finally been reassured his spine was fine, he'd cried for her. Yeah, he'd been an idiot not to let the CO call her. Pride had done that to him.

But he *was* working at making amends in the only way he knew, and she was turning him down. One of them had got it all wrong. Worse, it might be him. Not a lot he could do except return to Sydney, go for the final interview and await the outcome of that before making any rash decisions that could backfire on him.

Vicki heard a car door slam and rolled onto her back, glad that the sun was finally lightening the room. Not wanting to bump into Cole and swap more anger and bitterness, she'd stayed in bed long after wanting to get up and do something, anything, to ease the tightness gripping her body. She hadn't had a wink of sleep and knew he hadn't used the bedroom next to hers so must've stayed in the lounge all night after they'd returned from Sandra's.

The house was too quiet as she made her way to the kitchen, where she reached for the kettle. Two empty beer bottles stood neatly on the bench. Where was Cole? Then she saw the pad on the table, and her heart slowed. He'd left without saying goodbye. Of course she'd told him to go. She'd meant it, and she hadn't. Well, she had if they couldn't find a way out of the hole they found themselves in. At least she could be proud for sticking up for what she wanted. Couldn't she? This was so crazy. Needing to look out for herself definitely came with consequences.

Her fingers were shaking when she picked up the note.

*I got an early flight so ordered a taxi. Take care.*
*Cole XX*

'Take care' as in have a good life? Was their marriage really over? Sinking onto a dining chair, she dropped her head into her hands and let the tears come. She'd got what she'd asked for. And hated it. She should've tried harder. One more honest, share-everything conversation surely could've saved their marriage? They'd talked about many things, shared a lot, yet still it hadn't been enough. Deep down she really hadn't wanted, or expected, them to come to this. He hadn't even let her take him to the airport when they might've been able to talk some more and come out the right side of their problems.

Now what?

She needed to get on with her plans for the nursing agency. Find a job to support herself in the interim. Where was the excitement she'd known when thinking about her own business? Gone in a cloud of longing for Cole. It seemed she couldn't have both.

Lifting her head, she stared around the dining room and then into the lounge. Her gaze landed on her mother's painting of Palm Beach in a storm. Her heart stalled. Since Mum had finally begun following her dreams she'd become like a flower in the sun, bright, pretty. Looking into the picture, Vicki felt the wind on her face, the rain on her skin, hear the waves breaking on the beach. How did someone do that with a paintbrush? Because Mum believed in herself, in her talent, her passion for art.

*I have to believe I can have my dream. And hopefully my man.*

# CHAPTER ELEVEN

MONDAY MORNING COLE was up early, dressed in a navy suit and tie with a crisp white shirt, ready for the interview with hours to spare.

He wandered around the apartment, picking up photos Vicki had left behind. The two of them at their wedding, on their honeymoon, riding the waves at Bondi Beach—make that trying to ride them.

There was another taken the day he'd joined the army. He wore his officer's uniform and Vicki wore an enormous smile. Yes, they'd been okay back then. More than okay. They'd been so in love that even in the middle of a crowd there had been times they hadn't noticed anyone else.

*I miss that so much I ache all the time.*

Was it worth going to this appointment when, if he got the position, chances were Vicki wouldn't join him here in Sydney?

Jumping to conclusions here. He might not get the job. That wasn't a problem. He'd been on the net and seen other opportunities within the city and further out in the suburbs. Though Rose Bay did fit the bill of what he'd thought would be right for him and Vicki and their family when children came along. Right now, all he could do was wait and see how the interview unfolded. Only then could he talk to Vicki about making a commitment to living here. 'Together,' he added under his breath.

Putting the last photo back on the sideboard, he picked up his phone. No messages from Vicki. Not that he'd expected any, but a man was allowed to hope. Of course she wouldn't wish him luck if she didn't want to move back here. But then again, Vicki was usually fair, and always supported him in any endeavours he chose to undertake, so this was unlike her.

There hadn't been a peep out of her yesterday either. He'd respected her silence, and hadn't tried to get in touch. But he'd checked his phone numerous times until finally he'd left it in the bedroom so as not to pick it up every five minutes.

*To hell with this hanging around.*

He'd head to Rose Bay now. There were cafés there and by the time he'd made it to the township his stomach might be ready to take in some breakfast. If not, he'd go for a walk along the beach until it was nine o'clock, get a feel for the place he wanted to make home.

He did neither. His stomach wasn't playing ball, neither was the weather. Rain seemed to be the favourite pastime of the skies wherever he went at the moment. But at least this was a passing squall, not a monsoon. He actually smiled. Was this Vicki dumping on him to get his attention? Giving in to his need, he tugged his phone out of his pocket, and texted.

How's things up there?

She came straight back, making him wonder if she'd been waiting to hear from him.

Drying out slowly. You?

Getting rained on.

LOL

The phone went quiet. No good luck wishes. No questions about yesterday and what he might've got up to. Not a lot, but she might've asked. He hadn't even made it over here for a look around, had been too busy on the internet looking up other vacancies around the city— and in Cairns.

He went and found a coffee, to hell with his grizzly stomach.

Vicki set her phone aside and scanned the notes for her next patient. Cole would be on his way to his interview. She should've wished him luck. Not that he'd likely need it. He had a strong CV, and his time in the army might be a plus as he was used to different situations where patients were under trying conditions making them fearful and nervous. Maybe not what he'd see in Rose Bay often, but it gave him insight into people's mindsets he might not have gained otherwise.

'Vicki, Amelia Green's here,' the receptionist called through the door.

'Coming.' Quickly scanning the notes on the screen in front of her, Vicki focused on work and Amelia, putting Cole on hold. 'Hello, Amelia, come through.' She led the twenty-two-year-old through to her room. 'I see you're heading to Vietnam.'

'I can't wait. I've heard nothing but wonderful comments about the place.'

'So have I. Take a seat. So you're here for your Hep A and B shot? You know it's all in one now?'

'Yes. The doctor told me that when I first asked what

I needed. He said to be aware of rabies and if I get a dog or monkey bite to go straight to the nearest hospital for an injection. Or I could have the vaccination before I go, but I think I'll go with the first suggestion.' Amelia handed over her vaccination card. 'I had the typhoid shot when I went to Eastern Europe.'

'Right, I'll fetch the vaccine and we'll do this. Was it explained that we like you to wait for twenty minutes afterwards in case of an adverse reaction?'

Amelia nodded. 'I can finish an article on Iceland I started reading before you called me in.'

'That your next country to visit?' Vicki asked. She'd never had the travel bug the way Amelia seemed to. Too busy training and then being married to think about disappearing overseas. Europe and Britain had been fun, but hadn't lit a spark to be dashing off all over the world.

'I'm thinking about it. The Northern Lights look spectacular in photos.'

'Right, a sharp prick here.' Vicki inserted the needle, pressed the plunger, and it was done. She stuck a small plaster over the site. 'There you go.'

'Just like that. Thanks.' Amelia was gone, no doubt eager to get back to that article.

Vicki checked her phone. Lots of texts. Nothing from Cole. Eight forty-five. He wouldn't be at the medical centre yet. Was he nervous? Cole? He hadn't changed that much. Would he get in touch after the interview? She had to talk to him, to hear his voice, to know what was going on.

After filling in notes on Amelia's file, she clicked on the appointments screen. Next was thirty-three-year-old Mandy Stanaway, requiring external sutures removed post-mastectomy. Ouch. That was young. The patient file showed the results had come back and that Mandy had been referred for chemo and radiotherapy.

In the waiting room sat a woman in a wheelchair who looked Vicki's way the moment she entered. 'Mandy?'

'That's me.' She began wheeling towards her. 'I haven't met you before.'

Vicki put her hand out to shake. 'Vicki Halliday. I'm a temp nurse while Sarah's on maternity leave.'

Returning the handshake, Mandy smiled. 'Her daughter's gorgeous. I bumped into them in the supermarket yesterday.'

Crikey, the woman might look wan and worried but she wasn't sitting at home, fretting about her future.

*I could learn something from her.*

'Come on, let's get you sorted.'

It didn't take long to remove the stitches. 'All done.' Vicki pulled her gloves off while Mandy awkwardly pulled her top back on. 'Want a hand?'

'No, I'm fine. The stretching just gives me a nudge, that's all.'

'Any concerns about anything? You all right for pain meds?' One of the GP's would write a script if needed.

'Meds are good, got more than enough. And the stuff worrying me you can't help with. The chemo is the unknown factor: how I'll react to it and how long it'll take to get over the effects. Only time will tell.'

'I'm afraid you're right. Though we can arrange an appointment with a counsellor if you'd like.'

'The hospital offered the same, but I'd rather talk to family and friends first.'

'Fair enough, but know help is there if it gets too much. Is your partner supportive?' The notes said Mandy lived with a truck driver who was away a lot.

'He's brilliant.' Then Mandy's face fell. 'When he's

at home. His work takes him all over Northern Australia for days at a time. We talk at least twice a day but sometimes it's not enough, you know?'

All too well. 'Will he be able to get time off when you're having treatment?'

*Please tell me yes.*

'The company's promised to juggle the roster as soon as I have a date to start chemo so that he can be with me for a few days around each treatment.' Mandy pulled herself up and fixed a smile on her face.

*Like I would've for Cole, given half a chance.*

Excellent coffee in hand, Cole sat with the three partners of the medical centre in the cramped office of one of the doctors, and waited for the opening gambit. It seemed odd having a third interview, which had him wondering if there was more to this.

'You picked the wrong weekend to visit Northern Queensland,' Jill said with a welcoming smile. 'We half expected to hear that you hadn't made it back.'

'The airport was open on and off Saturday, and all day yesterday. Vicki and I were kept busy helping the emergency services a lot of the time I was in Cairns.'

David asked, 'She's a nurse, isn't she?'

They knew that from a previous meeting, and from what he'd seen with these people they would not forget. Cole nodded, and waited.

'Where's Vicki working at the moment?'

'Temping at a family medical centre in Cairns.' What was this about?

Jill looked at the other two men and nodded.

Jason sat forward and clasped his hands under his chin. 'Here's the thing, Cole. We're impressed with your medical record, and more importantly we believe you'll fit in well with our patients.'

Unsure where this was going, Cole merely said, 'Thank you,' and sipped his coffee while he waited.

Jason continued. 'We have decided to bring in a fourth partner. We'd like to offer the opportunity to you. Obviously, the terms and conditions would be different and entail an initial financial cost to you, but the benefits would make that worthwhile.'

Just as well he'd swallowed the mouthful of coffee. Spluttering it across the desk would not look good. 'Thank you.' A partnership had been in his plans but he'd believed that would be well into the future. 'I'm interested.'

*'You never discuss things with me.'*

Vicki's accusation echoed around his skull. He hadn't said he'd take the partnership. There was a lot to find out about what was on offer before anything else. Couldn't deny his pulse was racing with excitement, though. Who'd have thought he'd get an offer like this so soon after quitting the army? When he hadn't experienced general practice work? It could be perfect. If Vicki went with the idea. 'You'd better fill me in on the details.' First things first.

An hour later Cole stepped out into brilliant sunshine and stood on the steps leading to the centre's parking area, taking deep breaths as the offer he'd just been made buzzed around his head. It was a very good proposal. He could afford to buy into the business, and the returns would be way beyond what he'd have earned if he signed on simply as a GP with the practice. The amount of leave available was more than he'd have expected for a partner, which could be beneficial if he and Vicki had children.

The location fitted his idea of a good family suburb. He liked the partners, and the other staff he'd met at the end of the meeting. It had even been suggested Vicki could work there. What was there not to be thrilled about?

What would Vicki think? Would she jump on board, or say she wasn't prepared to move back to Sydney? One thing he was certain about. She wasn't about to forego her agency.

Anguish filled him. It was a hurdle to overcome. Admiration nudged at his anguish. She wasn't going along with his needs without fighting for her own. She'd not done that before, and it was probably gnawing away at her determination to keep focused. She needed his support, not his selfishness.

There was one way to find out. Staring at his phone, he debated with himself. Ring her with the news? Or fly back up there to tell her face to face? Gauge her reactions and try to answer any negatives she came up with? He wasn't accepting the position without talking to her first. He *had* learned that much.

Striding out along the steaming street, he headed for the town centre, looking around at the homes he passed, then the stores where people stopped and chatted to each other. A good sign of a friendly neighbourhood.

With a takeout coffee and a salad roll in hand, he headed for the beach to sit on a damp bench and enjoy the view of Sydney Harbour. Ferries plied between many of the bays and downtown Sydney, churning up the water as they zipped back and forth. Above, seagulls squawked as they swooped for any scraps lying around. Adults walked their dogs on the beach. Picture perfect. And he'd had a very tempting offer to become a part of the scene. To establish himself as a GP in a lovely neighbourhood was something he'd been dreaming about for a while.

Yet now it so close to happening, he felt uncomfortable. As though something wasn't right. Something was missing. Vicki. Yes, absolutely. But there something else itching at his excitement and he didn't know what it was. Tossing the paper cup and paper bag into a rubbish bin, Cole strolled along the beach, nodding to those who said hello, patting dogs that came to sniff him. It was easy to feel he might belong here. But…

*Vicki.*

The woman he loved, had sworn to love for the rest of their lives. The woman he'd fallen for the moment he'd set eyes upon her. She'd been there for him every time he'd returned from an overseas posting, had listened as he'd poured out his grief and anguish about the sights he'd witnessed, the desolate people he'd tried to help. Basically, she'd backed him all the way, all the time, until she couldn't take it any more. And look how he'd repaid her. Badly.

The warm sun on his back loosened some of the tightness in his muscles, but it didn't help the sense he was making a mistake. There was something else going on here. If only it would stand up and let him identify what it was.

*Go to Camperdown.*

With no idea why that had popped into his head, Cole turned around and headed back to town and the car, sensing that a visit where his time in Sydney had begun might help solve his dilemma.

The old stone brick building of the medical school Cole had trained at loomed large when he strolled up to the front. Memories of the first time he'd ever walked through the main entrance filled his head. He'd been nervous, excited, and glad to be starting there. He was starting afresh. In a large city where most people remained anonymous, where he could hide in plain daylight, and not be approached regularly to be asked how he was getting on now his name had been cleared, or told it was so sad what had happened and how he had to let it go and forgive every one for thinking he could ever commit such a crime.

Cole jammed his hands in his pockets and stood staring around, his legs splayed, his head spinning, and his heart beating slowly as he absorbed the familiar surroundings.

*I chose this medical school because of its location in a large city where I was a stranger.*

It helped that it was one of the best in the country, too, but that had come second to the need to just be a medical student learning his trade. It had worked. He'd made friends, met Nathan who had eventually became his closest mate. And he'd finally put everything on the line by telling Nathan what had gone down back in Adelaide when he'd been a teen. Nathan, being the guy he was, had clapped him on the back and dragged him down to the pub for a beer. No criticism, no unctuous comments about how he was sure Cole wouldn't have stolen the money, just a bloke's way of saying *You're fine, mate.*

It had felt good and it had been the last time he'd felt the need to explain himself to anyone as a test of friendship.

*Sorry, Vicki. I made a mistake there.*

Driving along the streets towards the rundown house he'd shared with four other students, he stared around. So familiar, so different. He wouldn't like to live here again. He was a doctor now, didn't need the shambolic lifestyle of a student. Neither did he need to hide any more. Now he could walk down any street anywhere, head held high.

Cole pulled to the side of the street and pulled on the handbrake, leaving the motor idling. He was getting closer to whatever had begun to irk him as he'd walked on the beach. It took time to make friends in a neighbourhood where everyone was intent on their families and careers and getting ahead. Especially in a huge city. Not like Cairns. Bet if he bumped into Merv or one of the other rescue crew members he'd worked alongside during the weekend, they'd stop and chat, probably suggest a beer at the pub or to go round for a barbecue. They'd certainly acknowledge him.

*Am I ready for that?*

More than ready, he realised. He wanted it, for himself and Vicki. For their children. To be comfortable, relaxed, and happy. The army hadn't given him that picture. It hadn't been bad, just not what he'd been looking for. It hadn't included Vicki, for one. And there wasn't anyone more important to him.

No one.

'Jack, the crutch is not a bat,' Vicki admonished as her patient flicked a large stone down the medical centre's drive.

'Not a very good one, anyway.' Jack laughed. 'I couldn't get the dog's bowl up the steps this morning.' He'd been in to get his dressings changed.

Rolling her eyes, she grinned. 'You're hopeless.'

'I hear you and your man were busy Friday night, rescuing that family from their ruined house. Everyone's been singing your praises at the station.'

'We did no more than the fire crew did. It was a joint effort, with good results.'

*We.* As in her and Cole. *We.*

A sigh slid across her lips, and her mood dipped. Again. Still not a word from him. She'd given up checking her phone for messages last night, tried to accept he wasn't rushing to tell her how the interview had gone. Except every time the phone pinged her heart would leap and she snatch it up only to be disappointed. Everyone but Cole seemed to be in touch. This morning she'd left the phone in her bag and refused to take it out all day. There could be a message from Cole by now, for all she knew, but she wasn't looking until she walked out of here in half an hour's time to go home.

Did his silence indicate she'd got what she'd asked for? What if she was wrong to demand he sort himself out before they went any further? What if he never called her again?

Jack was still talking. 'So the guys are wondering if you'd be interested.'

'In what?'

Now it was Jack's turn to do the eye-roll thing. 'Sorry if I'm boring you.' His smile told her he wasn't cross. 'Would you like to join our station as a voluntary medic?'

Become a part of the fire crews? Sounded exciting. Bit like working in an emergency department without all the modern equipment and a whole hospital to back the medics. It would fill in some more hours. 'Yes, I think I would.'

'Right, let Damon know. We're having a meeting on Wednesday. I'll put a word in for you.'

Guilt reared. 'Um…slow down. I would like to help, but I'm not sure how long I'm here for. I might be returning to Sydney soon.'

*Might. Probably won't, because Cole has given up on me.*

'Come on board anyway. We'll put you through the training, and if you leave town your time, and ours, won't have been wasted. We need people like you, Vicki. We really do.'

Pride swelled in her chest. 'Thanks. Okay, count me in for as long as I'm here.'

'Need a doctor as well?'

Vicki spun around, lost her balance, would've fallen if Cole hadn't caught her.

'Steady, sweetheart.' He gazed down at her with an intensity that tightened every muscle in her body.

'You didn't call me once.'

'Thought it better to come in person. Far more intimate.' He leaned closer, brushed his lips over hers.

She had to fight not to press back, to devour him with a kiss. Every cell ached with the need to touch him, feel his tenderness, to believe he really was here, holding her. 'Cole?'

'Yes, Vicki, I'm here, hopefully for good.' His gaze remained on her. 'If you'll have me.'

'Yes.' Just like that? Well, she wasn't carrying on feeling lonely and sad when this was the one person who made her happy. And he was here. 'With some changes,' she added through a smile.

Cole's return smile filled her with gladness. They would make this work.

'I can see I'm in the way here,' Jack interrupted them. 'I'll get in touch tomorrow. And, yes, we can always use a doctor. Now, where's Barbara got to?'

'She went next door to the pharmacy,' Vicki told him, and instinctively headed out to help him get into the car, feeling a loss as Cole's hands slid away from her arms.

Cole followed. 'I'm Cole Halliday, Vicki's husband,' he told Jack.

Jack grunted with pain as he lifted his cast leg inside the car. 'Jack Henderson. I've heard about you. Talk later when you've got a spare moment.' He grinned at her, then nodded to Cole. 'Go on. Seems you've got things to sort out.'

'You stay off those quad bikes, and bend down to pick up the dog bowl. There's nothing wrong with your waist.' She closed the door on Jack and turned to face the love of her life. Had she given in too quickly? When she shouldn't be giving in at all?

'Relax. I'm not here to demand we do everything my way. What time do you finish for the day?'

Joe was walking up the drive with a pharmacy pack in his hand. 'You can go now, Vicki. I'll cover for you if anyone needs a plaster put on a cut. Good to see you, Cole.'

'There's no one else booked in for me,' she said in a wobbly voice. 'So thanks, I'll grab my bag and get out of here.' She didn't look at Cole, just headed inside as quickly as possible, her head spinning at his sudden appearance. She'd said yes, she'd have him back, without thinking it through. She'd acted on her love for him. It was right. Now she still had to make sure he understood she wasn't backing down from her plans.

When she returned Joe and Cole were talking.

Joe held out his hand to shake Cole's 'Talk again.'

'Sure.'

'What was that about?' Vicki asked as they walked to her car.

'Work.'

'Right.' Back to not telling her what was going on? A timely reminder they hadn't resolved everything. But... she breathed out hard... Cole was here, with her, and he wanted to fix what was keeping them apart.

Clasping her hand, he said, 'It's okay, I promise. I just want to start at the beginning.'

'Then jump in and I'll drive as fast as I can because I need to hear this.'

'How about we find a quiet corner in a bar along the waterfront instead?'

'Sounds like a plan.' She knew exactly where to take them. As long as she wasn't getting her hopes up too high. Sneaking a sideways glance, she saw that Cole appeared relaxed yet edgy at the same time, giving no clues about what had gone down in Sydney so she hung onto his words back at the medical centre and tried to relax. Yeah, right.

Cole sat beside Vicki at a table on the pavement and looked at her. There were deep shadows staining her cheeks, and her mouth drooped. Equally, her eyes gleamed with what he could only recognise as love.

'I've been offered a partnership at the Rose Bay Medical Centre.'

She flinched, then rallied. 'You must be thrilled. That's great news.' Locking her eyes with his, she said, 'I mean it, Cole. I'm proud of you. Not that I'm surprised. You're a great doctor with the people skills required to make patients trust you.'

'I haven't accepted. I'm probably not going to.'

Her eyes widened.

'I haven't said anything to the partners yet. I wanted to talk to you first. To decide together where to live.' This was about their future, not just his.

'Tell me more.' Could those beautiful blue eyes get any wider?

'The contract has everything I want, yet it doesn't sit right with me.' Sipping his wine, he reached for Vicki's free hand, entwined their fingers. She didn't jerk away. 'That's wrong. It was Sydney I needed to look at properly. I went there as a teen to get lost in the crowds, to be free of people approaching me to talk about the theft I didn't commit. Being in a large city worked. I got on with study and making friends who knew nothing of my past.'

'Then I don't see what the problem is for you to continue living there.'

'I'm not saying I've made up my mind not to. But the other night, helping the rescue crew, I felt right at home with everyone without having to prove anything to myself or them. It's as simple as that.' Turning to face her, he locked his gaze with hers. 'I want to live where we'll both be happy. Have a job that fits round your dreams too. I love you, Vicki, and that's all that matters. Everything else can be worked around, but not my love for you.'

She studied him with an intensity he was coming to know. There was no anger or sadness, only hope in that expression. 'I never stopped loving you, Cole. I needed to be heard, that's all.'

'And hugged when everything was going belly up.'

She nodded. 'That too.' A devastating smile broke out on her face, and knocked his heart sideways.

Leaning closer, he wound his arms around his woman and covered her mouth with his, and kissed her long and deep, like he'd never kissed her before.

Pressing against him, her breasts on his chest, Vicki returned the kiss with equal vigour and love. The longer they kissed, the more his body softened—though some areas tightened. The months of tension evaporated, to be replaced with the love he hadn't stopped holding for this beautiful woman.

The sound of a metal chair leg scraping on concrete cut through the wonder 'I love you,' he whispered as he lifted his head to look around.

Beside their table an old man was getting to his feet. 'Good luck, you two.'

Vicki laughed. 'Thank you, but I don't think we'll need it now.'

Cole grinned. They were back on track. He waved to the waitress. 'Could we have two glasses of your best champagne, please?'

'Coming right up.' The young woman was smiling. 'Very quickly.'

Vicki pushed her barely touched glass of wine aside. 'That'll have to take a back seat if I'm having bubbles. I'm driving, remember?'

He slid it across to her hand. 'We're not going back to Palm Beach today. We're going to spend the night here in town at that hotel you can see.' They'd be together, make love, eat in bed, drink some more champagne in the hotel where there wouldn't be any interruptions from Vicki's family or friends. 'Ironic when I said I didn't need to re-main isolated any more and here I am, wanting a night totally to ourselves.'

'Here you go, you two.' Champagne flutes appeared before them. 'Enjoy.'

'Oh, we will,' Vicki lifted a glass and wound her arm through his. 'To us.'

They sipped.

'That's nectar.' She smiled.

'It is.' Hang on. He still had something to say. 'Vicki, wherever we choose to live, I will help with your proj-ect, give support in any way you require. When we have a baby I'll do my share of parenting so you don't have to juggle everything too much.'

'We can do all of this in Sydney, if you would like to take up the partnership. I have no beef against Sydney. It's a great place to live—together.'

'We'll talk about it. Later.' He tapped their glasses together. 'To us,' he repeated her words. 'I love you.'

'I love you too.' Then she burst into tears.

# EPILOGUE

*Twelve months later...*

VICKI STEPPED OUT of the car and smoothed the skirt of her cream full-length dress over her six-month baby bump and down to her new cream suede, solid-heeled shoes. The heels, thicker than normal, were to keep her upright in the sand. Anyway, they looked awesome.

'Are we ready?' Damon looked directly at her, a cheeky grin on his face.

She laughed. Did that a lot lately. Then she looked around at the group standing with her on the walkway leading down to the white sands of Palm Beach. 'What do you think?' she asked her brother. She was as excited as the first time she'd done this. More so, really, now that she and Cole had resolved their differences and were living together all the time, sharing their lives as she'd always hoped for.

'Then let's do this.' He took her arm as Phil stepped up to take the other.

'Can't have you falling flat on your face.' Phil grinned.

'I wouldn't be flat with junior in there, making a hill out of my stomach.'

Behind them, her father said, 'Anna, Julie, let me escort you both down to the beach. I've been made redundant with Vicki by my sons.'

Everyone laughed. It had been decided days ago that her brothers were walking her along to Cole where he waited on the beach with his father, and Nathan and Molly with the twins, to renew their vows. Cheeky guys that they were, Phil and Damon reckoned they might bring a bit more luck to the equation this time.

'Let's go.' She laughed. 'Can't keep Cole waiting.'

'Why change now?' Damon quipped.

'Because today, and only today, he can have everything his way.' Tomorrow they were going on a second honeymoon, back to Rarotonga and the same luxurious resort.

'Bet he'll be too busy making sure you have everything you want to be thinking of himself,' Julie said from behind her.

Yes, Cole put her first so often now it could get embarrassing. Despite being busy with the medical clinic he'd bought into here in Cairns, he'd backed her all the way with the agency, which was already doing well. Not so busy there weren't days when she had no jobs to fill, but those were becoming fewer and fewer.

Stepping onto the sand, Vicki looked along the beach to the small group waiting for them all. Her heart lurched with all the love spilling out. How could she once have thought they were over? It wasn't possible. She loved that man waiting for her more than life itself. And now they were going to be parents, were expecting a tiny miracle to love and cherish for ever.

She stumbled. Love was so wonderful.

'Hey, clumsy, look where you're going.' Phil grinned.

'There's a big distraction just ahead.' She grinned back.

'You two…' Damon rolled his eyes '…need to find a hotel quick smart.'

'Not until after the ceremony,' she retorted. Then she was standing in front of Cole, her heart flapping around in her chest like a fish on sand, and nothing else, no one else, mattered. Reaching for his hand, she held on tight, never wanting to let him go again. 'I love you,' she whispered.

Cole leaned close to brush his lips across hers. 'And I you.'

'Hey, you two. Enough of that. There are decent people present,' Damon's laughter broke through the haze taking over her head. 'And the marriage celebrant.'

'You saying I'm not decent?' Karen asked with a twinkle in her eye.

They didn't legally require a marriage celebrant to renew their vows, but she and Cole had become friends with Karen and Arlo since the monsoon, and when Karen had heard about the ceremony there had been no stopping her partaking in it. Not that either of them had wanted to turn down her offer.

'Right, let's do this.' Karen shuffled the pages in her hands as she waited.

Vicki and Cole turned to face her, still holding hands. *Here we go, second time lucky*, Vicki thought. *Luckier.*

Karen started with something unexpected. 'I am so glad you picked a beautiful, sunny day for this celebration, nothing like the night we met under a hill.' When everyone chuckled, she added, 'That was the worst time of my life and yet Arlo and I now have two wonderful friends we didn't have before.' She glanced across to her husband with a tender smile just for him.

Arlo winked. 'Get on with it, woman. The champagne's getting warm.' His foot tapped the Esky at his side.

'Cole and Vicki, do you both vow to love and cherish each other for the rest of your lives? To support and care for one another? To raise your family surrounded by love and understanding? To share the good, the bad, and everything in between with love and have a smile for each other every morning?'

Vicki's breasts rose as she drew in sun-warmed air and gazed at the man who was her husband, her support, her soul mate, her love. 'Yes, absolutely. I'll always love you, Cole. Always have, always will.' Her throat clogged up with unshed tears. She wasn't going to cry today. This was a joyous occasion.

Cole's hands were shaking as he held hers. 'Vicki, my heart. I promise to do all those things and more. I love you with everything I have. And some,' he added as a tear slid slowly down his cheek.

She rose on her toes to wipe the tear away with her finger, then leaned up to kiss him. Another tear appeared on his cheek. Okay, maybe crying was allowed.

'Not so fast,' Karen interrupted.

Laughter bubbled up from Vicki's tummy. 'Like Arlo said—hurry up.'

'Cole and Vicki, man and wife, we all wish you both the very best for the future and in everything you do. Your love is strong and beautiful. Enjoy.' Karen stepped back. 'Cole, you may kiss your wife.'

'About time.' His arms wound around her and she was hauled close to his strong body that had continued to strengthen back to normal over the past year.

Vicki knew nothing but Cole. His lips on hers, his man scent, his love pouring into her. This was her man, her life, her everything. They'd done it. Overcome the odds and found a stronger happiness together where each felt comfortable to talk about anything that worried them, which was surprisingly little these days.

Then someone tapped her on the shoulder. 'I'm so happy for you.' Molly. There was a river streaming down her face.

Turning in Cole's arms, she reached for her friend and hugged her tight. 'Thank you for everything.' The support, the understanding, and the celebration when she and Cole had learned they were having a baby.

'How is baby? Any reaction to her parents' special day?'

Looking down at her swollen belly, she had to laugh. 'Last time I swapped vows with Cole I could see my shoes. Not a chance today.'

Cole swung her up into his arms, lifting her legs so she could see her feet. 'There you go. Looking glam, if I might say so.'

'Not bad for a pair of swollen feet and toes like little sausages.' Then she leaned in against his chest and returned to kissing him. To heck with the champagne. Kisses were far more exciting. And important. 'Here's to us.'

'To us.'

And his mouth claimed hers, giving her a taste of their future. All good and exciting and filled with love.

\* \* \* \* \*

# COMING SOON!

We really hope you enjoyed reading this book. If you're looking for more romance, be sure to head to the shops when new books are available on

## Thursday 26th June

To see which titles are coming soon, please visit
**millsandboon.co.uk/nextmonth**

MILLS & BOON

# MILLS & BOON

## Coming next month

### TEMPTED BY THE BROODING VET

Shelley Rivers Good grief, could the man make it any clearer that he regretted asking to kiss her? What other reason explained his disagreeable attitude since her arrival? Was he scared she might take it into her head to embrace him in front of the other staff members? Or perhaps try and seduce him in a consultation room when no one was looking?

She'd never attempted such behaviour in her life, and she didn't plan to start with him.

'With me?' she asked, just to be certain.

'I'm not sure how to act around you,' he admitted. 'But, seeing as we're going to be working together, maybe we should just forget that last night I asked to...'

'Kiss me?' she taunted, unable to stop herself from reminding him. A perverse imp filled her with mischief. 'And you held me snugly against your half naked body.'

Alex cleared his throat. 'Yes.'

'Fine,' she said brightly. 'Because until you mentioned it I hadn't considered it a big deal or wasted much thought over it.'

Pleased she'd managed to keep her voice casual and indifferent throughout the lie, she resumed cleaning the area. No reason for Alex to know she'd relived that moment over and over for most of the night. Mentally rerunning each stimulating second until she'd wanted to scream with frustration and track him down to demand he give her the proposed kiss.

He frowned at her reply. 'Really?'

She bit hard on her inner lip to prevent a smile. The man certainly didn't like hearing that she found his romantic moves unmemorable.

'If you want to forget what happened—or rather didn't—then just be yourself when we're in the same room. Otherwise people might start to notice and that would create talk.'

'Are you sure I should?' he asked, not sounding convinced.

Unable to stop herself, she laughed. Alex's self-consciousness was rather refreshing and endearing. Every time the man forgot his stiff reserve passion smouldered from him. It intrigued her how his personality had two such different sides.

'I swear my hesitation had nothing to do with you or your request,' she said. 'It was all me—I promise. So I'll help you on Saturday at the stud farm?'

'Thanks. I'd appreciate it.'

*Continue reading*
**TEMPTED BY THE BROODING VET**
Shelley Rivers

*Available next month*
**www.millsandboon.co.uk**